INVASION

"Two hundred yards!" yelled the navy bo'sun from the stern, his deep baritone ringing out over the huddled GI's. Sinclair forgot his own worries and looked around at the youthful faces of the rifle platoon changing from affected indifference to tense expectation.

He looked up as wave after endless wave of Allied fighters screamed toward the beaches, their wingtips spitting fire. *Five thousand* ships lay off Normandy. *Nine thousand* aircraft filled the skies over Europe. *Three million* troops in all waited in suspense on land, sea, and air between the southeast counties of England and the shores of occupied France for news of the fate of the three thousand men who would be the spearhead of the greatest invasion effort in human history.

BOOK YOUR PLACE ON OUR WEBSITE AND MAKE THE READING CONNECTION!

We've created a customized website just for our very special readers, where you can get the inside scoop on everything that's going on with Zebra, Pinnacle and Kensington books.

When you come online, you'll have the exciting opportunity to:

- View covers of upcoming books
- Read sample chapters
- Learn about our future publishing schedule (listed by publication month *and author*)
- Find out when your favorite authors will be visiting a city near you
- Search for and order backlist books from our online catalog
- Check out author bios and background information
- Send e-mail to your favorite authors
- Meet the Kensington staff online
- Join us in weekly chats with authors, readers and other guests
- Get writing guidelines
- AND MUCH MORE!

**Visit our website at
http://www.kensingtonbooks.com**

THE TRIUMPH AND THE GLORY

Steven Edward Rustad

Kensington Books
Kensington Publishing Corp.
http://www.kensingtonbooks.com

KENSINGTON BOOKS are published by

Kensington Publishing Corp.
850 Third Avenue
New York, NY 10022

First Printing: March, 1999
10 9 8 7 6 5 4 3 2 1

Printed in the United States of America

This book is dedicated to my father,
Kenneth Allen Rustad
1929-1997.
God bless him.

I would like to express my gratitude to everyone whose support and encouragement helped make this book possible. Denice, whom I love beyond all measure, has been magnificent. My mother Florence has blessed me with all of the care and devotion a son could ever hope to have, she is a priceless treasure to me. If they awarded medals for brotherhood above and beyond the call of duty, my brother Craig would have a garage full of them. My brother Mitch's unfailing energy and optimism have always been a source of strength. Paul Rambeck and Alan Hendrickson have been great friends of mine ever since JFK was president, if we all had friends like them, this world would be a lot better place. I will always remember Marcie Larson's kindness and words of encouragement, they've meant a lot to me. I am grateful for Kent Larson's generosity and friendship, he is a true gentleman. My respect and affection for Connie LaRue grows with every passing day, her consideration and patience are greatly appreciated. John Ramberg read the manuscript and provided valued advice and counsel; the book is better for his efforts. The hard work, dedication, and talent of my editors at Kensington, Ann La Farge and Howard Mittelmark, have impressed me beyond words. I thank you all.

Steve Rustad
October 1998

Prologue

Wolf's Lair
East Prussia
January 1, 1944

The steady crunch of hobnail boots on brittle snow stopped as the visitor paused to be recognized by the grim pair of armed SS guards at the cabin door. Overhead, a gibbous moon rode the midnight clouds. German shepherd guard dogs barked somewhere across the compound, triggering distant howls from the wolves prowling the Prussian forest surrounding *Wolfshanze,* Adolf Hitler's field headquarters for the Eastern Front.

A brisk wind carried away their vaporized breath as the visitor exchanged peremptory salutes with the shivering guards. Then Field Marshal Wilhelm Keitel strode through the opened door into the warmth of the Fuhrer's quarters.

Weary faces glanced his way from the circle of officers seated around Hitler. The Fuhrer greeted him with a nod and gestured toward a vacant chair. "Sit down, Keitel. We were just discussing Wagner."

Keitel sat down next to young Strausser, Hitler's newest aide-de-camp. The field marshal stifled a sigh. These evening "discussions" were nothing more than brutally boring monologues as Hitler held forth, sometimes for hours, on whatever topic struck his fancy.

Attendance was expected, unless some military matter could

be produced which required attention elsewhere. Keitel had been spared an hour of banality while he read the latest dispatches from the front.

Hitler looked at him expectantly. "Well, have things been quiet then, Keitel?" he asked, leaning forward slightly in the black leather armchair.

"Yes, *Mein Fuhrer.*"

"Ah, that is good." An awkward silence fell over the small group as the Fuhrer stared past Keitel, savoring some unknown thought. A twinkle came to his eye. "Our enemies had better enjoy this solitude while they can, for the new year will bring them little opportunity for rest."

The officers chuckled dutifully. Wagner and his operas apparently forgotten, Hitler rose from his chair. "We will deal them blows this year which will leave them reeling," he declared, his voice rising in pitch as he warmed to this newest topic. "By February our V-1s will be operational, *then* we shall see that gangster Churchill change his tune. London will burn! We will raze it to the ground!" He began to pace excitedly, envisioning the chaos his new wonder weapons would wreak. "Our new Messerschmitt jets will crush the American air pirates, they will lay waste to *Generalissimo* Stalin's tanks." Hitler frowned as he spat out the Russian leader's new self-bestowed title. "A *generalissimo!*" he mocked, drawing renewed laughter from his guests. "What on earth is a *generalissimo,* some sort of Russian pastry . . . ?"

"I believe it is a type of beet cupcake, Mein Fuhrer," observed Strausser, straight-faced. The others stared at him for a moment, then everyone howled.

When the jollity faded, Hitler resumed. "At any rate, comrades, whatever that drunken cobbler's son calls himself, he will find us ready to entertain him. Our new Tiger tanks are pouring out of the factories now. Nothing can stop them. Nothing! Our new Type 21 submarines will scour the Atlantic of Allied shipping with their magnetic torpedos, England will be starving by autumn."

Hitler stopped pacing. The animation faded from his face, replaced by a fierce certainty. "This unnatural alliance against us will crumble, comrades. The hammer blows we will deal our enemies will tear this false structure asunder. The natural distrust between Russian communists and Anglo-American capitalists is just below the surface; it always has been. Even the English and the Americans will fall out—the English are inherently imperialist, the Americans inherently isolationist. When our enemies feel our renewed fury, they will begin to bicker amongst themselves. The Americans have never seen *real* war. When those cowboys they call soldiers begin to fall by the thousands, they will start to wonder why they are fighting for the British Empire or the Soviet commissars. The Soviets in turn will see no need to lose further millions for the sake of the timid West. For two years Moscow has demanded of them the opening of a second front, but Churchill and that Jew Roosevelt have been content to stand by and let us bleed them white."

Hitler's right arm chopped the air, his voice boomed out over his listeners. "Our enemies will fall out just as Frederick the Great's enemies fell out, just when the night seemed darkest. The Reich will triumph! The Americans will seek terms and go home. The English will behold their burning capital, their starving children, and throw down their weapons. Then, comrades! *Then* we will be free to unleash our full might on Russia and crush her once and for all!"

Hitler's icy gaze shifted from man to man. "The lightning war we unleashed in nineteen-forty will be but a shadow of the storm to come! The earth itself will tremble at the roar of our jets, at the thunder of our rockets! The very heavens will quake at the vengeance of the Fatherland!"

Part I

The Grand Alliance

Chapter I

I

Five miles above the Rhine all was still. The blazing disk of the sun washed the frigid air in amber brilliance. Far below, a cottony layer of clouds drifted slowly eastward, casting rolling shadows across the patchwork image of the north German plain twenty-five thousand feet below.

From the west a faint murmur broke the cathedral stillness. A hazy, indistinct shadow appeared on the horizon. Slowly, relentlessly, as it swept eastward, it resolved into countless specks, which in time manifested wings and filled the air with the drone of piston engines.

The air was whipped into violent turbulence as the formations thundered into view. The lead elements flashed past at two-hundred-fifty knots, the vanguard of an aerial armada of six hundred heavy bombers and six thousand airmen.

In the cockpit of one of the lead B-17s, Captain Wilson Lindberg raised a gloved hand to the intercom switch at his throat. "That's the Third Reich down there, so let's be sharp. Gunners, check in." He pulled back on the control column between his knees and the Flying Fortress, christened *Rosie II* by its crew twenty-three missions earlier, drifted upward until it was tucked tightly into formation for the final run in to the target. Through his helmet earphones the familiar voices crackled.

"Tail gunner, Skip . . ."

"Right waist, sir . . ."

"Left waist . . ."

Several seconds of silence passed. Lindberg glanced at Phil Owens. The copilot shrugged. He pressed a gloved hand to the intercom button at his throat.

"Ball turret, you need a special invitation?"

"Sorry, sir, just got hooked up."

Seconds later the disembodied voices of the radioman, top turret gunner, and bombardier crackled in sequence into Wilson's helmet. Thirteen fifty-caliber machine guns were manned and ready. Twelve quarter-ton bombs hung in the bomb bay. Ten men, clad in heavy leather flight suits, scanned the vastness of sky at twenty-five thousand feet, searching for the first sign of the Luftwaffe.

It didn't take long for the black-crossed Messerschmitts to appear. Six hundred four-engined bombers weren't hard to find. . . .

"Fighters! Fighters, ten o'clock high!"

The warning crackled through Wilson's headset, the voice of top turret gunner Smoky Braddock was strained but decisive. He had the best set of eyes in the whole squadron and was always the first to spot the small specks which would grow with frightening speed as they hurtled head-on into the formation at a combined closing speed of nearly six hundred miles an hour.

Wilson glanced to his right, where Owens sat rigid in the copilot's seat, staring ahead at the onrushing fighters.

"Easy, Phil, easy . . ."

Owens's reply was drowned out as Braddock opened up with the twin fifty-caliber machine guns mounted in the top turret just above and behind the cockpit. The fuselage vibrated from the hammering of the twin fifties, bright orange tracers reached out toward the onrushing enemy.

Wilson fought the urge to duck, to find some protection from the terrible white-hot lights winking at him from the approaching Messerschmitts' wings. But there was nowhere to hide, nothing to do but plod ahead into the hail of cannon fire and hope the mass of firepower coming from the formation would dissuade the enemy fighters from venturing too close.

That had yet to happen, despite the fervent hope which surged through him every time. The enemy pilots were defending their homes and families. They pressed home every attack, charging head-on at the Americans, only at the last instant diving away for another pass.

But their adversaries were just as determined. Not one Eighth Air Force raid on Germany had ever been turned back. Too often this terrible winter the shattered formations had returned to England having lost a full third of their comrades. Morale had wavered, but never broke. Morning after morning, young Americans had climbed into their planes, knowing that, at best, there was one chance in ten death would claim them that day, and at worst, one chance in three.

Very few airmen looked beyond tomorrow, for the odds of surviving a twenty-five-mission tour and going home in one piece were low. Statistically, every last one of them would be dead after twenty missions, if not sooner. . . .

The leading fighters flashed past in a blur.

Owens's voice crackled suddenly over the intercom. *"Eight Ball* is hit. . . ."

His voice was steady. He always seemed to shake his terror after the first assault. Wilson looked up to his right to see the olive-drab B-17's right outboard engine on fire. He watched the shimmering disc of the propeller slow until the individual blades could be seen, whirling rapidly, but slowing with every second. Flames licked greedily at the engine and spread along the wing toward the fuel tank.

Braddock's voice crackled over the intercom again. "190s, twelve o'clock!"

Wilson tensed at the controls as *Eight Ball* drifted to the right, weaving drunkenly as the flames spread across the wing. The right landing gear dangled from beneath the inboard engine, its hydraulics apparently shot away.

"She's in trouble, Phil." He kicked the rudder pedal and shoved the control column forward to swing *Rosie II* away from *Eight Ball* as the crippled plane lost speed and loomed directly ahead. Its huge bulk eclipsed the sun and threw the cockpit of *Rosie II* into shadow.

As *Eight Ball* staggered toward *Rosie II*, the second wave of fighters, green-mottled Focke-Wulf 190s, hurtled into range and opened up. Tracers tore through the formation. Wilson felt *Rosie II* shudder, and saw jagged holes walk across the left wing. An instant later, the 190s slashed past them and dove sharply downward.

He looked to his right just in time to see *Eight Ball* stagger from more hits. The huge bomber was no more than a wingspan away, its entire right wing ablaze. It seemed to blot out the sky.

In the last instant before collision, *Eight Ball* banked away. The pilot, framed in *Eight Ball*'s port cockpit window as he struggled to prevent the doomed plane from taking another with it to destruction, glanced quickly out the window. His eyes locked for an instant on Wilson's.

The glance spoke volumes. Those staring eyes seemed to convey every range of emotion man was capable of, all in an instant. *Eight Ball* rolled over and fell slowly into a fatal spin, weaving a swirling trail of black smoke across the blue sky.

"Anybody see any chutes?"

"I saw three," replied Owens, craning his neck to peer out the right cockpit window at *Eight Ball* spinning earthward far below. He looked back at Wilson. "No one's getting out now. . . ."

Wilson stared ahead. Once a B-17 fell into a spin at 250 miles an hour the poor bastards who hadn't made it to a hatch would be pinned inside by centrifugal force and would ride the wreck all the way to the ground. The image of the doomed pilot, Carl O'Reilly, burned in his mind, despite the constant shouts crackling through his earphones over the intercom as his crew called out the fighters and hammered away with their fifty-calibers.

He was sweating heavily inside his heavy leather flightsuit despite the subzero cold of the cockpit. Steam rose from his gloves as he fought at the controls to keep *Rosie II* level for the final approach to the target.

He and Carl had just had a couple drinks at the O Club the night before and made plans for a double date that Saturday with a couple of local girls to celebrate Wilson's finishing his tour. Maybe Carl had been one of the lucky three. . . .

A violent shudder shook *Rosie II* and Wilson kicked the rudder pedal hard to compensate for the sudden lurch to port. Wind whistled through a dozen holes in the cockpit wall. Dumbfounded, he glanced down and saw his left leg spattered with red blotches.

"We're hit! We're hit!" screamed Owens. "Feather two! Feather two!"

Dazed, Wilson stared out the left window at the inboard engine. Not ten feet away, bright flames licked at the cowling of number two. The wing and fuselage were shredded with shrapnel holes.

Sharp needles of pain stabbed at his left side. Warm blood oozed from his left hip and leg. His training taking over, he flipped the switch that would feather the number two prop.

"I'm hit, Phil. . . ."

Bright flames reflected off the frosted cockpit Plexiglas, shimmering like some image of hell. Wilson heard Owens curse softly as he shoved the throttle control levers between them full forward in a desperate effort to squeeze all the power they could from their three remaining engines.

"How bad?" shouted Owens, his eyes wide, his face suddenly gone white.

Wilson grimaced. "Hurts like hell, that's all I know." He glanced out the window. Number two was ablaze. "Cutting fuel flow! If that doesn't work . . ."

He toggled a switch to cut the fuel supply to the blazing engine, ignoring the clammy feeling spreading along his left side as the blood from a dozen shrapnel wounds began to freeze in the frigid air.

For what seemed an eternity they stared at the flames. A power dive was the last resort to extinguish an engine fire. The alternative was to watch helplessly until the flames reached the wing fuel tank and the bomber and its ten men vanished in a blinding explosion.

The flames, whipped by the slipstream, began to blister the olive-drab paint off the left wing. Green bubbles oozed off the aluminum skin of the wing, spattering about like grease on a hot griddle. Fed now by the paint as well as the oil leaking from the shattered engine, it began to spread.

Wilson looked over at Owens. There was only one thing to do now. The copilot glared past him at the stubborn fire as if it opened into the gates of hell itself.

"We leave formation, they'll cut us to ribbons, Lindy."

Wilson ignored the warning and shoved the control column forward. *Rosie II*'s nose dropped and she screamed earthward.

They were alone. They were on fire.

And they were scared to death. . . .

Five miles to the southeast, Oberstleutnant Gunther Dietrich shoved the throttle full forward, then yanked back on the stick, and felt the Focke-Wulf 190 surge upward. Squinting from the sun's glare, he could just make out the countless vapor trails filling the bright sky high above. The earth dropped away rapidly as the black-crossed fighter strained for altitude, clawing its way upward through the increasingly thin air.

The altimeter needle rotated past five-thousand meters before he could make out the silvery shapes of the Boeings, high above yet and far to the northwest.

He needed another four thousand meters of altitude before he could bank into a firing run on the formation. Terse commands from Staffel Leader Kurt Heinrich crackled over his helmet earphones as, somewhere high above, the lead 190s of Home Defense of the Reich Jagdschwader 52 swung into their four-abreast, head-on firing runs on the enemy.

Dietrich fumed. Through some blunder his Focke-Wulf hadn't been refueled, and he'd been forced to cool his heels for precious minutes while the oversight was rectified. By the time he'd lifted off from the base, his comrades were too high to catch.

Before steeling himself for the harrowing prospect of attacking hundreds of Boeings all alone, he allowed his thoughts to drift briefly to Kathe. To Gunther, Berlin wasn't the capital of the Reich so much as it was Kathe's home—*their* home now since the simple wedding during his last, too brief leave. He remembered the warm kisses, the scent of her hair, the silkiness of her skin.

The air raid sirens would be wailing down there now. She would be, God willing, in the bomb shelter of their apartment building, relatively safe. He told himself once more that only a direct hit on the building itself could penetrate the thick, concrete walls.

A glance at the armada of B-17s took from him any small comfort that thought had held. As he banked the fighter into a tight turn and leveled off at nine thousand meters, directly in the path of the bomber horde, he muttered a silent prayer for her.

He stared in grim fascination—there were hundreds of them! As far to the west as he could see, the sunwashed sky was filled with four-engined monsters from whose bellies thousands of tons of explosives would soon rain down on Berlin.

He had to get one. At least one. For one less bomber meant twelve less bombs that might take his Kathe from him.

Ignoring the familiar, coppery taste of fear, Gunther Dietrich peered through the gunsight as the Focke-Wulf tore through the sky on a collision course with the lead formation. His gloved hand gripped the stick, his thumb poised above the button that would trigger the fighter's four heavy machine guns.

Through the silvery disk of the spinning prop, Gunther

watched the lead bomber seem to expand menacingly across his windshield as he closed range. Bright lights winked from the bomber's nose and top turret. What had seconds ago been a black speck in his windscreen was now startlingly distinct. Wings and engine cowlings appeared, the sun glinted off the polished Plexiglas nose—

He pressed the trigger and watched four streams of glowing tracer shells tear across the sky toward the target. He had a fleeting impression of impacts before the bomber flashed past in a blur. He pulled the fighter into a half roll and yanked back on the stick. The 190 dove, belly up, from the formation. Black spots danced before his eyes as the blood drained from his head. Through tunnel vision forced by the high g's of the dive, he watched the altimeter needle swing past seven thousand meters before he did another half-roll and leveled off.

Craning his neck, he peered above and behind him at the formation leader, but could see no sign that his first attack had inflicted any serious damage. The lead Boeings swept relentlessly eastward.

He pulled the 190 into a tight turn for another run. Ahead, far to the east, he could just make out the layer of haze that was Berlin.

There would be no time for another pass on the lead bombers—he would have to brave the intense firepower of the middle formations. His heart racing, he began to pull the Focke-Wulf into a climb. Then, out of the corner of his eye, he spotted a lone bomber pulling out of a dive far below him.

A cripple? If so, why was it headed east for Berlin instead of west for home? He hesitated; then, his mind made up, he shoved the fighter into a steep dive. The lone American's bomb bay was as filled with death as any of those in the formation, and it seemed intent upon releasing that cargo on Berlin. . . .

Owens stared at Wilson Lindberg in disbelief. Beyond him, framed in the left cockpit window, the feathered, motionless prop of the number two engine hung lifelessly from the engine mount.

"What the hell are you doing, Lindy?"

Wilson glanced out at the charred cowling of number two before replying. The fire was out, the prop safely feathered.

"What we came to do, Phil."

"Are you nuts? Let's get the hell out of here!"

"I'm not going to turn back fifty miles from the damned target."

"We're five hundred feet off the ground, Lindy! A one-eyed monkey with a Luger could take us out!"

Wilson stared straight ahead, anxious to pick out the wide, gray ribbon of the *Unter den Linden*. He was going to follow it all the way into the center of Berlin and drop a dozen five-hundred pounders right on the damned Chancellery. He owed their buddies in *Eight Ball* his best—he wouldn't be able to live with himself if he turned tail now. Not after seeing them blown out of the sky by the damned Nazis.

He looked over at Owens for a moment. "We're going in, Phil."

Seconds later, top turret gunner Braddock's voice crackled over the intercom.

"190, six o'clock high!"

The top turret directly behind the cockpit swiveled with a hydraulic whine. Its twin fifties spat to life with ear-pounding urgency.

"Shit on a stick!" Owens muttered, before glancing back at Lindberg. Blood was still oozing from several jagged tears in his flight suit. His face was pasty white, his lips compressed tightly, his gaze directed at the hazy outlines of the city dead ahead.

"How's your leg, Lindy?"

Lindberg managed a wry grin. "Which one?"

Tracers whipped past the cockpit. Muffled curses sounded from the top turret as Braddock struggled to keep the diving Focke-Wulf in his sights. Seconds later, the German fighter swept past them and soared into a climbing turn for another run.

The horizon out the left cockpit window suddenly erupted in fire and smoke. Ugly black geysers of soil and debris shot suddenly skyward in long columns, the explosions seeming to walk their way from northwest to southeast across the edge of the city.

Wilson Lindberg braced for the coming concussion waves. He edged back on the stick until *Rosie II* was a thousand feet over the rooftops. As the big bomber shuddered from the shock waves, he spotted Hitler's Chancellery building almost dead ahead.

He pressed the intercom button. "Pilot to bombardier, open the bay doors."

"Yes, sir." Lieutenant Richard Lowell's voice was strained. Up forward in the cramped nose of the aircraft, he pushed aside the swing arm upon which was mounted his Norden bombsight. At this altitude, it was useless. He'd have to drop by dead reckoning. He toggled the switch on the panel at his left elbow and heard the bomb bay doors swing open.

"Lindy?"

Wilson banked *Rosie II* until the distant Chancellery appeared in the middle of the windscreen, then leveled off. "What?"

"The target, Lindy . . . what's the target?"

Wilson frowned. Everything had happened so quickly, he'd forgotten to inform his bombardier what he was supposed to bomb.

"The Chancellery, Richie boy, unless you got any better ideas."

"I hope the bastard is in there," Lowell muttered.

"So do I, Richie," Wilson replied. "So do I."

Oberstleutnant Dietrich pulled his Focke-Wulf out of its turn and sped back over the outer city at four hundred knots. To his left, the factory complexes in the northeast suburbs had vanished beneath a manmade cataclysm of fire and thunder. To his relief, he noted that the residential areas of the capital seemed untouched.

Kathe should be safe. For now . . .

From one thousand meters he swept his fighter into a shallow dive. Two kilometers ahead and just below him the American bomber was on a final run into the center of Berlin. He shoved the throttle control forward to close the range.

His mind raced. What was this rogue Boeing up to? Crippled bombers always turned for home once they lost an engine. This pilot was either very brave or very stupid. . . .

As the olive-drab bomber grew larger in his sights, he noted that the American seemed headed for the government area of the capital. The Americans didn't seem to be the butchers the RAF were. At least they tried to restrict their bombing to military targets, unlike the Britishers who carpet bombed entire cities. . . .

Oberstleutnant Dietrich's thumb hovered over the firing button on his control stick. He would soon be in range. He hesitated. Beyond the Boeing the Chancellery loomed into sight. Was the American going to bomb the Fuhrer's own headquarters or was it just coincidence that the building was ahead?

Bombs falling from the B-17 told him the answer. He pulled up and banked to his right, just in time to see a series of explosions walk their way across the plaza of the Chancellery, the last three impacting on the building itself.

Owens turned from the right window. "Damned if we didn't hit it, Lindy!"

"We got it?"

"Three direct hits."

Wilson pulled *Rosie II* into a bank. "Okay, let's get the hell out of Dodge."

"Where's that 190, Smoky?" asked Owens.

In the top turret, Smoky Braddock watched as the Focke-Wulf matched their turn, staying just out of range.

"He's dogging us, sir."

Wilson glanced at Owens. "What do you think he's up to?"

"Probably doesn't want to splatter us over half of Berlin. . . . He'll wait until we're over open country."

"I bet he's calling all his pals right now for help," Braddock added.

For the first time since being forced out of the formation, Wilson Lindberg had time to think about their chances of getting home. England was several hundred kilometers away. They had already lost one engine. Scores of hostile fighters were airborne between them and safety.

And he was bleeding from at least a dozen puncture wounds in his leg and left side. The adrenaline of the power dive and target run had sustained him through those long minutes of crisis, but now the pain was beginning in earnest. From his left heel to his left shoulder throbbing pain shot through him with every vibration of the bomber.

"Bing, get up here, and bring the first-aid kit with you, the skipper's hurt." Owens's gloved hand dropped from the intercom switch at his throat and reached out for Lindberg. "You look like hell, Lindy."

Wilson blinked his eyes in an effort to clear the spots that danced across his vision. How much blood had he lost? How much more would he lose before they got home?

If they got home.

He heard movement behind him, then Radioman Randall "Bing" Crosby appeared in the gap between the pilots' seats.

"I'll take it, Lindy," said Owens. He turned to Crosby. "See what you can do for the skip, Bing."

"Sure thing." Crosby stared at the jagged holes in the cabin wall next to Lindberg's seat.

Wilson tried to smile. It came out more like a wince. "Got any aspirin in there, Bing?"

"I don't think aspirin is going to help, Skip. You're going to need morphine." He opened the small kit and took out a syringe and a vial of clear liquid.

"No morphine, I need a clear head. Just see if you can keep the bleeding under control."

Crosby glanced at Owens, then leaned across Lindberg for a better look at his wounds. Out the cockpit windows open countryside flashed past.

"Can you turn toward me a bit, Skip?"

Wilson grunted from the effort, but managed to pivot enough to half face Crosby. He looked down at his bloody leg. It felt as though it was twice its size, but oddly, it looked the same as ever, except for the caked blood all over the pants leg.

"Doesn't look too bad," grunted Crosby, relief in his voice. "You've got some puncture wounds, but no sign of heavy bleeding. Just the same, I think you should come back with me so we can get some sulfa on you and patch you up."

"Not with that 190 hanging around."

Crosby frowned as Wilson asked Braddock where their shadow was.

"He's still following us, Skip."

"I can't leave the cockpit, Bing."

Crosby frowned. "Well at least let me give you a half-dose of morphine. It'll kill some of the pain, but won't fog your head."

Wilson nodded. The throbbing pain was getting unbearable.

Crosby injected him and soon a warm feeling spread through him, dulling the pain until it was merely annoying.

"Thanks, Bing."

"I'd better get back to my gun, Skip."

"Yeah."

Open fields raced by below, broken only by occasional copses of bare trees and scattered farmyards. He scanned the instrument panel, content for the moment to let Owens do the flying.

"What do you think our best bet is, Phil? Stay low and hug the treetops or get some altitude in case we get hit bad and have to bail out?"

Owens checked their fuel gauge, then their speed indicator. "Unless we get more company, I think we ought to stay below the kraut radar, Lindy. We go high enough to bail out, we'll pop up on every screen between here and Antwerp."

"We'll burn a lot more fuel at a thousand feet than we would at ten or fifteen. I'd hate to get away from the Luftwaffe only to have to ditch in the North Sea."

"It's your call, Lindy."

Wilson did some mental arithmetic. "It's going to be tight if we stay on the deck. Real tight."

"How about if we stay low until we get across the Rhine, then climb?"

Wilson thought it over. He knew the Nazis had thrown every available fighter aloft to defend Berlin. He also had a good idea of the range of a 109 or 190. By the time *Rosie II* reached the Rhine, the enemy fighters would have to return to base, their fuel running low. . . .

"Sounds good to me. All we'll have to worry about then is a couple of fighter bases in France."

Then Smoky Braddock's voice crackled into his earphones. "109s! Three o'clock!"

Wilson looked past Owens through the right cockpit window—several specks were closing on them.

"Aw shit!" He grabbed the wheel. "I've got her, Phil." He ignored the sudden surge of dull pain in his leg as he kicked the rudder and pulled *Rosie II* into a sharp left bank.

From three thousand meters Dietrich watched the Boeing bank suddenly into a climbing turn. Seconds later he saw the reason for the sudden evasive action. Five Messerschmitts were closing in from the northeast.

He frowned—a pity. . . .

Somehow, he had been unable to bring himself to attack a second time. The American had displayed courage. He could have dumped his bombs and run for home, and no one would have blamed him, but he had flown alone into the very heart of his enemy's homeland and dropped his bombs on Hitler's Chancellery itself.

And he, Oberstleutnant Gunther Klaus Dietrich, sworn to defend the Reich, had done nothing but watch while the American plastered the Fuhrer's lair with five-hundred-pound bombs.

He had committed treason.

Or had he? Would not the Fatherland be better off without Herr Hitler? Or Göring or Goebbels for that matter? Did not the Nazi leadership care more about their precious party than they did their own Fatherland? If not, why had they not even considered a negotiated peace? After all, any military man, but for the most fanatic zealot could see that the war was lost. The Western Allies were pounding German cities around the clock, the Red Army hordes were on the borders of Poland, and a massive invasion of France was imminent.

And what was there left to oppose these legions? The Russians had decimated the Wehrmacht on the eastern front; the divisions there were broken shells. The Luftwaffe was being ground to dust by relentless attrition, outnumbered in every theater of war. Only the brilliance of a few generals and the courage of the common German soldier and airman had delayed the inevitable for even this long.

Dietrich's gloved hand rose in salute to the lone American. Only the death of Hitler could save Germany. Maybe, just maybe, these Americans had done the job and saved the German people from the gotterdammerung that awaited them.

He kicked right rudder and banked away, unwilling to watch the end of such gallant airmen. The Focke-Wulf 190 descended through the clouds, bound for Bitburg Field and home.

The sickening death rattle of cannon shells ripping through the thin aluminum skin of *Rosie II* smothered the steady whine of three engines straining at full throttle. As the crescendo of battle roared around him, Wilson Lindberg pulled the B-17 into a climb, desperate to reach the cover of the cloud layer five thousand feet over the Rhine valley.

He kicked the rudder to throw off the aim of the pursuing Messerschmitts, jinking the heavy bomber side to side. Suddenly, the canopy roof seemed to explode and he heard a dull, wet thump, like the sound of a hammer whacking a watermelon. Then the cockpit windows were splattered with blood and gore. From the corner of his eye he saw Owens slumped forward in his seat.

The top of his head was gone.

Lindberg stared as two 109s, wingtip to wingtip, hurtled past and banked into steep climbing turns. Fighting the sour taste in his throat, he reached forward and wiped the blood and brain matter from the windshield.

Jackhammer blows shook the plane as the three trailing fighters stitched jagged holes across the left wing. The outboard engine screamed in protest as slugs tore into its vitals. *Rosie II* careened to the left as the engine quit. Lindberg jammed full right rudder to retain some semblance of control, then reached for his intercom button.

"Pilot to crew! Bail out! Bail out!"

With all his strength he fought to steady the doomed plane so his men could get out. He glanced at the altimeter.

Forty-two hundred feet.

They were high enough for their chutes to deploy. They'd have a chance. Wind whipped through the cockpit from below as the navigator and bombardier dropped through the lower hatch. Despite Lindberg's efforts, *Rosie II* began to bank into a shallow dive.

"Smoky! Burns! Kowalski! Get out! Now!"

He heard no response from aft. Were they all wounded? Dead?

The earth tilted crazily out the left cockpit window, alarmingly close. Too low to bail out now. Somehow, he managed to level off the dying bomber again, his mind racing.

His frantic gaze fell on an open area—a field! Just past the trees across the river. Crashland her, it was the only hope. Keep full right rudder. Ease forward on the stick. Chop throttle. Easy now . . . easy . . .

A thousand feet . . . still holding together. Where are the damned fighters? The river swept past below, sunlight glistening off the frozen surface.

Keep the nose down. Don't stall her now! Cut the throttle more . . . glide her in. . . .

Seconds later, *Rosie II* slammed belly first into the snow, crushing the lower ball turret into pulp. She careened into the air, hit again with a thud, and bounced wildly across the snow-blanketed furrows. The right wing struck a lone tree and sheared off just beyond the outboard engine. The plane whipped into a clockwise motion, riding its left wing across the barren, lifeless field.

Rosie II slammed into a hedgerow, rocked violently, then staggered to a halt on the far side, her right wing jutting into the air, her left buried in the snow. Acrid smoke drifted through the silent cockpit from the flames licking the shattered wreck. The choking smoke seeped through the smashed Plexiglas of the windshield and drifted westward on the wind.

II

Sinclair Robertson had just ordered his second scotch when he saw Ian Prestwick come through the door, pause as his eyes adjusted to the dimly lit pub, then begin to make his way through the late-afternoon crowd to the corner table.

Ian slumped into the chair across from the American. "Sorry I'm late, Robertson. Couldn't be helped, I'm afraid."

Robertson caught the waitress's attention and held up two fingers. She nodded from the bar. He made a mental note to ask for her phone number, and then smiled at Prestwick.

"My solution to a bad day is a drink or a dame—*both* if it can be arranged."

Prestwick shrugged. "Not all of us are blessed with your silver tongue, Robertson. I'll settle for a drink, though."

"On the way." Robertson glanced past Prestwick at the waitress. He'd definitely have to try to get her number.

They made small talk until the drinks arrived. Robertson pulled out a five-pound note and told the girl to keep the change. She smiled prettily, and her hand seemed to linger an extra moment on his as she took the note.

"Thank you, sir!"

He flashed his best smile. "Nothing is too good for an ally, that's my motto."

His smile faded as he returned his attention to Prestwick. His source in MI6, British Intelligence, seemed even glummer than usual. "Here now, Prestwick, drink up. Forget about the damn war for a few minutes."

Prestwick took a sip of his gin. "I lost a brother at Dunkirk, Robertson, and another one at Singapore. You'll have to forgive me my reluctance to forget the war."

Robertson fumbled for his cigarettes, deeply embarrassed at his insensitivity. His lighter flared to life, and the aroma of Virginia tobacco surrounded them. "Hey, I'm sorry. I didn't—"

Prestwick waved aside his apology. "No need to apologize, Robertson, you didn't know."

The American was the first to break the strained silence. "Grapevine has it that the Eighth is going to Berlin this week, maybe today. I guess that's why I'm on edge. I've got friends in the Eighth."

Prestwick took another sip of gin. "The RAF has been bombing Berlin for two years. . . ."

"Not in broad daylight."

Prestwick sighed. "We've been trying to talk your bomber chaps out of daylight bombing, Robertson. They won't listen. Spaatz and Arnold are convinced daylight strategic bombing can win this war without a ground campaign."

Robertson took a long drink of his scotch. "I wish I shared their optimism," he said, setting his glass down on a soggy napkin. "The fact is the Luftwaffe is kicking the daylights out of us over Germany."

Prestwick nodded in sympathy. "Still, the matter is far from settled—the Eighth Air Force chaps only started bombing Germany in force six months ago. Nevertheless, if I were running the show, I'd bomb at night."

"Problem is, you can't bomb with precision at night."

Prestwick shrugged. "If you'd been here during the Blitz, you wouldn't be too concerned with precision. The Germans weren't then; why should we be now?"

"Two wrongs don't make a right, Prestwick."

Prestwick finished his gin, then nodded at the waitress, who'd been glancing at them from the bar. He paid for the next round.

"My dear Robertson, war is not a tidy business. Civilians are going to get killed. . . ." He stuffed his wallet back in his vest pocket. "But I didn't come here to defend RAF Bomber Command—carpet bombing German cities at night is all they are capable of at this point. If your chaps in the Eighth can destroy German industry in daylight while reducing civilian casualties, my hat is off to them. But I don't think *this* war will decide the issue one way or another."

" 'This war?' You expecting *another* war, Prestwick?"

Prestwick stared glumly at his glass. "I fear that all this might just be a rehearsal for the real showdown, Mr. Robertson. . . ."

Sinclair Robertson set down his drink. " 'Real showdown?' "

"The real struggle of our time is between communism and capitalist democracy. Fascism is too extreme a response to communism to succeed. Hitler blundered by trying to destroy both systems at once; had he managed to control his hatred for the French and struck at Stalin alone, the West might have seen him as useful. Very useful."

"If one overlooks his anti-Semitism."

"A convenient political tactic that has gone tragically out of control. The Jews have been a scapegoat in Europe for centuries."

"What do you think of these death camp rumors?"

"Exaggerations."

"Maybe. Maybe not . . ."

"At any rate, once Hitler and Mussolini are disposed of, we'll be back at square one, communism versus capitalist democracy, with the whole world as the battlefield."

"You think so?"

"It's inevitable. In a few years we'll be fighting the Russians."

"I doubt that. . . ."

"Stalin is a menace, old chap. Before Hitler came along, the Soviet Union was a backward, divided society on the verge of revolt. Now it's a military juggernaut the likes of which the world has never seen. Stalin has learned the hard way that the only way he can unify the Soviet people behind communism is to have a foreign threat to focus on. Once Hitler is gone, he will simply replace the fascist threat to the USSR with the capitalist-imperialist threat. The man is a monster; he will do anything to stay in power."

Sinclair glanced around the dimly lit pub, filling rapidly now. Uniformed officers from the various staffs planning the invasion of Europe were filling the tables and already two deep at the bar.

"Perhaps, but he's *our* monster. He's gutted the Wehrmacht for us, hasn't he?"

"And we're next, if we don't play our hand right." Prestwick frowned and took a long drink of his gin. "We are enemies, Mr. Robertson, threatened for the time being by a greater enemy. Once the ultimate, immediate threat is destroyed, our only reason for cooperation will vanish. East and West, armed to the teeth from the present struggle, will be staring at one another amidst the rubble of the Third Reich."

It was Sinclair's turn to frown. "If we ever get back across the Channel."

Prestwick shook his head. "I don't envy Eisenhower—no invasion force has succeeded in crossing the Channel in a thousand years. If Rommel hurls his panzer divisions at the beaches early enough, Overlord will be a catastrophe. . . . Stalin would be in Paris before we could recover."

"Churchill and Roosevelt wouldn't stand for that."

Prestwick leaned forward. "Diplomacy is a poor substitute for military realities, my friend. We'd better get ashore and on our way to the Rhine, or we'll find the hammer and sickle flying from the Eiffel Tower. If you'll recall your history, the Russians drove Napoleon all the way from Moscow to Paris in a year and a half. Don't think for a moment they can't do the same to Hitler. The Wehrmacht is a broken shell. If Zhukov throws caution to the winds and throws everything he has into a spring offensive, Berlin could be his by summer. Then what would stop him from going all the way to the Channel?"

Robertson's eyebrows rose. "The Russians have twenty million dead, Ian. I hardly think those poor footsloggers in the Red Army would have the stomach to fight any more, once Germany is beaten."

Prestwick frowned. "They'll do what Stalin tells them to do."

"To a point," Sinclair conceded. He took a drink of scotch. "Look, when they're attacked, when they find their country invaded, they fight like the devil, they simply don't give up until the invader is defeated. But when the average Ivan is thrown into a war of conquest, like the war with Finland in nineteen-forty, or like a drive to the Channel would be, they just don't have the stomach for it. Granted, Stalin is ruthless. He would take what there was for the taking, *if* Roosevelt and Churchill let him. But would his troops fight, or would they simply go through the motions? Those poor bastards have been fighting and dying for four long years, Ian. I just can't believe they'd be willing to fight once Berlin falls."

"What choice would they have? If they don't obey orders they're stood up against a wall and shot."

"Stalin fears the Red Army, Ian. Hell, he liquidated seventy-five percent of the officer corps in thirty-seven. If he pushes his generals too far, they'll revolt. God knows they haven't forgotten the purges. The top-ranking marshals—Zhukov, Koniev,

Rosokovssky, and Chuikov—are very popular with the Russian people. Stalin would risk a military coup d'état if he pushed them too far."

"You make a good case, Sinclair, I'll give you that." Prestwick drained the last of his drink. "But I'll feel a lot better once we get into France and head for the Rhine. If the temptation isn't there, Stalin will be more likely to behave himself and leave Western Europe alone. But I'd bet my last pound he grabs everything east of the Rhine and keeps it."

"We'll see."

"I'm afraid we will."

Chapter II

Third Guards Tank Army
Vozgorod, Byelorussia
March 7, 1944

I

Private Yuri Arkadovich Rostov crouched in the shadows of the birch forest with his squad as the Katyusha rocket salvos screamed overhead. A hundred meters to the rear, the trio of flatbed Ford trucks lurched as their rocket launchers unleashed death at the Nazi lines just over the river.

Yuri clutched his rifle tightly as he peered across the open valley toward the invisible enemy. Winter still held an icy grip on the marshes of the western Soviet Union. Snow carpeted the frozen ground in a brittle blanket of white. A biting wind stung his face as he shivered, awaiting the order to advance.

He saw the flashes of the rocket impacts on the far bank of the river seconds before the dull rumble of the explosions reached his ears. There was no return fire; the Nazis would wait until the Katyushas fell silent and the infantry advanced before opening up with their deadly 88s to rain hot steel on the charging infantrymen.

He leaned against a tree and opened his canteen, trying to ignore the trembling of his hand as he twisted the cap off and took a drink of the icy water. He winced as the slushy liquid stung his cracked lips, weather-beaten from months of exposure to the biting winter winds.

He capped the canteen and hooked it in place to the utility belt of his greatcoat, looking up as the last of the rockets blasted the far riverbank. As the distant rumble from the final salvo faded, the bark of the battalion's noncoms echoed through the wood. To his left and right, figures began to stir. The ground seemed to sprout soldiers as his comrades rose to their feet from positions of concealment, unslung their rifles, and began to edge forward.

"Off we go, Yurochka."

Yuri looked up to see a huge bear of a man, brushing the snow off his tattered greatcoat. His weathered face broke into a grim smile as he scanned the open field between the wood and the river. "Let us not keep the fascists waiting."

Yuri nodded, gripping his rifle tightly to control the trembling in his hands. "Where is Dmitri?"

A stocky soldier appeared from behind a tree, buttoning his fly as he emerged from the shadows. "Taking a leak so I won't ruin my trousers out there."

The big man, Pavel Ilyitch Samsonov, unslung his rifle, eyed Dmitri Konstaninovich Azov, but said nothing. He turned to Yuri instead. "Stay with me, Yurochka. When we get to the river, take what cover you can. Wait for the Katyushas to sing. When they hit the fascist positions again, we dash across the ice."

Yuri nodded again, stamping his feet in an effort to return some feeling to his toes. His boots left deep footprints in the snow as he stamped about, rubbing his numb hands together. The ritual was a physical necessity, but also served to take his mind off his fear.

Sergeant Grigoriev's voice rang out behind them. Their squad leader stalked past the ranks, his eyes blazing with an unearthly light as he led his men from cover.

"Forward, comrades!"

The ragged lines emerged from the shadow of the trees into

sunlight, two hundred meters of open ground to cover before they could cross the frozen river and reach the enemy positions hacked out of the frozen ground atop the steep slope of the far riverbank.

Yuri stumbled forward with his comrades, blinking as his eyes, accustomed to the protective shadows of the woods, adjusted to the glare of the open field. He heard the first shell whistle earthward somewhere to his left. In seconds, the field was ringed with explosions. Screams pierced the air as shrapnel tore through the charging ranks, opening gaping holes in the lines of humanity struggling over the uneven ground.

He broke into a dead run, his heart pounding, his ears ringing from the violence of the enemy barrage. His greatcoat flapped about his legs as he sprinted over the snow, his canteen swinging wildly at his waist. Bullets began to kick up spurts of snow ahead as the enemy machine guns on the far bank opened up.

His stomach churned, bile rose in his throat as he raced head-on into the maelstrom. He had to prove to his comrades that he was worthy of the regiment, that he was every bit the soldier his comrades were, that he was a man, even if he was only sixteen.

The frigid air burned his lungs, his eyes watered from the biting wind, but he kept up with Pavel and Dmitri. A shell screamed earthward alarmingly close.

"Down!" Pavel screamed.

Yuri dropped instantly, trying to bury himself under the snow. The world seemed to explode. He felt something heavy slam onto his back, and warm liquid ran onto his neck. He froze.

"I'm hit!"

His breath came in sobbing gasps. Why was there no pain? His gloved hand reached for his neck and came away soaked with blood. Something grabbed him by the arm and pulled him to his feet. He squinted in the brilliance of the sun. A leg, sheared off above the knee, lay in the snow at his feet, oozing blood from the stump.

"Run!"

Yuri stared at the obscene limb in horror—how can he run with one leg?

Pavel shoved Yuri forward and he ran, amazed, until it hit him that the near miss had flung some other poor devil's leg his way. He darted forward behind Pavel and Dmitri. The bullets whined overhead. Pinpoints of light winked at him from the far riverbank. The whole Nazi army must be there.

The river seemed an eternity away.

Shells screamed overhead, but the impacts began to fall behind the assault waves as they neared the enemy's position. The German machine gun and small arms fire redoubled in urgency. Yuri saw his lead comrades dive for cover at the riverbank. Some burrowed into the snow; many others lay still where they fell.

"Down!" yelled Pavel.

Yuri threw himself in the snow behind the sprawled form of a comrade. Bullets kicked up geysers of dirty snow all around him. He shook the man, realized he was dead, and hugged the ground, thankful for the cover his dead comrade provided.

Pavel crawled over to him. Ten meters away Dmitri was prone behind another corpse. Beyond him scores of olive-clad figures lay in the snow on the bank, firing back at the hidden enemy. When would their covering fire start? He looked behind him to the dark woods, expecting to see the Katyusha salvos scream westward at any moment.

But his gaze was drawn to the sundrenched field they'd just crossed. A lump rose in his throat at the sight of his fallen comrades littering the field. Half the battalion lay sprawled in death across the open field.

"Keep your head down!"

He looked away to see Pavel glaring at him and realized he'd half risen, stunned at the price they'd paid to reach the river. He ducked behind the corpse just as the snow around him erupted as machine gun slugs tore into the ground. The corpse twitched lifelessly as two dull thuds slammed home.

Yuri buried his head in the snow as more rounds ripped into the body. He gagged at the sickening sound. A dull roar drifted over the field from the east, drowning out the enemy fire. Seconds later, the sky overhead was filled with arcing vapor trails. Dozens of Katyusha rockets screeched overhead and fell upon the far bank, obliterating it in fire and smoke. Debris cartwheeled into the air; the bank disappeared in geysers of dirty white.

"Now!" yelled Pavel.

Yuri forced himself to his feet, stumbled over the mangled body, and darted forward behind Pavel down the east bank and onto the frozen river. Dmitri sprinted to his side. "Don't fire unless you see a target!" he gasped, straining from the all-out sprint.

The thinned ranks reached the far side and charged up the bank to find the shattered woods suddenly empty of the enemy. Random shots echoed through the trees as wounded Germans, resisting to the last, were dispatched.

Yuri slumped against the white trunk of a birch tree, his heart pounding. His head began to spin. He leaned forward and retched. When the spasms stopped, he sank to his knees and grabbed a handful of snow. The icy coldness melted slowly in his mouth and he spat out the sourness.

He saw Pavel leaning over him, his face dark with fury. "The commissar will claim a great victory," he muttered. He mimicked the arrogant tone of the company's ambitious political officer, Captain Boris Pugo. " 'We drove the fascists back another three hundred meters this morning, Comrade Colonel.' "

He spat in disgust. "The bastard! He had no business assaulting this position without tank support."

Yuri staggered to his feet. Pugo was notorious for spending the lives of his men in frontal assaults. He'd made a name for himself with his superiors by taking ground and hiding the battalion's losses afterward, filling the depleted ranks with poorly trained conscripts, without anyone but his own men the wiser. To the out-of-touch officers at division he had become known as a man who could take any position.

"Are you all right, Yurochka?"

Yuri nodded woodenly. "I think so. . . ."

Pavel looked back across the frozen river at the corpse-strewn field. His mouth quivered at the waste, but his eyes were hard. "One of these days I am going to kill that devil Pugo. I'll slit the throat of that murdering bastard if it's the last thing I do."

II

Colonel Aleksei Petrovich Kriminov stood stiffly at attention as he waited for the balding, bespectacled man seated at the massive desk to acknowledge his presence. He stared at the portrait of Stalin on the wall over Lavrenti Beria's head, burning with resentment as the chief of the NKVD finished reading the open file before him.

The office smelled of stale cigarettes. Mixed with the odor of smoke-drenched upholstery was the ever-present aroma of expensive cognac. Outside the office's frosted windows, a heavy snow was falling. It was twilight, the lights of the Church of St. Basil glowing dimly in the distance.

Kriminov managed to hide his disgust. The daily ritual was calculated to humiliate him, that much was certain. The idea of a full colonel in State Security having to stand at attention before his superior's desk like some flunky for minutes at a time before being acknowledged was demeaning.

But was there more to it than met the eye? Was someone watching him from some hidden peephole to see if he tried to sneak a look at some of the documents scattered so invitingly atop Beria's desk? People had gone to the Gulag for less.

He forced himself to refrain from even glancing at the desk, occupying the time with a mental rehearsal of the report he'd been summoned to present. There was little in the way of good news coming out of London from the network of Soviet agents stationed in the British capital. He reminded himself that it wasn't his job to furnish good news to his superiors, but rather to pass along the intelligence his agents had gathered.

Beria finally looked up. "Well, what do you have for me then, comrade colonel?"

Kriminov looked down from Stalin's portrait to find Lavrenti Beria's eyes appraising him. The NKVD chief's glare was that of a predator eyeing its prey, coldly calculating, bereft of any emotion except perhaps suspicion.

"You requested the weekly report from our London network, Comrade Beria."

"Out with it then. I don't have all day."

Kriminov ignored the pompous attitude—Beria was the martinet of all martinets. "Our latest data, Comrade Beria, indicates that the Western Allies will indeed open a second front this year, most likely in late May or early June. The initial force will comprise several divisions, and plans call for a buildup in the first week to a force of substantial strength, perhaps as many as three army corps."

"So, Churchill has stalled the Americans as long as he could." Beria spat out the name of the English prime minister with loathing. "So, where will this magnificent display of imperialist bravery finally occur?"

Beria's sarcasm was heavy. Thousands of Russians were dying every day while western generals fretted over losing a few thousand men on the beaches of France. To a man, the Soviet leadership was embittered over the reluctance of the West to suffer the heavy casualties a ground campaign across Europe would incur. At best, it was seen as simple cowardice; at worst as a devilish scheme to stand aside as long as possible in order for the Nazis and Soviets to bleed themselves white on the eastern front. Most of the party elite, Stalin most of all, firmly believed the latter to be the case.

"Our people have been unable to confirm the location, Comrade Beria."

Beria's eyes narrowed. "It has to be the Pas de Calais."

"Either there or Normandy, Comrade Beria."

Beria scowled. "Normandy! Why the devil would they land in Normandy?"

"Perhaps because the Nazis expect them to land in the Pas de Calais."

Beria glared, distrust etched across his pink face. *"Your* sources, comrade, have sent us detailed reports of the huge buildup of material in the Dover area, directly across the Channel from Calais. Furthermore, the best general they have, Patton, is in command of the effort there. Any indication that Normandy is the target is simply a diversion. If Patton is opposite Calais, then Calais will be the invasion site."

"Patton is out of favor at present, Comrade Beria."

Beria laughed. His eyes regarded Kriminov in amusement. Kriminov stiffened at the reaction—Beria seldom laughed, unless the Great Stalin told a joke.

"Comrade Kriminov . . ." Beria's laughter faded, his eyes narrowed. "Only a fool would believe all that Western press nonsense about General Patton being disciplined for striking a common private."

Kriminov backtracked. It *did* sound ridiculous, even for the Americans. "If it is a ruse, Comrade Beria, it is a very clumsy one."

"Well, the Germans certainly don't believe such nonsense." He took off his glasses and tossed them on the desk. "Neither do I."

Kriminov felt trapped. His career depended on his prediction of the invasion site. His gut feeling was that it would be Normandy. Despite the risk, he wasn't going to allow Beria to bully him into a judgment that ran against his well-honed instincts. But if he was wrong . . .

"Well?" demanded Beria. "Calais, then? We are in agreement?"

"With all due respect, Comrade Beria, I would still have to say Normandy."

The head of the Soviet Secret Police, the second most powerful man in the Soviet Union, glared at his subordinate. "I am not about to tell Comrade Stalin that the Anglo-Americans will land in Normandy!"

"It is your decision, Comrade Beria. . . ."

Beria waved him away in disgust. "I'll give you another week or so to get your facts straight."

Kriminov saluted, turned on his heel, and left.

Beria fumed for several minutes, pacing the red carpet. It was nearly eight o'clock—his dinner hadn't arrived yet and he was due at Stalin's *dacha* at nine. He leaned over his desk and barked an inquiry into the intercom box, then continued his pacing. Stalin would keep him up until all hours, drinking, and he would need a full stomach to soak up the torrents of vodka that would flow.

By the time a hapless aide finally rolled in the serving cart at eight-thirty, Beria was in the blackest of moods. He dismissed the aide with a curt nod, then called Stalin's *dacha* and told the duty officer he was delayed, but that he'd be there by ten. Finally, he sat down at the table in his inner office and looked over the spread.

His rage eased as he breathed in the aroma of borscht, caviar, roast pork, honeyed yams, warm rye bread topped with melting butter, and sweet corn. He poured himself a glass of Napoleon brandy, unbuttoned the top button of his collar, and tucked into the meal.

But by the time he'd begun the main course, his mind had wandered to the coming meeting with Stalin. His thick lips turned down in a frown, twin dimples shadowing the flesh of his heavy jowls. He found himself unable to fully savor the food that only the highest in the Party hierarchy could command, for the luxuries he enjoyed, the power he held—second only to Stalin himself—could vanish on a whim of the Georgian peasant.

He shook his head—Stalin . . . the *Man of Steel,* indeed! The Bolshevik name Joseph Vissarionovich Djugashvili had bestowed upon himself as a young revolutionary was ironic in the extreme, for he was anything but a decisive leader—more a living, breathing case study of complexes. Stalin was paranoid, manic-depressive, compulsive, willful, alcoholic, incapable of

any emotion save hatred, suspicion, jealousy, and vengeful-
ness. . . .

Beria chewed his pork with detachment, his eyes distant, as-
sessing his past and future. For years he'd been able to use
Stalin's many weaknesses to bolster his own career. He'd risen
through the ranks of the NKVD by appealing to Stalin's paranoia, clearing his own path to the top through subtle campaigns
against his superiors—a provocation here, a timely accusation
there, a frame-up or two, or three, until he had risen above them
all. Yagoda, Yezhov, all the rest, were gone to their graves, victims of Stalin's deadly mistrust.

Beria wiped away a bead of pork juice running down his
double chin, then reached for his brandy. Was he next?

Stalin used his inner circle to conduct his purges, to murder
his enemies, to cow the people into numb subservience. Then,
to keep his own position safe against the powerful circle he'd
created, he raised ambitious newcomers to the heights of power
in order to replace their predecessors. The cycle repeated itself
at Stalin's leisure, for there were always plenty of men eager to
dispatch a rival if it meant moving upward. . . .

Beria speared a yam and chewed distractedly, then washed it
down with more brandy. He had only survived by eliminating
his own lieutenants frequently and dispersing NKVD operations
into so many hands that he was the only man who saw the whole
picture. Stalin undoubtedly understood this and had been com-
pelled to keep Beria in order to avoid the chaos his elimination
would bring.

But how long would it be before Stalin's suspicions out-
weighed his pragmatism? When would he decide that Lavrenti
Beria had become too great a threat to his own power to let live
and resolve to replace him, despite the turmoil it would cause
at Dzerzhinsky Square?

Beria shuddered. He pushed his bulk away from the table,
rose to his feet, lit a cigarette and puffed away, trailing clouds
of American tobacco smoke behind him as he began to stalk
back and forth. It was a deadly game they were playing, a deadly

game they had played for the last several years, a game which would only end when one or the other was gone. So far, each had prospered. Each had risen at the expense of countless millions thrown into the Gulag or executed outright—nameless, faceless millions, pawns in the contest of power, herds of human cattle to be butchered in order to slake the appetite of the revolution for enemies. . . .

Beria frowned. *Enemies*. If they didn't exist, they had to be created, for they were all that held the Party united behind Stalin. *Someone* had to be blamed for the years of starvation, the endless cycle of poverty, and the defeats of '41 and '42, for was not Great Stalin all-knowing, all-seeing, the infallible architect of world socialism, the true heir of Lenin? Surely, he was above reproach. Therefore the catastrophes of everyday life, falling like a plague from Minsk to Vladivostok, must be due to hidden enemies of the State, working their insidious evil at every level of Soviet life. . . .

So the blood had flowed. And flowed. And flowed. Lavrenti Beria had spilled oceans of it at the behest of Joseph Stalin and would soon drown in that sea of gore himself, for only the war had halted the cycle of death in Stalin's inner circle— the *Man of Steel* had needed stability to contend with the Hitlerite threat. But the war would not last forever, the end was even now in distant sight, and when it came, Stalin would return to his proven methods. Then it would come to a showdown. Stalin would eliminate his lieutenants, or they would eliminate him.

Beria sank into the thick leather cushion of his desk chair and massaged his temples to ease the dull pounding in his head. None of the men around Stalin trusted each other; they would never be able to combine against him. Khrushchev would frame Malenkov, or Malenkov would frame Voroshilov, or Voroshilov would betray Molotov, or Molotov would betray Khrushchev. The only certainty was that all of them would sink the knife in Lavrenti Beria, for he was the greatest threat to each of them.

Beria's eyes narrowed—the only way to survive would be to

act alone, to find some way to move against them all at once. But even then there would be the marshals to deal with. But how?

Beria closed his eyes. Some threat had to be unearthed that would solidify his position and buy time to maneuver. Slowly, a course clarified itself in his mind. He must expand foreign espionage . . . build the Americans into the new threat . . . methodically frame his rivals one by one until only Stalin was left to deal with. Then some subtle poison, administered in small doses, would send Joseph Vissarionovich Djugashvili to his waiting niche in the Kremlin Wall. . . .

Beria rose from his desk, a gleam of new confidence in his eyes. A constant stream of reports of American duplicity would begin to cross Stalin's desk, intelligence of such massive treachery that he would have to depend even more than ever on his NKVD chief.

He smiled, contemplating Stalin's reaction to tales of American legions poised to strike across the ruins of Germany at the heart of the Motherland, of hordes of American bombers ready to wing toward Moscow, or countless Western spies infiltrating the party apparatus, of Soviet soldiers turned against their comrades by Western dollars. . . .

Stalin would lick it up; he would see Beria as his only shield against the insidious machinations of the imperialist West. The others, Khrushchev, Molotov, Malenkov, would all fall from favor as their respective power bases become suspect, for the NKVD would implicate them all.

Beria punched the intercom and called for his car and driver. He would start tonight. At Stalin's *dacha* he would weave a concoction of such dizzying proportions as to light a smoldering fuse in Stalin's mind until his own paranoia sparked it to open flame. The rest was inevitable—more purges, more work for the NKVD, and fewer rivals standing between Lavrenti Beria and the ultimate prize, leadership of the Soviet Union.

He pulled on his greatcoat. By the time the smoke had cleared, only Stalin would remain to be dealt with. And who could say when a man in his late sixties, burdened by the trials of world war, might not succumb to a sudden stroke or heart attack?

Beria was smiling as he stepped into the heated limousine. As it rolled through the Borodivisky Gate onto Red Square, Lavrenti Beria indulged himself with a vision of the grand state funeral he would organize for Joseph Vissarionovich Djugashvili. He may even have the peasant embalmed and lain to rest beside Lenin.

Chapter III

I

Wilson Lindberg awoke in darkness. Blinking, he sat up in confusion. The pungent odor of cow dung was strong. As his senses adjusted, he became aware of the more pleasant smell of straw; his eyes began to make out the dim interior of a barn. His left side ached with a dull pain that became sharper as he moved.

The bed of straw shifted as he lay back down. He shivered—it was cold despite the heavy woolen blanket that lay in disarray at his waist. He pulled it up over his chest.

Tangled images flashed through his mind—Phil Owens's brains splattered over the cockpit windshield . . . the Messer-schmitts screaming past them . . . the shot-up wing of *Rosie II* . . . the ground rushing up to meet him . . . being tossed like a rag doll in his seat as the world careened crazily out the cockpit windows. . . .

Then nothing. A blank.

He heard footsteps and stiffened. The creak of a hinge drew his eyes toward the barn door some twenty feet away. A lantern appeared, swaying slowly in the darkness. He squinted, his eyes adjusting to the sudden light, then made out the dim figure of a man in the doorway.

The man approached slowly, his features shadowed by the glow of the flame. He was short, broad shouldered, his ruddy face dominated by a luxurious gray mustache. He wore a worn but clean blue suit, white shirt, and tie, but the callused hand holding the lantern revealed his profession—a farmer, a man who'd seen long years of toil. He kneeled on the straw next to Wilson, his eyes watery in the lantern's glow.

"You are feeling ho-kay, *capitan?*" he asked in broken English, holding the lantern high as he looked closely at his guest.

Wilson stared vacantly beyond him for a moment, his thoughts jumbled as first impressions of the Frenchman mixed with images of the crash. He blinked as the horror of those seconds flashed vividly through his mind.

"Monsieur?"

"Yes, I . . . I'm okay, I think." He shook the cobwebs loose and looked into the misty eyes of the farmer. "My friends, sir . . . my crew. Where are they?"

The Frenchman's gaze dropped to the dirt floor. "You are the only one left, *capitan.*"

Wilson drew back. How could that be? He stared in disbelief, trying to remember the crash.

"We heard the engines and ran to the plane, my daughter and I. . . ." The Frenchman set the lantern down; the flame flickered, then steadied. "We saw you through cockpit window, yes? We . . . we find door below. There is fire at back, fire at middle, fire on wing. I'm too old to go up, you see? But helped daughter up into plane and she pulled you out. We bring you away, then"—his hands swept outward—"Whoosh! Fire everywhere . . . petrol explode." His hands flew across his chest and face, signing the cross. "Your comrades . . . we could not help them. I am sorry, *capitan.* . . ."

Wilson's chin dropped to his chest. He closed his eyes as he absorbed this latest shock. "Thank you for trying," he said at last.

The Frenchman shrugged. "I was a soldier once myself—in the Great War. . . ." His eyes glowed with pride as distant memories surfaced. "I only wish I could have saved your friends."

Wilson extended his hand. "Wilson Lindberg, United States Army Air Force."

"Henri Lafleur." They shook hands.

"Are . . . I mean, did they burn . . . ?"

Lafleur's eyes glazed. He nodded.

Wilson took a ragged breath. A trembling hand rose to brush away the shock of blond hair that hung in his eyes as he looked down.

"They did not suffer, *Capitan* Lindberg," said Lafleur quickly. "The explosion, it was terrible. They died at once, I am sure."

"Yes . . ." Wilson blinked away tears. Their last mission. Their last damn mission . . .

"The Boche came at dawn. We had you hidden here. . . . They saw the destruction of your bomber and left quickly enough. But they may be back." He paused. "As soon as you feel able to travel, the Resistance will come for you."

Wilson winced as he shifted weight. Needles of pain rippled along his side from a dozen shrapnel wounds. He groaned and sat still, breathing shallowly.

"You have lost blood, but not badly," said Lafleur.

"I don't want to put you or your family in any more danger, Monsieur Lafleur. I will leave as soon as your friends can come."

Lafleur stroked his mustache thoughtfully. "It will be a day or two, matters must be arranged." He smiled proudly. "Our local people have smuggled fourteen airmen out of France this last year. We contact the English and they send small plane. So it will be with you."

Wilson nodded. "We've been briefed about you guys. But don't the Krauts hear the plane?"

"Most times, no. But sometimes the Boche manage to locate our . . . our rendezvous site, yes? We have lost two poor Englisher pilots, and five Resistance." Lefleur shrugged. "We grieve for our heroes, but it is war, no?"

"Papa . . . ?"

Lafleur turned and Wilson looked up as a young girl appeared in the doorway, wrapped in a black woolen cloak. Her manner was timid as her brown eyes met her father's, then focused on Wilson.

"Ah, Gabrielle," Lafleur, then he said in French, "You have brought some soup then?"

Her eyes remained on Wilson, curious, awed, shining in the glow of her lantern. "Yes, Papa . . ."

"Are you going to stare at our guest all night, girl?" Lefleur waved her over. "Come, come, before he drops dead from starvation."

Solemnly, Gabrielle set a wooden tray down on the straw next to Wilson. He inhaled the aroma of steaming bouillon and freshly baked bread, and flashed a smile of gratitude at her. "Thank you, Gabrielle."

She blushed, mumbled something in French, and rose, glancing at her father.

Amused at his daughter's awkwardness, he winked at Wilson. "I must apologize for my daughter, *capitan*. She is at that age where the opposite sex is a source of wonder." He chuckled. "And here before her she finds not only a living, breathing male specimen of the human race, but a gallant foreigner in the bargain, handsome, heroic, mysterious. . . . You must forgive her manner—she is apparently quite under your spell."

Wilson stared blankly at Lafleur. What was all this? A subtle warning against giving in to temptation? Or an even more subtle invitation? Before he could form a reply, Lafleur pulled away the cloth covering the tray.

"Eat now, you must be starving." He turned toward Gabrielle. "Pour *Capitan* Lindberg some wine, *cherie.*"

Ravenous, Wilson ate, trying to ignore their well-meant but unnerving attention to his every wish. He devoured two bowls of bouillon, a quarter loaf of rich, dark bread, and two glasses of wine before his hunger was satiated.

"It was satisfactory, then?" asked Lafleur as Wilson drained the last of the Burgundy in his goblet and set it down on the tray.

"It was fantastic. I've never had a better meal. Thank you, thank you very much."

Lafleur beamed. He translated for Gabrielle, whose face glowed with happiness as he concluded. "Gabrielle's mother is away in Paris, her sister is ill," he explained. "This is the first time my daughter has prepared food for a stranger. She scurried about the kitchen all day like a girl possessed."

Gabrielle stared anxiously at her father, then asked him something in French when he finished. He replied in a tone of reassurance.

"I tease her often," Lafleur explained, a twinkle in his eye. "She is anxious that I not reveal how much effort she put into this. She wishes you to think that she whipped up your dinner effortlessly. Do you perhaps have a sister her age, *capitan?* If so, you will understand."

"No, but I understand."

"No sisters?"

"One brother."

"Ah . . . a pity." Lafleur shrugged. "I had three sisters. It helped me to understand women. When the time came to court the *mademoiselles,* I had the advantage of some valuable experience in divining the mysterious workings of the feminine mind."

Wilson laughed, drawing a trace of alarm from Gabrielle. She glared at her father. They exchanged rapid phrases, then Gabrielle took the tray and rose to leave.

"You must rest now, *capitan,*" said Lafleur, rising as well. "Your wounds, are they too painful?"

"I feel okay, considering. Thanks for patching me up."

"I learned some first aid in the trenches, enough to get you by until a doctor from the Resistance comes. The bleeding, it has stopped?"

"Seems to have. You say a doctor is being arranged?"

"Yes, as soon as possible. Two days, perhaps three. . . ."

"I don't want anyone risking their neck on my account."

"The Resistance know what they are about, *capitan.* They've been doing this sort of thing for three years now, so don't give it another thought. Rest now, you must regain your strength."

"Yes . . . thank you."

Exhausted, Wilson dozed off soon after they left. He awoke to find Gabrielle sitting nearby, her form softly lit by the flickering lantern at her feet. Groggy, he rubbed his eyes. Was this a dream? Was it all a dream, the mission, the crash-landing, the Frenchman and his daughter? Wasn't he really still back in England, in his barracks bunk, his mind playing tricks on him?

But the dull pain in his side was too vivid, too real. He *was* in France, he *had* been shot down, his plane destroyed, his crew dead. . . .

He winced as he rose on an elbow and peered at his watch. It was 0530. It would be dawn soon. Ignoring the pain and stiffness, he sat up. Gabrielle smiled shyly.

"Oh-kay?" she asked.

"I think so." He smiled. She didn't seem to understand. He nodded, drawing a smile in return. She raised a finger to her mouth and pursed her lips in the universal gesture for silence, rose to her feet and came up to him. He looked up at her in confusion until she withdrew a piece of paper from her cloak, handed it to him, and waited expectantly.

He looked down at the paper. It was a note; several cursive lines of awkward phrasing evidently pieced together with the aid of a French-English dictionary. When he looked up again, he found her picking up the lantern. She gestured him to silence, smiled, then turned toward the door. She paused a moment, then waved shyly and left, closing the barn door softly behind her.

Charmed, Wilson read the note:

Captain Wilson,

    I am a young women lonely, you are a brave soldier who saves France. Father is gone when I come to you. I am not to be pretty, I know, but I am to be thank you for fighting the *Allemande*. You will go, I will to miss you then. I will be love with you if you wish for this. When we good-bye tell I will to remember brave captain always.

Gabrielle

Wilson reread the note, then tucked it into his tunic pocket. She was lovely, but he didn't want to take advantage of her, especially in light of the risks her father was taking to hide him from the Nazis.

He slept fitfully, unsure of how to respond.

Early the next morning Henri Lafleur returned with a boiled egg and tea. He sat down next to Wilson.

"They can come for you a week from this day, *capitan*."

Still troubled by Gabrielle's offer, Wilson sipped the steaming tea. "It's arranged, then?" he asked, forcing his thoughts from her.

"I will confirm it with the appropriate people today, if you think you can travel by then. . . ."

"I can."

Henri Lafleur sliced some bread for them, produced a jar of preserves, and indicated for Wilson to help himself. "I met Raoul Lufbury once, you know," he said, smiling proudly. "He force-landed his Neivport near our lines one day. The Boche had shot up his engine."

Wilson spread some rhubarb jam on his bread. "Lufbury? The Lafayette Escadrille ace?"

"Yes. Twenty victories he had before he was killed."

"I remember reading about him as a kid." Wilson grinned. "I read everything about the great aces I could get my hands on. Guynemer, Nungesser, Ball, Lufbury, Rickenbacker . . . I idolized them, wanted to be a fighter pilot but the Army Air Corps had its own ideas, put me in bomber training. . . ."

Lafleur shrugged. "You have taken the war to Allemande

itself, in your great bombers. The great Lufbury would be proud of you."

Wilson finished his bread, uncomfortable with martial praise. He fumbled in his flight jacket until he found his pack of Pall Malls. "Cigarette?" he asked, anxious to change the subject.

Lafleur's eyes widened. "Ah . . . a cigarette." He took one with alacrity. "They are like precious gems these days. The Boche keep them for themselves, except for those who sell to the black market."

"Keep the pack."

"I couldn't, they are yours, *capitan.*"

Wilson grinned. "Hell, you saved my life. What's a pack of smokes compared to that?"

"You are too kind. Thank you, *Capitan* Lindberg." Lafleur tucked the cigarettes into his trouser pocket. "I must go now. Gabrielle will come with soup and bread later. Until then you must stay here. The Boche, they might, how you say . . . snoop around?"

"I'll stay out of sight."

"Au revoir. I return at dark, yes?"

"Okay."

The sun was high, casting shafts of gold through the barn windows by the time Gabrielle Lafleur appeared. She smiled in greeting, set down a cloth-covered basket next to Wilson and dropped to her knees. Before she could remove the cloth, he took her in his arms and kissed her. . . .

II

Sinclair Robertson stirred as the sounds of early morning traffic drifted upward from the street below. A lorry's brakes squealed, a horn blared in the distance, the soprano voice of a Cockney newsboy rang out over the dull rumble of grinding gears and purring engines.

"Papuh's 'eah! Yanks bomb Buhlin! Papuh's 'eah!"

He opened his eyes. A shaft of sunlight from the hotel room window described a square of pale yellow on the rumpled bed. His head pounding, he closed his eyes again and rolled over. His hand fell on a soft, warm back. The scent of perfume stirred him to open his eyes again.

Maggie.

He raised his arm carefully and glanced at the Rolex on his wrist. Seven-twelve. What day was it? Tuesday? Wednesday? He slipped quietly out of bed so as not to wake Miss Margaret O'Reilly and stumbled to the bathroom. He ran the faucet, splashing cold water on his face as he struggled to remember what day it was.

"Sinclair?" Maggie's voice carried to the bathroom over the sound of the gurgling faucet. He wiped his face and hands dry and, mustering a smile, poked his head through the doorway.

"Good morning."

"Good morning." She stretched luxuriously, smiling at him. The sunlight seemed to glow off her silky skin; her hair shone like a halo of red about the soft peach complexion of her face.

She *was* beautiful. Too many other mornings had found him waking up next to a woman who somehow wasn't the beauty queen he'd brought to his room the night before.

"I'll be right with you, Maggie." Sinclair toweled off and stared at the face in the mirror a moment, frowning at the stubble on his chin. He decided to put off shaving until he faced Miss Margaret O'Reilly and sorted out what was going to happen next between them, if anything. . . .

He returned to the bed and sat on the edge of the mattress beside her. She sat up and leaned against the headboard, the sheets pulled up demurely over her breasts. "I suppose you'll be wanting me to leave soon. . . ."

"What makes you say that?" Sinclair heard himself say. He stroked her hair, brushing the bangs away from those amazing green eyes.

"I don't know . . . you must be a busy man." She hesitated,

then reached up for his hand and took it in hers. "Are you really a Yank war correspondent, Sinclair Robertson?"

Sinclair grinned. "No, Maggie, I'm a Nazi spy."

She hit him with a pillow. The sheet fell away, revealing her breasts. "You tell *me* the truth, Sinclair, and I'll tell *you* the truth." She pulled the sheet back up and looked at him, challenge in her eyes. "What do you say?"

"I have nothing to hide, Maggie. I'm a war correspondent." He kissed her on the forehead. "But are *you* really a pub waitress? How do I know you aren't just using your position to impress poor dumb Yanks just off the farm?"

She laughed. "I *have* noticed that the average GI is quite taken with pub waitresses, Sinclair." She kissed him on the lips. He drank in the intoxicating scent of her perfume, the warmth of her hand on his shoulder. He pulled himself away reluctantly. Her hand dropped from his shoulder to her lap. "Are you married, Mr. Sinclair Robertson, War Correspondent?"

"No, Miss Margaret O'Reilly."

Maggie leaned back against the headboard again, her eyes staring vacantly ahead. "I guess it's my turn now . . ." Her voice dropped, the teasing tone gone. She sighed. "I haven't been honest with you Sinclair. *I'm* married . . . at least I think I am. . . ."

Sinclair started to reply, but she held up her hand. "Please, let me finish, I want to explain. My husband left three years ago for North Africa. I haven't seen him since. The War Office declared him missing in action after El Alamein. I got a letter from his commander after the battle; he wrote that I shouldn't give up hope, but that witnesses reported that Ian's tank was hit by artillery fire and was last seen burning, its turret blown completely off. No remains of any of the crew were ever found. . . ."

Sinclair took her hand. "I'm sorry, Maggie. It must be awful for you."

She squeezed his hand, grateful for his understanding. "If I only *knew* that he'd fallen, or that he was alive! But I'm in this terrible suspension, Sinclair, this purgatory in between."

"Maggie, I . . . well, it would seem that after, what, more

than two years, that if he had survived, you would know. The Germans in most cases inform the International Red Cross of prisoners of war."

"I know, I know. . . . But there's still part of me that refuses to believe he's gone." She withdrew her hand from his and began to cry softly. "I'm sorry . . . I shouldn't be telling you all this. In fact, I shouldn't be here at all. . . ."

Sinclair, unsure of what to do, sat quietly beside her on the bed. Presently, she wiped her eyes and managed a brave smile. "You must think I'm frightfully daft, Sinclair, for seducing you and then carrying on the next morning about my husband. Please forgive me."

"I don't think we're the only people the war has thrown together like this, Maggie."

"Of course, you're right. I'm being an old ninny, feeling sorry for myself. At least I have *hope*, and that's a lot more than too many poor wives have been left with." She leaned over and kissed him on the cheek. *"And,* I can count as a friend a gentleman as considerate and understanding as you, Sinclair. Thank you for being here, for listening. For last night . . ."

She clutched the bedsheet to her chest, rose, gathered up her clothes from the carpet, and retreated to the bathroom to dress.

Sinclair found his shirt in the corner and his trousers flung onto the desk near the window. He scratched his head, trying to recall the sequence of events which had led to such a disbursement, but gave up when Maggie reemerged from the bathroom. She found him standing by the desk in his shirttails, holding his slacks, a look of bewilderment on his face.

"Most people put them on one leg at a time," she observed, her eyes as animated as when he'd first seen her at the pub. "Do you, Sinclair?"

"Afraid so."

She watched with a bemused smile as he pulled on his slacks. "Do you have time for a little breakfast?" she asked as he hunted for his shoes.

"I have to run down to the Western Union office this morning, Maggie. I'm expecting a telegram from the States. Is there someplace nearby we could grab something?"

She thought for a moment. "I know a place right across the street."

"Okay, you're on." He pulled on his socks.

"New assignment, Sinclair?" She handed him a brown wing-tip shoe.

"Yeah." He tied the laces, then looked around for the other shoe. "I think they've got me lined up with SHAEF to cover the invasion."

Maggie found the shoe under the bed and handed it to him. "Whoever was here last night was certainly in a hurry. . . ."

He felt his face flush hotly. "Sure was." Odd. He couldn't remember the last time any remark concerning sex had embarrassed him.

"The invasion, huh?" she asked, noting his reaction and changing the subject. "You must be looking forward to covering such a big story. The whole world will be watching."

Sinclair tied his shoe, stood up, and gave her a kiss on the forehead. "It's a great opportunity, Maggie, a plum assignment, that's for sure. Problem is, my editors want me going ashore with the first wave."

Maggie stared at him. "You mean you'd be one of the first people into France? You'd have to go ashore before most of the soldiers?"

Sinclair laughed. "My editors prefer to call it 'first wave credentials.' It doesn't sound so suicidal that way."

"My Lord, you aren't going to accept, are you?"

Sinclair shrugged. "I have to go where my editors want me to go, Maggie. That's how the system works. A newspaper can't have the reporters telling the editors what they'll cover. If they think I'm the best qualified man for the job, I go. Period."

Maggie sighed, then put her arms around him and hugged him tightly. "Why do you men think you have to be such heroes all the time? Why? What does it prove?" She looked up into his eyes. "I *know* you don't want to go, Sinclair, but I know you *will,* simply because you think your colleagues would think you're a coward if you didn't. Just like Ian. He didn't really want armor—he knew he was a better administrator than field officer, but he was afraid his comrades would think he was a coward if he applied for a staff job. Then once in tanks, he *had* to be in the worst of the fighting because he felt it was expected of armor officers. He *had* to take chances, he *had* be aggressive, because a C.O. sets the example for his men."

Her voice fell. "And it probably got him killed, this mutually deceptive show you men insist upon putting on for each other. You call it courage, but it's not really courage. It's something far deeper than that, something primeval, some deep-seated male trait that was needed for survival when we lived in caves, but now serves little purpose other than to ensure that small disputes become world wars."

Sinclair stared at her. "My. That was quite a discourse."

"I'm sorry, I just get so frustrated. Maybe I'm wrong, maybe I'm off base, but I really have to wonder what it would be like if everyone just admitted that they were afraid to fight and left the politicians with no armies to threaten each other with."

"Maybe it'll happen someday." Wilson threw on his coat. "But I don't think it's going to before I get my telegram."

After breakfast, they walked together to the Western Union Office. Maggie waited on the sidewalk while Sinclair went inside. She looked down the street toward Trafalgar Square, bustling with pedestrian traffic. She bought *The Times* from a passing newsboy, glanced at the lead stories, then folded it and stuffed it in her bag.

"Just like I thought."

She turned to find Sinclair behind her, a pale but determined expression on his face.

"Invasion?"

He nodded.

"First wave?"

"First wave."

Chapter IV

I

He paced the floor, a pipe clenched in his teeth. His boot heels clicked steadily upon the hardwood floor of the *dacha*. The bowl of his pipe glowed cherry red as he puffed away, trailing clouds of smoke in his wake. A fire crackled in the fireplace, the hickory smell of burning logs mingled with the aroma of tobacco.

His yellow eyes darted about the room as he paced, his withered left arm, damaged at birth, hung uselessly at his side. He wore a simple military tunic with no insignia, his matching khaki trousers were tucked into boots of Georgian leather.

Joseph Vissarionovich Djugashvili, known to the world as Stalin, was drunk. By three in the morning he was usually drunk, and tonight was no exception.

He glared at the portly figure sitting bleary eyed by the fire. Stalin's eyes, often likened to those of a tiger, managed to focus on his guest.

"Nikita Sergeivich, are you listening!"

It was a demand. The supreme leader of the Soviet Union's questions always had the intonation of a demand. One who held absolute power of life or death over tens of millions did not lower himself to ask questions as mere mortals must.

The rumpled figure stiffened. A beefy hand rose in supplication. "Of course, Joseph Vissarionovich."

Stalin's eyes narrowed. "What were we discussing!" He couldn't remember, but that couldn't be admitted. He must never show weakness, not even in his cups. Who knew what plots were being hatched against him? What deviltry his own circle of "yes" men were planning? To a man, they lusted to be rid of him and take his power for their own, the schemers! Well! He would show them when the time was ripe. He'd made them and he could break them. Beria. Khrushchev. Mikoyan. Molotov. The whole rotten lot of them held power at his whim.

Other names surfaced. Men raised by his own hand to the pinnacle of authority who'd turned against him and paid the ultimate price for their treason. That strutting pretty boy Kirov . . . that fiendish dwarf Yezhov . . . that sinister puppet Yagoda. He'd seen through them and he would see through their successors, and their successor's successors.

Stalin smiled. Georgians were blessed with long life. He could fully expect to see his nineties. He would outlast them all, every last one of them. He would turn ninety in, what was it?—1970. He would live to see a world under communism, a world led by a Georgian peasant whose father had been a peddler of shoes.

He looked smugly at Khrushchev. He would rule the world long after the Ukrainian buffoon was food for the worms. "Well, Nikita Sergeivich! What is your opinion, then!"

"It is plain, Comrade Stalin," Khrushchev offered after some hesitation, "that we must push as far into Europe as possible. The, uh . . . the Motherland must establish a buffer zone to protect our frontiers from any future aggressor."

Stalin's bloodshot eyes narrowed. Had they been talking of buffer zones . . . ? No matter, it was as good a topic as any. The real object was to keep Nikita Sergeivich talking—he had trapped many a subordinate into revealing disloyalty through such means.

He frowned as he pulled a worn tobacco pouch from his tunic and began to fill the bowl of his pipe. Frowning, followed by a lengthy silence, was also an effective tactic. It never failed to instill fear, which in itself was a sign that the subordinate was indeed hiding something from him.

"Are you implying that we should have had a buffer zone in '41, Nikita Sergeivich?"

Krushchev paled. He shook his head emphatically, his meathook hands rose in denial. "No, not at all."

Stalin frowned again as he struck a match on the rough cedar paneling next to his chair. He stoked his pipe, drawing the flame into the bowl until the tobacco glowed and the smoke drew down the stem. "We shouldn't have had a buffer zone in '41 . . . ?" He eyed Khrushchev, his eyebrows raised. "We should have let the fascists take all of Poland? We should have pushed farther into Finland in '40? We should have opposed the Hitlerites when they invaded the Balkans?"

Stalin rose unsteadily from the chair and turned to the window. Across the compound he saw the NKVD guards at the main gate, stamping their feet for warmth in the bitter wind. "It seems clear," he muttered, his back to Khrushchev, "that our policies before the war don't meet with your approval, Nikita Sergeivich. Perhaps someone else should have been in charge . . . ?"

He turned quickly to catch Khrushchev's reaction. The Ukrainian was silhouetted against the fire behind him, his face in shadow. But his hands were shaking badly, that much was evident. Looking like a sparrow caught in the talons of a hawk, Khrushchev stalled. "I . . . I didn't hear you, Joseph Vissarionovich. The fire is crackling so. What did you say?"

Clever. I'll give the fat goose that much. . . . Stalin cleared his throat and spoke up, slowly and distinctly. "You imply, comrade, that mistakes were made in the years before the war. You have criticized the policy of the party. You have criticized *my* policy."

"Not at all, Joseph Vissarionovich," stammered Khrushchev. "What is clear to me is that we were ill served by the NKVD. They let us all down by not warning us of the true situation."

Stalin nodded. The NKVD *had* failed him.

Khrushchev plunged onward, sensing he'd deflected Stalin's paranoia from himself to the secret police. "Your non-aggression pact with Berlin was a masterstroke, Joseph Vissarionovich. It turned the fascists against the West. We would have had several years to strengthen the Red Army, had the decadent French put up a real fight instead of collapsing like a house of cards."

Stalin's bushy eyebrows rose again. "Ah, so the Red Army was too weak? I suppose I should have let the nest of traitors in the officer cadre alone then, to plot against the party?"

Khrushchev's lips compressed tightly. "No . . . that is—"

"You are saying that I weakened the army on the eve of war, Nikita Sergeivich; that by purging the ranks of counterrevolutionaries and hidden Trotskyites I caused our early military reverses."

"No, Comrade Stalin. I, after all, cleansed the Ukraine myself, on your orders." Khrushchev was breathing hard, he was on the edge of a precipice. Stalin was in one of those moods, when heads rolled no matter what was said. "The traitors would have handed the Motherland over to the fascists had we not rooted them out."

Stalin stared at him, his pipe bowl glowing on and off as he stoked the embers. He swayed unsteadily as the room went in and out of focus. After what seemed an eternity, he turned and sank into his chair. He reached for his wine bottle, took a swig from the neck, then waved it in front of his face as he spoke again. "Another purge will be necessary when this is all over, Nikita Sergeivich." Stalin blinked in an effort to focus his eyes. When he could see Khrushchev's fat form fairly clearly, he continued, his voice slurred but menacing. "Zhukov, Koniev,

Chuikov, Rossokovsky . . . they would be rid of me tomorrow if they had their way. Well, we shall see who gets rid of whom."

Khrushchev glanced surreptitiously at his watch. It was 0445—he had to be at his post at 0700, while Stalin would sleep it off until noon, as was his habit. He noticed Stalin glaring at him.

"Uh . . . you are right, Joseph Vissarionovich. They cannot be trusted."

"Unfortunately, their military skills are necessary right now . . . but we can keep them in line by playing one off against the other, Zhukov against Koniev, Chuikov against Rossokovsky, and so forth." Stalin laughed. The bottle danced in front of his face. "They are like schoolgirls, Nikita Sergeivich, jealous over the same beau. Zhukov cannot stand it when Koniev advances more kilometers than he does; Koniev resents Zhukov for taking *this* city before he can take *that* city; Rossokovsky resents them both for outranking him; and Chuikov thinks *he* saved Stalingrad and Zhukov got all the credit. . . ."

"Yes, Joseph Vissarionovich."

Stalin sank back in his chair, his laughter rang hollow, then faded. "It *would* be simple to deal with my marshals, once and for all, were it not for the West . . . that devil Churchill."

Khrushchev stiffened. Stalin was about to go off on another lengthy tangent, keeping him up till the dawn. Unless he passed out from the wine first.

"The swine . . ." Stalin nodded off for a moment, then jerked awake. His yellow eyes searched the room in suspicion until he made out Khrushchev. "He wanted to finish us in '19 and won't rest until . . ." He faded away again, his words dwindling to mumbled incoherence.

Khrushchev sat in silence for several minutes, waiting. Finally, he hauled himself to his feet, staggered to the telephone, and picked up the receiver. "Yes . . . bring my car around . . . No, he is passed out at last. . . . All right. You'll see to him then?"

Five minutes later, Nikita Sergeivich Khrushchev stepped out into the bitter twilight, frowning at the dim glow in the eastern sky. He pulled his greatcoat collar up around his face as he stumbled to the idling limousine, shivering in the wind. He was asleep before they passed through the gate.

II

In Leningrad, five hundred kilometers to the northwest, Arkady Pavlovich Rostov rolled over in bed and moaned softly at the muffled rapping in the darkness. He snuggled deeper under the covers, savoring the warmth of the blankets. A dream . . . a dream . . . He drifted back toward oblivion, his senses dulled by sleep.

The sound grew louder. He mumbled, a part of him annoyed at the realness of this nocturnal intrusion. The sound persisted, breaking into his sleep. His eyes fluttered open. He felt his wife stir beside him. Then he sat up in alarm as a guttural voice rang out from beyond the door. In the pitch darkness of the flat, Arkady fumbled for the lamp on the bedside table. His heart pounding, befuddled from being awakened from a sound sleep, he finally felt the lamp switch and twisted it on, blinking at the harshness of the light. One thought stood out in the confusion of being wrenched from sleep, one terrifying thought.

The NKVD always made their arrests in the middle of the night.

His wife, Nina, touched his arm. "Arkasha . . ." Arkady picked up his pocket watch lying on the bedside table and peered through bleary eyes at the faded face. Perhaps it was nearly dawn. Perhaps he'd overslept and it was only Yakov, annoyed that he hadn't met him on the corner for their daily walk to the Institute. . . .

But the hands read three a.m.

Three more sharp raps echoed through the stillness. Nina clung to him. Their eyes met—she knew as well as he, all of Russia knew that only the dreaded NKVD came calling in the middle of the night. "A mistake . . . ?" she whispered, hardly daring to hope. "Could they have come to the wrong place?"

"Of course," he agreed, despite the hammering of his heart, the dry fear in his throat.

"Don't answer, Arkasha. Maybe they will go away."

The thought tempted him for only a moment. "They will see the light under the door," he replied, throwing a tattered robe over his shoulders. He silently berated himself for switching on the lamp as he stumbled barefoot toward the door, shivering in the chill. The door quivered in its frame as a heavy fist slammed against it from the communal hallway. Arkady steeled himself for the confrontation. One must guard against even the *appearance* of guilt, he reminded himself. Perhaps, just perhaps, they simply needed directions; after all, none of the apartment doors were numbered. Maybe they had come for 112, or 205, and simply needed a neighbor to point the way. . . .

His hands shaking, Arkady worked the lock, turned the latch, and opened the door just wide enough to see past it.

Three men stood in the dimly lit hallway, the bare lightbulb on the ceiling just behind them cast their faces into shadow, their forms into dark silhouettes. But he could make out the infamous sky-blue shoulder boards, stitched with the Cyrillic initials of the NKVD, Stalin's secret police.

"Are you Arkady Pavlovich Rostov?" the center shadow demanded.

Arkady blinked at the questioner, a lanky officer with a face like a ferret. His voice was businesslike, almost bored. His two associates looked past Arkady with expressions of affected indifference, surveying the one-room flat behind him.

"You are Rostov, this is flat 113?"

Arkady realized he'd been standing there mute. He stepped back involuntarily, his hope crushed, his bowels watery. They *did* have the correct address. . . . They were looking for *him,* they had come for *him.*

"Yes . . . ?" he heard himself say.

The leader pushed the door fully open and stepped into the

flat, flanked by his comrades. "You will come with us, citizen Rostov." The banal tone was chilling.

Arkady retreated, keeping his distance from the intruders. "There must be some mistake, comrade."

But his words, more a plea than a statement, had no visible affect on the visitors. They stamped the icy slush of the street from their boots. The man on the right, a sturdy Asiatic, his face scarred with pockmarks, closed the door behind them.

"Your papers." The leader pulled off his gloves. Glistening slush pooled at his feet, slowly melting on the hardwood floor.

Arkady's mind raced—what could he possibly have said or done to bring the NKVD to his door? His hands, clammy with fear, rose outstretched, palms up. "I don't understand, comrades."

"They all say that." The officer stepped past Arkady. His gaze fell on Nina standing next to the rumpled bed of the one-room flat. "He may take one small bag of personal things. See to it, citizeness."

Nina's eyes filled, tears began to course down her pale cheeks. "Arkady," she whimpered, "what do they want with us? What . . . ?" Her frail form, silhouetted by the glare of the lamp behind her, trembled uncontrollably.

Arkady went quickly to her. "Hush now, Nina. It will be all right. I will go with them and sort all this out." He held her close, stroking her gray hair.

"We have done nothing, Arkasha," she sobbed. "We are loyal citizens, our Yurochka is serving in the army. . . ." She stiffened in his embrace, seeming to gather her courage, then stepped out from behind her husband to confront the intruders. "You have no business with us."

"Citizen! Your papers!" Ferret-face glared at Arkady, ignoring Nina's challenge.

"Do as they say, Nina, they have their orders." Their eyes met. "Don't make a fuss now—we can't sort this out here. I will have to speak with their superiors." He retrieved the obligatory documents from his coat, lying on the back of a kitchen chair, and handed them to the leader.

Nina pulled at his arm. "Arkasha, if you go with them, you will never come back. . . ."

Arkady held her close, rocking her gently. "Nonsense. I have done nothing to warrant arrest. I—"

"Do you think *that* matters to these beasts!" she cried, her chest heaving anew as the tears flowed freely again. "Do you think they *care* about guilt or innocence?"

Arkady pulled her face to his chest in alarm, but the men heard. Ferret-face stepped forward. "Watch yourself, citizeness, or we will take you as well."

"My Nina is upset, comrade," Arkady pleaded, turning toward the agents. "You understand. . . ."

"Get dressed!" The voice had lost its bored indifference. Ferret-face glared at Nina. "Citizeness! I will have to report your slander of the state, you—"

"Leave her be!" Arkady roared. He returned Ferret-face's glare, his fists clenched. It was one thing to question him, but these louts weren't going to terrify poor Nina any more than they already had. "I will go peaceably, comrade."

Ferret-face nodded curtly. Arkady turned to Nina, his eyes imploring her to cooperate. She walked stiffly to the washbasin and carefully packed a bar of soap, a towel, extra stockings, a washcloth, and a change of underwear into Arkady's drawstring shopping bag. Arkady pulled on trousers, a heavy flannel shirt, his warmest pair of stockings, and winter boots. Nina handed him his bag and his winter coat. He hugged her tightly, praying for self-control.

"Have breakfast ready for me, will you, Ninochka?"

She nodded. Her mouth quivered as she kissed him good-bye. "Arkasha. . . ."

"It will be all right."

She clung to him, her eyes squeezed tightly shut. He felt her heart pounding through the thin cotton nightdress. He drew back at last and looked at her, memorizing every line of her face. Though he refused to admit it to her, for fear of tempting fate, they both knew the NKVD had little regard for guilt or innocence. The *Yezhovschina,* the great purge of the thirties, had proven *that* much. If the worst came to pass and he never saw her again, he would carry the image of her face to his grave, would remember the beating of her heart, the scent of her hair, the salt dew of her tears on his lips. . . .

Chapter V

I

A sliver of crescent moon shone weakly through the hazy overcast. A soft breeze rustled through the budding treetops, carrying the distant song of crickets to the two men crouched in the darkness.

"Are you sure this is the right place?" Wilson Lindberg whispered, fearing they'd botched the pickup, leaving him stranded in occupied France for God only knew how much longer. He'd lost all sense of direction since they'd left the LaFleur farm just after dusk.

The shadow that was Jacques Dubois flashed a penlight for a second on his watch, muttering Gallic curses. "Yes, *mon frère,* but we are late. The Britisher may have flown over already and left." He spat on the ground in disgust. "They cannot circle long. The Germans would hear the engine and investigate."

They searched the starry sky for what seemed an eternity before the distant drone of an aircraft sounded faintly from the northwest. Dubois pulled a large flashlight from his satchel and pointed it toward the sound, flipping the switch on and off in a prearranged sequence. They waited.

"He's too far away. . . ." Wilson's eyes scanned the moonlit clouds on the horizon. A front looked to be moving in from the English Channel; a thick overcast blotted out the stars to the north and west.

The drone grew gradually louder. Dubois flashed away, his thumb working the flashlight switch back and forth. Overhead, the sky was still clear and Wilson's hopes rose. He fought the urge to jump up, shout, wave his arms. It would be pointless, but he felt so helpless just sitting there. The sound grew louder, the steady hum of the plane's engine was now alarmingly loud, it seemed to reverberate off the trees, to vibrate off the wet grass.

"My God, he'll wake up half of France."

Dubois flashed a frown at his charge, and muttered something in French. Wilson instantly regretted his remark.

First he had been afraid the pilot wouldn't see them; now he was worried that the plane was too loud and too close. He looked up as a dark shape flashed by directly overhead, then watched with growing tension as the noisy shadow banked and came around in a tight turn over the distant treeline.

The engine noise faded as the pilot cut the throttle back and swooped lower. Faint moonlight lit the rescue craft as it glided to earth, then bounced once, twice, three times, before rolling along the damp meadow.

They edged toward the taxiing plane, which Wilson recognized as an RAF Lysander by its fixed landing gear and the gull-wings placed high on the fuselage.

"Merde!"

Wilson turned to see Dubois gesturing frantically at a pair of distant headlights bobbing along the road from St. Quentin. "The Boche! Go! Go!" He slapped Wilson on the back. Their eyes met for a moment. Wilson barely had time to utter a hasty thank-you before the Frenchman, with a nervous grin, shoved him toward the idling Lysander.

He sprinted to the plane. Through the cockpit windows, he saw the pilot lean to his right and shove open the small side door. Wilson ran around the nose, keeping well clear of the shimmering disc of the propeller, and scrambled aboard. "I think the Krauts are coming!" he shouted over the noise, pointing to the west. He yanked the door shut as the pilot shoved the throttle down.

"Jerry's on his way, eh?" The pilot glanced to the west as he swung the Lysander into a turn. "I say, not too sporting of them to make us take off with the wind."

Wilson stared at the closing headlights. "Maybe they're just some drunk Krauts heading home from town."

"Let's hope so, old chap." The Englishman thrust out a gloved hand as he shoved the throttle all the way down with the other. "By the way, the name's Watson, Flight Lieutenant Ian Watson."

"Lindberg, Captain Wilson Lindberg." They shook hands.

Watson began to work the rudder pedals and the stick as the Lysander bounced toward takeoff speed. The headlights were close. Whoever was in the truck had certainly heard the noise by now. Wilson wondered where Dubois was.

Suddenly, ugly yellow tracers spat from behind the headlights. Menacing beads of light reached out for them, flashed past overhead, and slammed into the ground all around them. Wilson ducked instinctively. They'd just started their takeoff roll and were terribly vulnerable. From a hundred yards away the Germans could hardly miss the lumbering target straining for speed just across the flat field.

"Bloody bastards aren't cooperating at all, are they?" Watson's voice was matter-of-fact as he indulged in typical British understatement. Over the bursts from the truck and the screaming whine of the engine, Wilson heard the distinctive bark of Dubois's tommy gun. A headlight winked out, then the other. The tracers arced wildly high for a moment. The Lysander swept past the darkened truck, gaining speed with every second as it bounced roughly over the meadow.

"Get 'em, Jacques!" he shouted, hunched low in his seat, his head just above the window.

But the tracers leveled off again, arcing relentlessly lower. They buzzed angrily past the cockpit, and the night came alive with supersonic fireflies as the Germans found the range. The Lysander shuddered as several rounds found the right wing. At the same instant, Watson yanked back on the stick. The plane staggered into the air, ringed by tracers.

Once again the tracers wavered, suddenly spraying wildly awry. Wilson's hopes soared as he looked behind them to see that Jacques's tommy gun winked steadily from the edge of the woods. But his heart pounded with renewed fury as two more pairs of headlights appeared to the south. Jacques had better run for it before it was too late. . . .

"Bugger me if we're going to make it over the trees," remarked Watson.

Wilson tore his gaze from behind them, turning in time to see the forbidding shadow of a wood looming directly ahead, not a hundred yards away. A quick look at the ground, then another at the approaching treeline told him they were in trouble. He braced himself as the Lysander clawed for altitude, its engine whining at full throttle, wind whistling through the jagged bullet holes in its wing. He no longer noticed the tracers tearing after them. His gaze was locked on the solid wall of forest rushing up at them.

He held his breath, every thought, every muscle straining to coax the plane over the heavy branches blocking their path. His gaze shot to the airspeed indicator; the dim-lit dial showed eighty knots. Was it enough?

"Bloody hell," said Watson, a trace of annoyance in his voice. At the last moment, he yanked the stick back. The nose rose sluggishly. Seconds later, they were jolted as the landing gear slammed across the top branches of an oak.

The Lysander staggered from the blow. Watson fought for control as the plane pitched forward and yawed to the left, just above the trees. He kicked right rudder to compensate, eased the stick back, and managed to bring the nose up just enough to maintain altitude. The forest swept past below them as the Lysander slowly gained airspeed and altitude.

Wilson exhaled in relief.

"Looks like the old girl is going to hold together, Lindberg." Watson grinned broadly at Wilson.

"That was some fancy flying."

"Thought we'd bought the farm, mate."

"What's the stall speed on these things?"

Watson shook his head in wonder. "Lower than advertised. We just proved that." He kept the nose up until the altimeter needle passed two hundred feet, then banked north toward the Channel. "Got to keep low until we're out of range of Jerry's night-fighter radar."

"Sounds good to me." Wilson turned to search the darkness behind them. "I hope they didn't get Jacques."

"They won't. Those Resistance blokes are good. Old Jacques will lead them on a merry chase, just to entertain himself, then disappear without a bloody trace."

"You know the guy?"

"Never met the chap." Watson pulled the Lysander out of the turn, leveled off, set the trim, and stretched to ease the stiffness of two hours in the cramped cockpit. He checked his watch. "Bomber Command is going full strength to the Ruhr tonight. Should keep the night fighters too busy to come snooping around for small fry like us."

Wilson cleared his throat self-consciously. He owed his life to this unassuming Briton, and searched for words to express his gratitude.

"Captain Watson, I'd like to thank you again, I—"

Watson waved off his halting attempt. "When did Jerry get you, mate?" he asked.

"March sixth over Berlin." The faces of his crew came to mind. Owens . . . Smoky . . . Bing . . . He blinked away the images. This wasn't the time for more grief. It was a time for satisfaction. He'd been snatched away from occupied France, right out from under the noses of the Nazis. He was going back to England, his tour done at last. In a matter of weeks he would be home. . . .

"Heard it was rough." Watson regarded Wilson with a look somewhere between awe and incredulousness.

"It was no picnic."

"I've got to hand it to you Yanks going over the bloody Reich in broad daylight. Bomber Command gave that up after one raid."

Wilson shrugged. "We just do what they tell us."

"Well, if it's any consolation, the Eighth hammered Berlin twice more after Jerry did for you blokes." Watson coughed, wishing he could take back that last phrase. "Sorry about your crew," he added, not wanting to come across as insensitive.

"We damn near made it, Watson. Twenty-four missions. Then we get it on the last one. . . ."

"Bloody bad luck. . . ."

"Yeah." Wilson stared ahead at the building overcast. Might get rough over the Channel, he thought, forcing aside once again the memory of his friends. But Watson didn't seem worried.

By the time they reached the seacoast, raindrops were beginning to spatter against the canopy windshield. The world outside soon vanished as the Lysander flew into heavy cloud. Watson pulled the nose up as he scanned the instrument panel, whose glowing dials had become his only means of guiding them home safely.

"Think we can get above this soup?" Wilson asked. Turbulence began to buffet the plane, sleet slapped steadily against the Plexiglas around them.

"Ceiling was angels five on the way over." Watson frowned. "Damned near got bloody lost. That's why I was a bit late. . . ." He climbed to seven thousand feet before he gave up breaking through the weather. "Don't have enough petrol left to keep this up, Lindberg, old chap."

Wilson glanced uneasily at the ice beginning to form on the wings. Didn't Lysanders have deicing boots? He was about to ask when Watson pushed them over into a thirty-degree dive.

The Lysander swept past two thousand feet before he pulled it level. The sleet changed to rain once again as they dropped through the swollen clouds. Sheets of it pounded against the canopy, driving Wilson to distraction.

The wind picked up, tossing the plane about like a toy. How were they going to find their way down in such a deluge? He'd brought *Rosie II* down in bad English weather before, but never like this, and certainly never in the middle of the night.

"Pretty bad, huh?" he asked, anxious to measure Watson's reaction to the mounting fury of the storm.

"Never seen it worse." Watson pulled a candy bar from his tunic pocket, tore away the wrapper, and began to eat. "I'd hate to waste a perfectly good Hershey Bar." His grin seemed a little forced. He thrust the bar at Wilson. "Care for a bite?"

Wilson shook his head. "No, thanks." He peered out into the blackness. "We hit the coast yet?"

Watson scanned the dimly lit instrument panel for several moments, his brow furrowed in thought. He took a bite of the chocolate bar, then turned to Wilson "Can't tell for sure, mate. We'll just have to wait until we can smell the chalk."

"The chalk . . . ?"

"You know, the cliffs of Dover."

Wilson stared blankly.

"In the rain," Watson explained, "the chalk of the Dover cliffs give off a rather distinctive smell."

Wilson laughed, but Watson seemed serious. "You're pulling my leg, right?"

"No, it's true."

"You're the boss." Wilson looked out the canopy Plexiglas again. Somewhere down in the murk were the freezing waters of the English Channel. It would be hell to go down in the sea now, after all he'd come through. But Watson's devil-may-care demeanor had rubbed off on him already. He liked the Englishman's style—stiff upper lip in the face of adversity, and all that. After all, what else could they do but try their damnedest? If fate decreed it wasn't enough, then wasn't it better leave this world proud rather then bitter . . . ?

Watson eased them lower, feeling his way for the Dover coast. Several minutes passed before he seemed to relax and eased the nose up. Wilson watched in astonishment as they broke through the overcast and swept over the white cliffs of Dover.

"Petrol's about gone, mate. Afraid we're going to have to set down here." He cut the throttle and brought the Lysander into a shallow glide toward an empty stretch of farmland. "At a thousand feet, I knew we'd clear the cliffs, but still be low enough to catch the chalk odor." He laughed. "It *was* a bit dramatic that the overcast chose to clear when it did."

The Lysander touched down on English soil and rolled to a stop in the rain. Watson cut the engine, reached below his seat for a thermos, unscrewed the cap, and passed the steaming cylinder to Wilson.

"Care for a spot of tea?"

II

Oberstleutnant Gunther Dietrich climbed wearily from the cockpit, stepped onto the wing, and jumped to the ground. A bedraggled noncom hurried up and came to a semblance of attention. His salute was perfunctory.

"Excuse me, Oberstleutnant, but Wing Commander Ruge wants to see you at once. He's in Hangar Eight."

Dietrich waved his hand in the direction of his service cap and nodded. He walked across the soggy grass to the hangar. The smell of fuel and grease was strong when he stepped into the shadow of number eight, despite the breeze blowing in through the open door.

Ruge saw him enter and stepped out from behind a wingless Messerschmitt, the squadron's "hangar queen," useless but for the spare parts they could scavenge from her aluminum carcass.

He nodded toward the small office in the rear. "I'll be right with you Dietrich."

Gunther saluted and headed for the office.

What was up? Ruge, a dedicated Nazi, had as little to do with him as possible, especially since he had openly criticized Göring at the Christmas party. . . . Gunther frowned. *The Fat One,* as Göring's detractors called him, had proven a disaster as Luftwaffe chief. The man simply had no concept of modern aerial warfare. His reputation had been made in the First World War and he was still trying to fight this one as he had that one, when he'd succeeded Manfred von Richtofen as commander of the famed Flying Circus.

Gunther stepped into the musty office and waited for Ruge next to his desk. Göring did nothing now but plunder art collections from the occupied territories of the Reich and indulge his morphine habit. . . .

"Dietrich."

Gunther turned as Ruge stepped past him, leaving a faint scent of expensive cologne in his wake. The commandant sat behind his desk and pulled a folder from his desk drawer. He leafed through it quickly, threw it atop the desk, and fixed a disdainful gaze on Gunther.

"Your combat report of six, March, states that you shot down a Boeing west of Berlin, Dietrich. Then damaged another before returning to base. . . ."

"That is correct, Herr Commandant."

Ruge's well-manicured hand tapped the top of the manila folder. "Yet this *eyewitness* report states that a 190 with your markings was seen pursuing a Boeing directly over the center of Berlin. This Focke-Wulf followed the enemy bomber right over the Chancellery and did nothing to prevent the American air pirate from bombing it, then flew off. Have you any explanation, Dietrich?"

Gunther tried desperately to remember if he'd expended all of his ammunition before landing. If he had, he could claim he'd been helpless—but that still left the matter of filing a false combat report. . . . But *had* there been ammunition left over when the ground crew had serviced his plane? If so, it would be in their report, and Ruge would have him cold. Better to claim jammed guns. That happened often enough. Besides, a ground crewman could not always tell one way or another if a 190's guns had jammed and then cleared later in the sortie.

"I forgot to mention the incident, Herr Commandant. I was ashamed because I had fired too long a burst at the second Boeing and jammed my guns. I . . . followed the third Boeing over Berlin, hoping they would clear, but when they didn't, I felt too stupid to admit my blunder and omitted the whole incident from my report."

Ruge shook his head in disgust. "A trainee might have been so stupid, Dietrich, but I find it difficult to believe a pilot of your experience would have committed such an idiocy." His eyes narrowed. "I don't believe your story."

Gunther stared past Ruge as he stiffened to attention. "I am sorry, Herr Commandant, but that is what happened."

Ruge rose to his feet. "I have insisted upon your transfer, Dietrich. You are a liar, a traitor to the Reich! If I had my way, you would find yourself in front of a firing squad, but that would leave the German people one less pilot to defend them against the enemy. You *have* served with some distinction in the past and this fact is all that has saved you from a traitor's death. For the sake of squadron morale, this will be kept quiet. My men deserve better than to learn their ranks have been smeared by your treachery. You will report to Jagdschwader 2 in Normandy. Now get out of my sight!"

Gunther clicked his heels, saluted smartly, pivoted, then paused. He turned to face Ruge. "Herr Commandant, I will go of course; it will be a pleasure to fight for a commandant who does more than fly a *desk* while he sends his men out to die."

Ruge colored. He started to speak, but Gunther cut him off. "I have flown for Germany ever since '39, Ruge! I shot down four Spitfires over England in '40 while you were drinking

French wine on the *Fat One's* fancy train and helping him screw his French whores. Since '41, I've accounted for eight Boeings, four Liberators, two Lancasters, seven Lightnings, and six Thunderbolts. I have flown three hundred and sixteen combat missions! How many have you flown, Ruge? Thirty? Maybe forty?"

"The Reich has seen fit to make use of my administrative skills," blustered Ruge. "I—"

"You are a poseur, Ruge! A two-faced hypocrite who sends men out to die while you kiss Goring's fat ass and wheedle promotions for yourself by stealing paintings for him. So don't preach to me about honor and duty. You know nothing about either!"

Gunther stalked out and headed for his quarters. By the time he'd packed his belongings, he wondered if his loss of temper would earn him a visit from the SS. Open criticism of the Nazi leadership was a court-martial offense, a transgression that could indeed get him shot. Perhaps he should have just bit his tongue and left, but Ruge was such a snake he simply couldn't leave without defending himself.

"Herr Oberstleutnant?"

Gunther turned to see Staff Sergeant Willi Braun standing in the door. Braun saluted and handed him a paper. "Your transfer, Herr Oberstleutnant."

"Thank you, Braun." Gunther glanced at the orders.

"The commandant is in a rage, Herr Oberstleutnant. He is threatening to have you arrested. . . ."

Gunther smiled bleakly. "Is my plane fueled up, Willi?"

Braun nodded. He stiffened to attention and saluted. "It has been an honor to have been your crew chief. . . . I . . . I hope you are not in trouble. . . ."

"I will get by, Willi." Gunther shook his hand. "You have been a good crew chief, the best a man could ask for. I'll miss you." He picked up his duffel bag, put on his service cap, and slapped Willi on the shoulder as he passed. "Take care of yourself, Willi."

* * *

Ten minutes later, he was airborne. The sky was a brilliant blue at four thousand meters, the land far below a patchwork quilt of green and rich brown squares. Spring in France was paradise. A man could almost forget the war as he drank in the beauty of the countryside.

But bastards like Ruge ruined even the few moments of rest and relaxation a pilot thought he could look forward to on the ground. It was bad enough facing the American armadas, risking death every day without having to wonder if Nazis like the commandant would have the SS waiting for one when he returned, simply for honest criticism of the leadership. *They* were the culprits responsible for losing the war. *They* were the ones whose blunders had plunged Germany into a two-front war. *They* were the ones who had criminally delayed production of the ME-262 jet. . . . Time and again the Nazi leadership, hypnotized by Hitler's insane ramblings, had betrayed the soldiers and airmen of Germany. And *now,* when Germany was forced to harvest the bitter fruits of their work, they turned viciously on the men at the front for telling the truth.

Thirty minutes later, Gunther saw the JG 2's airfield through the broken cumulus and eased the nose down, still bitter at the injustice of it all. War took all the good men, he mused. They fell in battle while the political soldiers at the top survived and prospered, surrounded by comforts, by women, by liquor.

The landing gear lowered with a hydraulic whine. He eased the throttle forward to lose speed and swept over the treetops at the downwind end of the field. The 190 touched down with a jolt and rolled across the grass to a halt. Gunther kicked rudder to turn, then taxied toward the hangars.

He killed the engine in front of the nearest hangar and yanked the canopy back. The air was fresh, a hint of salt drifted into the cockpit from the Channel, just fifteen kilometers to the north. Gunther climbed out onto the wing, dropped to the ground, and looked around. Finally, a noncom emerged from the hangar, walked slowly up to the Messerschmitt, and saluted.

"Oberstleutnant . . . ?"

"Gunther Dietrich, Sergeant." Gunther returned the salute. "Reassigned from JG 54."

"Follow me, Oberstleutnant Dietrich. The commandant is in Paris, but we expect him shortly. You can wait in the chalet if you wish."

"Fine." Gunther followed the limping sergeant to an imposing chalet at the edge of the field. Priller in Paris? That figured.

He recalled what he'd heard of Pips Priller, his new commanding officer. He had a well-earned reputation as a playboy, a carouser of the first rank. But also an excellent fighter pilot, one of the best. . . .

The sergeant left him alone in the chalet foyer. He sank into a chair and settled down to wait, impatient that his new C.O. was absent, but gratified to be rid of Ruge. Playboy or not, Priller was bound to be better to fight under than that Nazi fanatic. At least under Priller one knew for sure that one's enemies flew Mustangs and Boeings, not a desk. . . .

Chapter VI

Sinclair Robertson stepped out onto the weather deck of the troop transport *New Amsterdam,* desperate for some fresh air. The Channel weather, to his dismay, was as hideous as ever. Heavy rain lashed the decks, whipped by gale force winds. The sea seemed a malevolent beast, intent on savaging these impudent ships which dared to venture into her domain.

He grasped the bulkhead to steady himself on the heaving deck and stared into the murk. Was the invasion to turn into a catastrophe right before his eyes? Was the fleet doomed to share the fate of the Spanish Armada, beaten to pulp on these very seas, its commander's invasion plans shattered, his mighty legions drowned like so many rats?

Sinclair shuddered, thankful he wasn't Dwight David Eisenhower this night. As if storming ashore on a continent full of hardened Nazi troops wasn't enough to worry about, he had to fight the weather too. . . .

He grabbed a deck stanchion for support as the *New Amsterdam* plunged into the trough of a huge wave then pitched upward, riding out the crest. Green seawater sloshed along the deck, sweeping amidships to break into white froth against the gray superstructure of the bridge. From somewhere below, he heard the muffled clang as the ship's bells began to toll midnight.

D-Day had come . . . but what would it bring?

Sinclair stared ahead through the stinging rain. Somewhere out there was the rest of the convoy, stretching for mile after mile in line astern formation, plodding through the night toward France. Within the hour, scores of C-47s, loaded with the paratroopers of the 82nd and 101st Airborne, were due to take off. . . .

He stepped back through the hatch and pulled it shut with a metallic clang. The atrocious weather showed no signs of breaking—at least here, in the western reaches of the Channel. Maybe it was better to the east, where the airborne bases were . . . but how could that be? The weather systems came over England and the Continent from the west. If it was horrendous here, it had to be the same all over England and northern France.

Poor Ike was at the mercy of his staff weather people, who in turn were at the mercy of the capricious Channel weather itself. Pressing the Supreme Allied Commander as well was the requirement of low tides at dawn for his assault craft, plus enough moonlight the evening before to allow the airborne troops to drop accurately into their assigned zones.

It was common knowledge throughout the waiting legions in southern England that the invasion would have to come off sometime between June fifth and seventh, or weeks would pass before critical tide and moonlight conditions would combine to make another attempt possible. But the weather had to cooperate.

It wasn't doing so.

Sinclair turned at the sound of footsteps clumping down the ladder at the far end of the narrow passageway. A navy lieutenant approached, his peacoat hanging sodden and heavy on his shoulders, his young face flushed red from the biting wind.

"Rough night, eh?" Sinclair said as the officer came up to him.

"A bitch." The lieutenant squeezed past him.

"The invasion still on, Lieutenant?"

The officer paused, glancing at Sinclair's khaki trenchcoat, devoid of any military insignia of rank. "What outfit are you with . . . sir?"

"I'm a correspondent attached to the First Division, Lieutenant. Sinclair Robertson."

"Well, I guess you'll find out anyway. . . ." He frowned. "Big snafu, Robertson. Ike postponed the damned invasion last night, but we didn't get the word. We're going back to port. You might as well hit your rack, we're not goin' anywhere tonight." The lieutenant hurried aft toward the radio room. Sinclair stared after him in confusion. How could a whole convoy have been overlooked?

He trudged down the passageway toward the ladder leading to the lower berthing decks, mulling over the news. The more he thought about it, the less unlikely their situation appeared. An operation as massive and complex as the invasion required a strict timetable to organize the movement of thousands of ships from scores of ports and have them appear off the beaches at the same time and in the right places. Convoys which had a farther distance to steam, like this one, had to leave earlier than those based further to the east. Perhaps they'd left England when the invasion was still on and the callback orders had stalled somewhere along the labyrinth of bureaucracy between Ike and convoy commanders. . . .

Sinclair stepped from the dim passageway into the darkness of his assigned platoon's compartment. At any rate, the snafu had been rectified and they wouldn't find themselves alone at dawn off occupied France, giving away by their presence the location of the delayed invasion.

He took off his soaked coat, hung it on a post of the three-tiered bunk, and sank onto the lower berth. The middle bunk creaked as its occupant, a GI from Massachusetts, leaned down to peer over the edge.

"Can't sleep either, huh?"

"Was out checking the weather. . . ."

Shadows up and down the long row of bunks stirred. The GI

dropped to the deck and grabbed the frame of his bunk to steady himself against the ship's constant rolling and pitching. "Ike must be nuts to send us out in this shit. . . ."

Sinclair sighed. The men, despite their bitching about the weather, were ready to go. Long months of training had left them primed and anxious to get on with the job. The waiting, especially the last few tense days when they'd been quarantined on their bases, was worse, they felt, than anything they might face on the beaches of France.

He looked up at the GI. "We're turning back."

"What?"

Soldiers within earshot sat up in their bunks. The news spread in no time through the whole compartment.

"We didn't get the postponement orders like the rest of the fleet," Sinclair explained.

The GI stared at him, then shook his head in disbelief. "Snafu . . ." he muttered at last. "Situation normal—all fucked up!"

No one knew for sure who had first coined the acronym, but it was now constantly uttered around the world in every theater of war as millions of soldiers indulged their God-given right to bitch.

Someone threw on the light switch, revealing scores of wide-awake faces, most of them various shades of green from seasickness. The GIs blinked their eyes in the sudden brightness; the compartment soon buzzed with arguments for and against the recall.

They might disagree on the merits of Ike's postponement, Sinclair mused as he listened to the bitching, but they all had *one* thing in common. If the army gave Purple Hearts for puking to death, they'd all be heroes.

He lay down on his bunk. As he'd expected, the complaining died out rather quickly. The men were seasick, worn out from days of mounting tension, and every one of them, deep down, was relieved at the unexpected gift of another day or two of life. The postponement gave them one certainty to cling to amidst all the other uncertainties of their young lives—tomorrow was not going to be their last day on earth. The sixth or seventh might well be, but not tomorrow. Not the fifth of June.

He closed his eyes. The uncertainty was Ike's once more. The bowstring, drawn taut, had not been released, the arrow of Overlord was back in its quiver.

Part II

The Great Crusade

Chapter VII

Overlord First Wave
Omaha Beach
June 6, 1944

I

Sinclair Robertson tried to ignore the salt spray cascading over the bow ramp of landing craft PA-478 as it churned through the surf toward the Normandy beaches. His face reddened from the raw wind and stinging spray, his fatigues soaked through from the steady drenching, he looked out over the crowded deck from the last row of GIs. Thirty sodden, seasick, shivering riflemen swayed in rank with the rolling sea. Behind him, three navy bo'sun's mates manned the rear deck, one in the port steering compartment, and the others blasting away at the shore with twin fifty-caliber machine guns.

Sinclair winced from the steady hammering of the twin fifties. His ears rang from the concussion, his eyes blinked in rhythm to the staccato bursts. He clenched them shut in annoyance—what in God's name was he doing here? What could have possessed him to agree to tag along with the poor bastards fate had chosen to ride the first wave of Operation Overlord to the beaches of Nazi-occupied France?

He ducked as another onslaught of cold Channel spray smashed over the bow ramp and drenched the huddled GIs of

PA-478. Exasperated, soaked to the skin, teeth chattering in the dawn twilight, he came out of his crouch, put a boot on the framed side of the boat, grasped the hull, and pulled himself up until he could see over the bow ramp.

Through the Norman mist, the beach was just visible some five hundred yards away. From the clammy shoreline to the seawall inland, it was littered with inverted V-shaped beams upon which other beams were mounted, their blunt ends pointed seaward.

A GI grabbed his sleeve. "Are you nuts?"

He was yanked roughly to the deck and found himself looking into the wide eyes of a young PFC. SANDERS was etched on his tunic breast above the left pocket. "For crissakes, sir!" the soldier exclaimed. "If the army is expecting me to be a hero today, you could at least have the common courtesy to keep yourself alive to witness it."

"Sorry . . . I just want to get ashore."

Sanders looked at him like he was some strange new exhibit in a zoo. "You volunteered for this, sir?"

"Wasn't my idea, son. My editor more or less volunteered me."

PFC Sanders looked oddly relieved. He turned toward the soldier two men to his right. "Hey, Wallace! You owe me ten bucks."

PFC Wallace looked their way, a frown on his freckled face. "For cryin' out loud, Sanders, we're four hundred yards off the beach! Can I pay you later?!"

A titter of nervous laughter drifted over the GIs. Several pale faces, almost hidden under helmets glistening from the spray, turned toward Sanders.

"Better collect while you still can, Sanders," one shouted over the rumbling engine. Everyone ducked as a howitzer shell slammed into the broiling sea fifty yards ahead, throwing up a geyser of dirty green water.

Sanders's reply was drowned out by the freight-train roar of sixteen-inch battleship shells ripping through the mist high overhead, bound for targets far inland. Seconds later, the drone of aircraft began to emerge over the din of the naval bombardment. Suddenly, waves of fighters swept overhead toward the beaches, swooped down on the dim shore, and began to strafe the bunkers hidden along the sea wall.

Sinclair made mental notes of the sights and sounds of D-Day. For the moment, his notepads were useless, tucked away in waterproof plastic pouches stuffed into his pockets. But the drama of the moment was so vivid that the least of his worries was forgetting anything. The number-one concern was getting killed, number two was getting maimed, number three was the question of how scared he would be when the bullets started flying, whether he would be able to function or whether he would freeze up with fear. . . .

"Two hundred yards!" yelled the navy bo'sun from the stern, his deep baritone ringing out over the huddled GIs. Sinclair forgot his own worries and looked around at the youthful faces of the rifle platoon changing from affected indifference to tense expectation.

He looked up as wave after endless wave of Allied fighters screamed toward the beaches, their wingtips spitting fire. *Five thousand* ships lay off Normandy. *Nine thousand* aircraft filled the skies over Europe. *Three million* troops in all waited in suspense on land, sea, and air between the southeast counties of England and the shores of occupied France for news of the fate of the three thousand men who would be the spearhead of the greatest invasion effort in human history.

Robertson stared in wonder at the soldiers of PA-478. The awesome arsenal produced by the greatest industrial nation in the world and all the military skills of the accomplished graduates of West Point and Annapolis would be utterly useless if eighteen-year-old kids like Sanders and Wallace couldn't find it within themselves to wade onto a hostile foreign beach, with nothing but a rifle and a pouch of bullets, to liberate a continent.

His eyes welled up in quiet pride. They were young, they

were scared to death, but when that bow ramp dropped, they would do their jobs.

And he would do his.

"One hundred yards!"

More enemy artillery rounds began to fall into the sea around them. He glanced at his watch. It read 0625 . . . the first wave was on schedule for H-Hour at 0630. For a moment, he thought of his nice warm hotel room bed in London. Proud or not, he damned well wished he was there instead of here.

The lieutenant's voice rang out from the bow. "Lock and load!" Thirty rounds clicked into the muzzles of thirty Garand M-1 rifles. Thirty bolts snapped back into place.

Sanders nudged him. "Too bad your editor isn't here with you. He have something better to do today?"

Sinclair swallowed hard. He hoped his voice would be steady. "Guess so." He hardly recognized the croak that emerged. He cleared his throat in embarrassment.

A round slammed into the sea not thirty yards away, throwing a huge gray spout of water skyward. He felt his stomach and sphincter muscles contract. He closed his eyes.

"You okay, sir?"

He opened his eyes and managed a weak grin. "Ask me later, Sanders."

"Just remember, sir, if you close your eyes, you won't be able to see me and Wallace here win the war."

PA-478's hull hit bottom with a creaking shudder. The bow ramp slapped down into the surf with a splash, revealing fifty yards of water to wade through to reach the dirty brown beach.

Lieutenant Billings half turned toward his men, his eyes wide. "Move it! Move it! Move it!" He leaped off the ramp, plunging into the chest-deep water, and headed for shore, struggling for footing on the muddy bottom. In seconds, the landing craft was empty, the bullet-sprayed water filled with thirty men slogging through the surf toward the soil of France.

Sinclair, the last man out, gasped as he hit the ice-cold water and went in over his head. He staggered to the surface, spluttering and coughing. His eyes stinging from the brine, he blinked in an effort to focus on the blurred image of the shore. His eyes cleared in time to see the surf ahead ripped to angry froth by a hail of machine-gun fire.

Cover . . . find some cover . . .

He heard a series of sickening thuds and saw the man ahead of him slip below the surface. He struggled forward, groped in the murky water for the GI, and managed to grab his arm and pull him up. Four neat holes had been stitched in the man's chest.

Can't just leave him . . . at least drag him to shore. . . .

A mortar round screamed down and Sinclair dove underwater. The concussion slammed him against the tripod beams of a beach obstruction. His ears pounded painfully. Dazed, he huddled behind the tripod, staring toward the shore where the first ranks had reached the beach and stumbled forward into a firestorm of resistance.

Gathering his senses, he crouched behind the beam and took in the scene. Omaha Beach was already littered with shattered landing craft. Lifeless bodies bobbed in the surf all up and down the shoreline. On the beach itself, a few squads of GIs were darting inland toward the seawall, but most were huddled behind whatever cover they could find. Behind him, he could see the second wave churning steadily toward him. Beyond the Higgin's boats, the thunder and lightning from the warships continued unabated as they hurled shells onto the German positions.

Sinclair looked back to the beach. The first wave was pinned down; the tanks that were supposed to be first ashore to lead the way were nowhere to be seen. A murderous crossfire raked the beach, cutting down the few GIs who tried to charge inland.

Better stay here . . . if this is really as bad as it looks, the poor bastards on shore are finished. Did Sanders make it? Or Wallace?

A corpse bobbed past him, carried toward the beach by the surf. Facedown, it floated in an ugly pool of dark red. Dry heaves wracked Sinclair. He clutched his stomach in agony.

Behind him, the second wave, wreathed in ugly spouts of mortar fire, plodded doggedly shoreward. Overhead, a wave of Thunderbolts streaked past. The heights above bloody Omaha erupted seconds later as they plastered the Nazi pillboxes and machine-gun nests with bombs.

He recovered from the spasms in time to see the survivors of the first wave scurry a few more precious yards inland under the air cover. They had to get off the beach or the second wave would suffer as badly as they had. . . . Sinclair watched the tiny figures struggle toward the heights. Men fell, but more and more of them were making the seawall as the German fire began to shift to the swarms of men dashing into the surf from the open bow ramps of the second wave.

More Thunderbolts screamed overhead.

Sinclair hunched forward as the heights thundered with the impact of two-hundred-fifty-pound bombs. Got to get to the beach . . . head in when the Germans have their heads down. . . .

He staggered through the waist-high surf toward a wallowing Higgins boat, stranded just off the beach with a knocked-out engine, and reached the welcome cover of its bulk just as the guns on the heights opened up again. The second-wave landing craft surged past him. Bow ramps thudded into the muck.

Now or never . . .

He summoned his resolve and sloshed past the boat, then broke into a run when the water receded to his knees. On either side of him, a human wave charged into the fury of Omaha. Darting through the maze of beach obstacles, stopping only to catch his breath, he made his way toward the seawall, anxious to find the men of PA-478.

The sky seemed filled with Allied airpower now. Thunderbolts and Mustangs, black-and-white ID stripes on the undersides of their wings, kept the cliffs overlooking Omaha saturated with explosions. Destroyers a mile offshore blazed away with their five-inch guns, adding to the close-range firepower directed at the German positions. Between the sleek gray warships and the beach, the third wave was churning relentlessly forward.

"Robertson!"

The shout drew his eyes to a squad of soaked GIs crouching at the base of the seawall thirty yards up the beach. Sinclair recognized Sanders and darted across the last stretch of open beach. He'd just slumped onto his knees at the seawall when a mortar round obliterated the tripod beams he'd just left. The color drained from his face as he stared at the smoking crater in the sand.

Sanders tossed him a rifle. "You'll need this."

Sinclair hefted the unfamiliar weight of the M-1 as he stared slack-jawed back down the beach.

"Wallace didn't make it," muttered Sanders. "Bastards got him before he got ten yards. . . ."

The words didn't register through Sinclair's shock. Sanders shook him. "Hey!"

He stared vacantly at the face before him. Slowly, the image of the smoking crater faded from his mind. Wallace was dead . . . how many others? He looked around. No more than fifteen men crouched in the shadow of the seawall. Half of the assault unit had fallen in the first five minutes. . . .

Sanders shoved his helmet back on his head and scanned the beach behind them. "Where are the tanks?"

"At the bottom of the damn channel. . . ." The soldier next to Sanders spat in the dirt. "Saw 'em comin' off the LCTs a while back. Sank like stones, every last one of 'em."

Sinclair recalled the exhibition he'd seen back in England. Sherman tanks had been fitted with inflatable sponsons which would enable them to deploy from the deep-hulled LCTs and "swim" to shore. The experiment had worked. But the sea had been calm that day, nothing like the chop that greeted the invasion force the morning of D-Day. . . .

He looked down the line of huddled GIs as the raspy voice of Sergeant Bill Brady rang out over the roar of the Thunderbolts overhead, the crash of the shells, and the bursts of machine-gun fire. "All right, listen up!" he yelled, scurrying in a crouch down the seawall toward Sanders and Sinclair. "The lieutenant's dead, you saw what happened to the damn Shermans. It's up to the Goddamned grunts again." He slammed a fresh clip into his Thompson. "Okay, let's go, boys, let's get off this beach."

The squad hesitated. Men looked at Brady, then glanced white faced at one another. No one moved. Brady edged past Sinclair and climbed up over the seawall, oblivious to the rounds whining past his head. He stood up, fully exposing himself to the enemy fire and glared down at his men, still huddled in the shadows. "What's the matter with you bastards, you want to live forever?"

Sanders looked at Sinclair for a moment, his face tense with fear. "Goddamn it," he muttered, "sounds like a good idea to me." He leaned forward, stricken with the dry heaves. Then, gasping for breath, bent over double from the spasms, he worked the bolt of his M-1, spat the acid remains of his breakfast onto the wet sand, and climbed over the seawall into the hail of bullets.

Sinclair watched the rest of the squad rise to their feet as one and clamber over the wall to follow their sergeant. Suddenly alone, he glanced back at the beach. As far as he could see in each direction, Higgins boats were surging ashore, disgorging GIs onto the sodden shores of France. He turned and peered over the seawall, expecting the worst. But the smoke and haze of battle had already swept over his friends, hiding them from sight. . . .

II

Thirty miles to the southeast, Gunther Dietrich stood next to his Focke-Wulf 190 as the ground crew started it up. The Jumo engine coughed, the prop turned hesitantly, then spun to life. The propwash rippled his leather jacket and he turned away as the dust flew past him, just in time to see Wing Commander Priller's Mercedes roadster careen to a halt next to the pair of idling Focke-Wulfs.

Priller jumped out of the driver's side and dashed up to Gunther. His face was pale, his eyes blazed in fury. "It's the invasion, Dietrich, just like I suspected. Right here in Normandy."

Gunther's heart started hammering in his chest. Priller couldn't be considering heading for the beaches, not with the rest of the squadron transferred to the Pas de Calais. . . .

Priller pulled on his flying helmet, then tossed his roadster keys to Sergeant Kampf, his ground crew-chief. "It's yours, Fritz." Kampf stared wide-eyed at Priller, but the squadron commander had already turned toward Gunther. "Now listen, Dietrich," he shouted over the rumble of the Jumos, "thanks to those onionheads at Wing, there's just the two of us. We can't afford to break up. For God's sake, do as I do! Fly behind me and follow every move. We're going in alone—and I don't think we're coming back."

He dashed off to his 190 before Gunther could respond. Dazed, his mouth dry with fear, Gunther climbed into the cockpit of his 190. His crew chief, Walther Schmidt, helped him strap in. The task finished, their eyes met.

"God be with you, Gunther. . . ."

Gunther swallowed hard. He managed a nod. Schmidt jumped off the wing, snapped to attention and saluted. Gunther's hand wavered toward his forehead, then he leaned over the cockpit sill. "Wish I had a Mercedes to leave you, Walther!" he shouted.

The corner of Schmidt's mouth quivered, but he held his salute as Gunther pulled the canopy closed and taxied off into the mist.

They swept over the hedgerow country of Normandy at treetop height, the ground rushing in a blur below them as they roared at full throttle toward the sea. Gunther stayed on Priller's tail, his hand clutching the stick, his boots trembling against the rudder pedals.

Astonished faces looked up from the streets of St. Lo as they buzzed over the town, low enough for the French to see the black crosses on their wings, low enough for them to see the astonishment turn to fear. Gunther flinched as they screamed past a German antiaircraft bunker, its quad machine guns pivoting quickly to follow the intruders. Seconds later, tracers whipped past the canopy and he kicked the rudder pedals to jink evasively.

We're German, you stupid bastards!

The gun crew hammered away, nonetheless, until the 190's vanished over the treetops. The skies were filled with Allied aircraft, and gun crews all over Normandy were firing at anything that flew.

The nose of Priller's 190 rose and Gunther pulled up on the stick to follow. They shot over the cliffs—

Gunther gasped at the sight of the Channel. From the shore to the horizon the gray chop was dotted with ships. The sky was filled with barrage balloons, swinging from cables over the enemy fleet. Priller pulled into a sharp bank, turning to make a pass lengthwise over the beach. They had no bombs; the best they could do this day was strafe the vehicles swarming over the beaches.

Leveling out, Priller lined up on a trio of tanks chugging their way toward the seawall. Gunther's thumb twitched over the firing button on his stick as he sighted the target through the Plexiglas windshield. Just ahead and slightly above and to the left, Priller's 190 spat fire from its wingtips. Tracers shot downward. The beach around the tanks spurted geysers of dirt as the rounds walked their way toward their targets.

Gunther squeezed his thumb on the button and the 190 shuddered as its wingtip cannon erupted. The tanks grew large and then flashed by below, ringed by spurting sand.

They shot over an empty section of beach, then climbed slightly as another long stretch of white sand loomed into view. Gunther stared in amazement at the multitude of targets—more landing craft, more tanks, more soldiers . . . as far as he could see the shore was swarming with the enemy. The might of the Allies was mind boggling; it was the end for Germany in the West if the panzers couldn't somehow throw these legions back into the sea. . . .

They strafed the landing craft along the shoreline. Gunther made out a Union Jack whipping from the mast of one of the boats. A British beach . . . the second British landing zone. At least twenty kilometers of beach were under assault and they hadn't even seen the Americans yet.

Dodging scattered antiaircraft fire, Gunther followed Priller over another open stretch of beach. He took the opportunity to check above and behind him for Allied fighters. None yet. That couldn't last.

"Another beach ahead, Dietrich," crackled Priller's voice over his earphones. "Save the rest of your ammunition for the Americans; they must be farther west."

"Yes, Herr Commandant."

They dodged more desultory fire over the third British beach. Gunther kicked rudder every few seconds to jink the 190 side to side. Where was the Wehrmacht? The Tommies on all three beaches seemed to be rushing inland like it was some sort of exercise. There had been little sign of losses.

"Hug the beach, Gunther. There are the Yanks dead ahead."

Gunther eased the stick forward, following Priller down to the deck. His heart hammered away as the ground raced past in a blur just fifteen meters below the spinning disc of the prop. One mistake now . . . one lucky shot . . . He lined up an a long row of gray landing craft, pressed the trigger on his stick, and watched the tracers sweep across and through the boats. No time to worry about getting hit now . . . this low I'll be a smoking furrow in the ground before I know what hit me. . . .

The 190 shuddered and Gunther yanked back on the stick as it nosed down for an instant. I'm hit! Check the panel. Looks good . . . no holes in the right wing . . . none in the left . . . no sign of fire. . . . The engine roared steadily.

"One more beach, Dietrich, then we run for it."

Gunther heard himself acknowledge Priller's call. He breathed deeply, trying to calm himself. Whatever it was that had hit him, it hadn't done any major damage. He twisted in the seat and checked the sky above and behind them again. So far so good, no enemy fighters. . . .

The next beach swept into sight. Gunther stared open mouthed at the twisted wrecks littering the shoreline. *This* beach was being defended. Casualties lay sprawled on the sand and in clusters below the seawall. Scores of bodies bobbed in the surf offshore. Several landing craft drifted aimlessly on the choppy waves, bright flames licking at them. His gaze was drawn to the leading waves, huddled for cover in the shadows of knocked-out concrete bunkers and smoking pillboxes.

Was the Wehrmacht already hitting the right flank of the invasion zone with its panzers? Had someone done something right for once?

Priller banked left toward the soldiers farthest inland and opened up ahead of him, his guns spitting neon-green tracers toward the Americans sweeping through the Wehrmacht's first line of defense. Gunther flinched as bodies were slammed backwards like rag dolls. Grim-faced, he squeezed his own trigger. . . .

"Christ, they're Germans!"

Sanders yanked Sinclair to the dirt as the onrushing fighters opened up. The air sang with ricochets as shells careened wildly off the concrete bunker beside them. Sickening thuds mixed with cries of pain as other shells pierced flesh to spatter blood and gore on the white sand.

Sinclair felt something whistle past his head as he hugged the ground. He froze, his eyes squeezed tightly shut as he waited for the inevitable. An eternity seemed to pass as the hail of fire swept through, scything its way through the men of Bravo Company. The roar of the planes grew to a thunderous climax, then faded to a distant drone as they vanished over the cliff walls to the west.

He opened his eyes and looked over at Sanders. Sanders

looked back, then got slowly to his feet, careful to stay in the shadow of the smoldering bunker. Heavy machine-gun fire rattled relentlessly from the German pillboxes south of them.

"You all right, Robertson?"

Sinclair dragged himself to his feet. "I think so." He looked around. Nine or ten GIs were still facedown in the sand. Four of them weren't moving. The fallen men were quickly surrounded by buddies tearing open first-aid kits. Others down the beach cried for medics.

As he watched a couple of medics darting toward them from the littered wreckage of the beach his gaze was drawn skyward. Fighters, black-and-white stripes on their wings, roaring westward just offshore. Three groups of four Mustangs each disappeared over the cliffs in pursuit of the fleeing 190s.

"Hope they get the bastards." Sanders spat on the ground, then turned again toward Sinclair. He shook his head. "If you had any brains at all, Robertson, you'd be back at the seawall. You did your job, you came ashore with us. So what the hell are you trying to prove following us up here? You can't write any damn dispatches if you get your head blown off."

"I just thought—"

"Listen! You got nothin' to prove. You're a reporter, so let us do the fightin' and we'll let you do the writin', all right?"

Touched, Sinclair nodded. From somewhere up ahead Sergeant Brady barked another order and the men began to move out. Sanders shot Sinclair a last look. "Now stay here, dammit, or I'll shoot you myself and save the Krauts the trouble, all right?"

Sanders slapped him on the back as he rose. "Gotta go." He scampered forward, leaving a trail in the wet sand behind him, and was gone from sight again. Sinclair stared at the footprints for a moment, then pulled a notepad from his tunic, a pencil from his helmet liner, and began to write:

Omaha Beach, 6 June, 1944.

At dawn this cold spring morning three thousand GIs of Operation *OVERLORD'S* first assault wave stormed

ashore onto the beaches of Normandy, taking the first
bold step of a journey, the end of which many of them
will never see. . . .

The hedgerows of Normandy flashing by a thousand meters
below him, Gunther followed Priller into a steep banking turn
to the east, sickened by the slaughter of helpless soldiers. He'd
never strafed infantry before; he'd always fought the enemy high
in the clouds, machine against machine, where death was im-
personal, where his enemy was seldom seen, hidden by an enclosed cockpit from sight.

"Keep your eyes open, Dietrich," crackled Priller's voice over
his earphones. "We aren't out of this yet. How are your fuel
and ammunition?"

Gunther checked his instruments. "Plenty of fuel, Herr Commandant. Not much ammunition though. Four or five bursts
perhaps. . . ." He checked the small mirror just above his head
and froze at its reflection of enemy fighters closing fast from
behind and above. "Enemy fighters! Enemy fighters, Priller!"
He jerked around to see the first fighter, an olive-green Mustang, attach itself to his tail and open fire. Desperate to escape,
he dropped his flaps and landing gear. The 190 staggered in a
near stall and the Mustang shot past, but not before more rounds
slammed into his engine. Flames licked at the cowling and
streamed back past the canopy.

The engine sputtered and died.

He yanked back the canopy frame, unbuckled his harness,
and kicked rudder until the plane half rolled, then dropped into
space. The slipstream slammed into him as he fell free, hurling
him violently backward, but he managed to pull the ripcord of
his chute. By the time he'd gathered his senses, the silk had
ballooned out behind him and filled with air. He grasped the
nylon shroud lines and swayed beneath the parachute as it carried him south on the wind, directly toward an approaching
Mercedes staff car. The ground came up fast. He braced himself

for the impact, then thudded into a ditch next to a road and rolled to ease the blow.

The chute fluttered down beside him and he lay there in the black earth, not daring to move as the Mercedes screeched to a stop. *"Deutsch! Deutsch!"* he yelled, throwing his hands into the air. American paratroopers had landed during the night and he didn't want to be taken for the enemy.

A moment later, he found himself looking into the barrel of a drawn Luger. He closed his eyes, hoping the soldier would recognize a Luftwaffe uniform. "He's one of ours!" a voice yelled. Hands helped him to his feet. A Wehrmacht major regarded him in amazement. "We almost shot you."

Gunther breathed a sigh of relief. "The Americans beat you to it, Major."

"You were over the beaches?"

"Yes."

"The Allies are really landing? You saw them?"

Gunther nodded.

"Mein Gott! Here?"

"Here. In Normandy."

The major stared in disbelief. "It must be a feint, everyone knows the Pas de Calais is the real target."

Gunther shook his head. "There were thousands of ships offshore, Major. The beaches were swarming with troops. I saw them. If this is just a feint, I would hate to see the *real* invasion."

The major turned pale. "Come with me, Oberstleutnant, I want you to tell the general what you saw." He helped Gunther into the staff car and the Mercedes tore off down the road to the south.

Chapter VIII

Third Guards Tank Army
Kartovsk, Byelorussia
June 8, 1944

I

The early summer heat hung heavily over the drying marsh-lands of Byelorussia. As far as the eye could see across the vast flatlands, scattered columns of grimy smoke curled lazily into the azure skies, pinpointing the death of another Russian village or collective farm torched by the retreating Nazis.

The Wehrmacht was carrying out Adolf Hitler's scorched-earth policy to the letter. No hamlet was too small, no building too far off the road to avoid the torch. No livestock were spared, no grain bins left intact. What the Germans couldn't carry off was destroyed. Nothing was left in their wake which might provide sustenance or shelter to the pursuing Red Army.

Roving bands of SS death squads butchered every Russian they found, leaving riddled corpses on village streets, in farm fields, in countless ditches beside countless roads. The bodies blackened in the sun, the stench of their decomposing flesh drawing flocks of crows earthward to peck at their remains.

As the Germans fell back, keeping mainly to the sparse network of roads crisscrossing the marshes, advance patrols of Marshal of the Soviet Union Ivan Koniev's 1st Ukrainian Front probed westward on these same roads, slogging through the mud, seeking out the German rearguard units, pushing relentlessly forward, driven by the frequent specter of Nazi atrocities to hot pursuit of the fleeing enemy.

On the outskirts of a smoldering village, as the midday sun beat mercilessly down on his back, Yuri Rostov took a long pull from his canteen, slaking the thirst of the long march from Viashk. Bone-weary, he hooked the canteen back onto his webbed utility belt and tried to kick the gobs of mud from his boots.

The first bursts of machine-gun fire from the village sent his comrades diving for the cover of the roadside ditch. Startled, Yuri scrambled after them and threw himself to the ground beside Pavel Samsonov and Dmitri Azov. Pinned down, they huddled in the ditch with the rest of the platoon while units on their flanks deployed to converge on the village from the north and south.

"Stubborn bastards, these Nazis," Pavel muttered, rising to his elbows and peering over the road toward the smoking ruins.

Dmitri glared at the barrel of his rifle, jammed with mud from his unceremonious dive for cover. "What do you expect?" he asked, struggling out of his backpack so he could get to his cleaning gear. "The devils know we won't take them alive."

"Then why don't the stupid shits just run for it? Why do they have to fight for every pigsty between here and the Dnieper?"

"Same reason we do," observed Dmitri, swabbing out his rifle barrel. "They have their own Pugos."

Pavel Samsonov spat on the ground at the mention of the company commissar. "Where is the lout, anyway? I haven't seen him since yesterday morning."

"He was back at division." Yuri listened to the random firing, hoping the Germans would be flushed out before their platoon got sent in.

"Who told you that?"

Yuri shrugged. "Shadrin."

Pavel rolled his eyes. "That old hen always knows what's going on."

"Pugo's up to something," said Dmitri. "He's been running back and forth to division all week."

"The swine is probably offering to parachute us into Berlin to snatch Hitler himself." Pavel snorted.

Yuri noticed the sudden silence to the west and crawled to the top of the ditch. To his astonishment, he saw a German emerge from a burning *izhba,* his hands in the air. A handful of others appeared behind him. The field-gray figures were soon surrounded by a ring of olive-drab Soviets.

"Prisoners!" he exclaimed. "We took some prisoners!"

Pavel and Dmitri rose to stare at the apparition. "Devils are in for it now," muttered Pavel.

They joined the growing crowd around the cowed Germans. Yuri counted five of them. Three were wounded; the other two, no older than he, looked dazed. Scowling, Sergeant Grigoriev pushed his way through the circle of curious soldiers and began to bark questions at them in pidgin German. In the excitement, no one noticed the lend-lease jeep approaching from the east.

Harried squad leaders broke up most of the gathering, waving their reluctant troops forward to check the rest of the village. Only Grigoriev's squad remained by the time Commissar Boris Pugo's driver braked to a halt behind them. Pugo jumped from the jeep and strode toward the prisoners and their guards.

"Comrade Sergeant!"

Grigoriev stiffened. He turned and came to attention as Pugo stepped past Yuri and Pavel.

"Comrade Captain." He saluted smartly. "We have taken prisoners."

Pugo glared at him for a moment, then glanced at the trembling Germans. Seeing no officers among them, he yanked his Makarov from its holster. "What are you doing?" he demanded.

"Interrogating them, Comrade Captain. I thought—"

"You are *wasting time,* comrade!" He raised his pistol and shot a German in the mouth. The soldier, the back of his head gone, dropped like a stone. "These are privates and noncoms, comrade! They don't know shit!" He shot the next one in the groin and a third between the eyes. The two survivors fell to their knees. The odor of voided bowels drifted on the air. Pugo dispatched them with shots through the head, then finished off the writhing figure clutching his midsection in agony.

Sickened, Yuri looked away.

Pugo slammed his pistol back in its holster and resumed screaming at the hapless Grigoriev. "Leave the interrogations to the NKVD, comrade! *Your* job is to *kill* fascists, not *chat* with them! Now move your squad out before I arrest you for delaying the advance of the whole regiment!"

Yuri fought the bile rising in his throat, glancing at the commissar with a look of loathing as Pugo brushed past him. Their eyes met.

"What is wrong with *you,* comrade?" The commissar sneered. It was not a question. Yuri swallowed hard and came to attention. Pugo glared at him in disgust, noting his pallor, the look of pity in his eyes.

"The lad has dysentery, Comrade Captain," lied Pavel, thinking quickly. Yuri despised Pugo as much as anyone, but was too young to know when to watch his mouth. He seized Yuri's arm and started to lead him away.

"Dysentery . . . ?" Pugo's look halted Pavel in his tracks. His contemptuous gaze shifted from Pavel to Yuri, then toward the marshes beyond the road. "It is a criminal offense to fill one's canteen with marsh water," he said, fixing hard eyes once again on Yuri. "It deprives the Motherland of her soldiers through self-inflicted illness." His voice grew menacing. "If this man has dysentery, I will be forced to charge him with anti-Soviet conspiracy."

Sergeant Grigoriev, on the edge of panic, stepped in. If Rostov were arrested on such a charge, *he* could be charged as well for allowing his troops to drink contaminated water, thus depriving the Motherland of a *whole platoon* of her soldiers. It didn't matter if no one had actually done so; the charge would be sufficient to ensure conviction. On such logic was the massive slave-labor population of the Gulag built and sustained.

"Comrade Captain," he pleaded, glaring at Pavel, "no one in my unit has dysentery."

Pugo confronted Yuri. "Do you have dysentery!"

Yuri balked. Denial could doom Pavel to the camps for lying to a political officer; affirmation could land the whole platoon in the Gulag. He cursed his weak stomach, his sensitivity to death.

"Well!"

"I was mistaken," Pavel confessed, sparing Yuri a terrible decision. "Comrade Captain, the lad is a good soldier but he is young, he is only *sixteen*. He—"

"That is old enough to enjoy the extermination of fascist swine!" roared Pugo. "I saw his reaction, I saw the look in his eyes. This man is a fascist sympathizer, and your lies a scheme to cover your Hitlerite plots. I saw you cowering in that ditch when your comrades were attacking the enemy!" Pugo backed away, his hand on his holster. "I will have you arrested, I will have the lot of you arrested!"

He stalked toward his idling jeep, climbed in, then yelled a final warning. "You will pay for your treachery, every last one of you!" He snapped an order to the driver. The jeep wheeled about and sped down the road, leaving the stunned squad staring at the receding vehicle.

Grigoriev was first to break the strained silence. "Samsonov, you have the brains of a monkey," he muttered. "Dysentery? Was *that* the best you could do?"

"It was my fault, Comrade Sergeant," explained Yuri. "I—"

Grigoriev waved away the explanation in disgust. "I will speak to Captain Arbatov. He will sort it all out. Comrade Pugo cries 'wolf' so often, no one pays attention to his wild charges anymore."

He led the squad through the dying village and out onto the road to the west. Pavel Samsonov fell in beside Yuri as they trudged through the mud.

"Thank you for standing up for me, Pavel Iylitch."

Pavel spat on the ground. "I was afraid you would curse him out and get yourself in *real* trouble."

"I might have . . . that Pugo is a filthy lout."

Dmitri caught up with them. "Do you think Captain Arbatov will be able to deal with him?"

"He always has," Yuri replied. He looked toward Pavel for confirmation, but the big man was silent.

Dmitri glanced at Pavel. His concern was etched on his face as he then met Yuri's gaze. "Captain Arbatov is afraid of the commissar too. There's a limit to how often he'll be willing to stick his neck out."

"But Grigoriev said—"

"Yuri Arkadovich," Dmitri cut in, "it's true Pugo may have lost some credibility by making so many accusations, but sooner or later a commissar at regiment or division is bound to conclude that where there's smoke there's fire. Then the heads will roll. I just hope they aren't ours. . . ."

II

The interrogation cells at Butyrski Prison in Leningrad were in the basement. Cold, damp, functional, they contained nothing but a chair or two, a small writing desk, and a bare lightbulb hanging by a cord from the ceiling.

During his confinement, Arkady Rostov had seen several. They were all the same. The only things that changed were the tactics of his interrogators. Some were harsh and threatening one day; then sympathetic and comradely the next. His interrogator this day, a skeletally thin Muscovite by the name of Ivan Suslov, had ranged from one extreme to the other in the two hours Arkady had sat under the harsh light, listening in stoic resignation to the performance of the NKVD major.

Arkady sighed as Suslov launched again into the indictment, reading from the papers in a droning monologue. He stared at the gray cement floor, his arms folded across his chest for warmth against the chill of the basement cell. The clothes he'd worn since his arrest were rumpled and dirty, his hair was disheveled, and he had a three weeks' growth of beard. His breathing was labored—the head cold he'd contracted uncounted days ago had spread to his chest. His eyes watered, and his congested lungs ached from frequent coughing spells. His sinuses throbbed painfully with every spasm of coughing, and his nose was red and inflamed. Feverish, he waited for Suslov to conclude the farce, wanting nothing but to lie down and sleep.

The cement walls, beaded with condensation, seemed to swallow up the interrogator's words. When he finally finished, he walked from behind the desk and handed the five stapled pages to Arkady. "You will sign this," he said.

Arkady shook his head slowly. "I cannot sign a document that is nothing but a pack of lies, Suslov."

The major stiffened. His eyes, vacant and bored since the prisoner had been brought to him, grew hard. Didn't this stubborn fool know when to give up? Didn't he understand that it simply didn't matter whether the charges in the indictment were true or not? The unalterable fact was that he had been arrested under Article 58 of the Soviet Constitution for anti-Soviet activities. He had been accused by an anonymous informer and his name added to the quota list for the month of August. His arrest had sealed his fate. The motions they'd gone through the past week were not so much a trial as an effort to force from him the names of friends, neighbors, coworkers, or relatives who could be arrested as well. There was no chance of acquittal—only a chance for a reduced sentence if the prisoner cooperated.

Suslov waved the pages under Arkady's nose. "You have been

tried and convicted of anti-Soviet activities, Citizen Rostov. You have been sentenced to ten years for your crimes. But if you continue to insist upon protecting the identities of your fellow conspirators against the State, you will be given the maximum term."

Arkady sighed wearily. All right, if they wanted him to name some traitors to the Motherland, he would do so. He could think of several without any effort at all—men who schemed and plotted every waking hour to better themselves at the expense of their comrades and their country, men who had no motives that weren't self-serving, no morals that weren't corrupted, no words that weren't lies. He unfolded his arms, took the indictment from Suslov, and looked him square in the eyes.

"Do you have a pen, comrade?"

Suslov took one from his tunic pocket and handed it to Arkady. Suslov smirked—staring at a twenty-five-year term in the Gulag never failed to get the attention of these louts. "You will list your accomplices here, on page five," he explained, "then sign your name at the bottom." Arkady turned to the last page and began to write as Suslov went to the cell door and called for the guard waiting in the corridor to escort the prisoner back to his cell.

Under the *Conspirators* heading, in bold block Cyrillic letters he wrote *Josef Stalin, Lavrenti Beria, Georgi Malenkov, Lazar Kaganovich,* and *Nikita Khrushchev.* Where he was to sign his name, he wrote *Ivan Suslov.*

"I have identified the criminals, Suslov."

Suslov walked up to him. "Excellent! You have been wise to confess. Others would have continued to hide the identity of these traitors, but I knew you were not the kind to hide the truth."

Arkady nodded solemnly. "I have finally realized that we can no longer allow these vermin to contaminate the Russian people with their filth. I have fallen for their lies for too long. I have kept silent for too many years, looking the other way while they dragged us all down into the gutter." He glared at his persecutor. "You will arrest the traitors soon, I hope?"

Suslov, beaming, reached for the papers. "Twenty-five years was too big a pill to swallow, eh, Rostov? I knew you'd see the light."

Arkady raised defiant eyes to him. "Oh, I have. I have indeed. He handed the papers over. "Swallow *this,* Suslov."

The NKVD major's smirk faded as he scanned the last page. He stared at Arkady, livid with rage. "You bastard!" He crumpled the papers into a ball and flung them to the floor. "You will rot in the camps, Rostov! You will regret this treachery!

"Guard!" he bellowed. "Take the prisoner away!"

Arkady rose from his chair as the door began to open. He looked down on Suslov, several inches shorter than him. The major stepped back involuntarily, but not far enough to prevent Arkady's index finger from jabbing him in the chest. "I may die, Suslov, but your turn is coming. I may not live to see it, but Russia will. She is eternal, she will cleanse herself of your filth one day. She will climb out of the pit you and your kind have dug for us all, throw off her chains, and climb toward the light as I have. You can throw me in the camps, Suslov, you can kill me, but you can't kill the truth. It will shine on these black years of crime someday and all will see it."

For a moment, the guard stared dumbfounded at the spectacle of a prisoner berating his interrogator—then his training took over. Fearing an imminent assault on Major Suslov, he sprang forward. A meathook of a fist smashed into Arkady's face, sending him crumpling to the floor.

"Get this scum out of here!" raged Suslov, retrieving the crumpled confession from the cell floor. It would have to be destroyed before anyone saw it. Who knew what some ambitious rival might make of it? *His* signature was on a document accusing half the Politburo of anti-Soviet slander. . . .

Arkady was dragged from the cell, his nose broken, blood spouting from the smashed cartilage. The door slammed heavily behind him, leaving Suslov alone.

The NKVD major took a lighter from his trouser pocket and set the confession on fire. The flames licked greedily at the paper, flaring up until Suslov let it drop to the floor.

As the fire died, he ground the twisted remains into black powder with his boot, turned, and walked away.

Chapter IX

Grand Rapids
Michigan
June 10, 1944

I

The picnic table sat on the grass in the shade of an elm tree. Around the varnished table sat Wilson Lindberg, his brother, Bill, his parents, William Sr. and Elizabeth, and a neighbor girl, Carrie Anne Simmons. A pitcher of lemonade and plate of gingersnap cookies sat on a cotton, checkerboard-patterned tablecloth.

Wilson, dressed in his Army Air Corps uniform, sipping lemonade, glanced past his father at downtown Grand Rapids, just across the Grand River. It looked pretty much the same, a small city of two- or three-story brick buildings housing stores, offices, and banks. Along the river to the south were the long, warehouselike factory buildings which provided employment for most of the workforce of his hometown.

"They still all making furniture, Dad?"

The elder Lindberg nodded. Heavy-set, wearing a short-sleeved white shirt tucked into khaki chinos, the elder Lindberg was a man in his fifties, his once black hair now silver, yet as thick as ever. "Most of 'em, Willie, but not so much consumer stuff like before the war. These days its office stuff—desks, chairs, conference tables, that sort of thing. The military has more bases now than Carter has little liver pills, and they all need office furniture."

Bill Lindberg, Jr., seated next to his father, refilled his glass, a frown on his suntanned face. "Do we have to talk about furniture, for crying out loud?" He took a long drink of lemonade. "I'd like to hear more about the war."

"You'll get your bellyful soon enough, Junior," his father said. He slid the empty pitcher across to his wife. "Betty, we need more lemonade. . . ." He turned to his eldest son. "Junior here really upset his mother when he up and joined the Marines."

Wilson glanced at his mother. Elizabeth Lindberg was dressed in her Sunday best, a flowered dress with white belt and matching white high heels. Her smile faded at the reminder that her younger son would be gone soon, off to Parris Island, South Carolina, and then God only knew where. Not trusting herself to speak, she took the pitcher and headed for the house.

When the back porch screen door had slammed softly shut behind her, Bill Lindberg, Sr., was the first to break the strained silence.

"Your mother's friend from church, Mrs. Appleby, lost her son, Carl, at Saipan back in June." He sighed. "There have been others, of course. The Myers' boy Fred was killed at Kasserine; Frank Winslow, a guy I knew from work, was wounded bad in Sicily . . . oh, and Sam Kowalski, used to manage the Rexall Drug Store? He was on the Hornet when she went down off Guadalcanal. . . ."

"Poor Mrs. Appleby, she's been having a hard time of it, a widow and all. Carl was all she had," Carrie Anne Simmons said. "Betty has been over to see her almost every day since . . . it happened."

"I'm sure it helps a lot to have someone around, just to talk to. Mother's good at that sort of thing." Wilson looked across the table at his brother. Volunteering, instead of waiting for his draft notice, at least gave Bill his choice of which service to enter. But the marines?

Betty Lindberg returned with a fresh pitcher of lemonade. Her puffy eyes betrayed the tears that had flowed freely inside the house. She seemed a thousand miles away as Wilson asked Bill when he had to report.

"September fifth . . ." Bill glanced guiltily at his mother.

"Parris Island, huh?"

"Yeah."

Wilson smiled reassuringly at his mother. "War'll probably be over before you ever see action. Everyone in London figures the Germans will give up by Christmas. When they go, the Japs will have to throw in the towel too."

"Too bad those generals didn't get Hitler last month," Bill, Sr., grumbled, pouring himself a glass of lemonade. He waved at a fly buzzing around his head. "With that bastard dead— uh . . . sorry, ladies. . . . Anyway, with Hitler dead, there could have been a quick armistice, don't you think, Wilson?"

"They've lost the war, Dad, everyone knows it. But—" He noticed his mother hanging on his every word, hope alive in her eyes that her sons would both come back to her. He shifted gears quickly, unable to admit that the war in fact would likely be fought to the bitter end, maybe into '46. "But, Hitler or no Hitler, we'll have it wrapped up by the end of the year," he lied, rewarded by the evident relief on his mother's face.

Later, he poked his head into Bill's room. "Got a minute, Junior?" It was late. Down the hallway, their parents' room was dark and silent.

"Sure." Bill sat up on his bed and turned down the Glenn Miller music filtering softly from the old RCA. Wilson leaned against the edge of the desk and looked at his brother. Junior had grown a lot in the two years since he'd seen him last, yet he'd always be his kid brother—the kid brother who'd worshipped him from the great gulf of five years that had always made Wilson an idol of sorts. They had been far enough apart in age as they grew up to avoid the sibling rivalry that always seemed to simmer between brothers close in age. Junior had always listened to him before, sought him out for advice.

"Why the marines, Junior?" Wilson asked. He pulled a cigarette from a new pack and left it dangling from the corner of his mouth as he fumbled in his pockets for matches. Bill tossed him a book from his bedside table.

"I'd liked to have joined the Air Corps, Will, but figured by the time I got through training and all, the war would be over."

Wilson inhaled deeply, a frown creasing his handsome face. "Why this impatience to see action, Kid?"

"I wish you wouldn't call me that, Will. I'm eighteen now. I'm not a kid anymore."

"Sorry . . ." Wilson fumbled for words. "At any rate," he said finally, "I don't understand why you're in such a hurry to join up and get yourself shot at."

"You signed up the day after Pearl Harbor, Will. You didn't exactly let the screen door hit you on the way out."

Wilson's frown deepened. The kid had him there . . . but *that* was different—the country had been attacked. She *desperately needed* every able-bodied man she could get. But now, hell, the war was all but won.

"But Junior—"

"Bill."

Wilson's lips compressed. He hadn't expected a debate. Junior— Bill, had always reacted in abject misery to learn that he had disappointed his big brother. "Okay, *Bill,* I'll give it to you straight. I joined the Air Corps for three reasons: first, because I wanted to fly; second, because Carrie Anne wanted to get married; and third, because my country called. In *that* order." He crushed his cigarette in the ash tray, staring a moment at the dying butt as he collected his thoughts. "The only reason you seem to have is that you're afraid you'll be missing something. Well, believe me, you don't want to see what I've seen. Not by a long shot. You aren't missing a damn thing, Bill, except a lot of suffering, a lot of pain, a lot of death."

Bill Lindberg saw the distress on Wilson's face and watched spellbound as his brother struggled to control his emotions. "Wil—"

"No. Let me talk." He took a ragged breath. "Bill, when you've seen buddies of yours, *friends,* ride an out-of-control Fortress down to die. When you see them blown to hell by flak—there beside you one second, and gone in a fireball the next. . . . When you go back to the barracks and have to pack up their stuff to send to their families. When you see those empty bunks and empty chairs in the mess . . ."

He fumbled for another cigarette, his chest heaving. "I've seen ground crews hose out what's left of friends from the insides of Forts because there's nothing left big enough to pick up. . . ."

He lit his cigarette with trembling fingers, waiting until he was sure his voice wouldn't crack before going on. "I don't know how the papers here have handled things, but we were getting slaughtered last winter. Seemed like every day we flew, we lost fifty or sixty Fortresses, five to six hundred men. . . . More than one crew packed it up and flew to Switzerland or Sweden. I'll bet *that* never got in the papers. And don't think it never crossed my mind, or the guys on my crew. We thought about it. We thought about it a lot, damn near *everybody* did, even if some would never admit it."

Bill stared at Wilson in shocked silence, his eyes vacant as his mind struggled to absorb what he was hearing. Numb, he reached under the bed, pulled out a half-pint bottle of Wild Turkey, and handed the whiskey to Wilson.

Wilson unscrewed the top and knocked back a gulp, then another. He handed the half pint back. "I lost my whole crew, Bill. If we'd made a *navigational error* one day and landed in Stockholm, they'd still be around, not dead or rotting away in a POW camp."

"It was *that* bad?" Bill's voice was hushed. He took a drink and winced as the whiskey burned down his throat.

"A man can only take so much. . . . we all have our breaking point. Some guys can take a lot; others not so much, but sooner or later everybody cracks, one way or another. . . ." Wilson managed a bleak smile. "But most of us did our job, I guess. Somehow. . . . I guess you will too."

"I will." Bill took a long pull of whiskey. His eyes belied his words, though. An awkward silence fell.

"Just remember, Bill," Wilson said at last, "you won't be the only guy scared to death. Your buddies will be scared, and the *enemy* will be scared, just as scared as you are."

II

Sinclair Robertson lay in bed, listening to Maggie O'Reilly breathing softly beside him. The blackout curtains were drawn tightly over the hotel room window, leaving the room in pitch darkness. He closed his eyes, savoring the softness of her hair against his face, the scent of her perfume, the warmth of her body against his.

The sudden rumble of an explosion rattled the windowpanes. Sinclair sat up with a start. Maggie stirred beside him. He got up, padded through the darkened room to the window and peered out through the heavy curtains. Three blocks away a dull glow lit the rainy night. The glare of flames reflected off the glistening streets, wet with rain.

"Another buzz bomb."

Sinclair turned toward the bed. "Uh-huh." Maggie joined him at the window and they stared down the street, watching in helpless resignation as flames leaped skyward from the stricken building. A siren began to whine somewhere in the night, its wail growing louder and more insistent. In a matter of minutes, a symphony of sirens screamed in the night as London's fire and rescue teams responded to the latest V-1 attack.

Sighing, Sinclair let the curtains fall closed. "How often does this happen?"

Maggie held him close, her head resting against his chest. "Almost every night now. It's nothing like the Blitz of course, but the randomness of the destruction has everyone on edge." She looked up at him. "People are scared. Everyone thought London was safe, what with the Luftwaffe busy defending their own cities. Now, one never knows when one of those damned robot bombs might fall on their head out of a clear sky."

Sinclair guided her back to the bed. They lay down, listening to the sirens and the rumble of lorries in the night. "With any luck," he said, pulling the covers over them against the damp night chill, "the launch sites will be overrun soon and that'll be the end of it."

Maggie turned toward him, her breath soft on his neck, her hand resting on his chest. He kissed her forehead, then lay back, a jumble of images flitting through his mind—sinister V-1s droning through the night over the choppy Channel; Maggie's surprised smile as he'd walked into the pub; her clinging to him in breathless passion only an hour ago, and the formless face of her husband looking down on them from the darkened ceiling, silent accusation in haunted eyes. . . .

Sinclair blinked away the visions, but Maggie sensed his unease. Her hand drew away tentatively, then reached for his face, brushing against the rough stubble of his chin. She peered through the shadows, searching his darkened features. "Is something wrong, Sinclair?"

He fumbled for his cigarettes on the night table, then tapped out a Lucky Strike. His lighter flared to life, throwing their huddled shadows across the wall above the headboard. He exhaled, a cloud of tobacco smoke swirling over the rumpled bedspread before dissipating in the darkness. He looked into her eyes.

"Oh, I don't know," he said, rising on his elbow to face her, "when I'm with you, I just can't seem to keep your husband out of my thoughts." She started to speak, but he silenced her with a finger on her lips. "I know, I know, Ian was probably killed, but what if he wasn't? What if he's rotting away in some POW camp with nothing to cling to but the thought of coming home to you . . . ?"

"I've lived with that thought for two years, Sinclair," she said, her voice steady. "Don't think I haven't. I've tried to be the brave wife. I've put my life on hold for two years, but I just can't anymore." Her lips quivered, and she looked away. "Not knowing for sure one way or another is awful. . . . I loved Ian, but how long can you love a picture on your wall, a memory? We had so little time together . . . it seems like another lifetime, like some brief dream that flickered out, leaving nothing but emptiness."

Sinclair reached out for her, but she drew away.

"Look, I'm sorry," he said. "I shouldn't have brought it up."

She turned toward him again. "No, you shouldn't have."

"Must be the Puritan stock in me," he offered, a tentative smile on his face. "I come from a long line of New Englanders, Maggie. Most of the Robertsons have been Bible-thumping theologians ever since old Jonathon Robertson came over on the *Mayflower*. I'm the first in four generations of fire-and-brimstone believers to stray from the flock, to forsake the pulpit for the secular world of journalism. But I still have those Puritan genes in me, that inner self that's quick to judge and even quicker to feel guilt."

He leaned back and rested his head on the pillow. "I'm sorry, Maggie, I certainly didn't mean to imply that you're betraying your husband. It's just that, well, I've been in France with the troops, I've lived with those guys, more than a few of which have gotten 'Dear John' letters from home. . . . I've seen first-hand how devastating it is and sympathized with them. Yet here *I* am, maybe doing the same thing to Ian that some guy back in the States is doing to some poor GI in France. Do you understand why I feel caught in the middle here, why I feel like a hypocrite?"

Maggie began to cry softly. Sinclair reached for her again

and she responded this time, clinging to him. "This damned war," she sobbed, her chest heaving. The tears flowed freely. Sinclair held her, rocking her gently. He kissed her, brushed back the hair from her eyes.

"I'm sorry, Maggie, I'm sorry. . . . I'm such an idiot."

"You Americans are an odd lot," she sniffled, forcing a trembling smile through her tears. "Only a Yank would bring up a girl's husband when he's holding her in his arms." She wiped the tears from her cheeks. "We British are a tad more circumspect." She waved a finger in front of his nose, her tone one of mock scolding. "There's a time and place for everything, Sinclair. I really don't think this is the proper *time* or *place* to be thinking of poor Ian. . . ."

"You're quite right, Maggie."

She squeezed him even more tightly to her. "This is *our* time and we have so precious little o it." She looked up into his eyes. "While we're together, can't we just forget the war, Sinclair? Can't we just think of us? Heaven knows, the days—the weeks—we're apart give us plenty of time to brood about what might have been or what might be."

Sinclair smiled. "You have yourself a deal. From now on, Maggie O'Reilly, you and I are the only people in the world."

She kissed him. "Promise?"

"I promise."

Chapter X

I

Political Commissar Boris Pugo stamped most of the mud from his boots, then stalked through the doorway of the farmhouse to read the latest dispatches from division HQ. He cursed at the hard rain spattering through the blasted-out kitchen window and retreated to the remains of the main room, to find the battalion's company commanders being briefed by Major Samsonov.

He skulked back into the kitchen and leaned against a wall. Scanning the teletype messages, he stopped suddenly as he came to one initialed for immediate action by his immediate superior, Battalion Commissar Major Pyotr Boldev.

His eyes widened as he read; slowly, a smile of triumph spread across his face. One Arkady Pavlovich Rostov, the report stated, had been arrested in Leningrad, charged under Article 58 of the Soviet Constitution with anti-Soviet activities and sent off to the Gulag. . . .

Ignoring the murmur of voices from the next room, Pugo read the full report, then folded it carefully, and tucked it into his tunic pocket. He grinned savagely—this Arkady Rostov, un-

masked as a *traitor* to the State, it turned out, was the father of
the private in Grigoriev's squad, *and* Arbatov's platoon, involved
in the incident with the fascist prisoners. The younger Rostov
was the lout with the cow-eyes who'd protested his liquidation
of the Hitlerite enemy.

Well! Let's just see Grigoriev or Arbatov defend the little
bastard now!

Pugo closed his eyes for a moment, savoring the sudden gift
dropped into his lap from out of the blue. A plan began to form—
he would have to clear things with Boldev, of course, but that
was just a formality. It was a simple matter of forging an incrimi-
nating letter from the elder Rostov to his son, containing—

Pugo frowned. Why even make the effort? The younger Rostov's actions might have been enough to land him in a penal
battalion anyway—his fascist sympathies were there for all to
see. . . .

*But now his father had been exposed as a known traitor, by
the Leningrad NKVD, no less!*

It was delicious—an open-and-shut case if ever there was
one. Private Rostov displays Hitlerite sympathies on the battlefield; then within weeks his father is arrested for anti-Soviet
activities. Like father, like son. . . .

The briefing broke up in the other room. Pugo watched the
company commanders begin to emerge through the doorway
into the kitchen and waited until Arbatov appeared.

"Comrade Captain, a word with you . . . ?"

Arbatov stepped aside to let his comrades pass. He pulled on
his greatcoat, annoyed at the smug smile on Pugo's face. A
regular army officer, Arbatov, like most of his colleagues, resented the power of the commissars, political officers who had
the authority to countermand any of their orders. From platoons
all the way up through division, corps, and army levels, units
were co-commanded by a regular army officer and a commissar.
Most of the commissars had little military training—they existed for the sole purpose of maintaining Communist Party control over the Red Army.

"What is it, comrade?" Arbatov asked, glancing at the down-pour outside.

"It is my duty to arrest one of your men, Comrade Captain."

Arbatov's eyes narrowed. "If this is about the incident at that crossroads, I will have to protest. My soldiers—"

"Have a traitor among them," Pugo cut in. "It has come to my attention that Private Rostov's father has been arrested and sent to the camps under Article 58." He instantly regretted blurting out the information—he could have strung Arbatov along for a while. Who knew, he might have gone so far in defending one of his men as to bring suspicion down upon himself. Then the company might have gotten a commander more cooperative when it came to maintaining strict party discipline in the ranks. . . .

Arbatov blinked in surprise, then stiffened. Ever loyal to his troops, his instincts took over. "Well . . . that doesn't necessarily incriminate Private Rostov, Comrade Pugo. He is a good soldier; he has been with the company ever since Stalingrad. No one fights harder."

Pugo met Arbatov's glare. "And he will continue to fight, but not in *my* company! I must insist that he be charged and transferred to a penal battalion, where he can fight for the Motherland without infecting good Soviet soldiers with his disloyalty."

"I won't hear of it."

Pugo's eyebrows rose. "Political matters are my responsibility," he threatened, delighted at Arbatov's reaction. He just might fall into the trap after all.

Fearing Pugo, despite their equal rank, Arbatov shifted gears. "Look, comrade . . . Private Rostov is young, very young. His reaction to your justified execution of fascist prisoners shouldn't be interpreted as anything sinister. No soldier in my company has shown more devotion to the Motherland than Rostov."

"His father is a traitor." Pugo's eyes narrowed. "The son of a traitor cannot remain in a regular unit. It's as simple as that."

Arbatov stared at Pugo, measuring his determination. To protest too strongly was risky. Pugo could report him to the battalion commissar on a trumped-up charge of conspiring to conceal a traitor in the ranks. He could find himself in a penal battalion himself.

"It's settled then?" Pugo probed.

Fear won out over loyalty. Arbatov nodded.

"I will make the necessary arrangements. Rostov will be transferred tonight." Pugo turned to leave, then paused. He faced Arbatov again. "The others will bear watching. Rostov may have already contaminated some of his comrades with his views. . . ."

To Pugo's disappointment, Arbatov didn't rise to the bait. "I'm quite sure you won't neglect your duties." He sneered.

Pugo's eyes flashed at the insult. "Your attitude toward the NKVD will land you in hot water one day, comrade."

Not trusting himself with a response, Arbatov turned on his heel and stalked out into the deluge. Enraged at the casual manner in which the commissars consigned good troops to the penal battalions, but more angry at himself for buckling under to Pugo, he walked unseeing through the mud and slop of the camp, head down against the driving rain.

He pulled the collar of his greatcoat up around his ears. Rostov wouldn't last a week in a penal battalion—soldiers sent to the punishment units were nothing but fodder, nothing but hapless guinea pigs marched at gunpoint across fascist minefields to clear a path for the assault troops.

The poor bastard would be blown to quivering bits before he ever saw eighteen. . . .

II

Lavrenti Beria handed the latest dispatch from Poland back to Colonel Aleksei Kriminov with a curt nod of approval. "When will it be over?"

"The uprising has been crushed but for mopping up operations, Comrade Beria. We have been intercepting fascist reports since it began and have reliable information that the Poles in Warsaw have suffered some three-hundred-thousand casualties."

Beria beamed. "Excellent! Three hundred thousand, you say!"

"Yes, Comrade Beria."

"Joseph Vissarionovich will be pleased." Beria paused. "We must reduce those figures, of course. See that our estimates come closer to, say, fifty thousand."

"Fifty thousand?"

"Yes." Beria's smile faded. "The West has been giving us the devil over this enough as it is. Joseph Vissarionovich has had to send two personal letters to Churchill, explaining in detail Zhukov's difficulties with fascist counterattacks on the Vistula and the problems we are having with lengthy supply lines."

"The West will eventually find out how many were killed. . . ."

Beria shrugged. "We will stick to our story. At any rate, the necessary work has been accomplished, the pro-Western elements in Warsaw have been liquidated. *That* is what is important, not a few sniveling protests from Churchill. Warsaw was a nest of counterrevolutionaries who had to be eliminated so they wouldn't stand in the way of a socialist Poland. It was clever of Joseph Vissarionovich to let the Hitlerites do our dirty work for us. Now we can set our friends up in Warsaw without any internal opposition."

Beria dismissed Kriminov and hurried to Stalin's *dacha*. He was escorted to the grounds behind the main lodge, to find Stalin sitting at a table under the shade of a pine tree. Maps and dispatches from the front were scattered across the green tablecloth. A bottle of Georgian wine had been opened and left at the right edge of the table next to plates of smoked salmon, caviar, and *zakuski*. Two cigarettes smoldered in an ashtray at Stalin's elbow. His daughter, Svetlana, sat on the grass beside him, a book open on her lap.

They looked up as Beria approached. Stalin grunted a greeting, his yellow eyes expectant. He nodded toward the bench opposite him.

"Thank you, Joseph Vissarionovich." Beria sat down. He winked at Svetlana. "You are reading Lenin then, Lasha?" he joked, using his nickname for her.

Svetlana Stalin, a thin, blond ten-year-old, shook her head shyly. "Tolstoy, Uncle Lavrenti."

"Ah."

"Svetlana, go find Papa's pipe, will you?" Stalin said, shooing her away. "The Burnhill."

"Can't I—"

Stalin's look cut her off. She rolled her eyes in juvenile resignation and scampered toward the *dacha*.

Stalin turned eagerly toward Beria. "The latest."

Beria reported the news from Warsaw, and Stalin nodded silently, picking at the caviar. Chewing thoughtfully, he waited for Beria to finish, only half listening as he fumbled through the maps before him until he found the one he wanted. He spread it out over the others.

". . . that the uprising is completely crushed, Joseph Vissarionovich," Beria concluded, hiding his annoyance at Stalin's divided attention. What could be more important than the elimination of the pro-Western Poles in Warsaw?

"Well, that is *one* headache out of the way," Stalin replied. He reached for his cigarette, noting with a frown the burnt-out butts of two forgotten Lucky Strikes, and pulled his pack out from his tunic pocket. "Churchill will be hopping mad now. . . ." He lit up and left the cigarette dangling from the corner of his mouth. "Well fuck him, he'll just have to stew for a while."

Beria grinned. Stalin and Churchill were bitter enemies, thrown together by the common threat of Hitler's Reich. He had no doubt that the minute the war ended, all pretense would be dropped and they would be at each other's throats.

Stalin leaned over the map before him, scowling, Warsaw

forgotten. From Beria's position, it was upside-down so he walked around to Stalin's side of the table and stood beside him.

"Look at this," Stalin muttered, his cigarette bobbing up and down as he spoke. "The Americans have shot through France like shit through a goose. . . ."

Beria nodded solemnly, noting that the blue arrows denoting armored spearheads were already deep inside Belgium.

"The little Allies are less than a hundred kilometers from the German frontier, Lavrenti Davidovich." The tip of his cigarette glowed briefly as Stalin inhaled, then danced frantically up and down again as he continued, his voice rising in anger. "The fascists are running away! They've been in headlong retreat for six weeks! They've given up the fight in the West, while they hammer at us like demons in Poland. I smell a plot, Lavrenti Davidovich. The field marshals have muzzled Hitler. They're seeking accommodation with the West. They will hand Germany over to Eisenhower and march alongside the Americans to confront us on the Vistula!"

Svetlana appeared in the middle of her father's harangue, his pipe in her hands, a timid look on her face. Shaking with rage, Stalin didn't notice her. Knowing better than to interrupt her father at such times, she stood behind him uncertainly.

"Your pipe, Joseph Vissarionovich," said Beria at last, nodding behind them. Stalin turned around impatiently.

Svetlana held out the pipe. "Is this the Burnhill, Papa?"

Seeing his opening, Stalin shook his head. "No, girl, it's not," he lied, not wanting his daughter underfoot. "Go find Georgi Petrovich. He knows where it is."

Confused, Svetlana glanced at Beria, then at the pipe, then at her father. Stalin shooed her away, then turned again to his maps. She stared at his back for a moment. Then desperate to please, she ran off to find her father's aide.

"The little Allies are betraying us, Lavrenti Davidovich," Stalin growled, Svetlana forgotten. "They're in league with the fascists now. They'll combine forces and hurl nearly two hundred divisions at us, the bastards."

"Perhaps the Hitlerites will turn and fight on the Siegfried Line or the Rhine, Joseph Vissarionovich," ventured Beria, anxious to defuse Stalin's rampant paranoia. "Maybe things aren't what they appear. After all, the fascists' best troops are in the east, facing us. Maybe the troops in France simply aren't capable of standing up to determined assaults. . . ."

Stalin considered this for a moment. "It's a possibility," he conceded grudgingly. "From a purely military perspective, the Siegfried Line or the Rhine would be the best places to make a stand."

"Still, we must follow developments closely, Joseph Vissarionovich," Beria replied, indulging Stalin's suspicions. It didn't pay to be too contradictory."

"Oh, we will, we will. That lout Churchill will stab us in the back at the first opportunity."

"We will deal with *him,* when the time comes."

"His bark is far worse than his bite," said Stalin, reaching for the bottle of wine. "The English are no threat to us; their empire is dying. My only concern is Churchill's influence on Roosevelt."

"The Americans are the main threat," Beria agreed.

Stalin took a swig of wine. "We plan to meet at Yalta this winter, Lavrenti Davidovich. I will butter up Roosevelt like a roast goose." His eyes hardened as he set the wine down, remembering the situation in France. He stared down at the map again. "I just hope the cripple hasn't already betrayed us. . . ."

III

Adolf Hitler listened with growing detachment to the daily report of conditions on the Western Front. His eyes glazed over as Field Marshal von Rundstedt's patrician voice droned on and on, listing Wehrmacht and Allied dispositions from the English Channel to the Swiss border.

The Fuhrer of the Third Reich and his leading generals had

gathered in his quarters at *Wolfshanze,* The Wolf's Lair, Hitler's field headquarters deep in the forests of East Prussia. Dark and gloomy, shielded from the sun by the towering pines of the Prussian wilderness, the compound was an armed camp. Since the attempt on Hitler's life at Berchtesgaden, high in the Bavarian Alps, security had been tightened, armed SS guards now stood behind each of the generals present. Even field marshals were not beyond suspicion.

It was in this tense atmosphere that von Rundstedt, a Prussian aristocrat of the old school and less than ardent Nazi, began to describe the weakness of the Wehrmacht lines in the Ardennes.

The Fuhrer, hardly able to contain himself, waited for von Rundstedt to conclude. Then, finally, when his generals all turned expectantly toward him for any comments on the growing crisis in the west, Hitler paused theatrically.

"I have come to a momentous decision," he announced, jabbing a forefinger onto the map. "Here! In the Ardennes! This is where we will launch our counterattack."

The generals around him glanced nervously at one another. A counterattack . . . ? Now . . . ? When it was obvious that the Wehrmacht's only chance for survival was to fall back to the fortifications of the Siegfried Line or the natural barrier of the Rhine?

Oblivious, Hitler continued, his voice rising in excitement. "We will smash through the Ardennes between the English and American armies and drive to the Meuse, then from there to Antwerp. We will trap the English against the sea, it will be another Dunkirk!" He gazed triumphantly at von Rundstedt and the others. "With one mighty blow we will knock the English out of the war! Then we will be free to turn on the Americans and smash their cowboy army to pieces."

Hitler paused, savoring the vision of a dramatic end to the war in the west. "Once again," he crowed, indulging his self-image of the military genius surrounded by incompetent generals, *"I* was the only one to see this, the only one to grasp the significance of the Ardennes Forest, the only one to see the opportunity presented by the Allie's blunder of leaving a weak gap between their armies right in front of a region where we can gather our panzer divisions together without detection. The enemy won't know what hit them. We will strike a death blow at them from the mists of the Ardennes, fall upon them like wolves upon a flock of sheep! Before they can react, our panzers will have split them in two."

Von Rundstedt was the first to venture a comment. "A daring plan, *mein Fuhrer*," he conceded, avoiding the Fuhrer's eyes for the moment. "But what of the Allied air forces? They—"

"We will attack in November," Hitler replied, cutting him off. "The winter weather will ground the enemy fighter bombers."

Von Rundstedt blinked. One couldn't count on the weather. If the skies were clear, the panzer columns would be cut to ribbons by the Allie's overwhelming control of the air. "Perhaps . . ." he grunted, desperate for support from his colleagues. Someone must talk some sense into Hitler. If this colossal gamble failed, the Reich was finished.

"We must begin to pull some of our panzer divisions from the line," Hitler went on, scanning the map, examining the German deployments along the Western Front. "They must be sent to the rear to reform and resupply, then sent to the Ardennes."

Alarmed, von Rundstedt looked around for help. The German lines were desperately weak as it was. To pull even one or two armored divisions from the line was to invite disaster. He glanced briefly at Field Marshals Keitel and Jodl, but dismissed them at once. Two greater bootlickers of Hitler's couldn't be found in all of the Reich. He couldn't expect any help from those lackeys.

"Would that be wise, mein Fuhrer?" he inquired, resolved to make a stand all alone if need be. "Our gallant troops are spread painfully thin as it is."

Hitler glared at him. "My dear von Rundstedt," he replied, as one would speak to a child, "Germany's struggle for life cannot be won by defensive battles. We must strike a decisive blow; we must seize the initiative and go on the attack. Faced with military catastrophe, our enemies will fall out, they will take to bickering among themselves, laying blame on each other for the disaster. Only then will this unnatural alliance against us crumble."

Hitler sneered. "Don't you see? The *last* thing the Anglo-Americans expect is an *attack!* They think they have won the war; they think they have us on the run. Imagine their panic when we rise up, as if from the dead, and send our panzers slashing through their stunned troops and throw them into the sea!"

Von Rundstedt nodded grudgingly—the Fuhrer had a point there. . . . But the initial shock would soon wear off. What then? How could the decimated Wehrmacht defeat an enemy with heavy superiority in numbers of troops, tanks, artillery, and warplanes . . . ?

"It will buy us valuable time," said Jodl, rallying to Hitler's side. "Even a limited victory will earn us precious months to fully deploy all of our vengeance weapons."

Hitler frowned at Jodl's lukewarm appraisal of his knockout blow, but seized upon the idea of a stalemate to help justify the obvious risk of his plan. "Jodl is right. If fate turns against us and our Ardennes' offensive fails to end the war in the west, we will still have achieved a great victory. Our V-2 rockets are nearly ready, our new jets are arriving in increasing numbers at the front, our new Tiger IIs are now in full production. Even if the Allies escape defeat in the Ardennes, they won't survive the fury of our new wonder weapons."

Von Rundstedt saw that he had lost—nothing would sway the Fuhrer from staking Germany's future on one last desperate throw of the dice. With a sinking heart, he listened as Hitler rambled on, speaking with all the certainty of an Old Testament prophet.

Von Rundstedt shook his head. The problem was, Old Testament prophets always forecast disaster. . . .

Chapter XI

Smoky Hill Airfield
Salina, Kansas
September 17, 1944

I

The airfield sweltered under a brutal sun. Dust devils danced across the prairie, whipped up by the wind that buffeted Wilson Lindberg as he stood on the flight line, staring in awe at the gleaming silver monsters parked wingtip to wingtip astride the main runway.

He walked up to the nearest B-29 Superfortress and stepped into the shadow of the left wing to escape the blazing heat. The wind still howled like a blast furnace, but at least he was out of the sun.

"Can I help you, Major?"

He turned around, startled. A man appeared from behind the open, forward bomb-bay doors. He wore the bars of a captain on the collar of his khakis. "Hank Callahan," he said, holding out his hand. "You new here?"

"Yeah, just got here. The name's Lindberg, Wilson Lindberg." They shook hands.

Callahan grinned as Wilson touched the polished aluminum skin of the fuselage and ran his hand across the smooth warm metal. "Quite a bird, isn't it?"

"It's beautiful."

"She's got a range of thirty-eight-hundred miles, tops out at three-hundred-sixty miles an hour, handles like a fighter, and carries ten tons of bombs."

Wilson whistled in appreciation.

Callahan noted the service ribbons on Wilson's uniform. "You were over in England, huh?"

"Twenty-five missions in 17s. Then they promoted me and offered a transfer to 29s." He grinned. "I think I made the right decision."

"They're amazing machines all right." He stuck a pinch of Copenhagen into his mouth and worked it into place. "Was with the 15th in Italy myself. Liberators." Callahan waited for the jibe—there was a natural rivalry between Liberator and Fortress crews. Men assigned to B-17s often derided the ungainly, slab-sided B-24 Liberator as the shipping crates the graceful looking B-17s arrived in, while many B-24 crewmen resented the heavy press attention the more glamorous Flying Fortresses received.

Wilson avoided a comparison. To him it was simply the luck of the draw whether a man got assigned to Liberators or Forts. "You must have gone to Ploesti, then," he said instead, recalling the bloody raids on the Rumanian oil refineries.

Callahan regarded the newcomer with growing respect. *This* guy was no hot dog. "Three damn times. Glad I don't have to go *there* again."

"Must have been rough . . ."

"No fun, no fun at all." Callahan frowned.

"We heard you guys flew treetop level all the way in."

"You heard right." Callahan chewed his tobacco thoughtfully. Hell, he had time to swap a war story or two. . . . "You shoulda' seen it, Lindberg, a hundred and eighty B-24s screamin' across Greece, Bulgaria, and Rumania at two hundred knots, fifty feet off the damn ground all the way to the target."

Wilson whistled. "Don't think I'd want to try it myself. . . ."

"Wildest thing I ever saw. Half the formation missed a turn on the way, ended up doubling back and coming in from the northeast at the same time the rest of us were coming in from the west. Talk about a snafu! Looked like a big train wreck about to happen. There were 24s dodging each other all over the sky." He laughed. "God only knows what the Krauts must have thought, looking up from their flak batteries to see two swarms of Liberators on a collision course right over Ploesti."

Wilson grinned. "Who knows? They probably thought you guys planned it that way. Must have confused the hell out of the flak crews."

Callahan had to laugh. "A lot of them *were* too busy staring to shoot at us." He shook his head. "They must have thought we were stone crazy! At any rate, they started shooting at us soon enough."

"So how many collisions were there?"

"That's the strangest part—I only saw one midair. 'Course there was so much going on at once, who can say?" Callahan's grin faded. "Bottom line was they ended up shooting the hell out of us. We lost sixty planes."

"Didn't know it was that bad."

Callahan spat a stream of tobacco juice onto the concrete. "Don't know what the big secret was, but the brass hushed up the losses. Hell, the Germans knew how many of us they got. There were burning wrecks scattered all over the Balkans from Ploesti to Athens. I guess the generals just wanted to cover their asses. It wasn't exactly a mission for the training manual."

"They try their damnedest, Callahan, just like we do."

"Yeah, I suppose so." Callahan frowned again. *"I* sure as hell wouldn't want their job." He held out his can of Copenhagen. "Chew?"

"No thanks, got enough vices already."

"How about some Beeman's then." He pulled a pack of gum from his trousers.

"Sure."

"Well . . . enough about me," Callahan said, handing the pack over. "How was your tour?"

Wilson pulled a stick out, peeled the wrapper off, and popped the gum in his mouth. "Thanks. Can't remember the last time I had some Beeman's."

"Keep the pack, I got more."

"Thanks." Wilson paused—he'd thought little of his time in Europe since getting home, anxious to forget the war for a few weeks and enjoy the odd sensation of not having to wonder if each day might be his last. "Well, let's see . . ." he said, thinking back to the bitter winter of '43-'44, "our first mission was Schweinfurt in August. We made it back in one piece, but the Fort was so full of holes they had to write her off for spare parts."

"Black Thursday," Callahan muttered. "We heard about it."

Wilson shook his head, recalling the carnage. "Lost sixty planes over Germany, Callahan. Another thirty or forty were so shot up, they went right to the scrap heap like ours. Well, we stayed home for a while after that. Didn't have enough damn planes left to even *think* about going back to Krautland. . . . Anyway, we built up our strength for a month or so, then went at it. Hit Bremen, Hamburg, Schweinfurt again, Kassel, Hanover, Bremerhaven, Regensburg . . . you name it, we bombed it. Lost a lot of planes that winter, a lot of crews."

"Damn Krauts were tough bastards, I'll give them that." Callahan spat another stream of tobacco juice. "Ever get to *Big B?*"

"Last mission. That's where they got us. . . ." Wilson's voice fell. "Lost my whole crew."

"Christ . . ."

Wilson plunged ahead, forcing himself to purge some of the lingering horror by talking about it. "They shot the hell out of us, had to crash-land in France. . . . I was knocked unconscious, came to in a barn that night. A French farmer, guy named Lafleur, he and his daughter pulled me out, told me the plane blew up before they could get to my crew. . . . Anyway, they hid me for a week or so. Then the Resistance got me out on an RAF Lysander."

"Sorry about your crew, Lindberg," Callahan said, his voice

hushed. "Awful tough break to get shot down on your last damn mission."

"Yeah." Wilson thought of Owens, Smoky, Bing, the others . . . of the nine crosses in Lafleur's field . . . of Henri, of Gabrielle. . . .

He slapped the gleaming fuselage of the B-29. "Sure wish we could have had these babies. Things might have gone a lot better."

"Yeah . . . well, we've got 'em now."

Wilson managed a smile. "So, you got an hour? I'll buy you a beer."

"You're on, Lindberg. O-Club here isn't much to write home about, but they just might be able to scare up a beer or two for us."

"Great. By the way, my friends call me Lindy." Wilson frowned. "Used to be Lucky Lindy, after you know who, but I guess I wore *that* out a while back."

"I answer to Hank, Lindy."

"Hank, it is. Let's go see how the beer is in Kansas, huh?"

They walked off across the sweltering field toward the base officers' club, looking forward to drowning bitter memories, to forging new ties to replace old ones gone forever, torn away by the fortunes of war.

II

Sinclair Robertson sat on the ground, his back against a bogie wheel of a Sherman tank, and punched the *Record* button on his tape recorder. The wheels squeaked to life, and brown tape began to wind from reel to reel. He plugged in the microphone cord, composed his thoughts for a moment, and began to speak into the mike:

"Sixty miles from the borders of the Third Reich, the armored columns of General George Patton's Third Army sputtered to a halt this morning, the ninth of September, 1944. I am with the Third Armored Division near Avranches, France, sitting by the side of a dusty road this Indian summer morning, surrounded by idle armored vehicles, because the supply lines that have provided Third Army with the necessities of war these long weeks of headlong advance have been stretched to the breaking point. Simply put, we are out of gas. . . ."

A jeep pulled up in a cloud of dust, and Sinclair looked up to see a major looking down at him from behind the wheel. He punched the *Stop* button.

"Are you Robertson?" the officer shouted over the idling engine.

"Yeah. . . ."

"General Patton regrets that he'll have to postpone your interview."

"Again?"

"Sorry, pal, the general's got his hands full trying to round up some gas for us." The major grinned. "The mood he's in, you wouldn't want to be around him today anyway, believe me."

Sinclair rose to his feet. "He can't be half as mad as my editors will be when I have to tell them another interview's been canceled. I've been promising them one for weeks now."

The major shrugged. "If it's any consolation, no one else has been getting interviews either. Look, you're first in line once this supply problem is sorted out, okay?"

"Any idea when that might be?"

"Couldn't tell you if I knew." The major shoved in the clutch and ground the gearshift into first. "Interested in a consolation prize?"

Sinclair packed his recorder into his satchel bag, then slung it over his shoulder. "Maybe. What did you have in mind?"

The major gestured down the dusty road toward a farmhouse. "There's a wrecked Fortress sitting in that fellow's field. One of our patrols talked to the farmer yesterday. Scoop is he pulled a wounded pilot from the wreck last spring. Could be a story in it for you."

"Better than nothing I guess." He climbed in beside the major. "You say he pulled the pilot from the plane himself?"

The major gunned the engine and the jeep sprang forward. "That's what I heard. Apparently the plane blew up before they could get the rest of the crew out."

Sinclair gripped the windshield frame as the jeep bounced along the dirt road. "They?"

"His daughter helped."

"Ah . . ." Sinclair began to see the possibilities of the story. A heroic Frenchman and his daughter rescue a wounded American pilot from the clutches of the Nazis. . . . It was the type of story his editors would favor; they were always receptive to human interest stories.

"By the way, the name's Crowe, George Crowe."

Sinclair grinned at the transparent hint. "I'll work you into the story, Major. Where you from?"

"Jersey. Paterson, New Jersey."

Sinclair took out a notepad and jotted down the name and address. "Appreciate the tip, Major."

"No problem. "Crowe shrugged. "Kind of wanted to get away from HQ for an hour or two anyway. Things are a mite grim there today."

They pulled up to the simple two-story house and approached the door. The odor of hay and manure drifted across the yard from the barn. Chickens clucked across their path, heads bobbing as they darted away from the intruders. Sinclair and the major exchanged longing glances. Neither had enjoyed a real meal since the breakout from Normandy, and the sight of plump poultry set their mouths to watering.

Crowe sighed, then tapped on the door. It was opened, revealing a matronly woman in a blue dress. She smiled uncertainly, her hands fidgeting with the front of her apron. Sinclair listened as the major spoke to her in passable French. The woman nodded, glancing now and then at Sinclair as she listened. She held up a hand at last and shushed him.

"Oui, oui," she exclaimed, before a torrent of French left Sinclair bewildered.

"The old man and the girl are out back," explained the major. "Madame says we can talk to them if we wish, but that there isn't much to tell."

"You got time?"

The major glanced at his watch. "I guess I can spare an hour or so." He grinned. "Maybe the *mademoiselle* is a looker."

The climbed back into the jeep. "Wonder if there's anything we might be able to trade them for a chicken dinner," mused Sinclair, eyeing the chickens again as the major gunned the jeep into a turn and headed back down the path toward the road.

"Can't hurt to ask."

Following the woman's directions, the major drove a kilometer eastward, then pulled down a side road that ran north between waving fields of golden wheat. They spotted the pair across a sea of grain, their scythes at work harvesting. The sun gleamed off the metal blades as they swept to and fro over the ground, felling the ripe stalks.

Henri and Gabrielle Lafleur noticed the jeep approaching and halted their scything.

Crowe braked to a halt. They hopped out and made their way across the waving wheat toward the pair.

"Good afternoon," greeted Lafleur as they walked up.

Speaks English, Sinclair reflected. That would simplify things. He offered his hand. "Good afternoon, *monsieur*. My name is Robertson, Sinclair Robertson." They shook.

"My daughter, Gabrielle," said Lafleur, nodding toward the dark-haired girl at his side. She smiled gravely.

"Pleased to meet you." He turned toward Crowe. "And this is Major George Crowe."

"I congratulate you and your comrades, Major Crowe," Lafleur said, beaming. "You have the Boche on the run. The last of them went through here a week ago."

Crowe grinned. "Looks like they left your fields alone."

"Yes, thank God." Lafleur's eyes twinkled. "They were running away so fast, they had no time for mischief."

"Good, good." Crowe glanced at Sinclair, then back at Lafleur. "It's come to our attention that you helped an American flier last spring, *Monsieur* Lafleur. My companion here would like to write a story about it."

"Ah, yes, *Capitan* Lindberg." Lafleur turned toward his daughter, translating briefly. She began to smile. "The *capitan,* he is okay?"

Crowe looked at Sinclair uncertainly. "Uhhh . . ."

"He's fine," Sinclair offered. He had no idea what might have become of Lindberg, but why bring that up? He'd have to look into it.

"I am glad to hear this."

Sinclair set up his recorder and interviewed Lafleur. Proudly, he recounted the whole episode. Afterward, he insisted upon showing them the blackened, rusting hulk of *Rosie II*, lying at the far end of the wheat field.

"We buried the poor Americans over there," he explained, pointing to a cleared area. Nine simple crosses stood in the black soil. He paled, remembering the grisly task. "There wasn't much left of them, the poor boys. . . ."

"It was kind of you," said Sinclair.

Henri shrugged. "They gave their lives for France, for liberty . . . I could do no less."

They headed back toward the jeep. Gabrielle reached out and touched the recorder, a source of mystery to her. She smiled tentatively and asked something in French.

Henri smiled. "Gabrielle wants to know if you can play back a part for her to hear."

"Sure." Sinclair rewound the tape as they walked through the wheat. Henri and Gabrielle listened in fascination to the magic of their voices crackling from the small speaker. Sinclair let the tape run until they reached the jeep.

"I can send you a copy of the story if you like," he offered.

"It's for my wire service in the states, but should make the *Stars and Stripes* and *Yank* over here."

"Yes, yes, that would be good. We would like that."

They shook hands all around.

"Monsieur Robairtson . . . ?"

Sinclair returned the smile. "Yes, Gabrielle?"

"Capitan Lindbairg, you know he . . . ?" she asked hopefully.

"Not personally . . ." He glanced at Henri Lafleur. "But I should be able find out where he is." He smiled reassuringly at Gabrielle.

"We would like to write him," Henri explained.

"Of course. I'm sure he would like that." Sinclair climbed into the jeep. "I'll be back as soon as I can."

"We will have you to dinner." Henri beamed. "We will celebrate the defeat of the Boche, eh?"

Sinclair glanced at Crowe. Visions of succulent chicken danced through their heads. "Sounds great! Thank you!"

Gabrielle watched the jeep until it disappeared over the hill, hope glowing in her eyes. They would find her *Americain,* these kind men. Her *capitan* would write her! And she would write him, and then who could say what might happen . . . ?

III

The firing range of the Marine Corps Recruit Depot at Parris Island, North Carolina, popped with the sound of small-arms fire as the green-fatigues-clad recruits fired their M-2 carbines for the first time. One hundred yards from the long line of sweating recruits puffs of dirt kicked up around the row of bull's-eye targets. Some of the cardboard squares were stitched with holes, but far too few, especially at the east end of the line where Bill Lindberg lay prone in the red clay, jerking shot after shot at his untouched target.

His company drill instructor, Gunnery Sergeant Clay Boone,

a snarling bulldog of a man from Kentucky, stood behind him, hands on hips, staring in shaking rage at the rounds splattering the ground a good ten yards shy of the target.

"Lindberg, are your eyes open?" he asked with mock concern.

Bill jerked the trigger again, startled by the voice behind him. The next round went wildly high.

"Jesus Christ and General Jackson! This isn't antiaircraft drill, recruit! I don't see any Zeros diving down to strafe my rifle range! Your target is on the fucking ground, Lindberg, not up in the clouds! Now hit the damn target!"

The M-2 barked. The round was closer this time, but still five yards to the right.

"Give me your weapon, Lindberg!"

Bill, flustered, turned to hand the D.I. his carbine, the muzzle pointed right at the sergeant's chest. Boone's hand shot out and shoved the carbine barrel sideways before yanking it from Bill's grasp.

"You pointed that weapon at your sergeant, recruit! If I hadn't seen with my own eyes that you couldn't hit a bull in the butt with a baseball bat I'd have you up on charges!"

"Sir! Yes, sir!"

"Shut up!" Boone took quick aim at Bill's target and squeezed off five quick shots. Every round tore into the inner circles of the target. *"That* is how you use this weapon, recruit!"

Bill stared in awe at the display of marksmanship. Boone hadn't bothered raising the carbine to his chin, he'd shot from the hip.

"Sir! That's outstanding, sir!"

"Are you trying to kiss my ass, Lindberg?"

"Sir! No, sir!"

"Good! I don't like ass-kissers, Lindberg! Ass-kissers go right to the top of my shit list. Do you know where you are, Lindberg?"

"Sir! No, sir!"

"You occupy the top ten spots! You have set a new corps record!"

Humiliated, Bill said nothing. Boone shoved the carbine into his hands. "Reload!"

"Sir! Yes, sir!" Bill slammed another clip into the chamber of the M-2. "Sir! I'll do better, sir!"

"You'd gawddamned better, recruit! Some fine night you'll find your sorry ass in the jungle with a thousand Nips coming at you screaming *'Banzai'* and you'd sure as hell better be able to use that weapon! Your life depends on it! The lives of your squad depend on it!"

"Sir! Yes, sir!"

"When I come back, I'd better see your next target shredded, recruit!"

"Sir! Yes, sir!"

Boone stalked off, shaking his head in disgust. A veteran of Guadalcanal and Tarawa, he'd seen too many marines die because some D.I. hadn't been tough enough on them before they got thrown into combat against crack Jap troops.

He looked down the line of recruits, most of them eighteen- and nineteen-year-old kids, and knew that many were going to die on some damned beach. A lot of hard fighting lay ahead, a lot of islands had yet to be taken . . . and then there was Japan itself. . . .

Boone's lips compressed into a thin line. *That* would be a fight. Eighty million Japanese, every last one of them, man, woman, and child, ready and eager to die for their Emperor. . . .

His gaze fell on Lindberg again, his lips turned down in a dark frown as he watched. He shook his head as he watched the kid flinch every time he jerked the trigger. Couldn't hit a bull in the butt with a base fiddle.

He sighed. The kid was trying his damnedest, but just didn't seem to have it. Everyone in the company had beaten the crap out of him during pugil stick sessions. Bayonet drill was even worse. It was a wonder he hadn't run *himself* through instead of the stuffed dummy. The ten-mile hikes in full pack had damn near killed him. Then there was the obstacle course . . .

Boone walked up behind Lindberg. Mercifully, the hour on the firing range was about up. He watched Lindberg shove in his last clip.

"Squeeze 'em off, recruit, squeeze 'em off, nice an' easy."

The kid stiffened. He hesitated, then took careful aim. Boone stared at the pristine target, shining in the brutal heat, a hundred yards away. The carbine barked, then again, again, again. . . . Four holes magically appeared on the cardboard—nowhere near the bull's-eye, but at least on the target.

"Halleluleyah, recruit."

Lindberg squeezed off the last of the clip, most of the rounds finding the target. A grudging smile crossed Boone's face. He walked off, checking the other targets. The kids were improving. He took off his smoky hat and wiped his brow. The frown re-appeared.

Problem was, unlike Japs, cardboard targets didn't shoot back.

Chapter XII

Jagdverband 44
Munich, Germany
October 3, 1944

I

"Sit down, Oberstleutnant." Walter Novotny gestured to the chair next to his and Gunther accepted gratefully.

"Thank you."

The officers' mess was deserted. Muted jazz filtered across the room from a battered radio propped up on a dusty windowsill. The room smelled of stale beer and cigarettes.

"Schnapps?"

Before Gunther could reply, Nowotny was filling a glass for him. He set the liter bottle down and handed Gunther the glass.

"Thank you." He downed a mouthful and enjoyed the warm glow as it went down.

Nowotny leaned back on the rear legs of his chair, silently appraising his guest. "So," he said at least, flashing an engaging smile, "how is our Priller, then? Still chasing the *mademoiselles?*"

"Not as often as he'd like to, Herr Commandant." Gunther saw the smile fade from Nowotny's face and regretted the comment. It was clear that the commandant was simply trying to forget the war for a moment or two by engaging in comradely banter.

"Come now, "Nowotny insisted, forcing a smile, "one cannot fly day and night, even our Priller. I suspect he still finds an evening or two for the ladies, eh?"

Taking his cue this time, Gunther nodded. "Well, there *was* that night in Paris a few weeks back. . . ."

Nowotny fairly glowed. He listened with rapt attention as Gunther related Priller's account of the episode. In return, he described in detail the ace's escapades in Rome the summer before, roaring with laughter as he relived the week's leave they'd shared.

The bottle of schnapps was gone by the time Nowotny turned reluctantly to the business at hand. Lighting a cigar, he stoked it thoughtfully to life, then whipped the match out and sent it flying off into space.

"Well, Oberstleutnant Dietrich, I'm sure you know I didn't ask you here to trade Priller stories. There is a war on, eh, and we are soldiers." He paused, then frowned. "I didn't ask you here to listen to speeches either, so I'll come right to the point. Dietrich, I want you to join the squadron. Are you interested?"

Gunther's eyes widened. Join Nowotny? Fly the new Messerschmitt jets? He'd heard of the elite unit the two-hundred victory ace was forming, but had entertained no hope of being asked. True, he had one hundred and thirteen victories of his own, but that number couldn't even crack the top fifty aces.

Speechless, he stared at his host in astonished silence, drawing a good-natured chuckle from Nowotny. "Come now, Dietrich, don't be coy," he pressed. "I would like an answer before morning. . . ."

"I'd be honored to, Herr Commandant," said Gunther, his wits gathered at last. "But . . . well, there was this incident over Berlin, perhaps you are unaware—"

"Forget *that*," Nowotny replied, waving away the matter. "You come well-recommended by Priller, that's plenty good enough for me. So, it's settled?"

Gunther smiled proudly. "I guess so."

"Good! Now then, we'll get you started on training flights right away—we've got a couple of two-seater, dual-control units. You should be ready to solo in a few weeks."

In awed tones, Nowotny began to describe the new wonder jet. "You won't believe it, Dietrich, the 262 is *amazing!* She can climb faster than a Mustang can dive; she has six cannons in her nose that can tear a Fortress apart like so much tissue paper; and she can pounce on the enemy and be gone before they know what hit them. She is fantastic, the deadliest fighter in the world. Nothing else is even close to her."

"A pity there aren't more of them, Herr Commandant. If the whole fighter arm had them . . ." Gunther's voice trailed off as he saw the light seem to fade from Nowotny's eyes.

"Yes . . . a pity." Nowotny paused. "No, a tragedy, Dietrich, a tragedy." He seemed to measure Gunther for a moment, then an inner reserve seemed to give way. "No, more than a tragedy. If you ask my true opinion, it is nothing less than criminal that we don't have hundreds of them right now. Criminal! If it weren't for the idiots in Berlin, we would rule the skies of Europe right now, instead of fighting for our lives every time we go up."

Gunther winced inwardly at Nowotny's intensity. The commandant broke open a new bottle of schnapps, obviously seething. "Forgive me, Dietrich," he explained, pouring them each another glass, "but if you knew what I know, well, you would be fit to be tied as well."

"I imagine any aircraft as advanced as this new Messerschmitt takes some time to develop," Gunther replied, shaken by the revelation of such a lost opportunity. He put the delay in production down to the chaos wreaked on German industry by the Allied bombing. Nowotny must be furious at Goring for being unprepared to defend the Reich adequately.

"It was ready in '42, Dietrich." Nowotny tossed back his schnapps and slammed the glass down on the table in disgust.

"But our Fuhrer, in all his wisdom, decreed that it must be a bomber! Can you imagine? A bomber!"

Gunther stared, shocked at the open attack on Hitler himself. Several stunned seconds passed before the magnitude of the delay in deployment registered. "The 262 was ready for combat in '42?" he stammered.

"Yes."

Gunther had never heard so bitter a reply. "I don't understand, Herr Commandant. Why couldn't a bomber version have been looked into while the fighter arm was stocked?"

"Nazi politics!" Nowotny sneered. "The Fuhrer insisted upon full bomber production and those stooges around him backed him up, even Goring, who at least should have known better. He wouldn't allow any fighter production until the bomber version was perfected, which of course never happened because it was ludicrous in the first place!"

"I had no idea. . . ."

"Neither did I until General Galland told me about it." Nowotny relit his cigar, visibly struggling to control his temper.

"Has this been sorted out yet . . . ?"

"It's too late. The enemy is hammering our factories day and night. The Russians are deep inside Poland, the Americans and English astride the Meuse. . . . So here we sit, outnumbered twenty to one in the air, the enemy at the frontiers of the Reich, and all we're getting are a handful of 262s a month."

His euphoria long gone, Gunther downed his schnapps, stunned by the Hitler's colossal blunder. But was it too late? Even a few hundred jets could make the difference, couldn't they . . . ?

Nowotny saw the hope in his eyes. "Ah, you are a determined fellow, aren't you!" He sat up, and seemed to shake off the apathy of a moment ago. "Priller told me you had guts!" He got up from his chair, walked around to Gunther's chair, and slapped him on the back. "Your quarters are right across the way, Dietrich. Go get a good night's sleep and we'll start you off tomorrow. I'll take you up myself, by God!"

Gunther, buoyed by the praise, managed a smile. "Thank you, Herr Commandant."

"Off with you then." Nowotny saw him to the door. "0600 sharp!"

Gunther nodded. Nowotny watched him disappear into the night, then closed the door softly behind him. Sighing, he sank back into his chair to contemplate what might have been.

II

The penal battalion crept forward in the moonlight, a thousand shifting shadows on the snow. One hundred meters behind them, an NKVD company deployed at the edge of a birch forest until the soldiers were spread out in a long line at the perimeter of the dark woods. At a whispered command from the left flank, the troops, left to right, like a long line of dominos, dropped to their knees and trained their Kalashnikov assault rifles on the dim figures edging their way across the silent minefield toward the fascist positions in the treeline half a kilometer to the west.

In the middle ranks of the punishment battalion, Yuri Rostov, his heart hammering wildly in his chest, stepped gingerly over the snow, careful to follow the footprints ground into the drifts ahead. The only sound was the faint whistle of the wind through the bare trees and the soft crunch of boots on brittle snow.

The tentative advance, begun on a front one hundred meters wide, was quickly shrinking to half that width as the flanks edged in, the men trying to cheat fate by falling into step behind the comrade to his left or right.

Yuri's breath came in short gasps. His teeth clenched, every muscle tensed, he willed himself to take a step, then another, then another. His whole world had narrowed to the patch of snow directly ahead. His eyes searched out the precious footprints upon which existence depended. They watered from the strain and he brushed at them with his gloved hands, blinking away the blurred image of the snow.

When would the first sickening explosion come, to pierce the silence and alert the Nazis across the field? What would he do then, as the enemy flares sprang into the starry sky to turn day to night and leave the hapless battalion naked and exposed?

He halted suddenly as low hanging clouds, driven by the brisk north wind, drifted across the crescent moon. What precious little light there had been was gone; the shadows on the field ahead vanished. He peered across the field, waiting for his eyes to adjust to the blackness. His breath, vaporized in the frigid air, flared from his slack mouth and nostrils and drifted away on the breeze as he looked upward, searching the gathering overcast for the hidden moon.

"Maybe there's been a mistake," hissed a voice beside him. He turned to see a hulking shadow, crouching in the snow. "The maps have been wrong before—maybe there isn't a minefield here after all. . . ."

Yuri was about to reply when a sharp explosion up ahead pierced the silence. An instant later a brilliant burst of light broke the darkness, silhouetting the scores of shadows between them and the far wood. The explosion flared out amidst painful screams, leaving the survivors in pitch darkness for several seconds. Then, from the darkness ahead, green tendrils of light shot toward the stars.

Yuri froze. Blinding light exploded overhead as the flares burst to life, illuminating the field below in glaring, deadly light. Night became day. The leading ranks wavered. Some of the men dropped to the snow, some stood rooted in place, a few struggled forward, but most turned and began to run pell-mell toward Yuri and the cover of the woods behind him. Gunfire began to rattle menacingly from the far treeline, to be answered an instant later by the NKVD troops.

Yuri dropped to the ground as a violent crossfire of multi-colored tracer rounds swept overhead. A drumbeat of muffled explosions rolled over the snow as the hidden mines began to go off, triggered by panicked soldiers stumbling desperately about for cover.

A hand grasped his arm and yanked him to his feet. "Run, comrade!"

Yuri stared at the frenzied face. "Where?"

"Forward!" the man shouted over the din, shoving him toward the far treeline. "We go back, we're dead!"

Yuri blinked at the apocalypse ahead, his mind racing.

Bursts flared to evil light everywhere, hurling flailing shadows skyward to drop them in crumpled heaps on the snow. Angry tracers scoured the field, crisscrossing the open ground in a spiderweb of glowing lines. Screams of pain and death echoed over the *crumps* of explosions and whine of bullets.

He staggered forward, his rifle clutched in his gloved hands, his vaporized breath cascading in rapid bursts from his heaving lungs.

Forward . . . it *was* their only chance. The NKVD would mow them down like dogs if they turned and ran.

His comrade darted forward and Yuri followed, fear gripping his frozen heart like a vise. They dashed across the trampled snow, keeping well clear of the open, untouched drifts, leaping over bodies and parts of bodies. From behind them, scores of Katyusha rockets screamed overhead toward the Nazi-held treeline, to impact seconds later in volleys of flame among the trees.

The NKVD tracers rose above the ragged lines of the penal battalion survivors, their grisly work done. Voices howling in primitive fury, the NKVD company rose as one to follow the depleted ranks of their former targets toward the enemy. Behind them, several platoons of T-34 tanks creaked forward, emerging from the trees into the cleared minefield. Once in the open, the steel monsters sprang forward at full throttle, belching blue fingers of flame from their rear exhausts. Turrets pivoting to cover the far treeline, their cannon roaring, the T-34s burst through the gaps of the NKVD line and charged the enemy, adding their shellfire to the steady stream of rockets plunging on the treeline.

"Down!"

Yuri dove into the snow beside his comrade as the treeline, just fifty meters ahead, erupted. A hailstorm of fire swept over the trees. White-hot shrapnel whistled past his head. The nearest chunks tore into the drifts all around, hissing and sizzling in the snow.

"Fire! Fire!"

Yuri raised his head to see his comrade squeezing off shot after shot at the burning woods. He peered down his gun barrel, looking for a target, but could see nothing moving in the tangle of uprooted tree trunks, twisted branches, and burning under-brush. Dazed from the concussion of the shell bursts and rocket impacts, he fired round after round into the flames until the leading NKVD ranks burst past him.

His fingers numb from the cold, he fumbled with his ammu-nition pouch, withdrew another clip of ammunition, and began to reload. The firing began to fade. Behind him, the tanks clanked to a halt at the edge of the woods. Barked commands echoed through the fire-lit night and the trailing NKVD men began to round up the survivors of the penal battalion.

An NKVD sergeant pulled Yuri to his feet and pointed behind him. "Get behind the tanks and wait there!" He took Yuri's rifle and pushed him gently toward the idling tanks.

Slowly, singly and in ragged groups of two or three, the be-draggled survivors were rounded up. Weaponless again, ex-hausted, the small group milled about under the stars, guarded by a handful of NKVD soldiers.

Shivering in the cold, his hands stuffed into the pockets of his greatcoat, Yuri stumbled across the snow, looking for his friend.

"Over here," a voice called out as he trudged up to a lone figure sitting in the snow. Yuri sank to the ground beside him.

"Are you all right?"

The man nodded. His hands trembled, his eyes stared vacantly into the darkness of the field beyond the line of tanks.

Yuri looked across the snow drifts, just able to make out the dim forms of the fallen in the faint starlight. Here and there, pitiful moans drifted over the snow from the wounded, but most of the shadows were silent.

Shaken, the reality of his survival finally beginning to sink in, he drew his knees up to his chin, clasped his numb hands around them, hung his head, and closed his eyes. Time hung suspended. He wasn't sure how many minutes passed until he heard a commissar address the guard closest to him.

He looked up as the officer handed the guard a couple of canteens. "Give the poor devils some vodka, Comrade Sergeant," he said quietly, before walking off. When his turn came, Yuri took a long pull of the icy liquid, then handed the canteen to his friend. The vodka burned down his throat, then glowed warmly in his stomach. He longed for more, to erase all memory of the horror of this night, to warm his cold soul, to drown his mind in oblivion, but the small ration was gone quickly, consumed by the shivering survivors.

The crescent moon reappeared, to cast its soft silver light on the huddled men. Presently, they were roused to their feet and herded toward the rear. Yuri trudged wearily through the silent graveyard of half the battalion, forcing himself to think of home, to picture his mother and father, snug and warm in their kitchen, huddled by the steaming samovar, sipping tea.

At least *they* were safe at home, blissfully unaware of the fate of their son. Yuri clung to the vision, desperate for some shred of comfort to ease the pain, anxious to blot out the harsh reality of suffering and death.

Anything, even the mental torture of envisioning a home he would never see again, was better than thinking of the inevitability of the next minefield to cross, the next appointment with sudden death.

A mine, somehow missed during the initial assault, went off under the boot of a hapless comrade just to Yuri's right. He found himself suddenly on the ground, the blast still ringing in his ears. White-hot pain shot through his right leg. He looked down in alarm to see dark red blood spurting from his thigh.

The last sound he heard was his own muffled groan, then the world went black.

III

A thousand kilometers to the east, Arkady Rostov sat in a fetid boxcar, listening to the hypnotic rattle of iron wheels trundling over endless uneven rail joints. One of ninety-eight political prisoners jammed shoulder to shoulder into the rotting boxcar, he was bound for the slave labor camps of the Soviet Gulag.

The air reeked of human excrement, sweat, and decay. For the most part, the prisoners sat in stoic silence, worn down by the brutal journey, unwilling to expend precious energy on pointless conversation. Only a few scattered murmurs issued from their midst, prompted by someone's speculation as to their destination. Then, sides would be taken and opinions exchanged until a veteran *zek,* experienced in the ways of the camp system, would silence them all with a look and a blunt observation as to the futility of such talk.

As the boxcar rolled along the uneven rails, swaying steadily side to side, Arkady kept to himself. Wedged between a man named Kolya and a corpse, he leaned against the wall, thinking of poor Myushkin. The *zek* next to him had died that morning, just minutes after the guards had performed the daily ritual of tossing the newly deceased out into the snow. Myushkin had expired without sound or struggle, unnoticed by his neighbors until Arkady saw his glassy-eyed stare, pressed a mittened hand against his ribs, and felt no heartbeat.

It wasn't long before the emaciated body had been stripped of clothing and boots and left naked, propped up next to Arkady against the boxcar's sides. He'd protested, but Kolya had patiently explained that poor Myushkin didn't need his coat or trousers any longer, while too many in the car were slowly freezing to death. "It's the way of the Gulag, Arkady Pavlovich," he'd said. "They mean no disrespect."

Arkady shuddered, remembering the scene, and turned away from the corpse. His face pressed against the rough boards of the boxcar's wall, he hoped if he died his comrades wouldn't treat him with such disregard. Despite the logic of Kolya's observation, it just didn't seem right to treat the dead like that.

He breathed in the whisper of fresh air whistling through the cracks in the wall. Suddenly, the car lurched over a particularly bad coupling, throwing Arkady roughly against the wall. Pain shot through the left side of his face as a splinter pierced the flesh and embedded itself into his cheek, then tore free from the splintered board to hang free from his face.

Arkady tore off his mitten and reached with numb fingers toward the wound, then yanked out the two-inch-long sliver of wood and stared at it in impotent fury. Tears of rage streamed down his face, mixed with the blood oozing from the gash, and it started throbbing painfully.

For the first time since his arrest, he broke down. He hurled the offending splinter across the boxcar and slammed his fist onto the floor beside him, whimpering in helpless frustration.

"My God, how did it all come to this . . . ?" he spluttered. A sudden fury seized him. "The bastards, *the bastards!*" he bellowed, fists clenched, eyes wild with rage. "May Almighty God damn them all to hell for this!"

Kolya reached out to calm him, but he drew away and fell across Myushkin's corpse. Drops of tears and blood fell on the frozen blue flesh of the bony arm. He recoiled in horror at the sight and curled into a fetal position on the floor, sobbing in outrage. Perched on the edge of sanity, he clung to the images of Nina, of Yuri, of home. . . .

"Get hold of yourself, Arkady Pavlovich."

Kolya pulled him firmly but gently upward. The vision of home and family faded and the dim form of Kolya materialized. The pleasant scent of steaming tea and freshly baked bread gave way to the vile odor of the slop bucket.

He blinked. His mouth quivered as he tried to reply. Vivid condemnations sprang from his tortured mind, but only incoherent mumbles emerged. Strong hands gripped his shoulders and shook him. He looked into Kolya's eyes.

"You must be strong, Arkasha," Kolya pleaded. "Forget them, forget the devils who did this to you, or the hatred will eat at you day after day until you go mad!"

Arkady stared sullenly at Kolya. "Forget them?" he snarled. "How can I forget the bastards who have stolen my *life*, Kolya?"

"You must, Arkasha. They are beyond the reach of you or I. All you can do now is *survive*, Arkasha! *That* is the only vengeance left to a *zek.*"

Arkady looked away. Survival . . . ? How can one survive when one is already dead—torn from his world and cast headlong into the outer darkness of the camps? Was this not death? Was this not hell?

He glared at Kolya. Who was he to give advice? He'd been thrown to the same wolves; the only difference between them was that he'd been a soldier instead of a teacher.

Kolya seemed to see the accusation in his eyes. "I know, Arkasha. . . . I know how you feel. I felt the same way my first time."

Arkady's anger faded. "The *first time* . . . ?"

Kolya nodded.

"You've been arrested *twice?*"

"I was a major in the Red Army in '37, Arkasha," he explained, "an adjutant on the staff of Marshal Tukhachevsky."

Arkady stiffened. "My God . . ." It was an open secret in Soviet society that the Red Army officer corps had been decimated by the NKVD in the late thirties.

Kolya continued, his tone heavy with sarcasm. "I was blissfully unaware of my treasonous soul until the Great Stalin, vigilant as ever, discovered massive conspiracies afoot in the officer cadre. Wouldn't you know it? Three out of every four of us had been plotting to overthrow the party and set ourselves up as a ruling committee of fifteen thousand Bonapartes!"

He sighed. "Anyway, they shot most of us, packed the rest off to the camps. I was in the Gulag for six years until they combed the camps for veterans and threw those of us still alive into the fight for Stalingrad."

"Six years . . . ?"

"Six years, three months, twenty-seven days."

"How did you ever survive, Kolya?"

"I took one day at a time; it's the only way." He gestured toward the human debris huddled around them. " Most of us won't make it, Arkasha, but some of us will."

Arkady, the blood on his face already caked into a frozen clot, shook his head. "I won't."

"You will if you *believe* you will. I did."

"I'm a teacher, Kolya." Arkady frowned. "That is, I *was* a teacher. I'm simply not accustomed to hardship—my life was a cozy classroom, books, maps, children. . . . I won't last a month in a labor camp. You were a soldier, Kolya, you were used to a hard life."

"It's your *mind* that matters, Arkasha, not your body. Your mind rules your body, not the other way around."

"But—"

Kolya cut him off. "Listen! *Inner strength* will see you through. *Willpower! That* is the key, not physical strength! I have seen countless strong, vigorous men wither and die, while physically weaker men lived because they had strength of spirit, strength of will."

"Well, you've been through it before, Kolya. Who am I to argue?" For the first time since his sentencing, Arkady felt a glimmer of hope. Maybe there *was* a chance he could survive.

He looked at Kolya with new respect. Then the awful realization that his new friend faced a second term in the camps drove every other thought from his mind. "My God, Kolya, now you're here again."

Kolya sighed. "Leave it to the NKVD. . . ." His words trailed off.

"What happened, Kolya?"

He shrugged. "My unit was one of the first across the Vistula last August. We were to spearhead the drive into Warsaw. : . .

Well, it didn't quite work out that way. The fascists counterattacked, we were cut off. Some of us managed to elude capture, swim the river, and reach our comrades. Unknown to us, the commissars have a standing order to arrest anyone escaping fascist encirclement . . . To make a long story short, I was charged with espionage."

"Espionage!" Stunned, Arkady stared at Kolya. "They said you were a spy?"

"The fascists execute prisoners, Arkasha, "Kolya explained. "We all know this is so, as do the commissars. So it is their practice to arrest any soldier who survives encirclement and returns to his unit, the idea being that he *must have betrayed his comrades!* If he hadn't, the fascists would have killed him."

Kolya smiled bitterly. "You are looking at a fascist spy, Arkasha. A fascist spy *and* a Bonapartiste."

"What a mockery of justice," Arkady muttered, despair flooding over him. Was there no limit to the evil of the system? Was it not bad enough that innocent civilians were thrown into the camps? Must the NKVD now persecute the Motherland's own soldiers as well, even while they fought and died to save her?

He thought of Yuri, and his despair knew no bounds. What if his son fell victim to such perfidy?

He looked at Kolya, anxious to seek some reassurance, but Kolya was staring fixedly ahead, lost again to his surroundings, battling his own inner demons.

Arkady sank against the boxcar's wall. Despite the huddled humanity all around him, he'd never felt so alone, so abandoned. He closed his eyes and withdrew into himself, too drained to reach out to another comrade, too afraid at what he would find. . . .

Chapter XIII

101st Airborne Division
Bastogne, Belgium
December 29, 1944

I

The column of dirty white Sherman tanks rumbled into battered Bastogne under a hazy sky. Spitting diesel fumes from hot exhaust pipes, their treads crunching over the snowy streets, the lead elements of the Fourth Armored Division of Patton's Third Army entered the beleaguered city after slogging their way through the Nazi encirclement from the south to relieve the haggard defenders of the 101st Airborne.

Sinclair Robertson hopped off the rear deck of a half-track at the back of the column and struck out on foot.

The Belgian village had taken a terrible pounding. Most of its buildings had been reduced to smoking rubble, its narrow streets were scattered with chunks of masonry; over everything lay a powdery blanket of snow.

He approached several GIs standing in a group watching the Shermans roll past, anxious to get first-hand accounts of the heroic stand against Hitler's best panzer divisions. His eyes were drawn to the insignia patches on their shoulders—a black shield upon which the white head in profile of an American eagle, its eyes full of defiance, was emblazoned. Their uniforms hung on their gaunt frames like sackcloth, their eyes betrayed the harrowing experience of being cut off and pounded for over a week from all sides while the divisions on their flanks had been driven back, halfway to the Meuse, leaving them alone and surrounded. Yet they carried themselves with an air of studied indifference to the arrival of the Fourth Armored.

Sinclair nodded a greeting, unsure of what to say. These men were a different breed than the regular GI. They had been dropped into occupied France the night before D-Day, to pave the way for the Normandy invasion; they'd been parachuted deep inside Nazi lines into Holland in September during the gallant but disastrous effort to breach the Rhine and end the war by Christmas. They were accustomed to adversity. To these veterans, holding Bastogne was not something that should have amazed the world, it was their job.

A sergeant returned his nod, an unlit cigar clenched in his teeth. "Got a light, mac?"

"Sure." Sinclair took his Zippo from his tunic pocket and tossed it to the man. "How you fellows doing?"

The sergeant stoked his cigar and tossed the lighter back to Sinclair. "Wasn't one of our better holiday seasons."

"Didn't think the Krauts had it in 'em," remarked the soldier on the sergeant's right. "Reckon they shot their wad, though. We'll roll right to Berlin now."

The sergeant cast the private a baleful glance. "Gifford here's the master strategist in this outfit—just ask him."

Sinclair grinned. "That right, Gifford?"

Private Edwin Gifford spat on the ground in mock disgust. "The sarge slept through the whole damn fight. Didn't wake up 'til you folks rolled into town. Had to tell him he missed out on being a hero."

Laughter rang out, drawing curious stares from the tankers driving by. Despite their bravado, Sinclair could sense immense relief at surviving what had for days seemed certain to become a modern version of Custer's Last Stand.

"My name's Robertson. I'm a combat correspondent with

the AP." Sinclair shook hands all around. "If you fellas have time, I'd like to get your names, do a little story for the folks back home."

Their faces lit up. Sinclair hadn't met a GI yet who didn't jump at the chance to get his name in the papers.

"Sure." The sergeant nodded his head toward a relatively intact shop on the corner. "Been savin' some liberated French wine just for an occasion like this." He turned toward a tall, slender GI. "Johnson, go tell the lieutenant where I'll be."

Johnson's face fell. "Hell, Sarge . . ."

"We'll save you a glass. Now get your ass movin'."

Johnson scampered down the street, obviously determined to set a world record for message delivery. The others stepped out of the cold into the shadows of a confectionery shop.

"Not much merchandise left." Sinclair took in the empty shelves. The shop had apparently been abandoned in haste, but not before the proprietor had managed to collect his meager inventory and flee for the rear.

"Was in here in November, bought some cigars from the guy," replied the sergeant. "A mom-and-pop store. They sold tobacco, candy, yarn, odds and ends, ya know? Anything to scratch out a livin'."

The sat down wherever they could—on the counters, on the floor. The first bottle of wine was passed around as Sinclair jotted names and hometowns into his spiral notebook. He took a swig as it came by and handed it to a baby-faced private.

"So, what was it like?" he asked.

The young private, Ernie Waite, spoke up first. "I'll never forget the night Browne and I took Stanford back to the first-aid station in town here. We'd been out on the line all evening; the Krauts were shelling us from the woods. Anyway, Stanford got hit in the leg and the lieutenant told me and Browne to take him into Bastogne. We take him to the medics and one of 'em says to us, 'You guys heard?' 'Heard what?' we says. So this medic says, 'The Nazis got us surrounded, the poor bastards!' "

The GIs chuckled, savoring the now famous remark that had

spread by word of mouth through besieged Bastogne that first night of encirclement. It had rallied sagging spirits, lit a fire of determination in the frozen defenders, and already entered into army legend, along with General McAulliffe's equally, if not more famous response of "Nuts" to his German counterpart's surrender demand.

"To me, the cold was as bad as the Germans," offered Lloyd Bergen, a corporal in D Company, 506th Regiment. "The Krauts were shelling us, feeling us out, attacking in force a few times. But that damn cold was *always* there! It never let up. It froze your face, your fingers, your toes. At least the Germans let us be now and then."

"I remember all of us telling each other we wouldn't be taken alive," said Edwin Gifford. "And it wasn't just talk, either. We'd heard about Malmedy, about the SS shooting prisoners in cold blood. We figured, hell, giving up was no option."

"Nobody got much sleep," added PFC Wally Mahler. "It was too cold. The Krauts were shelling the whole area pretty much around the clock. . . . We were really dragging, getting by on fear and adrenaline, I guess."

Private William Johnson burst through the doorway, gasping for air from his errand to HQ.

Sergeant Paul Hauser rolled his eyes and tossed a fresh bottle of wine at Johnson. "Haven't seen you move that fast since you knocked out that Tiger, Christmas Eve, Johnson."

Johnson worked the cork free. "Lieutenant says we got an hour, Sarge." He took a long drink.

"Johnson here knocked out a Tiger with a bazooka. Pretty rare feat—they've got thick armor," said Hauser.

Johnson handed the bottle to Mahler. "Lucky shot. Let it roll past us and put a round between the tail pipes in back."

"Put him up for a Silver Star." Hauser took the bottle from Mahler. "Leave some for the rest of us, eh?"

Sinclair waited for the jibes and counter-jibes to die out before continuing his questions. "Were you guys aware of how outnumbered you really were? I've been told there were elements of at least four panzer divisions around Bastogne—*hundreds* of tanks—while you fellows were stuck here with hardly any artillery, tanks, or air support. It's amazing! Just amazing . . ."

Hauser shrugged. "Krauts couldn't have known how weak we were. If they had, they would have rolled right over us."

"Sarge is right," echoed Mahler. "We could see all the traffic on the roads all around—there had to have been several divisions coming through. But we caused enough commotion for them to think we had two or three divisions here ourselves."

"General McAuliffe's idea?"

"Hell, no disrespect toward the general," said Mahler, "but we didn't have to wait for the old man to tell us what to do, we knew what to do. We've been around the block, Robertson. We've learned a few tricks since Normandy. Every Kraut prisoner we've ever taken thinks we got two or three times the troops we've got."

"Mahler's right, you know. " Hauser took another swig of wine. "Every German I've talked to since August claims we've got a hundred-and-fifty-some divisions. I don't know where they get those numbers, but we're plenty happy to let them think they're right. It probably saved our asses here. In fact I *know* it did. We fought like hell, but there was no damn way we could have held out if the Germans had found out we only had a few thousand troops in Bastogne. They've been intimidated ever since Normandy, always thinking we've got more than we have."

"That doesn't take anything away from what you fellows accomplished here," said Sinclair. "Hanging on to a vital road and rail junction against the largest German attack in the West since 1940, while all around you Allied units were crumbling, whole divisions reeling backwards, communications cut, air support grounded by the weather. . . . You guys were front-page headline news for two weeks, did you know that?"

A wry smile crossed Hauser's face. "We didn't have much time to think about it."

Mahler shrugged. "We had to hang on—we knew the Krauts

were shooting prisoners." He handed Johnson the last of the wine.

"Big news, huh?" Johnson asked. "Front page, you say?"

"Biggest story since D-Day, no doubt about it."

Johnson whistled. He grinned at his buddies. "We're famous, guys!"

"Yeah, famous for gettin' surrounded," muttered Mahler. "Big deal. We're supposed to be winning the war, not hanging onto some Belgian crossroads town by our fingernails."

"A defensive victory is still a victory, Private." Sinclair rose to leave. "You took the best shot the Nazis could throw and stayed on your feet. Bastogne's as famous as Waterloo now, because of you guys. Anyone who had never heard of the 'Screaming Eagles' of the 101st sure as hell has now."

Sinclair shook hands all around. Despite their affected nonchalance, every GI's eyes gleamed with quiet pride. They *had* held the line when almost everyone else had run; they had stood up to the best the Wehrmacht could throw at them.

II

The troopship wallowed over the Pacific swells, her decks filled with prone marines doing pushups in the tropical sun. The hazy peak of Diamond Head, an emerald triangle almost lost on the eastern horizon, was just visible behind the *William McKinley*. Ahead, a long line of gray-painted transports plodded steadily westward. To the north and south, sleek destroyers patroled the flanks of the convoy, their sonar pinging the depths for Japanese submarines.

Bill Lindberg blinked the stinging sweat from his eyes, uninterested in the sights. His arms felt like lead, his stomach cramped from the strain as the voice of Gunnery Sergeant Boone rang out over the deck, counting the cadence in a barking monotone.

He glared at the deck. What kind of luck was it to have Boone assigned to his company? The bastard had seemed to single him out as his personal whipping boy all through basic. He'd thought he'd been rid of him, only to see Boone stride aboard the ship in San Diego, another stripe on his sleeve and fire in his eyes. The Corps, scuttlebutt had it, was going to throw the best it had at the Japs in '45, and had transferred scores of combat proven DIs from the training units in the States to combat-bound units in the Pacific.

"On your feet, marines!"

Bill staggered up with the rest and stood at attention, his head swimming from the exercise. The ranks stirred with scattered bitching about dying of sunstroke before ever seeing a Jap.

"Shut the hell up!" roared Boone. Instant silence fell over the crowded deck. "The damn Japs could hear you fairies pissing and moaning all the way from Tokyo!" His gaze drifted over his men—bare chested, boots shiny black, fatigue caps stuck at jaunty angles on their close-cropped heads. When he had their full attention, he turned and drew the canvas away from a tripod behind him, revealing a map. Taking a pointer, he whacked the tip against a pear-shaped island outlined in brown ink. Red contour lines, widely spaced over the island, bunched together tightly at its western tip.

"This is a chunk of volcanic rock called Iwo Jima. It will be assaulted and taken by elements of three marine divisions." Boone hesitated. When he spoke again, his voice had lost some of its hardness. "It will be the last place many of you see on this earth."

He had their undivided attention. The flush of exertion on their faces quickly faded to a pasty white. One hundred pairs of eyes stared past Boone at the map of the island with the odd name.

"Most of you will survive," continued Boone, "if you keep your heads and listen to your squad and platoon leaders. You will be supported by naval gunfire offshore, and by Marine and Navy pilots above you. You will be led by men who have survived the Canal, Tarawa, Peliuliu, Saipan, Tinian, and Guam. Listen to them! Do what they tell you! When they tell you to get your asses off the goddamned beach, get your asses off the goddamned beach! Marines are helpless on the beach; they are nothing but big fat targets for the Japs. No matter how bad the beach looks when you jump off that amtrack, get *across* the bastard! I don't want to hear any bullshit about being pinned down. Pinned down is just a longer way of saying dead."

He turned from the troops. His pointer slapped down on the west end of the island with a *whack.* "This is Mount Suribachi. It commands the entire landing zone. As long as the Japs control Suribachi, every marine on the island is a sitting duck. It is our first objective. It must be taken quickly, no matter what the cost, because the price of not taking it will mean dead marines all over Iwo instead of just dead marines on Suribachi."

Boone turned again toward his men. "We will not do it alone. The Navy will be pounding Suribachi from point-blank range offshore. Corsairs and Hellcats will bomb and strafe it from H-Hour on. The Japs will not be sitting up there fat and happy picking us off like flies. They'll be targets themselves.

"But supporting fire can only do so much. The Japs won't come out from cover until we are so close that supporting fire will have to be lifted to avoid hitting our own people. *That's* when a marine earns his dough. *That's* when your training will be put to the test, because that is when the Japs will throw everything they have at you. The Japanese soldier is tough, gentlemen, extremely capable and dedicated. He is on Iwo to die. He knows he will not leave that island. His goal is to take as many of you with him as he can, and he will do so by any means available to him. Do *not* approach a wounded Jap! Do *not* go near a Jap attempting to surrender! You have to assume that they are booby-trapped—they have pulled the same trick from Guadalcanal to Guam and some poor bastard falls for it every time."

Boone turned again to the map. His pointer fell on the shoreline just east of Suribachi. "Now to specifics. We will come ashore here, on Red Beach Two. . . ."

Chapter XIV

Litovia Palace
Yalta, USSR
February 5, 1945

Franklin Delano Roosevelt, a navy blue cape wrapped about his shoulders, was wheeled into the library of the Litovia Palace by his son. It was past midnight and the president was exhausted. The second day of the summit had been taxing—Churchill and Stalin had crossed rhetorical swords again and FDR had had to play arbitrator.

"By the fireplace would be fine. . . ."

"Can I get you anything?"

"Not right now, son." FDR smiled and waved his son to bed. "Get some rest."

"You should get some sleep too, Father."

FDR inserted a Tareyton into his cigarette holder. God knows I could use some, he thought. But there is much to do. . . . so much yet to do . . . His lighter flared and he flashed his trademark grin, full of confidence and assurance. "George will be around to order me to bed soon. I just need to think for a few minutes."

"All right, I'll see you at breakfast."

"Good night." FDR wheeled himself closer to the fire. Was it cold in this blasted palace or was it just him? He found himself staring at the crackling logs. Flames licked at the wood, glowing embers filling the hearth, and the aroma of burning hickory wafted across the huge library. The president closed his eyes.

I'm dying. . . . If I see another year I'll be fortunate. . . . The war in Europe will be over before I leave the scene. . . . But winning the peace will be as much of a challenge as defeating Hitler. . . . Stalin seems intent upon setting up puppet governments throughout all of eastern Europe. . . .

FDR's cigarette holder, ever jutting upward at a jaunty angle in public, dangled from the corner of his mouth, a cone of spent ashes dropping from the tip of his cigarette to the tile floor. He rubbed the bridge of his nose in a futile effort to soothe the almost constant headaches which now plagued him.

Then there is Japan. Her warlords showed no sign of giving in. . . . A massive invasion of the home islands would almost certainly be called for . . . unless the wizards at Los Alamos could get their atomic gizmo to function properly. . . . If Oppenheimer and Groves were right and this new bomb was as powerful as they claimed, perhaps the carnage of an invasion could be avoided. . . .

FDR shuddered at the memory of his debriefing of the Joint Chiefs before leaving for Yalta. Operations Olympic and Coronet, the amphibious assaults on Kyushu and Honshu, they'd told him, would cost an estimated *one million* casualties. . . .

A way must be found to avoid such a horror. . . . If only he could be certain that the bomb would end it all, he wouldn't be forced to pressure Stalin into invading Japan from Vladivostok. . . . It would certainly reduce American casualties . . . but a plethora of complications would result from dual occupation of Japan. . . . But the first obligation is to our boys—if their sacrifice can be reduced, it will be worth the price of having the Red Army in Tokyo. . . . I must have Stalin's promise that he will enter the war as soon as possible. If political compromises have to be made, they will be made; I owe it to our magnificent GIs. . . .

FDR opened his eyes to find his cigarette had smoldered down to the holder. He tapped it against the fireplace, shaking loose the remains, and inserted another as his thoughts drifted again to Europe. Bradley and Montgomery were approaching the Rhine, the last natural barrier before the final drive to Berlin. The Red Army was on the Oder, just sixty miles from the city.

The Nazis would put up a ferocious fight for Berlin. Ike had warned of a quarter of a million American casualties in the final battle.

The president stared at the fire. Was Berlin worth it?

Would it not be better if the Russians were first to the city? Oh, there was prestige involved, of course, and military egos. Ike's generals were determined to take Berlin before Zhukov, but Ike's generals weren't the ones who would die in the final assault. Eighteen- and nineteen-year-old kids would . . . kids who had survived North Africa . . . Sicily . . . Italy . . . Normandy . . . and the Bulge. Kids who deserved to go home in one piece, get married, and have kids of their own, not die in the last battle. . . .

Churchill would raise hell as well. . . . The closer victory came, the more he was returning to his rabid anticommunism. He had insisted that a final showdown between democracy and communism was inevitable, that everything possible must be done in the months before Germany collapsed to ensure that the West held as many cards as possible.

FDR frowned. Winston deserved the greatest respect. If any one man was responsible for pulling Britain through the black days of 1940 when she stood alone against the Nazi juggernaut, it was Winston. He had rallied a tiny island nation and faced down the greatest military power the world had ever seen. But the same fortitude that had won the Battle of Britain was being exercised in his determination to restore the British Empire to world prominence. He seemed unable to grasp that colonialism was dead, that the peoples of the dying empire were intent on independence. Britain's world-power status was gone, spent in the carnage of two world wars. The United States and the Soviet Union had replaced her as arbiters of the world.

FDR watched the fire die. Roaring logs were now but glowing embers in the hearth. As the logs had been consumed, so had Britain. The mantle of leadership of the free world now rested upon America's shoulders. An isolationist people, disdainful of the endless wars of Europe and Asia, had been thrust against their will into a position of responsibility for the very future of the human race.

Fascism was dying, but communism had replaced it as the ultimate threat to their future. How would they respond to such a challenge? Would they be willing to sacrifice their sons once again should Stalin prove determined to spread revolution and tyranny through Europe and Asia?

The president's thoughts drifted to his vice president. Harry Truman would bear that burden. Harry Truman would be president soon. . . .

He had done his best, Roosevelt thought. America had survived the Great Depression, fought a world war, and seen fit to elect him four times to her highest office. The threats of the Huey Longs, the Eugene Debs, and the Father Coughlins had been overcome. When the desperate peoples of Europe and Asia had turned to fascism or communism, he had done all he could to keep the spark of democracy alive in the land of Washington and Lincoln. It had been a harrowing trial, the pied piper song of fascist utopia or socialist utopia had turned many American heads in those dark days when the country was one spark away from social revolution. Democratic government had seemed helpless, unequipped to cope with the surging currents of unrest.

"We have nothing to fear but fear itself" . . . that one phrase, that simple declaration had somehow sparked a glow of determination to carry on, to keep alive the spirit of hope which had waned in the hearts of tens of millions.

Franklin Delano Roosevelt stirred from his reverie at the sound of footsteps behind him. George had come to pack him off to bed.

* * *

An hour later FDR lay awake in the darkness of the bedroom, the pain throbbing in his head once again, keeping sleep from coming. His thoughts drifted to Truman. Had his choice been wise? Would his successor be able to handle the crushing weight of the presidency?

Roosevelt stared at the darkened ceiling. Despite the heavy blankets, he felt cold, so cold. . . . He shivered in the night until sleep finally came, bringing dreams of Hyde Park, of home . . . of home. . . .

Part III

Götterdämmerung

Chapter XV

Third Marine Division
Iwo Jima
February 19, 1945

I

The smell of disinfectant, sprayed on every marine before leaving the troopships, hadn't done a whole lot for morale, mused Bill Lindberg as he stared at the malevolent bulk of Mount Suribachi, lurking like some forbidding sentinel on the first wave's left flank. Its rocky slopes seemed alive with fire, ugly red flashes sparkling all across its five-hundred-foot-high bulk.

The Corps had learned the hard way at Guadalcanal, at Tarawa, Saipan, and Tinian, that amphibious assaults on hostile island beaches inevitably left hundreds of corpses awash on steaming tropical shores. Why not disinfect the men before landing, some efficient officer had asked, when there was time? Was that not better than worrying about it when the survivors were fighting for their lives, with enough to concern them without having to think about epidemics of God only knew what from flesh-gorged flies feasting on too rapidly decomposing ex-marines?

Bill shuddered as the toxic odor assaulted his nostrils. Never mind that Iwo Jima was far from tropical and the temperature was a cold fifty degrees—when the gunnery sergeant called muster for disinfection, you got disinfected. And liked it.

Scattered mortar shells began to fall near the first wave of amtracks, throwing up frothy white geysers as the tracked amphibians churned to within one hundred yards of the shoreline. Waves of blue Corsairs and Hellcats swept over the beaches to bomb and strafe the dug-in enemy.

"Lock and load!" Clay Boone looked past Bill at the marines huddled behind them. Fifteen helmeted heads looked down as they slammed live rounds into their carbines. Bill worked the bolt action of his M-2 carbine. The first round snapped into the chamber at an angle and jammed.

Bill glanced up at Boone. The sergeant had turned forward again to face the approaching beach. He tried to pry the bullet free with numb fingers.

Damn . . .

He worked the bolt action several times, trying to jar the round free. Shouldn't have jerked the action so hard, now it's really jammed. . . . Get your bayonet, pry the damn thing out. . . .

"Fifty yards!"

Bill yanked his bayonet from its sheath, worked the point between the round and the chamber's sides, and tried to pry it loose. The round sprang free suddenly and dropped to the plywood deck. The sudden movement swung the carbine barrel upward. It jammed into Boone's back, knocking him forward against the amtrack bow.

Startled, he turned to see Bill's carbine pointed at him, a bayonet in his right hand. "Lindberg! What in hell are you doing?"

Bill stared at him, eyes wide. Boone's expression flashed from surprise to annoyance as he noticed the open chamber and the round on the deck. "Christ, Lindberg, sheath that bayonet before you decapitate yourself!" He grabbed the carbine in disgust, snapped the next round into the chamber, and shoved the weapon back at Bill.

"It jammed, Sarge," he stammered, sheepishly slipping the bayonet back into the sheath hanging from his combination belt.

The amtrack shuddered as its tracks struck bottom. It lurched forward, straining for traction in the black ashy soil of the beach, but foundered in place, its tracks only churning it deeper into the volcanic sand.

"Over the side!"

Bill grabbed the amtrack bulkhead and leaped over the side onto the beach. The water in the canteens hanging from his web belt sloshed as he charged forward behind Boone. Staggering from the weight of his backpack, entrenching shovel, and full ammo pouches, he struggled toward the dirty seawall.

The whole squad made it to the seawall without incident. Bill looked down the beach at the marines swarming ashore under the shadow of Suribachi. Very few had fallen; enemy fire was moderate. He glanced at Boone, who seemed amazed at the slack resistance. Offshore, the big guns of the navy hammered away at the mountain. The sky seemed filled with carrier planes.

The hammering of his heart faded toward normal. The pre-H-Hour bombardment had been furious. Maybe the defenders had been all but wiped out. . . . Several days of intense shelling were bound to take a toll. . . .

But an hour later, the sky itself seemed to burst open in a thunderstorm of shells. Every Japanese position on the island opened up, a hail of small arms, machine-gun, mortar, and artillery fire swept across the thousands of marines scattered from the beaches to a few hundred yards inland. Cries of "Corpsman! Corpsman!" rang out over the *crumps* of explosions and screams of bullets as hot metal found yielding flesh and marines began to fall in alarming numbers.

Two hundred yards from Red Beach One, at the base of Suribachi, Bill huddled with his squad in a narrow ravine, his head hunched into his shoulders, his eyes taking in the sudden debacle on the beaches behind them. Several waves of marines had come ashore, and now too many of them were packed into too small an area. The murderous fire had pinned down the leading units, stalling the drive inland and backing up the beaches with thousands of newly arrived troops who were crouched behind whatever cover they could find.

The beaches turned to a charnel house before his eyes. Countless amtracks, Higgins boats, and tanks were burning. Coils of black smoke swirled into the skies from the knocked-out vehicles. Fountains of black soil erupted everywhere. The beach looked as though it were boiling, so thick were the explosions. Direct hits on hastily dug foxholes hurled human debris in all directions. Bloody limbs thudded into the sand; mangled torsos quivered briefly, then stilled.

A shell screamed down and Bill hugged the ravine wall. The blast set his ears to ringing, a cascade of dirt showering down on them.

Clay Boone scampered past him, cursing, and dropped to his belly at the right end of the gully. He peered cautiously over the rim. Two more rounds exploded just behind them in quick succession. Clumps of black dirt plopped onto the squad.

"I see it!" Boone turned to his squad. "Mortar's got us zeroed in! They're up there by that cave mouth, a hundred yards up and just to the right." He emptied a clip from his carbine, but the rounds splattered harmlessly off the side of the mountain below the ledge. The mortar and its crew were protected by the ledge in front of the cave.

"We've got to get closer!" He looked down the line of marines leaning against the ravine wall to his left. "Brown! Diaz! Lindberg! Let's go! The rest of you cover us!" Bill, Carl Brown, and Ricardo Diaz gathered next to Boone. "Now look," he said, "we're gonna have to get close enough to grenade the bastards."

They ducked as a round whistled down. The mortar shell exploded just behind them. Diaz groaned, then slumped against Bill. A second, then a third exploded, hurling shrapnel into their ranks. Voices screamed down the line. "I'm hit! Christ! I'm hit!"

Bill, half stunned by the concussions, reached out to check Diaz. Blood oozed from several ragged holes in his green fatigues as he muttered something in Spanish, clutching his bleeding chest. Farther down, Oldham and Wright huddled over Kowalski, while Mac and Brady crawled over to see about Sims.

He suddenly noticed Boone was screaming in his ear. "Grab some extra grenades from Diaz and follow me!" Boone cupped his hands to his mouth and yelled toward a group of marines pinned down fifty yards behind them. "We need a corpsman up here! Now!"

Bill grabbed three grenades from Diaz's web belt, hooked them to his, then crawled to the edge of the ravine.

Boone screamed at Mac and Brady to lay down some covering fire, then threw himself over the ravine ledge and darted uphill, throwing himself behind a rock some twenty yards away. He fired another clip at the cave.

Bill swallowed hard, then leaped over the ravine and scurried off to the right toward a shell crater. A rattle of machine-gun fire from farther up Suribachi stitched a dancing column of geysers in the sand behind him as he covered the fifteen yards to the hole and dove in headfirst.

Please God, get me out of this . . . just get me out of this— "Lindberg!"

Bill peered over the edge of the hole at Boone, some thirty yards to his left and just uphill. He tried to reply, but his throat was dry as dust.

"Cover me!" Boone set himself for another dash forward. "Now!"

Bill aimed his carbine at the cave and squeezed off a burst, then another. Debris shot off the mountainside over the cave. A head popped up quickly, then vanished. Seconds later, three grenades arced out from the ledge and bounced down the slope toward them. Bill yelled a warning, but just a faint croak emerged. He saw Boone duck behind another boulder just as the first grenade went off between them.

Where were the other two?

A pair of sharp bursts just uphill told him they'd gone off before reaching him. He heard Boone yell at him to go when he opened fire. He peered over the top again, looking for another patch of cover and spotted a shallow ravine some twenty yards uphill, then looked down toward the squad.

Brady and Mac were watching him, their faces pasty white, their carbines pointed past him at the cave. He nodded and they opened up. An instant later, Boone's carbine cracked to life on his flank.

Just as he jumped up, an explosion behind him silenced the covering fire from the ravine. Bullets sang angrily past his head and he dove instinctively to the ground. He heard Boone screaming at him and scampered on his hands and knees up the hill. Something tore at one of his canteens, then his rifle jerked from his hands. He glanced back and say the carbine lying on the ground, its stock splintered by a slug.

"Leave it!"

He darted the last fifteen yards to the depression and threw himself into it, amazed he was still in one piece. But his rifle was gone. He checked his canteen and found it split nearly in two, a big round hole right in the middle of it. He looked haplessly over at Boone.

"Can you get a grenade that far?" Boone yelled.

Bill snatched a look up the hill. Had to be sixty yards to the cave . . . but if there was anything he did right at boot camp, it was grenade drill. He had the best arm in the company. . . .

He unhooked two grenades from his belt. "I'll try!" He looked down the hill again toward the squad. He saw Oldham poke his head over the top.

"Mac's hit! Brady's dead!" he yelled at Boone, an edge of panic in his voice.

"Cover us, dammit!" Boone screamed.

Oldham's carbine barrel appeared and he pointed it at the cave.

"We'll fire a short burst, then jump up and toss one!" he yelled at Bill. "Oldham! Fire when I do!"

Bill got his footing and crouched on his haunches, his hand clutching the firing pin of a grenade. He heard Boone open up, yanked the pin, sprung to full height and let fly. He let his follow-through drop him to the ground and waited for the explosion. Seconds later, a distant whump! sounded from above.

To his left, he saw Boone scamper from cover and charge uphill, firing from the hip. The sergeant raced another twenty yards up Suribachi before hurling himself into a crater. He threw two grenades in quick succession, then waved Bill forward as he got up himself and darted ahead.

Bill, armed with nothing but a grenade in his right hand, scurried uphill before he had time to change his mind. The ledge seemed oddly silent. He dove behind a boulder just thirty yards from the ledge, yanked the firing pin, tossed his last grenade, and watched it sail over the edge. The blast still ringing in his ears, he rose to his knees.

What now? He had no rifle, no grenades. . . .

His unspoken question was answered by Boone, who charged past him, carbine blazing. He scrambled over the edge and disappeared. A moment later, his head popped over the side. He waved the squad forward.

Bill reached the ledge first. Three bodies lay sprawled in death. The mortar was gone.

Boone nodded toward a small opening in the side of the mountain. "Tunnels," he grunted. "Whole damn island's one big rat's nest."

Bill stared at the hole in the cliff face, chilled.

How can you fight an enemy you can't even see . . . ?

II

That night, as Bill Lindberg and thousands of marines clung to their foothold on Iwo Jima, far to the southeast the taxiways of Tinian trembled from the roar of scores of B-29s, cueing in long lines for their turn on the twin runways of the sprawling airbase. At 2100 it was *Rosie III*'s turn.

As the big bomber reached the end of the runway, Major Wilson Lindberg eased back on the stick. He held her steady as she roared just over the waves, watching the dark water of the atoll flash by below.

"One hundred knots . . . one-ten . . ."

Not until a hundred-thirty knots was called off did Wilson pull back on the wheel and haul *Rosie III* into a steady climb toward the stars. He'd heard too many tales in the Tinian Officers' Club of fatal stalls just after liftoff. The B-29 handled so beautifully that pilots sometimes tended to forget they were flying a four-engined bomber loaded with tons of bombs and tried to climb too quickly. The tragic result was a spectacular explosion in the bay, eleven more empty bunks in the crew barracks, and the useless waste of a multi-million-dollar, state-of-the-art aircraft.

He eased back on the wheel as the airspeed needle rotated past one-hundred-eighty knots and *Rosie III*, her four huge props biting into the heavy tropical air, settled into a gradual climb toward cruising altitude.

At twenty-five-thousand feet, the Superforts, one-hundred-fifty strong, formed up and the formation headed northwestward for the Empire. With *Rosie III* tucked into position, Wilson handed control over to Hank Callahan, poured himself a steaming cup of coffee from the cockpit thermos, and took out his charts and briefing notes. The target for his first mission against Japan was the Nakajima aircraft plant at Musashino. The weather officer at the morning briefing had warned of a cold front moving over Japan from the Asian mainland and predicted a seventy percent likelihood of solid cloud cover over the target.

He checked his notes. If Musashino was socked in, they would be diverted to secondary targets, mainly railroad marshaling yards and bridges. He frowned. Sending a hundred and fifty Superforts against bridges and rail yards was like taking a shotgun after a pesky fly.

Weather, as he had learned in Europe, especially during the winter of '43-'44, had diverted many an Eighth Air Force raid from a critical target to pinprick attacks on scattered secondary targets of little importance. Too many aircrew and planes had been lost for little or no reward. He'd thought it would be different here, but had quickly learned from other pilots that the Twentieth Air Force was finding clear weather over their targets only an average of seven days a month.

At that pace, they couldn't hope to wage a successful strategic bombing campaign and batter the Japs to their knees through airpower. An invasion of the Empire itself would be necessary.

Wilson winced inwardly at the thought of Bill and hundreds of thousands of other poor footsloggers having to fight their way through millions of fanatic Japs. He frowned. First things first—Iwo Jima had to be taken, then Okinawa.

He reached behind the seat and pulled the latest letter from Bill out of his flight bag. The long flights to and from the Empire allowed free time for the crews to catch up on correspondence and Wilson always saved his mail for times like this. He checked the postmark. Bill had mailed it from the transport on the ninth. . . .

He opened the envelope and began reading.

Dear Will:

Well, we're all anxious to get this thing over with. Like you told me back home, it's the waiting around that's the hardest. We've got a lot of veterans in the outfit, guys who've seen action before, which makes us rookies feel a lot better about the whole thing.

Scuttlebutt has it that we're taking this place so you bomber guys will have an emergency base to land on if you have trouble. There's been no end of bitching about *that!* I have yet to mention that I have a brother in the Twentieth Air Force, ha-ha.

Anyway, the brass wants the island taken, so that's what we're going to do. We've had a lot of briefings about Iwo

Jima. Seems the Japs have been fortifying it for years, but the Navy's going to pound it for nine days before we land. Most of the guys figure that should take care of most of the Japs there.

I haven't gotten a letter from you for a while, Will. Maybe they've gotten delayed somewhere. God knows how late our mail gets to us. I suppose it's not easy for it to catch up to us once we're at sea. I know you guys are awful busy pounding the Japs, but try to write if you can. Seems like all the guys get more mail than me. The folks, Mom—that is, she writes for the both of them—send a letter every couple weeks, but it's hard to write them back because they just don't know or understand how things really are out here.

Well, I've got to wind this up. Will, if anything should happen to me, I wanted you to know how proud I am to have had you for a brother. I've always looked up to you, you know that, and I hope you understand why I joined the Corps. I just couldn't face not being a part of all this. I know it sounds corny, but I feel so alive, so excited at being in on something so momentous.

I'll write again as soon as I get a chance. Take care of yourself. Oh, I got a nice letter from Carrie Anne. This might be unsolicited advice, but I really think you should give her another chance, she's a sweetheart.

                Bill

Wilson folded the letter and put it back in his bag. The only news Tinian had of Iwo was that the marines had gone ashore that morning and were meeting stiff resistance.

"Who was the letter from, Lindy?"

Wilson glanced at Callahan as he made his way forward from the nose. "My brother, Bill. He's on Iwo. . . ."

"Ah." Callahan poured some coffee from the steaming cockpit thermos. "Hope he's okay. Heard they're having a rough time of it."

"Yeah."

"When did he mail it?"

Wilson glanced again at the postmark on the envelope. "The ninth." He took the proffered cup.

Callahan finally broke the heavy silence. "Well, it'll be good to have that airfield. We've lost too many Superforts that would have at least made it back to Iwo. They're going to base Mustangs there, too, I heard. We'll get better escort protection."

"Yeah."

Callahan patted Wilson on the shoulder. "He'll be okay, Lindy."

Wilson didn't trust his voice. He nodded.

An hour later, the formation passed near enough to the embattled island for Wilson to see the pinpoint flashes of artillery fire lighting the darkness far below to the west. He stared out through the Plexiglas. Was Bill down there right now, fighting for his life—or had his name already been added to the growing casualty lists . . . ?

The vision haunted him on the return trip as well.

The bomb-run over Musashino had been uneventful. The scarcity of flak and fighters had been a pleasant surprise. Wilson had counted his blessings, and as soon as *Rosie III* was safely at sea again, his thoughts returned to Iwo Jima.

Now, as they passed the island again, there seemed to be no letup at all in the fighting. Ugly points of light flared to life constantly in the darkness far below. Wilson checked his watch: 0220. It was going to be a long, brutal night on Iwo. . . .

Anxious for news of the fighting, Wilson handed the controls over to Callahan and made his way back to the radio compartment just aft of the cockpit. He roused Sergeant Walsh and asked him if he could find any ground frequencies.

"I'll try, Skip." Walsh twisted the frequency dial around until they could hear voices squawking through the static. They leaned closer as a harried voice called out map coordinates.

"Yeah, there's a howitzer up there," the voice explained over a background of heavy explosions. "They've got our positions zeroed in. . . ."

Wilson and Walsh glanced at one another. Someone was in trouble, big trouble.

Another voice, obviously that of a gunnery officer on an off-shore warship, replied. "Okay, map grid K-4?"

"Affirmative! Affirmative! For Christ's sake, hurry! They're—"

The line went dead.

"On the way . . ."

Walsh and Wilson stared at the radio. Presently, the second voice crackled over the air. "Popeye Four to Archie . . . Popeye Four to Archie, come in, Archie . . ."

No response. For several minutes the gunnery officer called the marine position, repeating the code name over and over.

"Maybe their radio's out. . . ." ventured Walsh.

Wilson nodded, unwilling to think the worst. "Try another frequency, will you, Sergeant?"

Walsh scanned the airwaves, getting nothing but static.

"We're getting out of range, Skip."

"Yeah . . ." Wilson turned to leave. "Thanks for trying."

"No problem."

He returned to the cockpit and slumped into the pilot's seat. Callahan looked across. "How's it going down there, Lindy?"

"Sounds bad, Hank. Sounds bad . . ."

Chapter XVI

I

Gunther Dietrich stared in awe at the bedraggled officer wrestling with the corkscrew and the bottle of wine. General Adolph Galland was a legend in the Luftwaffe. He had flown with the Condor Legion in Spain, led the Luftwaffe fighter wing in the Battle of Britain, and served since 1942 as the commanding general of all the Luftwaffe's fighters.

Yet here he was, just another pilot in a decimated fighter squadron, flying against the enemy alongside lowly majors and colonels.

The cork popped free at last and Galland filled their glasses. "Since our comrades are aloft, it falls to you, mein Oberstleutnant, to welcome the new recruit to the squadron." He raised the glass of sparkling white wine, a bemused smile on his face.

"Mein General, I . . . I don't understand. . . ."

Galland shrugged. "The Fuhrer and myself have had our last disagreement. I have resigned my position and come here to meet my fate with my comrades."

"But you are too valuable to the Luftwaffe . . . to us."

"I have accomplished nothing since '43 but dash my head

against a brick wall. The Fuhrer, the Fat One—they are so befuddled with drugs they cannot see straight, much less think. They have not heard a word I've said in two years and now we are paying the price for it." Galland walked to the window of the officers' mess and gazed fondly at the pair of Messerschmitt 262s hidden in the trees at the edge of the airfield. "The 262 would have been operational two years ago, Herr Oberstleutnant, had Hitler and Goring not been such dolts as to think it could be converted into a bomber. Think of it! With twenty or thirty squadrons of jets, we could have cleared the skies of the enemy, saved Germany's cities from ruin, halted the Russians in Poland, prevented the invasion of France."

Galland's eyes blazed. "We could have stopped the Allies cold, Dietrich! Instead, our cities are piles of rubble, the Russians are at the gates of Berlin, and we have nothing to give our children but a lifetime of despair. Germany will be split in two; she may never rise again. Can you still wonder, Dietrich, why I have come here to fight?"

"You do not want to live . . . ?"

"I did all I could in Berlin, but I have failed. I have failed myself, I have failed my pilots, I have failed the German people. A death in battle alongside my comrades is all I can offer now."

A bitter smile on his face, Galland turned to the window as the whine of approaching jets was heard. They stepped outside and searched the western sky for the first sign of the returning squadron. A low ceiling hid the approaching 262s from sight.

"Herr General, listen!" Gunther thought he heard the unmistakable rumble of piston engines over the higher-pitched whine of the 262s. A moment later, he was certain. "Mustangs! There are Mustangs about!" He turned and ran to the flight office, Galland on his heels. Breathless, he charged through the door. "Otto! Warn them! Mustangs are waiting to ambush them over the field!"

As the warning went out over the squadron frequency, Gunther explained the new American tactic to Galland. The American Mustangs and Thunderbolts, hopelessly outclassed by the 262s, had recently taken to orbiting entire squadrons over the known landing fields of the jets in order to jump them when they were most vulnerable. Only when in a low-speed landing approach, low on fuel and ammunition, could a 262 fall prey to the American fighters.

The voice of Heinz Gerhardt crackled over the radio speaker, informing them that he was on fumes and would have to come in. Hartmann and Brandenburg were in the same fix. As Gunther and Galland raced outside, they heard the staccato bursts from the airfields antiaircraft gunners.

"There!" Gunther pointed to the northwest. Just above the bare trees a 262 was coming in. Smoke trailed from its left engine nacelle. He watched the antiaircraft tracers arc skyward, reaching out to a point some one hundred meters behind the jet. Two Mustangs were on its tail, hammering away with their machine guns.

He watched helplessly as the jet staggered, dipped a wing, and plunged to the ground, cartwheeling viciously across the ground, scattering chunks of airframe about as it tore itself to pieces. The Mustangs banked away just as the other 262s appeared.

Gunther prayed. Let them get down . . . let them get down. . . . But Hartmann and Brandenburg were jumped as well. The lead jet exploded in midair as rounds from three more Mustangs tore into its vitals. Flaming debris showered earthward.

The lone survivor pulled into a banking climb and vanished through the overcast pursued by the first pair of American fighters. Bail out, thought Gunther. Get altitude and take to your chute, it's your only chance. He could just make out the whine of engines straining at full power over the rumble of the piston-engined Mustangs. The sounds faded as the Mustangs and their prey climbed through the murk.

Finally, Galland pointed to the north. A dark object tumbled through the overcast and impacted with a flash some three kilometers away. A dull rumble echoed through the woods a few seconds later.

"Maybe he got out," said Gunther, scanning the sky in the hopes of seeing a parachute drifting down. They watched anxiously for any sign of a silk canopy.

"The wind would have carried him east," observed Galland. He turned to his left to search the clouds in the direction of Essen.

"I'm going up," Gunther said.

Galland turned to see Gunther racing across the field toward the woods where his 262 was hidden. "Don't be a fool, they'll jump you too," he yelled. But Gunther was too far away. Galland hesitated only a second, then took off after him.

Gunther reached the clearing, gasping for breath. He saw his ground crew huddled under the wings of the jet. "Is she fueled and armed?"

They stared at him. The crew captain nodded. He looked past Gunther as Galland staggered to a stop, winded by the sprint across the snowy field. "I'll go, Oberstleutnant!"

"They were my friends, Herr General. I'm going."

"You are grounded. That's an order." The ground crew stiffened to attention, realizing suddenly who was standing amongst them. They stared in disbelief as Gunther ignored Galland and climbed onto the wing and into the cockpit.

"Take number five if you want, it's in the next clearing!" The whine of twin Jumo engines drowned out Galland's reply. The general was smiling, much to Gunther's relief. He raised his hand to his battered cap and Gunther returned the salute.

They climbed through the overcast and broke into sunlight at a thousand meters. Galland's voice crackled over Gunther's radio. "See anything?"

"No, Herr General."

"Follow me. They must be heading west for home." Galland's 262 banked into a turn and Gunther stayed on his tail. The jets climbed steadily, both pilots keeping a sharp eye sunward, the likeliest danger source. If Mustangs were waiting for them, they would be up sun, using the glare behind them to hide their attack.

Five minutes later, they were at thirteen thousand meters. Far below the dappled-green Messerschmitts, the earth was hidden in a shroud of white. Gunther scanned the sky ahead, hoping to see the glint of sunlight off aluminum.

"There they are!" shouted Galland. He waggled his wings and pushed over into a banking dive to the northwest. Gunther, in his wingman's position two hundred meters to Galland's right and a hundred meters behind and just above him, pushed the stick forward and searched the sky below. His airspeed needle was sweeping past five-hundred-and-eighty miles an hour before he saw the distant sparkle of sunlight reflecting off polished aluminum. Five Mustangs, spread out in an extended "finger four" formation, were cruising westward, unaware of the two jets plunging at them out of the sun.

As the range closed, Gunther peered through his gunsight, watching the image of the last Mustang on the right grow larger. He had just made out the red tail when the enemy fighter banked suddenly and peeled away. He looked up from the sight to see the formation scattering.

They'd seen them!

The two lead Mustangs pulled up sharply, the left pair dove away to the east, and his target was already in a banking turn to the right in an effort to get on his tail. The thought that the Mustangs which had jumped his friends were blue tailed flashed through his mind as he kicked rudder and pulled into a climbing turn to stay above his opponent. He craned his neck around to find Galland just as the general's voice crackled over his radio.

"There's one on your tail!"

He cursed, yanked the stick back to centerline, and shoved the throttle full forward, fighting the instinct to bank into a turn. A Mustang, being slower, could out-turn him; Gunther's advantage was superior speed. Green tracers shot past the cockpit.

He hunched low in the seat, jinking side to side to throw the American's aim off while he opened the range. At full thrust, the twin jet engines brought him quickly out of range.

He pulled into a climb and joined up with Galland. The Mustangs had vanished.

"They must be low on fuel, Dietrich," Galland's voice crackled into his helmet. "We could give chase, but I suspect they have plenty of friends about, just waiting to jump us. . . ."

Gunther searched the sky, feeling cheated. He *had* one of them right in his sights! He looked over at Galland, on station just off his wingtip.

"It's up to you, *kamerade,*" said Galland. "I'm with you, either way."

Gunther searched the sky again. The Americans had killed his friends; could he just let them get away? He glanced at the general. On the other hand, how could he lead the great Galland into a certain trap? The legendary ace had fought for the Fatherland ever since Poland, had downed over a hundred of the enemy. He was a beloved father figure to every fighter pilot in the Luftwaffe. . . .

Gunther glared at the scudding cloud formations to the west. Somewhere out there, hidden in the cumulus, were countless Mustangs and Thunderbolts, just waiting for them. He made his decision, knowing he couldn't live with himself if he got Galland killed in a hopeless fight. The American airforce was like a horde of locusts—they swallowed up everything in their path.

"They will be back tomorrow," he radioed glumly, kicking rudder and swinging the jet into a shallow turn to the east. Galland followed, flying wingman.

"Next time, *we* will jump *them,* Dietrich," Galland promised.

Frustrated, bitter at the losing, one-sided fight being waged over Germany, Gunther didn't trust himself with a reply. Would there even be a next time . . . ?

II

Yuri groaned as the throbbing pain in his leg stirred him to consciousness. He opened his eyes. Groggy, confused, he looked around.

He was in a tent. On a cot. The odor of iodine and the coppery smell of blood lingered in the cool air. He saw other cots, other men.

He was alive. . . .

The pain and, more insistently, the pressure in his bladder told him that the fascists hadn't done for him yet. He propped himself up on his elbows, struggling to get up so he could go outside and relieve himself.

"Careful, we don't want to have to stitch you up again."

Startled, Yuri turned toward the feminine voice. An auburn-haired nurse stood next to his cot. A small hand gently eased him down.

"What . . . happened . . . ?" His mouth was dry, his tongue felt stubbornly thick.

"We had to sew up your leg, Comrade Rostov," she explained. "It was opened up clear to the bone. You were lucky you didn't bleed to death."

Suddenly dizzy, Yuri closed his eyes for a moment, trying to make sense of things. Slowly, a nightmare image of bursting flares and barking machine guns formed in his mind. He stiffened, his leg throbbed suddenly, his eyes opened in alarm.

Reality flooded back. The penal battalion . . . the mine-field . . .

Yuri looked up at the nurse. "Water . . ." he croaked. She handed him a canteen and he drank greedily, wincing as moisture soaked into his cracked, chapped lips. "Thank you."

She took the canteen. He found himself staring at her. She was beautiful . . . the most beautiful thing he'd ever seen. Her blue eyes twinkled, her pretty mouth turned upward at the corners in a wry smile.

"Haven't you ever seen a girl before, comrade?"

Her melodic words seemed to take forever to register. Finally, subject and predicate merged into one and he blushed.

"I . . . uh . . ." But his throbbing leg, his bursting bladder, and her simple beauty overwhelmed his senses. He fumbled for words, transfixed by those blue eyes as she pulled back the woolen blanket to have a look at his leg. His hospital gown was hiked up past his waist. . . .

"I see Olga has taken your catheter out, and not too gently judging by the swelling. We'd better get you a bedpan."

Yuri felt his face flush even more hotly—no woman had ever had such intimate regard for his privates. He managed to recover some of his composure by the time she returned with the blessed implement.

"Do you need it right away?"

He nodded, his face coloring again.

Her eyes twinkled. "Do you need any help?"

"I think I can manage. . . ."

"My, a whole sentence!" She smiled indulgently. "I was starting to wonder if your vocabulary was limited to 'water,' 'thank you,' and 'I . . . uh . . .' "

She patted his hand and was gone before Yuri could reply. He used the bedpan and lay back in relief, finally able to focus his thoughts.

Who would have taken the trouble to haul a wounded penal battalion prisoner to a first-aid tent . . . ? How was it that he hadn't bled to death on the way?

But most important of all, who was this angel of mercy, this girl with the lilting voice, the sparkling eyes, the auburn hair?

Exhausted, weak from loss of blood, Yuri dozed off, thinking of her. When he came to again, she was standing over him.

"Good morning, Comrade Rostov."

He blinked. Was he still dreaming?

"You slept twelve hours straight," she clucked. "Olga was supposed to see that you were fed."

"Olga . . . ?"

"The night nurse, Comrade Rostov."

"Please, my name is Yuri."

"Well, Yuri, I am pleased to make your acquaintance." She held out her hand and he gave it a weak shake.

"And your name is . . . ?"

"Katya."

"Katya."

She smiled. "Can I have my hand back?"

"Oh . . ." He released his grip, embarrassed.

"I will try to find you something to eat, Yuri. Try your hardest not to fall asleep again, won't you?"

He laughed, then winced from the sudden pain in his leg. It seemed an eternity before she returned with a cup of steaming tea and plate of black bread. "Eat now. I must see to the others."

His ten days of recovery passed quickly. By the time the day came to leave, he was desperately in love. His brief moments with Katya, as she ministered to his dressings, brought his food, and raised his spirits with her smiles, had changed him forever.

His last morning there, she walked him outside into the late winter sunshine. An early thaw lay over Poland. The ground was soggy with melting snow, the faintest hint of spring hung in the brisk air.

"Good-bye, Yuri Rostov," she said. "Be sure to say hello to Captain Arbatov for me."

"Captain Arbatov? You know him?"

She smiled. "He's the one who brought you here."

Yuri stared.

"You certainly have a habit of staring at a girl, Yuri," she said, laughing.

"But I don't understand. . . . How could . . . how did he know where . . . Say hello to him . . . ?"

Katya pressed a finger to his lips. "You're going back to your old unit, Yuri." She kissed him on each cheek in the traditional Russian manner of farewell, her breath warm on his neck. "Your truck is here. Off with you now. Your comrades are waiting."

"Katya—"

"I know . . ." She pressed something into his hand. He

looked down at the folded letter. When he looked up, she'd disappeared into the tent.

"Are you Rostov?" He turned to find an impatient sergeant scowling at him from the idling Ford.

"Yes, Comrade Sergeant."

"Get aboard, comrade."

Yuri hesitated.

"Now!" the sergeant bellowed. Yuri scampered to the truck. Helping hands pulled him up into the canvas-topped flatbed. He sank onto the bench next to a grinning private.

"Don't you know the Hitlerites have been asking after you, Rostov?" the soldier joked, winking at the sergeant. "They've been wondering where you've been lately. Why, I hear Hitler asked von Bock the other day where that terror of the fascists Rostov was."

"Leave him alone, Zorin," growled the sergeant. "Can't you see he's already pining away for his little nurse?"

The truck lurched ahead. Gears ground together as the driver shifted into second, then third. Yuri stared out the open back of the Ford at the rapidly receding tents of the field hospital, watching until they faded from view.

He stuffed Katya's letter into his pocket, desperate to read it, but unwilling to invite more jokes. It would have to wait until he had some privacy.

Chapter XVII

Third Marine Division
Iwo Jima
March 1, 1945

I

Bill Lindberg crouched in his foxhole, shivering in the damp chill of dawn, hand raised to shield his eyes against the glare of the rising sun. Directly ahead, some two hundred yards away across a barren, crater-pocked no-man's-land lay Nishi Ridge, the battalion objective for D-Day plus ten. Behind him, two miles to the west, the blasted slopes of Mount Suribachi caught the early morning sunshine, providing a mocking background of peaceful tranquillity to the marines holding the front lines.

Bill turned and pulled his bayonet from the sheath on his web belt, snapped it into place at the tip of his M-2, and glanced up at the summit of Suribachi where a small American flag rippled silently in the offshore breeze, just visible from their foxholes.

"Hey Bill, you hear the latest . . . ?"

He looked over at Reggie Blackwell frowning at the sight from the next foxhole. "Maybe, Reg. Maybe not . . ."

Blackwell slammed a fresh clip into his carbine. "When I was back at the beach, I heard some guy from *Life* shot the flag-raising the other day, got it on film, you know, and, well, the shit is the picture's made about every front page in the world. They say it's already the most famous picture of the damned war."

Bill turned again to face Nishi Ridge. The complex of machine-gun nests and hidden bunkers had defied repeated marine assaults and sent a steady stream of litters of dead and wounded marines back to the beaches. "So what?" he muttered, scanning the forbidding ground ahead.

Blackwell shrugged. "Just thought I'd pass on some news, Bill."

Bill took several deep breaths to ease the growing tension. Down the line he could see Sergeant Boone scurrying from foxhole to foxhole—the company was minutes away from having to charge the enemy-infested ground ahead. "Sorry, Reg . . . guess I'm a little edgy. . . ." He managed a shaky grin—Reg was just trying to take his mind off the looming firefight. "So, did you see a copy?"

"Yeah. Looked pretty dramatic; like a painting or some scene from a movie." He shook his head. "Couldn't have been staged better if a Hollywood director had been up there."

"Recognize anybody?"

"Nope, couldn't really see anyone's face. But the scoop is they're all famous now. When the picture went big time, the papers back home wanted the names of the guys there."

"Bet *that* drove the brass nuts! We're in the fight of our lives and all the press wants to know is who was up on Suribachi ten days ago."

"Nothing like a few heroes to take everyone's mind back home off the casualty lists, at least for a while." Blackwell watched Sergeant Boone coming and tightened the chin strap of his helmet. "Problem is, half the guys in the picture got killed already. . . ."

Bill thought of the carnage he'd seen in nine days and nights of constant, close-quarters fighting. Marine assault rifle companies on Iwo were taking a terrible beating, casualty rates of eighty and ninety percent weren't unusual. Any company that had seen steady action and retained an effective strength of fifty percent could count itself lucky. "Figures, don't it . . . ?"

"Yeah."

Boone dropped to his knees between their foxholes, his knuckles white around the stock of his Thompson submachine gun. "We've got the left flank," he grunted, furiously working the gum in his mouth. "Baker and Charlie companies are going right up the gut; Easy company's got the right flank."

"Another frontal assault? Why can't we just outflank them?"

Boone's laugh was bitter. "Ain't no other damn way, unless you want to walk out there, Blackwell, and ask the Japs where there damned flanks are."

"No thanks, Sarge."

"Then quit bitching. You've seen the tunnel holes, you've seen how the sneaky bastards fight. If we don't take ground one position at a time, they let us go right past 'em, pop up behind us, and mow down whole platoons from behind." He rose to a crouch. "Just thank whatever God you got that your ass isn't in Baker or Charlie company this morning."

"Hell, we've pulled our share, Sarge."

"Yeah, and so have *they,* Blackwell. So has every last damned marine on Iwo!" Boone spat on the ground in frustration. "But today it's their turn again, and they're going to get shot to hell and there isn't a damned thing we can do about it because *somebody's* got to do it."

"Reg didn't mean anything, Sarge. . . ."

Boone turned toward Bill. "Ah hell, I know that. But I was the lucky stiff the major sent over there to tell the poor bastards in Baker and Charlie they've got to take the point again. They looked at me like I was some ghost from hell itself, come to welcome them into eternity."

"Shit, Sarge," Blackwell muttered. "Ain't one of us going to leave here alive anyway—Judgment Day will come and go before the last marine blasts the last Jap out of his last damn hole."

The dull thump of mortars began to echo from beyond Nishi Ridge. Seconds later, the first explosions tore through the marine positions. Cries of "Corpsman! Corpsman!" began to ring out over the noise of renewed shelling.

"First squad, follow me!" Boone shouted, edging forward in a crouch. "Second squad, cover us!"

Bill fell into line behind Reggie Blackwell, careful to leave a gap of several yards between them. A glance to his right revealed scattered squads of marines darting forward along the mile-long front. Within seconds, the air came alive with the hideous whine of bullets as the hidden enemy unleashed a murderous crossfire on the advancing marines.

He threw himself to the ground, then crawled forward behind Boone and Blackwell. They edged their way forward toward a shallow ravine some thirty yards ahead, the first real cover available.

A head popped up from the gulch. Bill froze. Before he could react, the head was gone and a grenade was arcing through the air toward them. It fell with a sickening thud in the sand not three feet from his face. He grabbed it without thinking and hurled it back toward the ravine. It sailed back over Boone and exploded with a muffled sound in the ditch.

Cursing, Boone grabbed one of his own from his belt, yanked the pin, and sent it flying into the ravine. "Now!" he roared. They sprang to their feet and charged the ravine, throwing themselves into the depression before the enemy machine gunners from the ridge beyond could single them out for special attention.

Gasping in fear, delayed shock coming over him, Bill stared as Boone crawled to the edge of a tunnel opening and slammed two more grenades down into the opening.

"Fire in the hole!"

The explosion was faint—the grenades had fallen several feet before going off somewhere below. Bill managed to gather his wits and crawled to the far edge of the gully where Boone and Blackwell were crouched against the sloping wall, facing Nishi Ridge.

Blackwell stared at Bill, pale, eyes wide. "Damn, Bill, thought you'd had it. . . ."

Bill shrugged, his mouth too dry to speak. He gripped his carbine tightly to hide the trembling of his hands. His heart still hammering wildly in his chest, he glanced at Boone. Thank God he'd thrown the damn thing hard enough to clear the sarge. He should have thrown it off to the side. . . .

Boone turned and yelled toward the foxholes behind them. "Second squad! Get moving!"

As marine howitzers pounded the ridge ahead, and Boone, Blackwell, and Bill laid down covering fire, the second squad darted forward, then piled into the ravine with them. The platoon assault gear was distributed—the sudden mortar attack had forced a hasty abandonment of the zeroed-in foxhole line before they were ready. Boone slung three satchel charges over his shoulder; Blackwell took the unit's second flame-thrower; and Bill loaded up with a dozen grenades. He'd proven himself on D-Day during the charge up bloody Suribachi—he had the best arm in the platoon, if not the whole company.

Through the long morning, the squads leapfrogged forward in turn, clearing the left flank of the main assault, pausing often to hold their positions as Baker and Charlie companies fought their way into the main line of concrete bunkers and hidden pillboxes. By noon, battalion runners passed the word for them to hold in place.

As Bill and his buddies relieved parched throats with canteen water, lit cigarettes, and reflected on the sudden gift of at least another hour of life, Boone tracked down a walkie-talkie to get details on the delay.

When he returned, he sank to the ground beside Bill and Reggie Blackwell. His face a grim mask, he lit a Pall Mall from Bill's smoldering Camel, handed the butt back, and stared silently into space.

After several minutes of tense silence, broken only by the occasional ringing shot from some hidden Japanese mortar tube, Bill cleared his throat and turned toward Boone. "What's up, Sarge?" he asked quietly.

Boone took a long drag from his Pall Mall. "Baker and Charlie caught it bad. . . . Battalion's sending up reinforcements."

"Are they pulling them out of the line . . . ?"

"No. Whoever can still carry a rifle is going in again this afternoon. Major's orders." Boone tossed the burnt-down butt aside in disgust. "Can't be more than thirty of the poor bastards left."

Bill glanced at Blackwell. Marine rifle companies carried a combat strength of some one-hundred-eighty marines. Baker and Charlie, like all rifle companies on Iwo, had lost people every day since D-Day, but still had gone into the morning assault with at least two hundred marines between them. . . .

Boone slammed a fresh clip into his Thompson. "Blackwell, you're in charge here until I get back."

Blackwell stared at him. "Where are you going, Sarge?"

Boone got wearily to his feet. "There isn't a damn sergeant left in Baker or Charlie, Blackwell. They need help over there."

"But, Sarge, you—"

"I'll be back later. Now listen, there shouldn't be much in front of you. The Japs ahead have gone through the tunnels to reinforce the center. Don't do anything stupid. If you run into anything you can't handle send someone back for artillery support, okay?"

Blackwell nodded dully. Boone slapped Bill on the back and winked. "If all else fails, have Cy Young here see if he can throw one of his grenades two hundred yards."

Before Bill could reply, Boone was gone, darting through the smoke and haze of battle toward the shattered remains of Baker and Charlie companies.

II

Sinclair Robertson stood alone on the windswept heights of the west bank of the Rhine and directed his field glasses onto the girdered span which beckoned so invitingly from the fog-filled valley below. The railroad bridge at Remagen was indeed still intact. . . .

He lowered his binoculars, buoyant at the incredible luck of happening to be covering the only Allied unit to find a Rhine bridge still standing. The last great natural barrier between the Allied armies and the heart of the Third Reich was being forced over an obscure railroad bridge, sparing the Allies the bloody alternative of a costly frontal assault by pontoon bridge and amphibious vehicle.

And he had the exclusive story all to himself! At least for a while.

Even better for all concerned, Remagen was far from the main Nazi armies. The enemy stood little chance of shifting panzer divisions southward in time to contain the expanding bridgehead. Instead of a desperately needed stalemate at the Rhine, the Germans were suddenly faced with military catastrophe, for Allied armored divisions could pour nearly unopposed through the gap at Remagen, swing north behind them, and trap the last Nazi armies between the great river and a solid wall of Allied tanks, troops, and artillery.

Sinclair sat down in the back of an idling half-track and began to jot down his impressions as he watched a steady stream of tanks, trucks, armored cars, and jeeps rumble past him toward the east. In the misty valley itself, the leading elements of the column, one olive-drab vehicle at a time, snaked across the bridge amidst light shelling from the eastern hills.

A half-track, its rear deck bristling with a quad-fifty, antiaircraft machine-gun turret, ground to a halt behind him. He looked up from his notebook for a moment, noting the arrival with approval. Despite the protective umbrella of Mustang fighters overhead, several Nazi fighter-bombers had managed to make bomb runs on the bridge—without success so far, but others would return and the more antiaircraft M-3s around the better. . . .

"Well! Damned if it isn't my old buddy from Omaha!"

Sinclair looked up again to see a grinning GI approaching

from the other half-track. He reached down to meet the upthrust hand of the soldier and shook it before he finally recognized him.

"Sanders! Long time, no see."

"How you been, Robertson?"

Sinclair grinned, happy to see that the kid had made it through France, Holland, and the Bulge in one piece. "Can't complain! And you?"

"Just might make it home, Robertson!" He slapped the side of his right leg. "Caught a round in the thigh back in Antwerp— didn't get me a ticket to the States, but got me out of the infantry at least." He nodded back toward the M-3. "I've been driving that baby since the Bulge."

"Hey, great!"

"Yeah." He looked down at the bridge. "Good to see the Nazis can pull off a snafu of their own now and then, huh?"

"Somebody really goofed all right."

"Cripes, I'd hate to be the poor bastard that had to tell ol' Adolf he forgot to blow up a Rhine bridge. . . ."

They laughed, drawing stares from an open truckload of GIs rumbling past.

"So, where are they going to deploy you guys, Sanders?"

"Right here on the high ground, at least for now. Guess we got plenty down by the bridge and four or five tracks on the far side already."

Sinclair glanced at the M-3 crew. A GI was seated in the turret, training the heavy machine guns around in a circle as he elevated the gun barrels to full vertical and back. Another soldier, apparently a loader, was checking the ammo boxes lining the inside of the rear deck, while another, obviously an observer, scanned the leaden skies through a pair of field glasses.

"You got time for a smoke, Sanders?" he asked, pulling a pack of Tareytons from his tunic. "Looks like you'll be unemployed for a while."

"Sure." He climbed up onto the deck and sat down next to Sinclair. "We're cross-trained, any of us can shoot, load, observe, or drive." He shrugged as he tapped a cigarette from the proffered box. "It's my day to drive."

"Pretty odd running into each other again like this," Sinclair remarked, lighting Sanders's cigarette.

Sanders exhaled. His white teeth flashed in a still-boyish grin as he looked down at the Remagen Bridge, then at Sinclair. "I should have known that if I ever wound up again where the action is, I'd run into you." He shook his head. "I still can't believe you went in with us at Normandy. First goddamn wave. Jeez Louise . . ."

"Wasn't my idea, remember?"

"And now you're gonna be the first reporter over the Rhine! Criminy, don't you ever quit?"

Sinclair looked down at the bridge, wondering when he'd get the okay to go across. "HQ hasn't approved it yet." He unscrewed his canteen and took a swig of Jack Daniels, then passed it over to Sanders. "By the time they do, there's bound to be other correspondents here."

"How's the bridge holding up?"

"Could go down anytime. Krauts tried to blow it, but only a few charges went off. There's been some near misses that have weakened it too. . . ."

"Hmmmm . . ." Sanders took a drink before realizing it wasn't water. "Damn! Where'd you get this stuff?"

Sinclair grinned. "I *have* gotten back to London a couple of times, you know."

"What? The ace war correspondent left the front lines?" Sanders flashed a look of mock horror.

The radio squawked suddenly in the cab of his M-3. He handed Sinclair his canteen, jumped to the ground, and darted over to the half-track. A minute later, he gunned the engine to sputtering life, then climbed out of the cab and walked up to Sinclair. "Guess what, hero. . . . ?"

"What . . . ?"

"Change of plans, we're goin' across."

Sinclair stared at him a moment. "Do you suppose I could tag along?"

"Now how did I know you'd ask me that?"

Sinclair began to think twice about it. "I don't want to get you in trouble. . . ."

"What the hell can they do to me, Robertson, send me across the Rhine?"

"Good point."

They climbed into the cab. Sanders shoved the M-3 into gear and they lurched forward to join the long column of white-starred vehicles winding down into the valley of the Rhine.

Chapter XVIII

I

They huddled against the steel turret of the lumbering T-34, heads down, greatcoat collars pulled up against the cold drizzle, fatigue caps pulled down low over their eyes. Acrid exhaust fumes swirled around the glistening deck from the tank's twin tail pipes, stinging their eyes and hiding the rest of the regiment's long column of tanks and assault guns behind a drifting shroud of white smoke.

In the gathering twilight, Yuri prodded Pavel with his rifle butt. "Wake up, Pasha . . . we'll be bivouacking any time now."

Pavel Samsonov's snoring stopped abruptly. "I was sleeping like a babe," he grumbled, rubbing his eyes. "First good nap I've had in weeks."

"Marshal Koniev himself was here," said Dmitri, sitting atop the turret just above his comrades. "He is putting you in for a medal for heroic snoring. You frightened the fascists so much, they've declared Berlin an open city and handed the Fuhrer over. Isn't that right, Yuroshka?"

Yuri nodded. "They thought it was some kind of sinister

secret weapon." Yuri slapped Pavel on the back. "Congratulations, Pasha, you have won the war!"

"Oh shut your trap. . . ."

"Just don't forget your old comrades when you're hobnobbing at the Bolshoi with STAVKA, eh?" Dmitri needled him, winking at Yuri.

Pavel rolled his eyes toward the leaden skies, then blinked as the cold rain fell on his face, driving away his lingering drowsiness.

"He's ignoring us already!" Yuri lamented, nudging Dmitri in the ribs, casting a sad look Pavel's way. "How quickly a hero forgets his old comrades once fame arrives."

Pavel peeled off his soggy gloves and wrung them out in disgust. "Why did you louts take that tarp off me? I'm drenched."

Dmitri nodded toward the canvas, twisted into a sodden tangle next to Pavel. "It must have fallen off while you were waking the dead with that rolling thunder you call snoring."

"My wife never complained," Pavel retorted.

"She was probably stone deaf after the first night, the poor thing!"

Yuri nodded solemnly. "The human eardrum can only take so many decibels."

"You two are a couple of real jokers tonight. If I didn't know better, I'd swear you found some vodka somewhere."

Dmitri's grin faded. "Don't I wish. . . ."

Pavel looked at him, then Yuri, realizing what they were up to. The final assault on Berlin loomed ahead, just days away now. Who wouldn't try to fend off his growing fear by indulging in banter? It was better than silent contemplation of the desperate fight the fascists would put up for Berlin.

Pavel grinned, deciding to join in the game. "I dreamed of Katya again, comrades," he said, mimicking Yuri's almost daily morning greeting to Dmitri and himself. He affected a look of lovesick longing, then sighed theatrically.

Yuri blushed. It was true—Katya had been a glow of happiness in his soul since they'd met. Thinking of her had kept him going through the daily misery and horror of the bitter fighting at the gates of Berlin—that, and mindless joking with his comrades.

"Leave him alone, Pavel, he's in love," said Dmitri, winking at Yuri. "He's read her letter so many times, he must have the whole thing memorized by now."

"I wish she'd write again. . . ."

Pavel glanced at Dmitri. Several weeks had passed since Yuri's return, without a letter from Katya. But who got regular letters? The logistical buildup for the final thrust into Berlin had swallowed up every last truck and rail car in Soviet Russia. To supply the two million soldiers of the three great armies of Marshals Koniev, Zhukov, and Rossokovsky with ammunition, fuel, and food took every resource available. Mail was last on the list.

The T-34 ground to a halt in the gathering darkness and Yuri and his comrades jumped from the rear deck to the ground. Stretching to relieve the stiffness of the long ride, they stood silently in the mud, waiting for Sergeant Grigoriev or Captain Arbatov to come by with orders for the night.

"I hope we don't draw sentry duty again," Pavel grumbled at last, peering down the line of idling tanks, searching the twilight for a sign of Grigoriev or Arbatov.

They stiffened as Commissar Pugo stalked past them toward the head of the column. Since Yuri's return from the penal battalion, Pugo had studiously ignored them.

Pavel spat on the ground, glaring at the receding shadow of the commissar. "Bastard . . ." he muttered.

Dmitri stamped his numb feet to get some circulation going. "Maybe our gallant commissar will catch a bullet in Berlin and we'll be rid of him."

"When pigs fly!" Pavel snorted. "His fancy armored car stays so far to the rear, it's a wonder he can keep up with the rest of us."

"Well, at least old Arbatov seems to have him in line now."

"I don't think Arbatov has anything to do with it. It's that new battalion commissar we've got. Ever since Boldev disappeared and Kalinovsky took over, Pugo's been meek as a lamb."

"Well, Arbatov saved Yuri anyway, give him credit for that."

Sergeant Grigoriev appeared out of the darkness. "Grab some sleep, comrades," he said, pausing for a moment beside them. "First squad has sentry duty tonight."

Dmitri grinned happily, anticipating a night of rest.

"And tomorrow . . . ?" Yuri asked, noting the grim expression on Grigoriev's face.

"We attack at first light—our company has the point."

They groaned in unison.

"Comrade Arbatov says there's a full SS panzer division dug in down the road," Grigoriev added. He shook his head slowly. "The fur will fly tomorrow, lads. Comrade Koniev wants to beat Comrade Zhukov to Berlin and we're the point of the spear."

"Pugo's handiwork again," Pavel grumbled.

Grigoriev shrugged. "Pugo's small peanuts now, comrade—the front will be thick with commissars tomorrow." He sighed. "The eyes of all Russia are upon us, thanks to Marshal Koniev's boast that we will be first to Berlin."

Pavel frowned. "I think I'll pull for Zhukov. . . ."

Dmitri laughed. "Second is just fine with me too."

A wry smile crossed Grigoriev's face. "You louts don't want the eternal glory of taking Berlin?"

"We don't want anything to do with eternity right now," Yuri replied. "We would be happy to have Zhukov's lads waiting to greet us in Berlin."

"*If* there are any of them left." Pavel smirked.

"*We* will greet *them,* comrades, or Marshal Koniev will know the reason why."

"Maybe the Americans will get there first. . . ."

Grigoriev rolled his eyes. "That would land us *all* in the Gulag, from marshal down to the last one-legged cook." He turned to leave. "Rest now, comrades. You will need it."

II

Arkady Rostov stood in formation in the bitter wind, numbed to his soul at the thought of another day of backbreaking timber cutting in the primeval forests surrounding the Ust-Izhma Penal Camp.

Like his fellow *zeks* shivering in the predawn darkness of the camp compound, he wore a ragged black uniform of pleated cotton. Both peacoat and trousers displayed white patches upon which his number, K-571, had been stenciled—above the left knee on his trousers, and larger patches on the chest and back of his peacoat.

The center of the compound, lit by perimeter lights strung atop high poles surrounding the camp, was awash in a sea of black as the various work gangs stood waiting to be herded toward the gate for count and inspection. Camp warders and guards stalked between the ragged squares of *zeks,* shouting commands at the work-gang leaders, organizing the gangs into a long column which stretched across the compound to the main gate.

Finally, Arkady's work gang reached the gate.

"Pair off in fives!" shouted a guard. Like robots, the leading *zeks* shuffled into rows of five and, one row at a time, stepped up to five warders, who frisked them.

In the fourth row from the front, Arkady stamped his feet to ward off the cold. Twenty-four below zero, old Shaprikov had said. Felt worse . . . the wind was howling like a banshee.

Counted and frisked, he waited with the others outside the main gate for the rest of the gang to come through. When all of work gang 58 was standing in rows of fives outside the barbed wire, the guards and warders counted them again, slowly, carefully. If the count was wrong and a *zek* turned up missing at evening roll call, the guards and warders responsible became *zeks* themselves, arrested, charged, and sentenced in one day to a ten-year term for aiding and abetting an escape.

Another freezing ten minutes passed before the supervisors were satisfied. Commands rang out in the brittle air and the column began to move out across the taiga toward the logging camp, three kilometers to the north. Ringed by machine-gun toting guards, the prisoners trudged forward silently, heads down to shield their faces from the biting wind

The commander of the escort, marching alongside the right flank, barked out the inevitable orders they had to listen to each morning. "Your attention, prisoners! You will stay in your own rank! You will not speak! You will keep your hands behind you! You will keep an interval of a meter between ranks! You will not look to either side! A step to right or left will be considered an attempt to escape and the escort will fire without warning!"

As he trudged over the snowdrifts, the only thought that kept Arkady clinging to sanity was the hope that the end of the war would move Stalin to issue the general amnesty he'd heard so much about. It was almost all that was spoken of in the barracks and the mess hall. Unspoken was the knowledge that no *zek* had ever survived a term in Ust-Izhma. Death or amnesty was the only escape from the frozen hell on the shores of the Pechora River.

By the time they reached the logging compound, the sun had peeked above the treetops to cast long, weak shadows through the forest. The guards took up stations around the temporary barbed wire ringing that day's section of wood. Two-man saws were handed out from the tool cart. The *zeks* were paired off by Mikhailov, the work-gang leader, and trudged off through the knee-deep snow to start cutting.

Arkady found himself with Igor Vasilyev and counted himself fortunate. The Muscovite was a bear of a man who could more than hold up his end of the job—the worst fate was to be paired off with a shirker, or a *zek* on his last legs. On those days, he barely had the energy to drag himself back to camp.

Quotas were quotas. The work gangs were evaluated as a unit and fed as a unit. Their weekly rations were measured by how much work they'd done the week before. At Ust-Izhma, food was life. If the quota wasn't made, the rations for the whole work gang were cut. Any pair of *zeks* not doing their fair share threatened the very existence of the entire work gang. . . .

Arkady frowned—coercion was the prime motivating force of the Gulag. What better way to get the *zeks* to slave away like Stakhanovites than to make them their own enforcers? A starving man had little sympathy for shirkers, not when they were taking bread from his mouth. Besides, in places like Ust-Izhma, working was the only way to stay warm.

He and Vasilyev set to work, each on one end of the long saw. Thirty minutes of pushing and pulling felled a giant conifer. The rest of the morning passed in trimming the branches and lopping off the trunk in thirty-foot sections. By the time the escort commander fired a machine-gun burst skyward to signal noon break, Arkady was sweating inside his peacoat, despite the bitter cold.

The *zeks* staggered into a column and were marched off in ranks of five to the edge of the wood, where a pair of rusty Ford trucks waited. They filed past the canvas-covered truck beds, took their bowls of cold gruel, and sank into the snow to drink the watery mixture. Arkady sipped slowly, he'd learned quickly to savor every ounce of food, no matter how tasteless, no matter how watery, no matter how stale the bread or scaly the piece of whitefish. Still, the bowl didn't last five minutes. When he'd finished, he pulled the small chunk of bread he'd saved from his breakfast ration out of his peacoat and sopped up the thin film of gruel coating the inside of the bowl.

Every last drop consumed, he set the bowl in the snow beside him and glanced with longing at the guards taking their turns at the second truck, where hot vegetable soup and fresh black bread were being served. Their comrades, those who'd already eaten and returned to the perimeter to guard the prisoners, were smoking. The tempting scent of tobacco drifted over the *zeks,* many of whom stared at the greatcoat-clad soldiers in sullen resentment. Some had tobacco back at the camp, sent from home every month or so, but by the time all the camp trusties took their cut, there was little left for the recipient. Most *zeks,*

if they had tobacco to smoke at all, savored a hand-rolled cigarette in the morning right after reveille. It took away some of
the despair out of facing another day.

The afternoon passed as the morning had, in numbing cold.
Arkady's back ached from the constant wrestling with the heavy
saw, the bending over to trim the branches, the lugging of the
wood to the central pile, the tedious slogging through the deep
snow.

It was dark again before the command to turn in their saws
rang out through the pines. Under a full moon, the *zeks* were
counted at the logging camp gate, marched the three kilometers
to the main camp, counted again at that gate, frisked, then sent
to the mess hall, to wait in the snow for the work gangs ahead
of them to file through the doorway for their evening ration of
tepid soup.

Arkady shivered in the cold, teeth chattering, toes and fingers
numb, staring at the sea of heads ahead of him. Another work-
day done, he thought, huddled in the midst of his fellow *zeks*
for whatever warmth the crowd offered. His forty-first at Ust-
Izhma.

Forty-one survived.

Three-thousand, six hundred, and nine to go. . . .

III

In his office in Berlin's Propaganda Ministry, Joseph Goebbels set down the teletype report with a trembling hand and
rushed to his desk to ring the Fuhrerbunker. His eyes blazed
triumphantly as he waited to be put through. Finally, he heard
Hitler's voice on the other end.

"Mein Fuhrer, I congratulate you!" he crowed. "Roosevelt
is dead!"

At the Fuhrerbunker, buried deep beneath the Reich Chancellery, Adolf Hitler stared blankly ahead for a moment.
"Dead?" he mumbled. "Roosevelt is dead?"

"Yes!" Goebbels cried. *"Mein Fuhrer,* the miracle has come!"

When Goebbels rang off, Hitler, his eyes alight in triumph, repeated the news to his secretary, Frau Trudl. In minutes, his inner circle had gathered around him in the bunker conference room. Martin Bormann, Herman Goring, Field Marshals Jodl and Keitel, Minister of Munitions Albert Speer, assorted military aides and personal staff, stood in a circle around the Fuhrer, amazed at the transformation. Hitler was no longer the shuffling, glassy-eyed robot of the past weeks of despair. He was once again the Fuhrer of the glory days of victory.

"It has come to pass!" he crowed. "As I knew it would!" A glare of challenge fell upon his advisers, one by one. "I was right, once again, to continue the struggle. I was right not to give up at five minutes to midnight. This unholy alliance against the Fatherland will crumble to dust now that the notorious Jew is dead. Dead!"

Martin Bormann, ever the bootlicker, was the first to echo Hitler's exultation. *"Mein Fuhrer,* history has indeed repeated itself. The Reich is saved, thanks to your genius, to your wisdom in seeing the real currents of history swirling beneath the surface!"

Hitler accepted the praise as a matter of course.

Ignoring the heavy thunder of Allied bombs blasting the capital far above them, he singled out Albert Speer, the only leading Nazi who'd ever dared speak the truth to him. "Well then, what do you have to say now, Speer?" he asked, chest puffed up with pride. "Have things not developed as I predicted?"

"I'm sorry, *Mein Fuhrer.* . . . I'm afraid I can't see how Roosevelt's death is going to change the military situation. The Russians are at the gates of Berlin, the Anglo-Americans are at the Elbe."

"Bah!" Hitler scowled. With a wave of his hand, he dismissed the reality of two million enemy troops poised to strike the death blow at Berlin itself. "The foundation of war is politics, Speer. If the political equation changes, the military equation must as well. Remember the Seven Year's War. When the Empress Catherine of Russia died, the coalition against Frederick the Great crumbled and the long struggle was won, just when things seemed darkest."

"But—"

Hitler cut off Speer with a glare. "It is in the stars, I tell you! My destiny is yet to be fulfilled." His tone shifted from combative to one of hushed revelation. "Herr Goebbels had an astrological forecast prepared for me on the date of my accession to the Chancellership. It foretold three years of great victories, followed by reverses, culminating in a great crisis in the spring of 1945. In the second half of April, my enemies would be shattered in a great battle and fall back in disarray. The next two years would be hard, but final victory would come in 1948. Don't you see, Speer? The death of that notorious Jew Roosevelt has triggered the breakup of the coalition against me. The cowboy armies will go home, freeing our divisions in the west for the titanic struggle against the Slavs. Then we will *smash them!* You'll see, Speer. Just as Frederick triumphed when all seemed lost, so will I. You'll see. You'll see."

Speer nodded dully. After going through the motions of congratulating Hitler for his foresight, he excused himself.

Once above ground, he stood in the Chancellery Garden, listening to the all-clear sirens wailing the departure of the RAF, breathing in the brisk night air, gathering his wits about him.

What madness reigned down there in that pit!

Speer's gaze fell on the ventilation shaft jutting up through the ground from the Fuhrerbunker sixty feet below the garden. He looked up to the top of the structure, some five meters above the surface.

Once again the thought seized him—if the intake vents were closer to the ground, it would be a simple matter of exposing a container of nerve gas next to them . . . the fatal mixture would be drawn down into the bunker and the nest of lunatics exterminated.

Germany would at least be saved the final insanity of a blood-bath over doomed Berlin. . . .

Speer noticed the SS guards eyeing him from across the garden and walked briskly off into the rubbled street, cursing himself for his cowardice. The act could have been accomplished months ago, before the shaft had been raised, but now it was impossible. The final madness would be played out to its bitter conclusion. The German people would pay in full for falling under the spell of their self-proclaimed messiah.

Once lord of Europe from the English Channel to the Volga, master of the mightiest legions in human history, sole arbiter of the fate of tens of millions of human beings, their Fuhrer now hid like a rabid rat in the moral cesspool of his bunker while Germany died. . . .

Chapter XIX

I

Sinclair Robertson finished the last of his coffee and nodded thanks to the GIs shooting the breeze around the open fire. The unit he was with had halted on the banks of the Elbe River to refuel and resupply before the last push to Berlin. On the outskirts of shattered Wiesbaden, hundreds of olive-green vehicles and thousands of troops were scattered over the rolling hills, awaiting the word to roll out.

The odor of diesel fuel mingled with the faint aroma of brewing coffee as he climbed the riverbank onto the road and trudged past a long line of tanks and half-tracks toward the press tent a mile away. He hadn't walked far before a jeep screeched to a halt beside him. The driver shoved the stick into neutral and leaned toward him.

"Need a lift, mac?"

"Sure, thanks." He climbed in and they roared off. The driver glanced at his tunic, noting the lack of rank insignia. "Correspondent?"

"That's right." They sped past a burned-out barn. The stench from dead livestock was thick.

"Where can I drop you off?"

Sinclair pointed at the two-story brick house on a wooded hill a half mile ahead. "Up there if you will."

"Sure thing." The driver downshifted as the jeep reached the bottom of a hollow and started uphill toward regimental headquarters. "Goin' to see the colonel, then?"

"If he's not too busy. . . ."

The driver grinned. "The old man's chompin' at the bit. Can't wait to get to Berlin." He gunned the jeep to the top of the hill and braked to a halt in front of the house. Two sentries flanked the doorway, regarding the jeep and its occupants with bored detachment.

Sinclair hopped out. "Thanks, Sergeant." The driver waved and was gone in a cloud of dust. A lieutenant greeted him at the door and took him through the house to the backyard. Colonel O'Brien was pacing the lawn, hands clasped behind his back.

"Colonel?"

O'Brien looked up distractedly. "What is it, Hodges?"

"Mr. Robertson is here, sir."

"Ah, yes." O'Brien strode briskly to the steps. "That will be all for now, Hodges." He nodded at Sinclair. "Let's go for a walk, shall we?"

O'Brien was uncharacteristically silent as they walked. Finally, the colonel stopped. They were some fifty yards from the house. From the summit of the hill they could look down on the Elbe and beyond to the spires of Wiesbaden in the distance.

"I need to blow off some steam, Robertson, and I didn't want any of my staff people within earshot." He turned to face Sinclair. "I just got word from division that we're to halt at the Elbe."

Sinclair looked at him blankly. "For how long, Colonel?" he asked, at a loss to understand why the colonel would be upset about a stop to resupply before the final push.

"Until the damn war is over, that's how long."

"I'm sorry, Colonel. I know how much you wanted to be along on the drive to Berlin."

O'Brien bristled. "I'm not referring to this unit, Robertson. I'm talking about the whole goddamned United States Army. Ike's going to let the Russians get Berlin."

"What?"

O'Brien gazed across the hazy hills to the east. "Fifty gawd-damned miles away and he pulls in the reins!" He spat on the ground in disgust. "Ain't *shit* between us and Berlin but a few beat-to-hell German divisions, and they're just itching to surrender to us before the Russians get them."

"Did Corps say why, Colonel?"

"I heard Ike's really catching hell about it. Simpson, Patton, Monty, they're fit to be tied! Even Bradley is pissed."

"There would have been a lot of casualties, Colonel. Maybe Ike doesn't want to lose tens of thousands of men now, with the war all but over."

O'Brien snorted. "Hell, the Germans would open the city to *us*. All this talk about heavy casualties is misguided bullshit. Sure, if the Russians go in there, the Germans will fight for every gawd-damned house, but if we get there first, they'll quit, happier than hell that we got there before Ivan."

Sinclair nodded. He hadn't looked at it from that angle. Everyone seemed to take heavy casualties for granted, but O'Brien had brought up a good point. The Germans *would* put up fanatic resistance to the Russians, knowing it was a fight to the death between the bitterest of enemies. After what the SS had done in Russia, they had nothing to gain by surrendering to the Russians, knowing it only meant summary execution or a long slow death in a slave labor camp. The Americans and British were another matter, however, another matter entirely.

"It's not the casualties that's stopping Ike, Robertson. He's seen the Germans falling all over themselves now to surrender to us. Whole army corps are fighting their way west through the Soviet lines so they can surrender to us, for chrissakes! The Berlin garrison wouldn't do any different. No. It's something political, some deal between FDR and Stalin. That's the only thing that makes any sense to me. . . ."

The faint droning of aircraft emerged over the soft rush of the river and the breeze rustling the budding trees. Sinclair shaded his eyes against the sun and looked up. Countless faint contrails stretched across the distant heights—the Eighth Air Force was out in force again, bound for some hapless target points east.

"Roosevelt *did* want Stalin to enter the war against Japan as soon as possible," Sinclair said, still taking in the sight of the vast armada filling the sky five miles overhead. "Maybe Berlin was the price. FDR was probably thinking of the casualties we'd take invading Japan, more than any losses we'd suffer taking Berlin. With the Russians tying down the Japs in Manchuria, they wouldn't be able to transfer hundreds of thousands of troops to defend the home islands."

O'Brien looked wistfully to the east. Berlin was less than fifty miles from the Elbe, just a day or two away. . . . Every officer worth his commission wanted to cap off the war by taking the capital. Such was the nature of the animal. On the other hand, the average GI would be satisfied to let the Russians have it. Why get killed the last week of the damn war?

He sighed. "Maybe it's for the best. Hell, I don't know, I just feel cheated somehow. We fought our way ashore in Normandy, battered our way through the damned hedgerows, got through Arnhem, the Bulge, the Siegfried Line, the Rhine . . . it seems a pity to stop now, fifty damn miles away from Berlin."

Sinclair nodded. "But think how the Russians must feel, Colonel. They had their backs to the wall outside Moscow in '41. Four years and twenty million dead later *they'd* sure as hell feel cheated if *they* didn't get Berlin." He shrugged. "No one can say they haven't earned the right to try."

"No." O'Brien pulled a pack of Pall Malls from his tunic pocket and lit one. "I just don't trust the bastards, that's all," he muttered, exhaling a cloud of tobacco smoke as he spoke. "Hell, I know how many people they've lost. I know how far they've come. But the bottom line is, the Nazis are the only reason we're on the same side. When the Third Reich goes down, what then?"

"I don't know, but I don't see how much difference it can make whether we take Berlin or the Russians do. Germany and Berlin are going to be divided into Allied zones anyway. If we can save lives both here *and* in the Pacific by letting the Russians take Berlin, then they can have it as far as I'm concerned."

"I hope you're right. I just don't have a good feeling about this business. Political issues aside, I shudder to think about all those poor *hausfraus* in Berlin. The Russians are going to rape every last one of them and won't quit till the whole damned Red Army's had a share. . . ."

II

Bill Lindberg walked slowly among the long rows of white crosses planted in the ashy soil of the Third Marine Division Cemetery on Iwo Jima, pausing here and there as a familiar name brought to mind the face of a lost friend.

Another dawn had come to Iwo Jima. To the east, the morning sun hovered just above the sparkling sea, throwing long shadows across the fresh graves. A cool breeze drifted across the shattered island, fluttering the flag atop the cemetery gate, stirring up the stench of death that clung to the blackened hulk of Suribachi.

Bill, shivering in the damp chill, read the etched names one by one, Harley, third cross from the gate . . . Kevin, middle of the first row . . . Fitzgerald, next to Kevin . . . Luke, last cross on the end . . . Jerry, eighth cross in the second row. . . .

He forced himself to go on, he would have expected the same of them. . . . Crowley, four crosses down from Jerry . . . Andy, third cross from the end of the second row . . . Richie, tenth cross in the third row . . . Carl, five crosses down from Richie . . . Sal, the Italian guy from boot camp, seven crosses down from Richie . . . Mickey, second cross in the fourth row . . . Randall, the guy from the troopship, middle of the fourth row . . . Tom, four crosses down from Randall . . . Daryl, one down from Tom. . . .

Bill, his spirit sagging, mouthed the names silently as he passed fresh grave after fresh grave. Harrison . . . Matthews . . . Rodgers . . . Osowski . . . Boone. . . .

His shadow fell upon the last cross in the last row. He read with brimming eyes the plain inscription on the white cross: CLAYTON DANIEL BOONE, GUNNERY SERGEANT, USMC, SEPTEMBER 3, 1922-MARCH 4, 1945.

Images of those terrible minutes on Nishi Ridge swam before his eyes . . . the mortar rounds falling like rain . . . the wild charge up the ridge, the bullets singing past his ears . . . the fear, the rage, the death. . . .

He turned from the last grave and headed toward the stone pillars of the gate. Gunnery Sergeant Boone wasn't going home to Kentucky. Six thousand marines would never go home again. Nineteen thousand more were in hospital beds, torn and bleeding from wounds.

Several Medals of Honor had been earned on Iwo. Scores of other decorations for valor had been bestowed on the men of the Third, Fourth, and Fifth Marine Divisions. But as General Smith had put it, "Uncommon valor was a common virtue on Iwo." Bill agreed. There weren't enough medals in the world to equal the courage and sacrifice he'd seen in the past month.

He put on his helmet as he passed the gate, then glanced toward the northern sky, his attention drawn by the distant drone of a plane. By the time he'd reached the bottom of the gentle slope, the speck on the horizon had resolved into the distinct lines of a B-29.

Wilson Lindberg took a last look at the winking red warning light, then pressed the intercom button at his throat. "Okay, fellas, we're going to have to belly in. Assume crash-landing positions."

In the copilot's seat to his right, Lieutenant Casey Peltier tightened his straps. "Thank God for Iwo."

"We're not down yet, Case." Wilson stared through the Plexi-glas nose—the pear-shaped island seemed to tip sideways as he banked *Rosie III* to the west to line up with the runway. He leveled off at three hundred feet and eased the control column forward, kicking rudder now and then to adjust to the crosswind. The Superfort crabbed slightly to the left, nose just toward the wind.

At the far end of the runway, he saw a fire truck and ambulance waiting. Another fire truck was racing for the runway from the hangars to the east, trailing a long cloud of dust in its wake as it barreled westward. Behind him, beyond the tunnel connecting the cockpit to the rear crew compartment, two crewman lay wounded, hit by the same flak blast that had knocked out number three engine and shattered the landing gear.

He eased the throttles forward and kept the nose up to bleed off all the speed he could without stalling. *Rosie III* crept lower, her three good props biting into the humid tropical air, her flaps down, her crew braced for the jarring impact with the runway. Wilson kept steady pressure on the rudder pedals, fighting the gusting crosswind, keeping the wings level. Out of the corner of his eye, he could see marines emerging from tents and Quonset huts all over the small island, their gaze drawn toward the east, their hands shielding their eyes as they squinted into the glare of the rising sun to spot the source of all the excitement.

The runway hove into view directly below the cockpit, the white centerlines a blur as they swept past. Wilson nudged the throttles forward, eased the control column back, and waited for the grinding crunch of impact.

"Hang on!" he yelled over the intercom. He shoved the throttles forward to cut power and *Rosie III* bellied onto the concrete at one-hundred-thirty knots. The uproar of metal airframe meeting asphalt runway was deafening. A rumbling earthquake seemed to shake the plane as it careened toward the distant fire trucks. The spinning props bit into solid ground, twisting the blades awry, slamming them to a sudden halt. The smell of friction-heated metal wafted into the cockpit.

Rosie III finally slid to a stop fifty yards from the fire engines. Wilson's senses balked at the sudden silence. He blinked as he tried to collect his wits.

"Let's get out of here, Lindy."

A form materialized before him, resolving into the figure of Hank Callahan. The bombardier shook him out of his daze. "You okay?"

"Yeah . . ." He followed Callahan and Peltier through the side hatch and dropped onto the runway. Grant and Wellesley were eased gently through the waist hatch and taken away in an ambulance. The rest of the crew then sank to the runway in the shade of the wing, exhausted by the fourteen-hour flight.

An Air Force major drove up in a jeep, hopped out, and hurried over to where Wilson, Callahan, and Peltier stood beneath number two engine. "Welcome to Iwo. You guys are already the fifteenth '29 to land here."

Wilson extended his hand. "I'm Major Lindberg, the pilot."

"Randolph, Exec." Introductions were made. Callahan and Peltier shook hands with Randolph.

"What happens now, Major?"

Randolph nodded toward the idling jeep. "We take you to Operations, your crew to the NCO Barracks. Medics check you over, we debrief you on the flight, then put you on the next flight to Tinian." He looked at *Rosie III*. "Doesn't look like she'll fly again. . . ."

"Wil!"

Wilson looked up from his cot to see Bill standing in the open doorway of the Quonset, a thin figure silhouetted by the fading evening light behind him.

"You *are* still here!" He jumped to his feet. "I asked them to check for me after debriefing, but I thought you'd be gone by now." They shook hands, grinning at one another.

"My unit's shipping out for Ulithi tomorrow."

"Damn! Well, here, sit down," he said, nodding toward his cot.

"Saw you come in, Wil. I was up at the cemetery and heard a plane, looked around, and here's this B-29 coming in with no wheels." He grinned happily. "Didn't think that much of it. Figured the odds it might be you were too low to even consider. When I saw the name on the nose, I couldn't believe it."

Wilson reached for a cigarette. "We were awfully glad to have this field waiting. Would have had to ditch in the sea if you guys hadn't taken Iwo."

"What happened, Wil?"

"Got hit by flak over Osaka. Lost an engine, some hydraulics. . . . Then got shot up by a couple of Tonys. Two of my gunners were wounded."

"Will they be all right?"

"Yeah. Saw them at eighteen hundred. Lost some blood, but they'll be okay."

"Well, it's good to see you, despite the circumstances."

Wilson grinned. "Good to see you too, Bill." The grin faded quickly. "You know, when I saw this place from the air, I just couldn't connect what I was seeing with the image we've all had of Iwo since February. Didn't seem real that this quiet little island was *Iwo Jima!*"

Bill looked at him blankly. Wilson frowned, trying to explain. "We heard all the reports, everyone did. I guess we formed impressions of some hell on earth, and then when . . ." He shrugged. "When we came in, it looked like just another island airfield to me, not at all like what I'd expected. Sounds stupid, I know. I guess this place is such a legend already that the reality of seeing it firsthand can't hope to match one's preconceptions. Am I making any sense?"

"I think I know what you're saying. I've been here since D-Day and seen Iwo change from a battlefield to a rear-area air base. But when I look around, I don't really see an air base. I still see dead marines. I still hear the mortar rounds screaming down, the flame-throwers blazing." Bill stared at the floor. "I'll be glad to leave. Too many ghosts. . . ."

Wilson put a hand on his shoulder. "You must have lost a lot of buddies."

"Yeah . . ."

"Not easy, is it?"

"No."

"It'll do you good to get to Ulithi. I know how you feel here. I was damn glad to leave England when the time came. Too many memories, too many sorrows. A guy has to move on or he'll go nuts." Wilson sighed. "You have the rest of your life to remember your buddies, so push them aside for now, concentrate on your job, or you'll be one of those memories yourself. It's hard, but you've got to do it."

Bill frowned as he checked his watch. "I'll try." He got up from the cot. "Gotta go, Wil, got guard duty at 1800."

Wilson walked him to the door. "What time are you leaving tomorrow?"

"At 0600." Bill gave his big brother a hug. "This'll be so long for now, Wil." He grinned despite the lump in his throat. "Don't wreck any more '29s, all right?"

"Don't plan to. . . . So . . . I suppose you'll be in the big show this fall."

Bill's grin faded. "I hope to hell old Tojo gives up by then."

"So do I, Bill." They shook hands and Wilson watched his kid brother walk away until he disappeared behind a row of Quonsets. His lips worked silently as he closed the door. "So do I. . . ."

Chapter XX

Third Guards Tank Army
Berlin, Germany
April 25, 1945

I

"The lair of the fascist beast. . . ." muttered Pavel as he and Yuri stared at the western horizon. It flashed steadily from the pounding of thousands of heavy shells, filling the drizzly night with man-made thunder. The ground trembled, overhead a full moon rode across the clouds, washing the Prussian woods in silvery light.

Yuri pulled up the collar of his greatcoat against the wind and stuffed his hands in his pockets, shivering. Was it the cold? Or was it the knowledge that, come the dawn, he would lead his squad into Berlin?

A match flared in the darkness. The smell of Pavel's crude *papirosu* drifted his way, the tip of the handrolled cigarette glowed cherry red. "Cat got your tongue, Yurochka?" he asked.

"No. I was just thinking, that's all." He checked his watch in the moonlight, the hands just visible. It was 0430; dawn was less than two hours away. Just over the horizon lay Berlin and their last battle. He had a terrible feeling that he would not survive it. A recurring nightmare had plagued him the past several nights. Each time he'd awoken in a cold sweat, the after-image of his crumpled body lying on a cobblestone street vividly etched in his mind's eye. . . .

They slogged their way into Berlin the next day, following the grinding columns of T-34 and Stalin heavy tanks into the outer suburbs, making steady but bloody progress against fanatic pockets of resistance. The assault companies pushed relentlessly forward, hounded by regimental headquarters to press for the Reichstag. Regiment, in turn, was under heavy pressure from division headquarters, which had to answer to Marshal Koniev himself at First Ukrainian Front headquarters. Koniev was determined to beat his rival Zhukov to the symbol of the hated Reich, to grab the glory of planting the hammer and sickle atop the Reichstag.

By dawn of the twenty-eighth, after three days of bitter house-to-house fighting, Yuri's company was stalled under heavy fire at the Towper Canal, six kilometers from the Reichstag. Orders soon filtered down the chain of command, transferring the main thrust to the companies on their left flank. The companies on the canal would "mop up" resistance in the canal and Tempelhof Airport sectors. The glory of seizing the Reichstag would go to someone else.

Under a watery sun, which shone weakly through the heavy shroud of smoke hanging over the city, Yuri and the rest of the squad refilled their ammunition pouches from the supply just brought forward by armored car. Across the Towper Canal lay Tempelhof Airport, two kilometers beyond it the Teirgarten and the Reichstag, so close, yet so far away.

Crouched next to Yuri, Pavel snapped the bulging pouches on his utility belt shut and picked up his Kalashnikov. "All the way from Stalingrad and we stop here," he muttered. "What a way to end the war."

Captain Ivanov came up, his face grim, his eyes bitter. "Rostov, round up your squad and follow me. We've got to clear out that street to the west."

"Just us?"

"No, the devil take you! Two companies, if you must know, *Comrade Marshal*. We're the point platoon, and you've got the point squad."

Kathe Dietrich sat alone in the darkness of the cellar, listening to the fading rumble of the Russian heavy guns. A thunderstorm of explosions had broken over the neighborhood early in the morning, hailing shells for nearly two hours, before moving off toward the northwest and the center of Berlin itself.

She stared at poor Herr Krause, still holding his wife in his arms, rocking the body gently to and fro as he stared vacantly ahead. Dead now three hours, Hilde Krause had been killed in the morning shelling that had obliterated the Krause home and destroyed the last bridge over the Towper Canal, stranding Kathe on the wrong side from Tempelhof Airport.

Kathe cried softly, as much for Karl and Hilde Krause as for herself. After all, what real chance had there been that Gunther would have been able to reach Tempelhof? But she'd clung to the slim hope ever since he'd somehow gotten a telegram through, telling her to wait there for him. He'd promised to fly a small Fieseler Storch into Berlin and take her out before the Russians arrived. But who could have imagined what a cauldron the city had become the past week? Since the Russian ring had closed around Berlin, the bombardment had been constant. To attempt to go anywhere above ground was tantamount to suicide.

She dabbed her eyes, scolding herself for believing for even one moment that they could pull off such a fantastic scheme. Poor Gunther might have made it, *if* he could have made himself abandon his comrades in the face of the enemy, *if* he could have found a light staff plane *and* enough fuel to get to Berlin and back, *if* he hadn't been shot down on the way, and *if* by some miracle a Tempelhof runway was still open.

Kathe walked over and tried to comfort Karl, anxious to forget about being rescued. The whole idea had been insane. But then everyone was insane these terrible days. The whole world had been insane for years. . . .

An ominous silence had fallen on the canal area. Only the dull rumble of distant guns sounded through the cellar walls. Kathe tried to speak to Karl, but he seemed in another world and she gave up.

She tried to think. Staying in the cellar seemed the only possibility, but if the artillery had lifted beyond the area, it could only mean that Russian troops were close. But where could she flee that wouldn't find her in the same situation in another few hours? Was it not better to stay where she was and hope for the best?

The sudden rattle of machine-gun fire made up her mind for her. It was too late to run now, the Russians were right down the street.

Yuri waved the squad forward, his eyes stinging from the heavy smoke drifting southward from burning Tempelhof. He sprinted down the right side of the debris-filled street, followed by Pavel, Dmitri, Arbatov, and Ranko. Mikhailov, Konstantinov, Rogev, and Tikhinov laid down fire to cover their advance, raking the houses up the street with machine-gun fire.

They halted, then laid down covering fire for Mikhailov's squad. Mikhailov and Tikhinov dashed toward the second house on the street, while Konstantinov and Rogev kicked in the door of the first and darted inside, to emerge a minute later, each of them holding up a bottle of wine.

"Not now!" Yuri yelled, waving them forward in case Mikhailov and Tikhinov ran into trouble. Konstantinov ignored him. He and Rogev smashed the bottle necks open and drank greedily. Furious, Yuri ran across the street, grabbed the bottle from Konstantinov and hurled it into the street, scattering shards of glass and dark red wine across the dusty cobblestones. He whirled on Rogev, who dropped his bottle in alarm, seized him by the back of the neck, and shoved him forward. "Get going! If I catch you drinking again, I'll have you up on charges before the commissar! Check the next house. Now!"

Muttering, Konstantinov led Rogev down the rubbled sidewalk. Yuri dashed back across the street, drawn by the rattle of machine-gun fire from the end of the block. Pavel and Dmitri must have flushed out some defenders.

Kathe stiffened at the sound of voices coming from the street above. Russian voices. She stared at Karl, but he just stared glassy eyed at the wall above her head, rocking his dead wife in his lap. He was in some other world, far from the horror of Berlin.

The voices grew louder, the thud of boots on wood flooring came from just overhead. She stared fearfully at the cellar door, edging farther into the shadows, willing it not to open. Heavy footsteps thumped toward her left, to the door.

It opened with a creak, and a shaft of light shot into the cellar. Her heart raced. She swallowed hard as a grimy boot appeared at the top of the stairs.

They're coming down! God, they're coming down!

Across the celler, Karl stirred. He looked up toward the stairs. "Heinrich, is that you, son?" His mouth turned up at the corners, a tentative smile appearing. The boot on the top step vanished. An instant later, a grenade sailed down the stairway, plopped onto the dirt floor, and rolled to a stop against the far wall.

Kathe threw herself behind a workbench. The world exploded.

Crouched in a doorway, Yuri heard the muffled blast from across the street. Konstantinov and Rogev had stumbled onto some Germans too. . . . He ducked as rounds whined over his head from the house on the corner. They'd have to fend for themselves for the moment, the bastards. He squeezed off a burst, then sprinted toward the next doorway. Pavel, Dmitri, and the others deserved his help more than those louts.

Igor Konstantinov crept cautiously down the stairs, Rogev right behind him. He peered through the swirling smoke, his finger tight on the trigger of his Kalashnikov. As the murk cleared he saw two bodies sprawled against the north wall. He shot them, just to be sure, then turned. Someone was moaning softly from behind the stairs.

"Rogev!"

Rogev crept toward the sound, the barrel of his Kalashnikov trained on the dim form lying next to an overturned workbench. "It's a woman, Igor. . . ."

Konstantinov hurried over. "Is she alive?"

Rogev poked the woman in the back with his machine gun. She groaned. He propped his machine gun against the stairway, reached down, and rolled her onto her back. "She's alive."

Konstantinov leaned over. "A young one." He winked lasciviously at Rogev. "Go up and keep an eye peeled for Rostov while I give the *frau* here some *first aid.*"

Rogev hesitated.

Konstantinov shoved him toward the stairs. "Go! You can have seconds!" He unbuckled his belt and dropped to his knees beside her.

Pavel waved Yuri back as Dmitri tossed a grenade, then another through the shattered front windows of the corner house. When they exploded, he charged through the doorway, followed by Arbatov and Ranko. Yuri tensed, waiting for the sound of shots, but seconds later his comrades emerged unharmed. Pavel walked up to him.

"A kid, Yurochka. Couldn't have been more than fourteen. . . ."

"Dead?"

"Dead."

"Hold here, I'm taking Dmitri back to help Konstantinov and Rogev." They scampered back across the street. Yuri saw Rogev's helmeted head poke out from the doorway, then vanish.

What the devil?

"Rogev!"

The doorway remained empty. Yuri and Dmitri ran up to the ruins of the first floor. "If those bastards are into some more wine, Misha, I'll arrest them," Yuri said.

"Now?"

Yuri ran into the house. "Soon as there's a breathing spell." He shouted over his shoulder. "I'll be damned if they'll get stinking drunk while we're getting shot at!"

In the cellar, Konstantinov had Kathe's dress hiked up past her hips when Rogev stumbled down the stairs. "Igor!" he cried, eyes wild in alarm. "Rostov's here!"

"Stall him!" Konstantinov half turned, an ugly leer on his face. *"Get up there!"* Rogev spun around and started back up the dusty stairs, leaving Kathe struggling under Konstantinov's hulking back.

Yuri heard voices from somewhere below, but couldn't make them out. "Rogev! Konstantinov!" He saw the cellar door ajar.

They're into some more wine. . . .

He dashed through the door and down the stairs, colliding with Rogev on his way up. He shoved him aside and took the steps two at a time, enraged that they could betray their comrades by guzzling wine in the midst of a firefight.

"Konstantinov!" He peered into the shadowy cellar, then halted at the foot of the stairs as his eyes adjusted to the darkness. He found himself staring at Konstantinov's back, then heard the terrified whimpering of a woman.

"Get *off* her!" he roared, realizing what was up. *"Now!"*

Konstantinov pawed at Kathe's blouse. "It's just a German whore, Comrade Sergeant."

Yuri jammed the barrel of his Kalashnikov into the base of Konstantinov's skull. "Get off her or I'll blow your head off!"

Konstantinov stiffened. Slowly, he rose to his knees, turned, and glared at Yuri. "You just want her for yourself!"

Yuri pulled the barrel away and slammed the stock of the machine gun onto Konstantinov's head, knocking him out cold. *"Rogev!"* He turned toward the stairs. "Drag this pig out of here before I kill him!"

Rogev scurried over and hauled the unconscious Konstantinov toward the stairs as Yuri leaned over the sobbing *fraulein*.

Kathe covered herself. Sobbing, her hands over her face, she edged away from him. Gently, in pidgin German, Yuri asked her name.

She stared at him. "K-K-Kathe," she stammered, watching him uncertainly. She froze as he reached toward his belt. To her relief he just unhooked his canteen and offered it to her.

"Here."

She shook her head, but Yuri pressed it into her hand. "I'm sorry, *fraulein*. . . ." He couldn't meet her eyes, so ashamed was he of his "comrades."

Kathe drank some water, then handed the canteen back.

"Keep it." Yuri picked Konstantinov's rifle up from the cellar floor and set it beside her, then pulled several days' worth of rations from his backpack and laid them by the gun.

"You must stay hidden, *fraulein*. Don't go into the streets." He cursed softly in Russian. The poor thing—who knew how many thousands of Konstantinovs were about? But what else could he tell her?

He started up the stairs.

"Thank you," she said, her voice a hoarse whisper.

He turned. The grateful look on her tear-stained face drew his first smile since leaving Katya. *"Nichevo,"* he said. She looked blankly at him and he fumbled for the right German phrase. "It . . . was nothing. . . ."

He nodded toward the sound of the guns. "I have to go." He disappeared up the stairs, his smile gone—a pretty one like her was in for a bad time of it unless some officer claimed her. Once the city fell and Koniev and Zhukov's elite assault units withdrew, the dregs of the Red Army would take over occupation duties and gang rape anything in a skirt.

He edged cautiously into the street, hoping some decent captain or major would find her and protect her—the alternative was too awful to contemplate. She'd be better off dead. . . .

II

The last ME-262 exploded into orange flame as the leading tanks of the American armored column crested the top of the hill. They slowed for a moment, then accelerated toward the pillars of oily smoke rising from the airfield.

Gunther Dietrich sat on the grass, watching the olive-drab Shermans clank down the hillside, their turrets rotating back and forth in a half circle to cover their flanks as they approached. Behind him, anxious Luftwaffe ground crewmen, gathered in tight clusters in front of their barracks, waved white sheets of surrender toward the Americans.

The smell of tank exhaust mixed with the acrid stench of burning fuel and rubber. Despite the steady drizzle, the five remaining 262s burned like funeral pyres—a last measure of defiance to the victors.

As the lead tank neared, a khaki-clad figure popped up through the turret hatch and beckoned for them to put their hands over their heads. Gunther rose slowly from the ground, his hands in the air. The Sherman, *Betty Boop* etched in neat white letters on its flank, ground to a halt in front of the assembled Germans. Four others deployed into a semicircle in front of the prisoners while half-tracks raced toward the burning jets.

Lieutenant Karl Graf, the only man who spoke English, stepped forward, his hands carefully held above his head.

"Thank God you got here before the Russians," he shouted over the rumble of the tank engines.

The American scowled. His unit had liberated the Nazi death camp at Dachau. "You Krauts lock your hands on the backs of your heads! Turn around and drop to your knees! You!" He pointed at Graf. "Wipe that smile off your face or I'll gaw-damned shoot it off!"

Graf repeated the orders to the others, and they complied. Gunther read the fury on the American's face. Who was this, Patton himself? He looked ready to mow them all down at the slightest excuse.

Armed Americans dismounted and moved among the prisoners, frisking them for weapons. Gunther knelt patiently while a towheaded private checked him. The kid looked more shaken than angry.

What did the American commander expect Galland to do, hand over five flight-worthy ME-262s? Surely they understood that it was customary to destroy weapons rather than have them taken intact by the enemy.

He saw a convoy of trucks come over the hill. The noncoms were rounded up and herded under guard toward the approaching line of vehicles. The officers were separated and taken to the field mess, where an American colonel awaited them.

Graf, Gunther, Krause, and von Kleist trooped into the room and came to attention before the officer. Gunther's eyebrows rose in surprise as the colonel addressed them in passable German.

"As of sixteen-hundred hours, twenty-four April, nineteen-forty-five, you are prisoners of war of the United States Army. You will be taken to an interrogation center and questioned. You will cooperate fully with the Allied authorities there. But first," he added, his face a grim mask, "we're going to take you to Dachau."

Gunther stared blankly at the American. The name meant nothing to him, his concern was when the Americans would get to Berlin. Kathe's fate had tortured him for weeks. He shuddered at the thought of the Russians reaching the city before the Americans.

He decided to risk further displeasure by inquiring. "Excuse me, Colonel. . . ."

The American glared silently at him.

"My wife is in Berlin. . . . I was wondering how far your comrades are from there . . . ?"

"Shut up and get moving!" The colonel nodded toward the trucks.

Shaken, Gunther climbed aboard the first in line, exchanging glances with the others. Two armed GIs climbed in after them, slammed the gate shut, and eyed their four charges with ill-disguised malice. The small convoy was soon rolling down the autobahn toward the southeast.

Determined, Gunther caught the eye of one of the guards. *"Sprechen zie Deutsche?"* he asked.

"Shut up, Kraut," replied the youngster.

Undaunted, Gunther tried again, mustering his limited English. "Your army . . . uh, to take Berlin now . . . ?"

"No."

"When?"

The soldier glared at him, then noted the pleading look in his eyes. "We've stopped at the Elbe. We're not goin' to Berlin."

Gunther's heart seemed to freeze in his chest. The cold wind whipping through the open truck felt suddenly colder. "Just your . . . own *kamerades?*"

"Nobody, mac! Your Russian friends got Berlin all to themselves, goddammit. Now shut up!"

Stunned, Gunther closed his eyes. "Kathe . . ." he mumbled. "Oh, Kathe."

The rest of the two-hour trip was a blur. The countryside passed by unseen by Gunther, plunged into horrified despair at the reality of the Red Army in Berlin. It wasn't until a strange odor began to manifest itself that he became aware again of his surroundings. As the stench grew stronger, forcing his thoughts from Kathe, he looked out to find the convoy headed toward some sort of camp. High barbed-wire fences enclosed a complex of Spartan buildings. Guard towers rose into the overcast from each corner of the facility.

With growing unease, Gunther stared at the sprawling grounds of the complex. By the time the truck rolled to within half a kilometer of the fenced-in compound, the source of the terrible stench was all too plain.

"Mein Gott . . ." He stared at the naked corpses, stacked like cordwood in obscene mounds beside the buildings . . . along the fences . . . next to hastily dug pits. . . . The pasty white bodies, stiffened with rigor mortis, skeletally thin, lay sprawled where they'd been dumped. Sticklike arms and legs protruded from the torsos of the dead. Sightless eyes open to heaven, mouths agape, the corpses lay everywhere in macabre piles.

The truck braked to a halt in the midst of the hellish scene. Dazed, sickened, Gunther and his comrades were herded from the truck and marched to the nearest victims.

The American colonel walked stiffly up to the shaken pilots. Pale, his hands trembling, he shoved Gunther toward the nearest pitiful mound of humanity.

"Take a look, superman, take a good look!"

Gunther stepped involuntarily back, repelled by the sight. A firm push between his shoulder blades forced him closer. The stench was appalling.

The American went down the line, shoving von Kleist, Graf, and Krause up to the sprawled tangle of corpses. "Murdering bastards," he growled. "Go on, get a good look at these people." He pointed to a frail female. "That was someone's grandmother . . . someone's sister . . . someone's wife . . . someone's mother. . . ." He glared at the Germans. "Look at the rest of them—sons . . . brothers . . . nephews . . . nieces . . . husbands . . . daughters . . . fathers. . . ."

Gunther fought the sour bile rising in his throat. He closed his eyes, teeth clenched in disbelief. An SS labor camp . . . ?

But it didn't look like a labor camp. There were no fields nearby, no manufactories. . . .

The reality slowly dawned on him. Himmler had taken the Fuhrer's anti-Semitism to inhuman extremes. . . . This was a *death camp* . . . a place of *extermination*.

"Open your eyes, Kraut!"

He forced his eyes open. The haunting vision was still there. From the edge of the mound, the glazed eyes of a small girl seemed to stare at him. His knees buckled and he dropped to the hard ground. The American yanked him back to his feet by his collar. "What's the matter, Kraut?"

Gunther couldn't meet the American's eyes. "I had no idea. . . ." he mumbled.

"These human slaughterhouses are all over the Reich, Kraut! Bergen-Belsen! Buchenwald! Nordhausen! Ohrdruf! God only knows where else!"

Gunther stared at the ground in abject horror.

"Look at them, dammit! Look at these people! Human beings . . . butchered like cattle."

"I didn't know. . . ."

"Why not, Kraut? Too busy flying your fancy jet to notice mass murder going on right under your nose? Too busy polishing your Iron Cross? Too busy painting victory marks on your Messerschmitt?"

"No . . ."

"What then? I'd like to know, these people would like to know."

"I'm a soldier, I—"

"Not anymore, Kraut! I've got a new job for you and your pals. You're going to help bury these people, by God! One at a time! One mother at a time, Kraut! One father at a time. One son at a time, one daughter at a time, one aunt at a time, one grandmother at a time, one sister at a time. One . . . slaughtered . . . human . . . being . . . at . . . a . . . time." The American looked around, tears streaming down his face. "I don't care if it takes all summer. By God, you're going to give these people a decent burial."

Gunther nodded woodenly. A GI shoved a spade into his hands. "You'll start with the females, superman. Little girls first. . . ."

Chapter XXI

B-29 *Superfortress* Gabrielle
Sea of Japan
May 3, 1945

I

Wilson Lindberg stared in stunned silence at the distant glow. Even from the dark cockpit of *Gabrielle,* one hundred and fifty miles out over the Sea of Japan, the howling inferno that had been Osaka could be seen clearly.

The last bomber in the last formation of the massive B-29 armada bound for the city, *Gabrielle* carried a full load of Mark V incendiaries in her two bomb bays, but her primary mission was to photograph the destruction and bring the results back to Tinian for study.

But Wilson wasn't thinking about photo interpretation as the Superfort swept northward, five thousand feet over the black sea. He stared through the framed Plexiglas nose, hypnotized by the evil glow of Osaka. It seemed as if a gaping tunnel to hell itself had burst through the earth's crust to light the night with pulsating fury.

As Wilson watched Osaka burn, copilot Matt Jowalski stirred from his catnap, sat up, and rubbed his face. "Ummmhhh . . ." he mumbled, stretching as much as the cramped cockpit permitted. He blinked his eyes, trying to focus on the instrument panel before him. "How far out are we, Lindy?"

"Hundred miles, give or take a few. . . ."

"Ummmhhh . . ." Jowalski leaned forward suddenly, his attention drawn to the distant horizon. "Hell's bells, is that the target?"

"What's left of it."

Jowalski whistled in awe. "No radar approach tonight!"

Wilson kept the nose pointed at the inferno as they approached Honshu. At a cruising speed of three hundred knots, *Gabrielle* closed the range quickly. Ten minutes after crossing the coast, they were thirty miles away. The whole horizon seemed ablaze. Particles of soot and ash, thrown up from the city in the violent updraft of the firestorm and carried downwind toward the sea, began to swirl past the nose. The darkness faded as they closed on the outskirts of Osaka, the polished wings and fuselage of the plane began to glow a shimmering orange as *Gabrielle*'s shiny aluminum skin reflected the raging fires a mile below.

"Getting rough," muttered Jowalski as they plunged into the tortured air over Osaka. Hurricane-force winds, created by the intense heat of the inferno, raged on the surface, sucking cooler surrounding air into the vortex. This fresh, oxygen-rich air fanned the flames further, raising the temperatures higher, which in turn drew in even more outside air, until Osaka and everything near it became a hellish typhoon of death.

The Superfort began to stagger crazily across the glowing sky. Wilson yanked the wheel back, anxious to climb above the worst of the turbulence. *Gabrielle* shuddered, then began to respond. A strange odor began to sift into the cockpit.

"What's that . . . ?" Jawolski sniffed the air. Hank Callahan crawled back from the tip of the Plexiglas nose and asked the same question.

Alarmed, Wilson scanned his panel displays. Were they on fire? "Instruments look okay."

"Burning insulation?" offered Callahan, looking from Wilson to Jowalski.

"Nope," Wilson replied, recalling the smell of the burning wire insulation aboard *Rosie II* as she'd careened across Henri Lafleur's field.

The bomber caught a violent updraft and soared upward, tossed like a toy. The odor grew to a stench. Their eyes began to sting as they flew through the heaviest of the smoke just downwind of the inner city.

Wilson wrestled with the wheel and finally managed to steady *Gabrielle.* All of a sudden it hit him.

Burning flesh . . . it was the odor of human flesh, roasting in the firestorm. . . .

"My God." He stared down at the inferno two miles below. Thousands, maybe tens of thousands of people were burning to death.

Callahan looked at Wilson, read his expression, and winced. "Gawd Awmighty . . . it's not *that.* . . . Is it *that* bad down there . . . ?"

"What?!" demanded Jowalski, still confused.

Wilson, gagging back the rising bile in his throat, sputtered incoherently.

"What? What?"

As Callahan crawled silently back to his bombsight, Wilson gasped for air, drawing in deep breaths to clear his head. "It's burning Japs, Matt, burning Japs. . . ."

Jowalski went deathly white. He swore softly.

Wilson couldn't look anymore at the hell on earth raging through Osaka. Shaken, he forced himself to focus on the job at hand. His training took over. "Pilot to bombardier," he said, stiffly formal, "open the bay doors. Let's get this over with."

Huddled in the very nose of the Superfort, Hank Callahan peered through the Norden bombsight, trying to find the squadron's assigned target through the raging sea of flame. It was useless, he couldn't spot one landmark.

"No good, Lindy."

"All right, just drop 'em."

"Roger." He flipped a toggle switch on the bombsight and the bay doors snapped open. Seconds later, fifty sticks of magnesium spiraled earthward. "Bombs away, Skip."

Wilson kicked rudder and pulled *Gabrielle* into a climbing turn. The cockpit was silent until he came in for another run over the dying city. They still had to take recon photos for General Lemay.

Shutters clicked in the four cameras mounted onboard. Wilson held the Superfort as steady as he could through the pass. Finally, mercifully, *Gabrielle* swept past the southern edge of the ring of fire.

Wilson pulled the wheel back to climb toward cruising altitude, seeking the clear, clean air of twenty-five thousand feet. No one spoke until they were high over the Sea of Japan.

Tonelessly, navigator Walter Jarrod called out the ETA to Tinian over the intercom. Wilson acknowledged him, set the plane on autopilot, and turned toward Jowalski. Their eyes met for the first time since the bomb run.

"Last time I volunteer us for recon duty, Matt." Wilson pulled out his thermos and drank some tepid coffee in a futile attempt to rinse the sour taste from his mouth. "God, I didn't know it got so bad."

"We've always been up front, Lindy."

Wilson nodded. His experience over Germany had led Lemay to consistently assign him to the leading squadrons. *Gabrielle* had always been one of the first '29s over the target, sparing her pilot and crew the haunting vision the trailing bombers experienced every mission.

Callahan reappeared from the nose and sank to the cockpit floor between them. "No one's going to sleep tonight, folks."

"I may never sleep again." Wilson offered Hank his thermos, but the bombardier waved it away.

"Wish to hell we had something stronger, Skip."

"Yeah . . ."

"It still stinks," muttered Jowalski. The sickening odor lingered in the cockpit. "Can't we go lower and crack the windows, Lindy?"

"Cost us too much fuel, Matt." For the first time Wilson regretted the pressurized cabin. In a '17 he could have aired out the cockpit. As it was, they had to stay at twenty-five or thirty thousand feet in order to take advantage of the thin air and stretch their range. There was no question of opening a window at an altitude of five miles—the pressure difference between the atmosphere and the cabin was far too great.

"Never seen anything like it," said Callahan. "I heard about firestorms. Hell those Jap cities burn like tinderboxes. But *seeing* one . . ." His voice trailed off.

Wilson tried not to think about it, but the images of Osaka were etched in his mind, branded into his brain by the first-hand experience into vivid scenes of hellish carnage. The long flight back to Tinian was a nightmare of silent guilt and horror. By the time *Gabrielle*'s landing gear's wheels touched down on Runway 2, Wilson wasn't sure he'd ever be able to face another. Robotlike, he taxied the bomber to its parking revetment.

As he dropped from the hatch onto the tarmac, his knees buckled and he sank to the warm asphalt, sobbing. His ground crew stared at him in shocked silence until Callahan and Jowalski helped him to his feet.

"Come on, Lindy, let's get a drink."

Wilson looked at his bombardier through bleary eyes. "We've got to go to debriefing," he spluttered.

"To hell with the debriefing. It can wait."

Gathering himself, ashamed of losing control in front of his ground crew, he turned toward the men, *his* men, anxious to apologize, to explain, but Callahan pulled him away. "Later, Lindy. Later . . ."

They walked off under the stars, breathing in the cool ocean air. Wilson looked up at the Southern Cross, twinkling placidly on high. He hung his head in shame and confusion—why did the God who could create such beauty allow such an obscenity as war? How could he let men do such things to each other . . . ?

"Forgive us," he whispered. "God forgive us."

II

Bill Lindberg took a tentative sip of his beer and spat it out in disgust. Two cans of ninety-degree Schlitz weren't his idea of a great reward for having survived the bloody carnage of Iwo Jima.

He looked down the dazzling brightness of the beach at Ulithi. Hundreds of marines and sailors were making the best of their precious R&R; some lay on the white sand, some splashed in the surf, but most gathered under whatever shade they could find to guzzle their ration of two beers, even if they were warm. A brisk trade had developed between those who didn't care for warm beer and those who reflected that beer was beer, and that a guy could get just as drunk on warm beer as cold beer.

Reggie Blackwell, sitting on the beach next to Bill, was one of the latter, having traded two weeks' pay, a singed Japanese flag, and a ceremonial sword to a couple of enterprising sailors from the *Bunker Hill* for the twelve cans of Schlitz sitting on the beach between them. Six were empty and crushed, the seventh was half empty and going down. "Never thought I'd see another beer, back on Nishi Ridge," he said, before draining his seventh and tossing it on the pile. He glanced bleary-eyed at Bill. "You gonna finish that or look at it all day?"

Bill handed him the can. "You can have it, Reg."

Blackwell grinned. "Trick is, you gotta *think* cold, imagine you're back home on the porch with a six-pack on ice, listening to the ball game." He laughed. "Then guzzle like hell before you burn your tongue."

"Ice"—Bill stared at the warm beer—"if we only had ice, Reg. . . ."

"Well, we don't. Except in my head."

Bill pulled a pack of Pall Malls from his tunic pocket and lit up. He stared out across the harbor at the warships sitting at anchor. The vast Ulithi Atoll was filled with the combined might of Task Force 58. Dazzle camouflaged in angular patterns of gray, navy blue, white, and black, flattops, battleships, cruisers, destroyers, and countless auxiliaries swung at the end of their anchor chains, refueling and reprovisioning for the coming assault on Okinawa.

"You heard the latest, Reg?"

Blackwell belched. "What's that, Bill?" He reached for another beer.

"We're going to Kyushu. In October or November, unless the Japs surrender first."

Blackwell set down the unopened beer. "Surrender, my ass. . . . Look, why kid yourself? Those bastards won't give up 'til we kill the last mama-san on top of Mount Fuji."

"A guy can hope, can't he? They got to know they're gonna lose, Reg. Why get killed for nothing?"

"Shit, you forget Iwo already? The Japs there knew they didn't have a prayer either, but they fought for every damn rathole on the island!" Blackwell tapped a finger against the side of his head. "Those folks are *different,* Billy boy, they don't think like you or me. They fought like demons for Iwo. They'll fight like *crazed demons* for Kyushu. Hell, they *live* there! If they fight like they did for some rock out in the middle of nowhere, what makes you think they won't for their own towns?"

"The brass knows that too, Reg. Maybe they'll just let the Superforts pound the Japs into submission. Then there's the blockade the navy's got set up. We could bomb and starve 'em until they're too damn beat up to fight."

"Not a chance." Blackwell propped himself up on his elbows and squinted at Bill. "You really think ol' MacArthur is going to stand by and let the navy and air force win the war? That prima donna? Hell, he's jus' dyin' ta wade ashore in Tokyo Bay in front of the newsreel cameras like he did at Leyte. Problem is, it's you and me that'll probably be doin' the dyin' ta get him there."

Bill watched a navy launch pull up to the shore to disgorge another load of sailors. "I hadn't thought of 'Dugout Doug.' "

"Well you'd better start, 'cause he's the guy who's gonna ship your ass to the Empire, carbine in hand, to take the Land of the Rising Sun, for God, the good old U.S. of A., and General Douglas MacArthur."

Bill fell silent. It made sense. He'd seen enough service rivalry to see how the army brass would be motivated to steal the navy's thunder and grab some glory of their own by taking the home islands. If the navy got their blockade and the air force got their bombing campaign, then by God the army would get its invasion. . . .

Blackwell tossed a beer at him. "Now drink that, Bambi, or I'll pour it down your throat myself. Maybe a few beers will burn some of that mush out of your brain so you can use it again."

Bill caught the beer. "Bambi? What the hell's that mean?"

"Hell, sometimes you're like a fawn lost in the woods, Billy boy. Christ, is everybody in Michigan as wet behind the ears as you?"

"No . . . I mean, none of—"

"Oh shut up and drink your beer. You're ruinin' my vacation. So quit worryin' about November and get drunk. We got better things ta do right now than think about the damn war."

"Okay, okay. But can you answer me a couple more questions?"

Blackwell groaned. "Do I have a choice?"

"No."

"All right, shoot . . ."

Bill grinned. "Is everybody from *Brooklyn* an asshole or is it just you?"

Blackwell laughed. "Fair enough. What's part two?"

"Are you going to toss me that opener, or am I supposed to chew the damn can open?"

"That's more like it." Blackwell chuckled, tossing the opener over. "There might be hope for you yet. . . ."

Chapter XXII

U.S. 3RD Army
Ingolstadt, Germany
May 5, 1945

I

General George S. Patton jumped down from the rear deck of his command half-track and pulled his goggles from his eyes. From his spit-shined tanker's boots to the top of his gleaming helmet, he was coated in dust.

"Ah, Robertson, isn't it? Haven't seen you since we ran out of gas back in France." He smiled perfunctorily.

"No, General." Sinclair returned the smile. "You still owe me an interview, sir. I saw your M-3 coming down the road and— well, here I am. Could you spare a few minutes?"

"I owe you an interview?" Patton checked his Rolex. "I suppose I can give you five minutes, Robertson. Come along to my tent."

Sinclair followed him off the road to a khaki canvas command tent struck in the shade of a copse of lindenwoods. "Always glad to talk to you fellows," Patton said over his shoulder. *"Some* of you, that is. There's always a few smart-ass bastards who misquote me and land me in the shithouse."

Sinclair took three long strides to catch up, deciding to let the remark pass. "I just wanted to ask a couple questions about the Russians and Berlin, sir."

Patton stopped. "It'll have to be on background then, Robertson."

"If you prefer, sir."

"Damn right I do. I don't want to see anything I might say about the damn Russians in print. Ike would have my ass back in the States so quick it'd make your head spin." His eyes narrowed. "You've been a straight shooter, Robertson. I've read most of your stuff since Normandy. It's been accurate and fair. You're not about to fall off the straight and narrow by sending in my opinion of the Russians, are you?"

"Certainly not, General."

"Then why that subject?"

"I've been thinking of writing a history of the campaign someday, sir. The attitudes of the American high command toward the Russians would have to be included. I can promise that whatever you might say won't get into print for years yet."

"I have your word?"

"You do."

"Well, all right, I've got a few things to get off my chest anyway." They entered the tent. Patton gestured Sinclair toward a folding chair next to his map-cluttered desk. Staff officers came and went, but knew better than to disturb Patton during the brief moments he was with the press.

They sat down. Patton took off his helmet, frowned at the dirt coated on the polished surface, then set it down next to his chair. "I'll get right to the point, Robertson. The Russians are our enemies. They're god-damned communists. I don't like the bastards, I don't trust the bastards, and I'll tell you right now that sooner or later we're going to have to fight the bastards. As far as I'm concerned, the sooner the better. Get it over with, that's what I say. We should go to Stalin and lay our cards right on the table—tell the son of a bitch exactly what will fly after the war and what won't! No more of this coddling, no more looking the other way while he breaks agreement after agreement. We've been kissing his ass long enough and I'm damned tired of it."

Sinclair reached for his notepad, then thought better of it. Patton might clam up if he saw notes being taken. Better to wait until right after the interview. Then write down everything while his memory was still fresh. "Can I play devil's advocate here, General?" he asked.

"Not if I have to listen to any bullshit about how the Russians have gutted the Wehrmacht and deserve political concessions for fighting the Nazis. Hell, they're not fighting the Nazis as a favor to us—they've been fighting to save their own hides. Why should we reward them for doing what any country would have to do?" Patton's eyes blazed, his high-pitched voice rose. "Stalin dug his own hole in '37 when he murdered three fourths of his officer corps. The paranoid bastard all but wipes out his own military leadership, then signs a nonaggression pact with Hitler, and *then,* when the damned Nazi bastard double-crosses him and attacks him, he comes to us, demanding help!" Patton sniffed in disgust. "He sure as hell wouldn't have lifted a finger to help *us* if Hitler had left him alone and turned on us, I'll tell you that!"

"So you weren't in favor of lend-lease?"

"Oh hell, we *had* to at first. But once it was clear that Hitler wasn't going to knock the Russians out of the war, we should have cut it off, let them go at it, locked in stalemate until they wiped each other out. Churchill has been right all along. I wish FDR would have listened to him and faced up to the fact that Stalin is as much of a threat to us as Hitler ever was. Our whole policy should have been based on doing everything in our power to see that they destroyed each other. Churchill is a realist. He knows Stalin will turn on us the first chance he gets. He's known it all along. FDR always used too much carrot and not enough stick, where Churchill would have thrown the damn carrot away and gotten the biggest stick he could find. I hope Truman listens to him, or we're going to have Munich all over again."

Patton glanced at his watch. "We're going to have to wind this up, Robertson."

"One more question, General."

"Shoot."

"What do you think Stalin's immediate plans are, say, for the next few years?"

Patton thought for a moment. "Well, you can bet he'll put his own puppets in power all through eastern Europe. He'll try to spread political unrest in France, Italy, Great Britain. He'll plunder Germany of everything that isn't nailed down and keep the Red Army on a war footing while we send our boys home to Mom and Pop. Then, when western Europe is defenseless, he'll take over, one way or another."

He rose. "I've got to go, Robertson."

"Thank you for your time, General." Patton walked him to the entrance. "I'll keep this all under my hat."

"See that you do." They shook hands. "Will you be coming along with us to Vienna, then? Third Army's got an appointment with our Russian friends in Austria." His eyes twinkled. "Should be interesting . . ."

"I go where they send me, sir."

Patton sighed. "I know how *that* goes. Thought sure as hell I'd be in Berlin right now, pissing on the Reichstag."

Sinclair smiled. "I wish we had time to talk about Berlin, General."

"Don't get me started." The laugh was bitter.

"Some other time, perhaps?"

"Perhaps."

Sinclair nodded. He turned and headed for the press tent. A sudden shower had fallen, a fresh breeze washed the air with the scent of spring. A rainbow shone in the east, beyond the breaking overcast. Somewhere beyond the glowing band of color lay Berlin and the Russians. . . .

He thought of George Patton, a warrior soon to be without a war. Did he want to fight the Russians because he really felt it was inevitable, or was some inner voice telling him he'd wither and die without another battle to fight? He looked at the rainbow. For George Patton there was no pot of gold at the end of it, only bitterness; bitterness that politicians had taken from him what could have been a glorious climax to his military career, the taking of Berlin by his beloved Third Army. . . .

II

Arkady Rostov trudged wearily through the mud toward the main camp, his hands stuffed deep in the pockets of his tattered coat, his head bent forward into the unceasing wind. The guard dogs barked menacingly around the clustered mass of *zeks*, straining at their leashes, jerking their handlers roughly. Their blood was up—right at the end of the work day a *zek* had attacked a guard, charging him with wild eyes, waving his saw overhead like a sword.

Arkady closed his eyes as the incident was replayed in his mind. The guard had leveled his Kalashnikov and cut down the man, inadvertently mowing down several other *zeks* behind him. The scent of blood had thrown the dogs into a frenzy. Even now, an hour later, they still snarled at the hapless prisoners, intent on tearing them limb from limb if given the chance.

Arkady kept to the center of the mass of *zeks*, as far from the dogs as possible. Madness or suicide . . . ? There was no escape from the camp, isolated in the middle of nowhere. A saw was no match for a machine gun. The poor bastard had either cracked or resolved to end things quickly.

At any rate, *that zek's* suffering was over. Arkady sighed. Not so for the rest of them. They still faced day after endless day of brutal labor until they grew too weakened and emaciated to work. Then the food, pathetic as it was, would stop and slow death by starvation would take them.

"Bad day, Arkasha. Bad day . . ."

Arkady turned to his friend Kolya and nodded woodenly. They slogged through the mud for several minutes in silence, waving haplessly at the clouds of mosquitoes hovering about the ranks.

"Poor Rabinski, lost his temper one time too many," Kolya said at last, his voice low so as not to provoke the edgy guards. "Pity he had to take others with him though, the fool. . . ." He noticed Arkady casting a curious glance at the *zek* to his right. "Oh . . . Arkasha, this is Aleksandr Ivanovich Solzhenitsyn, late of our heroic Red Army."

"Welcome to our little resort," said Arkady. "Arkady Pavlovich Rostov, late of Gymnasium 17, Leningrad. Article 58, myself."

"The same," Solzhenitsyn grunted. He glanced back at the five bodies left behind in the mud. "Are the guards just going to leave them there for the wolves?"

"Probably." Kolya swatted a mosquito feasting on the back of his neck. *"They* sure as the devil aren't going to carry them back to camp."

"Maybe we should round up some of the lads and bring them back. . . ."

Arkady stared at the newcomer, then at Kolya, who shrugged.

"Aleksandr Ivanovich has a lot to learn, eh, Arkasha? Next thing we know he'll be wanting to escape."

Kolya's thin lips turned up in a grim smile. "The last time our friend here escaped it was from the Germans, and look where it landed him—in the Gulag as a fascist spy." He turned toward Solzhenitsyn. "We mean no harm, Aleksandr Ivanovich, but the quicker you accept the way things are here, the better off you'll be."

"So we just give up? We just let them treat us like animals?"

"One is not an animal unless one believes himself one." Kolya nodded toward the guards. "They are the animals, Aleksandr Ivanovich." He spat on the ground. "The two-legged kind, with the guns. Not the dogs. *They* don't know any better."

"You! 319! Shut your yap! You're in column!"

Kolya glanced at the guard glaring at him from the right side of the column. His German shepherd strained at its leash, its low growl menacing, its teeth bared. The soldier, a stocky Mongolian, was the same one who'd cut down poor Rabinski.

Kolya's temper flared, but he bit back a retort. Murmurs drifted through the column of *zeks*. Angry looks flashed toward the guard from several of the men nearest him.

"You louts want more?" he shouted, his accent thick, but the challenge plain enough. He handed the leash to the next guard and pointed his Kalashnikov right at Kolya's head. "Just say another word!"

"Ushka!"

Heads turned as the escort commander trudged back toward them from the head of the column. Ushka stiffened, but the barrel remained trained on Kolya, Arkady, and Solzhenitsyn. The whole mass of *zeks* and guards kept walking, but the pace had slowed. Around the black-clad prisoners, the guards' fingers tightened on their guns' triggers as they edged away. There were fifteen of them, all armed with machine guns. But there were over one hundred and fifty-five prisoners. . . .

The escort commander fell into step beside Ushka. "Report!" he demanded.

"The prisoners were talking in rank, Comrade Captain!"

Zharkin's dark eyes scanned the slogging mass of *zeks*. "Who!"

"319, Comrade Captain!"

Zharkin glared at Ushka. "I don't imagine he was talking to himself, comrade. Who else!"

Ushka couldn't see the white number patches of Arkady or Solzhenitsyn from the side. "The pigs next to him," he stammered at last.

"Well, they must have been admiring your marksmanship, Ushka," Zharkin snarled, his tone scathing. "After all, it couldn't have been easy to wing five men with a Kalashnikov from three meters away! And one of them had a saw! If you hadn't reacted so quickly, he might have, given an hour or so, sawed your head clean off!"

Ushka blinked. His mouth worked, but no words emerged.

The column had slowed to a crawl. Zharkin turned toward the *zeks*. *"Keep moving! Eyes forward!"* he bellowed. The pace picked up, but all ears were listening. "You have cost this work gang five laborers, Ushka! What am I going to tell my superiors?!"

"I—"

"Silence!" Zharkin called the two closest guards over. "Give them your weapon!" Ushka complied, stunned. Zharkin reached out and ripped the sky-blue NKVD epaulettes from his shoulders. "Fall in!"

"What . . . ?"

"Fall in! Last rank!" Zharkin shoved Ushka toward the rear of the column of *zeks*. "You've destroyed state property for the last time, Ushka. You're a wrecker! That's worth a tenner at least, maybe twenty-five."

"But—"

"I should have you shot, but your new work gang seems to be short a few men. Consider yourself fortunate."

"Comrade Captain!"

Zharkin pointed the Kalashnikov at Ushka. "No talking in ranks, *zek!*"

Part IV

The Atomic Age

Chapter XXIII

Third Guards Tank Army
Berlin, Germany
May 5, 1945

I

Crouching behind the burned-out hulk of a Tiger tank, Yuri peered down the Wilhelmstrasse toward the upper floors of the building at the end of the street. His breathing was shallow—the better to avoid the heavy stench of death that hung over Berlin. He ducked quickly behind the charred Tiger as a sniper round ricocheted off the street right beside him.

The bastard *was* on the top floor, or maybe the roof. The puff of white smoke from the discharge betrayed his position. . . . He turned to Pavel, crouching beside him behind the smoldering Tiger. "Take Ivanov and Kerenski and work your way up the other side of the street." He trained his Kalashnikov on the building and let go a burst as Pavel darted across the rubble of the Wilhelmstrasse toward the rest of the squad.

Now, where were Konstantinov and Rogev? They were supposed to be working their way up the right side of the street. Yuri waved at Pavel to wait, then turned to scan the doorways behind him. Uneasiness came over him—Igor Konstantinov was the kind of bastard who'd put a bullet in a comrade's back if given half the chance. After saving that poor German woman from his tender attentions, he'd seen the malice in those cold eyes, the unspoken thirst for vengeance.

"Konstantinov! Rogev! Where the devil are you?!"

No reply.

Yuri cursed, the back of his neck tingling with fear. Rooting out the last fanatics still fighting was bad enough without having to worry about being done in by one of his own.

"Pavel! Cover me!"

Pavel and the others opened up on the upper floor of the building, splattering chunks of masonry to the street below. Yuri sprinted down the right side of the Wilhelmstrasse, darting from doorway to doorway until he reached the far end of the block. Then he crouched behind a burning Mercedes and snatched a quick look at the sniper's perch.

Bastard's probably gone to a different room by now—they seldom shot more than once or twice from one position. Not that *that* mattered. He'd have to search the damned building floor by floor, room by room anyway—division had made such tactics mandatory.

Yuri caught his breath. Oddly, he felt safer right under the nose of the sniper than he did farther back. Konstantinov seemed the worse threat. At least he knew where the sniper was. . . .

At the far end of the block, Igor Konstantinov drew a bead on Yuri from behind a pile of rubble. "I could get him, Boris, I could get him right now."

Rogev grabbed the rifle barrel and pushed it away. "Not now, Igor, the others will hear the shot and see us." He nodded toward Pavel and the rest of the squad working their way up the left side of the Wilhelmstrasse. "There will be chances to even the score."

Konstantinov raised the rifle again, squeezed his left eye shut, and sighted down the black barrel at the small figure firing at the sniper's nest from behind the overturned automobile. "It would be so easy, Rogev." His finger tensed on the trigger. If he only knew when the sniper would fire again, he could shoot at the same time.

Rogev yanked the barrel away again, his eyes pleading. "Just wait!"

Konstantinov glared at him. *It'll be a pleasure to do for* you *too, you lout. After I get Rostov, you'll be next. The devil take me if I leave a witness, especially one who'd turn in his own mother to save his skin.*

"Wait until night, Igor. We can do it with grenades. Wait until the bastard's asleep and—"

"What about the sentries, you idiot?! And the others?! They'd see soon enough that we aren't there camped with the squad. Rostov's friends would point the finger at us in a second." He stared down the street. "No, we have to get him now, while the bullets are flying. If only we had tank support, I could get him while the '85 is booming. No one would hear the shot over *that* kind of racket."

As if in answer to a prayer, a T-34 clanked around the corner and rumbled down the Wilhelmstrasse, treads creaking over the rubble, crushing chunks of masonry debris to dust.

Konstantinov's eyes widened at the apparition, then watched in anticipation as the tank lumbered past them, its turret training on the building ahead where Rostov and the squad waited.

"Let's get closer, Boris. I'll not want to miss." He shoved Rogev forward and waited until he was a few meters ahead, then followed, his gaze darting from the sniper perch, to Rostov, then Rogev, then the tank, which was stopped now, belching blue exhaust from its tail pipes, its eighty-five-millimeter cannon at full elevation. He pointed his rifle at Rogev. When the cannon thundered, he squeezed the trigger. Rogev's head exploded. He pitched forward, his rifle clattering off the street as he fell. Bright red arterial blood spurted onto the dirty concrete, mixing with the blue-gray gore splattered there like spilt cottage cheese.

He'll not rat on me now. . . . Better done with sooner than

later. Konstantinov scampered past the corpse, eyes on Rostov, and the squad deployed under cover at the end of the block, now only fifty meters away. The tank turret pivoted, then stopped, its barrel trained on the upper corner to blast another gaping hole in the wall.

He crouched behind the Tiger and raised his rifle, waiting for the T-34 to fire.

Yuri trained his field glasses on the shattered wall, searching the smoking shadows of the interior for any sign of a body. Thank God the tank had shown up. They were the best way to clear buildings of snipers. The steel monsters could just sit in the street and blast away until the building was demolished. No sniper, no matter how fanatic, would face down a tank. If he wasn't killed by the first few shots, he'd flee for some safer refuge to continue his sniping from somewhere else.

Yuri stared at the tank, waiting for it to fire. What the devil were they waiting for? He scampered from cover and leaped onto the back of the T-34, his eyes on the upper-floor windows, wary of a sudden shot. He pounded the butt of his Kalashnikov atop the turret hatch just as the cannon roared. An instant later a ricochet sang off the steel side of the turret. He dove to the ground, landing in a heap beside the rear bogie wheels. Pain shot through his ankle. He hobbled toward a pile of rubble.

Must have twisted it. . . . He peered over the top of the debris, holding his ankle. Sniper was still there after all. . . .

Konstantinov glared at the sight at Yuri, cursing the clean miss. He sucked in a breath, his finger tight on the trigger. Rostov was still in sight beside the tank. . . . Must have thought that the shot came from the building. . . . Easy now, wait for the next shot, let go a full burst this time and to the devil with who might hear. Rostov wasn't going to live to hand him over to the NKVD. Who did he think he was, anyway, taking the side of a Nazi woman over a comrade?

The eighty-five roared again. Konstantinov squeezed the trigger and held it, spraying a long burst.

Yuri flinched as the tank fired. The sudden pressure on his ankle shot white hot pain up his leg. It gave way and he fell to his left. The mound of rubble beside him erupted, riddled by machine-gun fire. He rolled against the tank treads.

That came from behind him. He was sure of it.

Konstantinov!

He peered through the bogie wheels and saw a helmet duck behind the smoldering Tiger fifty meters down the street. In a rage, he snatched several grenades from his utility belt, rose to a crouch behind the T-34, pulled the pin on the first, and hurled it toward the hulk. He threw a second as the first exploded, then a third.

Konstantinov heard something hard clank off the far side of the Tiger. An explosion rang in his ears. Something tore into his boot and he fell to the ground, screaming in pain. He clutched his right foot, blood oozing through the leather from several ragged holes. He looked up just in time to see another grenade plop onto the ground not five meters from him. His last scream was cut off in mid-breath as white hot shrapnel tore through his chest and face.

Yuri stared down at the bloody mess that had been Igor Konstantinov. Farther down the street, Rogev was sprawled in death, his head gone. Beside him, Pavel spat on the corpse. "Murdering devil!"

"The NKVD won't get him now," Dmitri muttered.

"Bastards wouldn't have done anything, anyway. They're too busy looting and raping themselves."

Yuri leaned against the Tiger, his ankle throbbing. "Let's go, we've got work to do."

"You're going to the rear, you can't even walk," said Pavel. "We're taking you back, we've done enough for one day."

II

Commissar Kriminov stood in the blasted-out garden of the Chancellery, staring down at the charred pit. The smell of decaying flesh hung over the city like a shroud, but the stench from the pit grew stronger than the general odor pervading Berlin as the soldiers' spades unearthed the blackened corpses.

He wrinkled his nose in disgust. Could it be Hitler? Some of his top henchmen? Or just some anonymous Berliners, cut down here by chance? Yet the bodies had been burned, then buried. Who in Berlin would take time to bury a body—cremate it, no less—amidst such a horrendous bombardment? Thousands of corpses lay where they'd fallen all over the city, yet these had been doused with gasoline, set afire, then buried. . . .

He stepped closer to the edge of the hole as one of the men cleared the last of the dirt from the upper torso of the larger body. Then he turned to Lieutenant Smirnov. "Go find the colonel, he'd better have a look at this."

By the time Colonel Nikolai Lermontov arrived with a coterie of aides, forensic specialists, and photographers, the charred corpses had been completely unearthed. Artillery rumbled in the distance, mixing with the thunder growling from the darkening east, but the group's attention was focused on identifying the bodies.

Kriminov stood aside as the medical people pushed past him. They set quickly to work. Photos were snapped, tissue samples scraped off. Soldiers came up with canvas tarpaulins and stretchers. The bodies were picked up and wrapped in the tarp, then placed on stretchers and carried toward the waiting convoy of army trucks, armored cars, and tanks.

Lermontov beckoned Kriminov to where he waited next to an idling armored car. "Come with me, Comrade Kriminov. I have some questions. Then you'll fill out a full report on the circumstances of discovery."

"Yes, Comrade Colonel." Kriminov climbed into the vehicle, his heart pounding in excitement. If one of those bodies *was* Hitler, his career was made. While other units had been racing one another for the Reichstag, he'd driven his regiment mercilessly toward the Chancellery, browbeating that fool Markov when necessary, but never straying from his goal—being the first to Hitler's bunker.

A driving rain began to fall as the convoy rumbled off. They rolled north toward the Brandenburg Gate, turned right onto the wide expanse of the tree-lined Under den Linden, and raced east several kilometers. They met a long armored column bound westward, led by JS-2 heavy tanks. Truckload after truckload of grim-faced soldiers followed, heads bowed against the downpour.

Finally, they pulled off into a sprawling encampment on the eastern outskirts of the city and stopped before a huge, olive-drab tent, surrounded by NKVD guards. The tarp-covered stretchers were taken inside. Kriminov followed Colonel Lermontov into the tent, where their papers were checked before they were permitted admittance.

"Come, Kriminov, we'll wait here." Lermontov nodded toward some folding chairs set against the left wall. They watched as the forensic team carried the corpses into a partitioned section, then dropped the flap down behind them.

They sat down. Lermontov lit a cigarette with trembling hands, then handed the pack to Kriminov. "I don't know if the initial examination will prove anything, but I wanted our division people to have a look before we send the bodies up to front HQ." He inhaled deeply, his eyes darting toward the canvas partition, then at Kriminov. "If one of those bodies *is* Hitler's, we may find ourselves in a bit of a mess, I fear."

Kriminov stared at Lermontov. What was this?

Visions of glory, of being decorated by Great Stalin himself faded. "I . . . don't understand, Comrade Colonel."

Lermontov frowned. He leaned closer to Kriminov, his voice low. "Certain people in Moscow, certain *very powerful people,* do not want Hitler's body found. If we cannot capture him alive, they prefer that Herr Adolf vanish mysteriously."

Kriminov's eyes fell, his shoulders sagged. He felt himself drawn toward some terrible abyss. If that *was* Hitler behind that tent flap, and Stalin or the Politburo hadn't wanted his body found, *he,* lowly Colonel Kriminov, could be the one to vanish without a trace. But how could Hitler's disappearance benefit Moscow?

"But why, Comrade Colonel?" he heard himself ask. "Why wouldn't they want the body found?"

Lermontov frowned. "Political reasons, what else? Look, if Hitler's body isn't found, certain people would find it useful to claim that he has escaped, that he is *still* a threat to us. They could then justify the harshest of measures against Germany, measures that the Western Allies are unlikely to accept, *unless* they are faced with the specter of endless guerrilla warfare throughout Germany, waged by Hitler and his fanatics against both of us."

"But if he *is* dead, the West would insist that fascism is indeed crushed and Germany should be treated with more lenience . . . ?"

"Exactly." Lermontov tossed his cigarette onto the dirt floor and crushed it out with his boot. "Our problem, Kriminov, is what position Stalin will take on this. I knew there was a huge risk all along . . . finding Hitler would make a career or break it, spectacularly, one way or another. I felt it was worth the gamble."

Chills ran down Kriminov's spine, the back of his neck tingled. If he'd found Hitler and Stalin hadn't wanted Hitler found, it only followed that eyewitnesses to the discovery would have to be silenced. He'd been nothing but a pawn in a high-stakes game, a chess piece to be crowned or swept off the board. . . .

One of the forensic team emerged through the partition and gestured for Lermontov to come over. Kriminov watched as the pair huddled, their voices too low to carry. Finally, Lermontov nodded. He disappeared behind the canvas wall for several minutes. When he came out again, his face was a pasty white. He sat down next to Kriminov and fumbled for a cigarette.

"Nasty business, that . . ." he muttered. He found his pouch of hand-rolled *papirosu*, pulled a "liberated" German lighter from his trouser pocket, and lit up.

"What did they say, comrade?"

Lermontov inhaled deeply, his eyes closed. "Nothing conclusive, as far as *I* can tell." He frowned. "They'll hedge until they sense which way the wind is blowing. I think they know already whether we have Hitler or not. They just don't want to go on record yet."

"What should *we* do?"

Lermontov shrugged. "We fill out a report stating that we found the bodies in the Chancellery Garden and brought them in for examination, suspecting that they could be high Nazi officials. We may have found Hitler, or we may not have . . . but that question is for others to decide. The thing for us to remember is that we must keep our heads down so they don't get chopped off. If the bosses don't want that corpse in there to be Hitler, it won't be. If they want it to be, it will be. Unless we go around blabbering that we found Hitler's body, they'll leave us alone, Kriminov."

"You think so?"

"I wasn't so sure . . . but it makes sense, does it not? I mean, are we forensic experts? No. So how could our opinion on who that might be in there carry any weight with anyone? It's not like the corpses were identifiable by sight. . . . If *that* were the case and Moscow wanted to hush the matter up, we'd be—" Lermontov drew his thumb across his throat.

"But the bodies were charred beyond recognition," said Kriminov, thinking aloud.

"Exactly." Lermontov nodded toward the canvas. "It's those lads who are on the spot, not us."

III

Three days later, Joseph Stalin examined the photographs. Two grisly corpses, charred beyond recognition, lay in the mud. He looked up in disdain at Lavrenti Beria.

"These could be two Berlin whores for all we know."

"The attached X rays are the ultimate proof, Joseph Vissarionovich." Beria handed the X rays to Stalin, along with detailed dental records of Adolph Hitler and Eva Braun. "The matter of the bridge is the decisive evidence," Beria explained. "The dental bridge on the corpse we found in the Chancellery garden is the same as shown on these X rays of Hitler taken at various times throughout the war."

Stalin glanced in disdain at the X rays and accompanying documents. Smoke curled from his pipe and twirled toward the ceiling. Then, caught in the draft coming in through the open window, it faded to nothingness. He leafed through the material, a frown spreading across his face. Beria of all people should know the dubious value of photographs and X rays; the NKVD had a whole department whose only duty was to provide just such false evidence if it benefited state security.

He tossed the file on his desk. "This will not be sufficient. It would have been simple to arrange to leave a charred corpse there with a dental bridge identical to Hitler's." Stalin glared at the chief of the NKVD. "I want real proof! The Soviet people demand real proof, not some blurred X ray and a bunch of forged medical records!"

"But Joseph Vissarionovich, our top forensic scientists have concluded beyond a doubt that—"

"*I* have not concluded beyond a doubt that that Austrian bastard is dead, comrade! Until *I* do, your people will investigate the matter. I want the survivors of the bunker brought to the

Kremlin. They will be interrogated in my presence. *They* know, comrade! *They* know if that corpse is actually Hitler or not, and they will tell me. Documents can lie; people in the hands of the NKVD cannot!"

"Most of them are dead, or missing, Joseph Vissarionovich. . . ."

Stalin rolled his eyes. "Were Hitler's cronies supposed to wait to greet the Red Army with tea and cupcakes? Should they have strolled out onto the Tiergarten and waved a big sign? 'Here we are! Come and arrest us, please.' " He shook his head in disgust. "Perhaps it is time for the NKVD to have a new chief. Someone whose brain has not been turned to borscht by too many late nights fornicating with schoolgirls."

Beria's face was expressionless, but Stalin caught the hint of guilt in his eyes. So it was true. . . . Malenkov and Khrushchev had not been telling tales out of school after all.

"Joseph Vissarionovich," said Beria, his voice dripping with false contrition, "a man has his weaknesses, but mine have never prevented me from fulfilling my duty toward you or the security of the Motherland. I—"

Stalin held up a beefy hand to silence him. Beria pushed his wire rims back to the bridge of his nose, a nervous habit often joked about in Stalin's inner circle.

"Comrade Beria," Stalin said, fixing him with an icy glare. "I don't care if you rut like a boar on every woman in Moscow, or girl for that matter. I *do* care when you come in here and waste my time with such obvious drivel as this." He picked up the Hitler file from his desk and tossed it toward Beria. The pages flopped out of the manila holder and fluttered all over the parquet tile. Beria stooped to collect the scattered documents.

"Leave them there. You are the head of the NKVD, not a maid! Start acting like one! Get your fat ass to Berlin and find those people. Dig up every rathole in the city if that's what it takes, but bring them back to me. And bring the corpses in the photos as well. Do you understand?"

"Yes, Joseph Vissarionovich."

Stalin waved Beria out in disgust.

Alone, he slumped into his chair, his elbows on the desk, his head resting in his hands. He closed his eyes in thought. The Red Army had found dozens of bunkers throughout Germany, all specially built for the use of Hitler and the Nazi leadership. Why spend hundreds of millions of deutschmarks building such elaborate hideouts if they were never meant to be used? Surely, sometime in April, that devil Hitler had fled Berlin. Such a fanatic would not have stayed there to die like a trapped rat, or worse, risk capture by the Red Army. . . .

Stalin rose from his desk and walked to the open window. Down below, beyond the turreted walls of the Kremlin, long evening shadows stretched across Red Square. Muted sounds of traffic drifted to the window from Marx Prospekt. The day was waning—another day without definitive knowledge of Hitler's fate. Even now, as Berlin burned, he was probably in some hidden bunker, smirking at the fantastic hoax he had pulled on the world, hatching some devilish plot.

He returned to his desk and sank into the red leather upholstery of his chair. The NKVD had discovered sinister weapons programs afoot in the Third Reich—rockets that could cross the Atlantic, atomic bomb research, perhaps even the beginnings of production, jet bombers that could outpace the Red Air Force's fastest fighter planes, invincible new U-boats, monster tanks with impenetrable armor plate. . . .

Stalin stared at the oil portrait of Lenin on the far wall. Even with the Reich in ruins, Nazi fanatics, spurred on by Hitler's ravings, could be launching a rocket at Moscow from some complex hidden in the Bavarian Alps. The Americans might even be aware of such deviltry and stand by while the last Nazis did their dirty work for them.

Ah, but what of Hitler? The thought obsessed him. Was the maniac dead after all? Was the report from Beria true? Could Hitler have actually resolved to die in his Berlin bunker? According to the NKVD, he'd been addicted to all manner of drugs, so who was to say what mental state he had been in when he'd chosen to stay in Berlin? Or *was in now,* hidden in some subterranean vault instead of dead in the ashes of his capital. . . .

Which really would be best? Hitler dead at the hands of the Red Army, slain in his lair by victorious communism? Or still at large, still a threat, still a means of crushing Germany under the jackboot?

Stalin rubbed his temples, trying to think. Would Hitler conceivably give himself up to the West? Try to work out some arrangement? His basic political creed had been anti-communist. He'd always claimed he had no argument with Germany's Anglo-Saxon "cousins," and had fought them only when they'd interfered with his plans by standing up for the Poles.

Now, could the most monstrous betrayal in all human history be in creation? Had Hitler fled to the Americans? Was he at this moment hounding them to turn on their allies, playing on their common bourgeoisie hatred of socialism?

Stalin frowned. Roosevelt would not have betrayed him, but Roosevelt was dead. This Truman was an unknown; if he fell under Churchill's spell, another war was unavoidable. Churchill, of course, despised Hitler, but the English pig had sided with us when Hitler was the greater threat. Why would he not side with Hitler now that we are the greater threat?

Stalin rose wearily from his desk and gathered up the papers lying on the red carpet. He paged through them, examining the photos, staring at the X rays, scanning the text. Beria was convinced the corpse was Hitler's; the other a female, his mistress's. But was he right? Or was he hatching some scheme himself?

But how would faking Hitler's death help him?

Stalin threw the file onto the desk in disgust. Was he getting too suspicious? Was he seeing plots where no plots existed?

No. Beria was a snake, that much was true. He would make his move someday. But not now, not at the end of the war. He would bide his time; he knew the marshals had to be weakened, he knew there would be much work for him to do, many enemies to deal with, many potential allies to recruit.

Stalin's mouth curled up in a smile. Better to let Beria have his lead, let him do as he would, while watching whom he kept counsel with, whom he cultivated, whom to arrest along with him as soon as the time was ripe. Then all the fish could be scooped up in one net.

And fried.

Chapter XXIV

The Kremlin, Moscow, USSR
May 1945

Joseph Stalin stared at the corpse on the slab. The forensic staff had pulled the white sheet down from the face and shoulders before leaving Stalin alone in the laboratory. The upper chest, somewhat protected from the flames of the Chancellery pit by clothing, was still human in appearance, despite the wax-like sheen.

Curious, Stalin tapped his knuckles against the sternum. The chest wall was hard as a rock—the corpse had been frozen to prevent decay after the initial autopsy had confirmed beyond reasonable doubt that it was indeed Adolf Hitler. Packed in ice, it had been flown to Moscow and brought to the Kremlin morgue, deep in a subterranean chamber beneath Lenin's Tomb.

The only facility used by Communist Party leaders and their families when death required skilled mortuary services, the morgue was seldom used. Lenin had been prepared here, as had Dzerzhinsky, the founder of the Cheka, the Secret Police. Recently however, the only activity in the facility were the comings and goings of the permanent staff people who maintained Lenin's embalmed corpse for the thousands of Soviets who filed through the upper chamber daily to view the remains.

Until the arrival of Hitler.

The leading forensic scientists of the Soviet Union had scurried busily about the lab, fussing over the corpse, taking tissue samples, x-raying the body, sectioning the brain and vital organs, examining and reexamining the teeth and dental bridge for comparison with captured Nazi dental records of the Fuhrer for thirteen days and nights before affirming its identity. In the days following the conclusion of the autopsy, a parade of Red Army marshals and generals had come through the morgue to look upon their dead enemy.

But Stalin had refrained. Until now . . .

Intrigued, Stalin knocked on the chest again. "Are you in there, you bastard?" He grinned in triumph—his deadliest enemy, his arch rival in tyranny, sworn to annihilate communism and turn the vast steppes of Soviet Russia into an agricultural province of the Thousand-Year Reich, was no more.

Stalin stared at the charred skull. The eye sockets were empty—the fire had melted the fluid of the eyeballs and burned away most of the hair on the singed scalp. But some of the infamous mustache remained, as did the decayed teeth. Hitler's blue lips had constricted as rigor mortis had set in and were drawn away from his teeth, giving the skull a hideous grin.

Stalin grinned back. "Thought you'd have *me* on a slab, didn't you, you devil . . . ?" He lit a Camel and exhaled a stream of tobacco smoke over the face. "They told me you despised smoking. . . . Well, get a snootful of that." His laughter echoed through the sparkling clean laboratory, but faded quickly as he remembered the dark days of 1941. Hitler's legions had been at the gates of Moscow; Wehrmacht patrols had penetrated the outer suburbs of the city before the desperate counterattack of the Red Army's newly arrived Asiatic divisions had thrown them back.

"It was you or me, you son of a bitch. With the world itself at stake." Stalin stepped closer. He'd always felt an odd affinity with Hitler. While they were at opposite extremes of the political spectrum, they had one thing in common—complete and utter contempt for the anarchy of democracy. Stalin had modeled his Great Purge of the thirties on Hitler's liquidation of the Nazi

SA. He'd admired Hitler's ruthless annihilation of his domestic political enemies.

"And I have won." Stalin reached out and flicked the smoldering ashes of his cigarette into Hitler's mouth. "You should have finished the English when you had the chance, you fool. Without a two-front war to fight, you may well have done for me. You may well have had your Thousand-Year Reich."

Stalin took another puff of his Camel. "But it's Germany that will wither away; it's Germany that will be the province of a Soviet World Union. *We* will rule a thousand-year empire, *we* will crush the West and bring order to the world. *I* will be a god a thousand years from today, while you will be long forgotten."

Stalin crushed out his cigarette on the corpse's forehead and tossed the butt onto the waxy chest. "A pity the flames did such messy work. If you were more presentable, I would have had you stuffed and propped up in a museum somewhere as an example to my enemies."

He turned to leave, then paused. He tapped another cigarette out of his pack, stuck it into the corner of the corpse's mouth, and lit the end with his Zippo. "Have a smoke on me, you bastard—one for the road, eh?"

Stalin closed the door behind him and strode through the hallway toward the waiting morticians. "Keep him on ice, comrades," he muttered as he passed. "I may have further use for him."

Chapter XXV

I

Harry Truman glanced across the conference table at Joseph Stalin, trying to measure the Soviet leader against the political and psychological profile drawn up by the OSS and Army G-2. He'd been poring over bulky briefing books for weeks, anxious to hold his own during the first postwar meeting of the Allied leadership, only too aware that his counterparts, Churchill and Stalin, were legendary figures with finely tuned diplomatic skills, crafty bargainers who would eat him alive if he wasn't ready for this high-stakes game of power politics.

Only half listening to the droning translation of Winston Churchill's opening remarks, Truman eyed Stalin surreptitiously—he'd found throughout his political career that there was no substitute for dealing face-to-face with a rival. Briefing books were fine, but they couldn't begin to compare with direct, one-on-one contact.

He saw a short, stocky man in his mid-sixties, resplendent in the white dress, high-collar uniform of a Soviet marshal. Stalin's hair, combed straight back, was gray, almost white. His bushy eyebrows and thick mustache were a darker gray, his complexion pallid from endless months of confinement behind the Kremlin walls.

Truman smiled inwardly—if nothing else, the OSS had been right about *one* thing: both Stalin and his Foreign Minister Vyacheslav Molotov had the pallor of men whose duties kept them indoors. Their "Kremlin tans" testified to that much.

But of what use was such trivia, other than testimony to the personal work habits of the Kremlin leadership?

Truman frowned. If his intelligence people had told him what Stalin was going to say about Germany's future, or Poland's, or Austria's, or Czechoslovakia's . . . or entering the war against Japan, or the United Nations, or Hitler's fate, or any of a multitude of real issues, that would have helped. Instead, he got half-baked psychological profiles and physical descriptions.

The president watched as Stalin began to reply to Churchill's remarks. He found his attention drawn at once to the eyes of the Soviet dictator. They had a glint of joviality in them, yet revealed the cunning of a man risen from peasant stock over rivals with more intelligence and scholastic training but perhaps with less of an intuitive grasp of the basic motives which drive human beings.

Stalin, his tone bantering, almost lighthearted, spoke briefly, then paused as his translator repeated his remarks in English.

A very confident man, Truman mused. A man fully aware of the might of his Red Army, of the clamor of the American people to "bring the boys home," of England's exhaustion. A man who knew how to play the game when he held a good hand.

The president smiled, drawing a curious glance from Churchill. Stalin might be holding good cards, but the recent news from Alamogordo, New Mexico, had given Truman a trump card to play. The atomic gizmo had actually worked. The United States had split the atom and acquired a weapon of indescribable power.

His smile faded. Stalin must be told—he *was* still an ally, despite his apparent intentions to ignore prior Big Three agreements and install procommunist governments in Eastern

Europe. The United States must not be perceived to be acting in bad faith—to fail to inform Stalin of the atomic bomb would trigger his instinctive distrust and paranoia, leading to God only knew what reaction.

But how to do so? Stalin saw any power not his own as a threat. He must be given the news in such a way as to avoid any inference that the United States intended to use the bomb as a means of pressuring the Soviet Union diplomatically.

Truman frowned. It was self-evident that the bomb was a trump card for the West, but it must not appear to be. He must under no condition act as though it was—to wave the issue in Stalin's face would be counterproductive. He must be told the news in such a way as to defuse his inherent suspicions before they could smolder into open flame.

The president decided not to bring it up when his turn came to speak. A setting less formal was required—to announce such news at a plenary session would only dramatize it needlessly, would only confront Stalin with an excuse to see it as a planned gesture of intimidation.

As the men around the table turned toward him for his opening remarks, Truman resolved to break the news at the evening reception. He would simply approach Stalin, engage him in conversation, then throw in, almost as an afterthought, that the United States had developed a new weapon for use against Japan. . . .

That evening, as the Big Three and their military and diplomatic advisers and staffs mingled under the sparkling chandeliers of the palace drawing room, the president waited for his opportunity. Standing with Secretary of State James Byrne near the buffet tables, Truman sipped his white wine and exchanged pleasantries with the steady stream of people drifting up to pay their respects.

As he chatted, he glanced occasionally at his counterparts. Winston Churchill, gleaming brandy snifter in one hand, smoldering cigar in the other, was holding forth before a large circle of people next to the champagne tables. Across the smoky room, Stalin stood in a corner, surrounded by Molotov and a solemn group of Russian officers, listening to the American ambassador to the Soviet Union, Averell Harriman.

Several minutes passed before Harriman glanced his way. Then most of the group, led by Harriman and Molotov, drifted toward the champagne tables, leaving Stalin alone, but for his interpreter and a pair of Soviet generals. Seeing his chance, Truman excused himself and approached the Russian leader.

Stalin greeted him with a smile. Through his interpreter they indulged in small talk for several minutes. Finally Truman affected to notice that his wineglass was empty and began to excuse himself, then paused.

"Oh, by the way, Generalissimo, I almost forgot to mention it. . . ."

The yellow eyes regarded him thoughtfully. Stalin listened to the translation, then smiled, revealing teeth yellowed by decades of smoking.

"Yes, Mr. President . . . ?"

Truman glanced past Stalin for a moment at Byrne watching them intently from the buffet tables, then plunged ahead, hoping his words wouldn't sound rehearsed. He returned Stalin's smile. "I wanted to tell you about this new weapon we've developed, Generalissimo. It should prove a nasty surprise to the Japanese."

"A new weapon you say?" Stalin asked as the translator finished, his tone one of polite interest.

"Yes. A powerful new bomb, Generalissimo."

To Truman's surprise, Stalin's expression remained unchanged as the interpreter spoke. Beneath his courteous attention, the Soviet leader seemed singularly unimpressed.

"I congratulate you, Mr. President."

Truman paused. Had Stalin grasped the significance of the revelation? "My people tell me it is far more destructive than any bomb ever used," he added, feeling oddly cheated at Stalin's lack of reaction.

Stalin nodded indulgently. "Thank you for telling me, Mr. President."

Truman politely took his leave and drifted back toward James Byrne. His Secretary of State noted the perplexed expression on his face and regarded him expectantly. "Well . . . ?"

Truman shrugged. "Jim, the fellow didn't even blink."

Byrne stared at him. "Maybe he didn't understand, Mr. President."

Truman glanced back at Stalin. The Soviet leader betrayed no sign of concern as he greeted British Foreign Minister Anthony Eden. Smiling broadly, he pounded the Englishman on the back, saying something that drew laughter from the group around them.

The president turned back to Byrne. "I made it as clear as I possibly could without making a big deal out of it, Jim."

"I'm sure you did, sir."

"Damn right, I did. And by God, when we drop one of those babies on the Japs, I'd better not hear Uncle Joe raising any hell about it."

Byrne frowned. "He'll be too busy trying to get into the war before it's all over, Mr. President. You know how badly he wants Manchuria, Korea, and Sakhalin Island."

"Well, he's not going to get them! He's got his paws on too much territory as it is."

"He'll play hardball, Mr. President. Japan and Germany are traditional enemies. At the very least, he's going to insist on buffer zones in Eastern Europe and the Far East."

"Then we'll have to play hardball too." Truman scowled. "Hell, if it were up to Stalin, the *whole world* would be a buffer zone. . . ."

II

Wilson Lindberg felt the eyes of the enlisted clerk on his back as he hesitated at the door of the squadron chaplain's inner office. Before he could change his mind and slink away in embarrassing retreat, he forced himself to knock on the doorframe. Father Riley looked up from his desk. "Yes, Major . . . what can I do for you?"

The Catholic priest, a army air force colonel for the duration, stood up, walked out from behind his cluttered desk, and greeted Wilson with a broad smile. "Come in, come in." He gestured toward the chair next to his desk. "Have a seat. Major . . . ?"

"Lindberg, sir. Major Wilson Lindberg." He sank wearily into the chair as Riley closed the door quietly, then took a seat himself.

"Is something troubling you, son?" he asked, dropping military formality once out of earshot of his aides. He noted the hesitation on Wilson's face, and an understanding smile appeared. "People don't come to me just to shoot the breeze, son. If they knock on my door, it's because they have problems. That's what I'm here for, to listen—to offer whatever advice I can, but mainly to listen."

"Yes, Padre."

Riley sighed. "I seem to be doing more business lately. My first months here I must have been the loneliest fellow on Tinian. Not anymore." He glanced at the silver wings on Wilson's uniform. "You are a pilot, then?"

Wilson's tension began to fade—Riley seemed to understand already. "Yes, Padre. I . . . thought I'd come by, I didn't know who else to turn to."

"If you'll pardon my frankness, I can see you don't look well, son."

"I haven't been sleeping well, Padre." Wilson poured it all out. "I'm having nightmares. I wake up in the middle of the night in a cold sweat. I get out of my bunk in the morning more tired than when I got in, and it's getting worse. It's been going on for weeks now. It's starting to affect my flying. I'm not sharp anymore. I can't stay alert, my reflexes are shot. I'm so worn down I'm afraid I'm going to foul up and get my whole crew killed."

"I have to ask you, son, have you been to sick bay? They could give you something to help you sleep, you know."

"More than once, but nothing helps." Wilson's hopes fell— was he going to be fobbed off onto the docs at sick bay, sent packing with a few clichés and a pat on the back?

Riley sighed, noting the doubt in Wilson's eyes. "Please understand, son." A sad smile crossed his face. "I'm required to advise medical solutions if I consider them warranted, but I suspect your troubles cannot be cured by medication."

"No, sir . . ."

"You are troubled by the bombing."

Wilson nodded. He groped for words of explanation, but before he could find any, Riley continued. "If I might ask, how long have you been here on Tinian, son?"

"About five months, Padre."

"I see. You've gone to Japan many times then . . . ?"

"Thirteen missions."

"And you've been troubled this whole time?"

Wilson felt his face flush. "No, Padre . . . I, that is, I guess I never thought much about it. I just did my job like the next fellow." He shook his head in bewilderment. "I flew my first mission in '44, completed a tour in England, lost a crew . . . damn near— Sorry . . . uh, almost got killed myself. Came out here, flew another thirteen against the Empire . . . and, I guess I was affected by things, you know. Who wouldn't be? But not like *this*."

"When did it start?"

"After Osaka." Wilson's gaze fell to the floor. "We were one of the last 29s over the city." His voice grew hushed. "I can still smell that burning flesh, Padre. . . . Every night, those fires burn again, every night that stench fills my nostrils, every night . . . every night. . . ."

"Have you gone to confession, son?"

Wilson looked up slowly. "I'm not Catholic, Padre."

Riley leaned toward him. "My bishop back home would throw a fit if he heard me say this, but I don't care what particular faith any of my flock here follows. We're all under trial out here. Many of us walk to death's door every night and too often it opens wide. . . ." Riley paused, his composure wavering for a moment. He cleared his throat, took off his glasses, and put them on again. "Even those," he added at last, "even those spared, who return to see another dawn on this earth, have to face another day with the knowledge that they themselves have opened death's door to others. And if they come to me, I tell them to pray to their God for solace and comfort, to lay their burdens on a stronger back than their own, to ask forgiveness and understanding, and go about their duty. We are the instruments of the Lord, son. Nothing happens in this world that is not meant to be. This struggle against tyranny, this world war we find ourselves in, is a portal through which mankind must pass to reach ultimate salvation. The history of mankind is not a series of accidents, son. It is not a wayward tangle of happenstance and circumstance. It doesn't stumble along from nowhere on the way to nowhere. There is meaning in every event; there is purpose. Do you follow me?"

"I think so. . . ."

"What I'm trying to say is, we are all part of a tapestry that was woven long ago. Each of us is but a thread of that tapestry; but without threads, one cannot have a tapestry, can one?"

"No, Padre."

"You are a thread, son. I am one. Everyone is. We are part of the greater whole, the unfathomable fabric of life and human history. Some threads are longer, some shorter, but each has purpose. In other words, if you are a soldier, you were meant to be one. If I am a priest, I was meant to be one. We must follow the course the Weaver has set for us, for He can see the entire tapestry while we cannot. If you have shed blood, you were meant to shed blood. If you are troubled, you were meant to be troubled. If you feel pain, you were meant to feel pain. If you die, you were meant to die. If you live, you were meant to live."

"But what of free choice?" Wilson asked. "Isn't it Christian doctrine that each of us is free to follow Satan or Christ? I mean, what is the purpose of living if we are just robots, programmed to a fulfill a function?"

Riley smiled. "We have freedom to choose, son. It's just that the Lord *knows* what choices we will make, while *we do not, until we make them.*"

"So He knew what carnage Hitler, Tojo, and the rest of them would wreak, the suffering they would cause to millions, because it was all part of the plan . . . ?"

"Yes."

"But why allow it?"

"For the greater good of mankind."

"I don't understand. . . ."

Riley sighed. "Sometimes one generation must suffer for the good of those to follow, son. Without pain, there cannot be healing. Without lessons, there cannot be learning. The coming generation may avoid a greater catastrophe than this terrible war, simply *because of it.*"

"Maybe. Maybe not . . . Did World War One teach *us* anything?"

Riley frowned. "Historians are mistaken in numbering them as though they were different conflicts. This war started in 1914 and has been going on ever since. One mustn't mistake the lull between battles for peace. By 1918 both sides were too exhausted to continue for a while, that's all.

"We have seen dark days, son, we children of this bloody century. Not one, but two generations, have suffered. I take your point. But mine remains. Without autumn and winter, there cannot be spring. Without death, there cannot be new life. Without darkness, what meaning would there be to light?"

Wilson began to feel a dull throb behind his eyes, but he had to smile. "You're throwing more questions at me than answers, Padre."

Riley smiled as well. "Without questions, there can be no answers, can there?"

"There's another one."

"We're put on this earth to seek answers, Major Lindberg." He glanced at his watch.

"Am I keeping you from something, Padre?"

"I have a funeral service at 1300 . . ." He sighed. "The poor fellows that crashed on takeoff yesterday."

Wilson rose from his chair. He shook his head sadly. *"They* don't have any more questions to ask."

Riley walked him to the door. "I have faith that they are beyond confusion now. The light of final understanding has come to them."

"I hope so."

Riley opened the door. "Feel free to come back tomorrow, son."

"I fly tomorrow, Padre."

"Ah . . . well, God be with you and your crew."

"Thank you. Maybe the day after."

"Yes, that would be fine."

Outside the quonset hut, Wilson blinked in the midday glare, wondering if he should try sick bay again, head for the barracks, or take whatever comfort he could find in the boozy camaraderie of the Officers' Club.

He frowned. "Eat, drink, and be merry, for tomorrow you die. . . ."?

He turned toward the O-Club. The odds were heavy that he'd have a whole sleepless night ahead of him to contemplate Father Riley's words. In the meantime, a glass or two of beer wasn't going to be as hard to understand as life, death, or God were.

Chapter XXVI

Yaroslavsky Station
Lenningrad, USSR
July 24, 1945

I

Yuri looked across the crowded platform of the Yaroslavsky Station, searching the mingling Leningraders for a familiar face. The smell of unwashed bodies and wet wool was strong. A soft drizzle was falling from twilight skies, but the crowd meeting the troop train was oblivious to the weather. Joyous reunions were taking place everywhere as clusters of people hugged weary soldiers returning from the war.

Leningrad was in the middle of summer's "white nights," the period of weeks before and after the summer solstice when the northern city on the Baltic enjoyed twenty-one hours of daylight out of twenty-four.

He checked his watch. It was past midnight, but surely someone would be here. He'd written from Berlin two weeks ago when he'd learned he'd get leave, telling his parents and sister that he expected to be home by the twenty-third or fourth.

After an hour of waiting, Yuri began to worry. The crowd was thinning rapidly, most of them already homeward bound with long-lost fathers, brothers, and sons.

He slumped onto a bench, worn out by the long train trip and the emotional excitement of imminent reunion with his family. Maybe they hadn't gotten his letter, maybe they were at home, oblivious to his arrival. . . . Perhaps he'd better start out. Were any buses still running, or would he have to walk the whole way?

He heard a trembling voice behind him call his name uncertainly. He whirled around.

"Natasha?"

"Yuri?"

He jumped to his feet and wrapped his arms around his sister. She was frail, her frame gaunt. He could feel her ribs through her tattered coat. He pulled gently away and looked down at her. "You have grown, Natasha, I hardly recognize you."

She smiled through her tears of joy and relief. "I was only twelve when you left, Yurochka. I'm almost sixteen now."

He looked past her. "Where are Mother and Father?"

Natasha blinked at him, her smile fading. "What?"

Yuri grinned. "Mother. Father. You know, our parents," he joked, overjoyed at being home at last.

Natasha stared at him. "You don't know . . . ?"

Yuri stared back. "Know what?"

"You didn't get my letters?"

A faint sense of apprehension surfaced in Yuri's mind. The few letters he'd received had been heavily censored, whole sections blacked out by some anonymous political officer. It was commonplace.

"I got some letters, but . . ." Yuri's voice trailed off when he saw Natasha's stricken reaction.

"Oh, Yuri . . . I thought you knew. . . ."

Yuri braced himself for the worst. "What happened?" he choked out.

"Father was arrested, Yuri."

The news hit him like a hammer blow. "Arrested?"

"They took him away over a year ago. . . ."

Dazed, Yuri sank back onto the bench. "Where is he?"

"We don't know, Yuri." Natasha sat down beside him. "All

we know is they sentenced Father to ten years for anti-Soviet activity."

"Impossible . . ." Then Yuri thought of Pugo . . . no, it wasn't impossible, it wasn't impossible at all, not with thugs like Boris Pugo running around loose.

"Mother . . . ?"

"She is home. She is not well, Yurochka. . . . Since Father was taken, she hardly eats." Natasha frowned. "Not that there is much to eat anyway."

"Have you heard from Father at *all?*"

Natasha began to cry again. "One letter, Yurochka, one letter is all they have forwarded to us."

"What did he say . . . ?"

"All they allowed was a short note. . . . He is alive, somewhere in the camps. That's all we know."

Yuri's shock turned to growing rage. A harmless school teacher thrown into the Gulag like a common criminal. . . . He rose to his feet. "Come, Natasha." Arm in arm, they walked off the platform into the twilight of the streets. Yaroslavsky Station was no place to discuss such things. Informers were everywhere, but especially at places like train depots, where people, tongues loosened by reunions and happiness, might say something they shouldn't.

In the cruel half-light, Natasha told Yuri of the ordeal of Leningrad, of the nine-hundred-day siege, of the mass starvation that first terrible winter of '41-'42.

"They say a million died, Yurochka. . . ."

Beyond shock, Yuri nodded grimly. He'd heard terrible rumors, but had believed the official communiques concerning "heroic Leningrad," standing fast against the Hitlerite hordes.

The brief night had fallen by the time they reached the third-floor flat Yuri had left over four years before, an oversized thirteen-year-old off to join the Red Army. Yuri followed Natasha through the doorway. The flat was dark but for an oil lamp glowing atop the kitchen table.

There at the table, her face lit softly by the lamp, sat his mother, thin lips trembling with emotion at the sight of her son. He rushed up to her as she rose from the chair and wrapped his arms around her. Her frail shoulders shook with her sobs.

"Mother . . ."

"You're home, Yurochka!" she cried, looking up into his eyes. "You're really home. . . . Oh Lord in heaven, you're home at last." She clung to him, her long years of desperate hope rewarded, her countless prayers answered. "If only your father were here, Yurochka . . . if only. . . ." Her voice trailed away, and she buried her face in his chest, wetting his tunic with her tears.

"There will be an amnesty, Mother," Yuri whispered, hardly daring to hope. "There always is after a great victory. Father will be home too. He will be with us soon."

II

Arkady looked up from his bowl of turnip gruel as the shadow of a fellow *zek* swept across the mess table. He blinked his eyes from the brightness of the naked light bulb hanging from the ceiling above and behind the man, then froze, his spoon poised midway between his bowl and his mouth, as he looked up into the hard eyes of Sakar Ushka.

The Mongolian sat down across from Arkady and leaned forward menacingly. "Where's your friend, shithead?"

Arkady lowered his spoon to his bowl, flinching from the odor of rotting teeth wafting toward him as he fumbled for a reply. "Which friend?" he finally managed.

"The bastard who earned me a tenner, that's who!"

His breath was overpowering. Arkady leaned away in disgust. "Well, you've got about ten years to find him, Ushka," he replied, determined not to be intimidated. A *zek* who let himself get pushed around would never see the end of his sentence. "I wouldn't worry about it if I were you."

"Careful, old man, or I might have to pound your face in for you."

Arkady returned the glare. Ushka scared him: the ex-guard was a powerful brute, broad shouldered, with hands like bear paws. But he was a marked man himself. It was a miracle he'd survived as long as he had in the camp population—former guards were inevitably found dead in their bunks one morning, throats slashed from ear to ear by some *zek's* homemade knife.

"Why don't you just let it be, Ushka?"

Just then Kolya entered through the mess hall door, saw Arkady, and headed his way. Ushka was sitting with his back to the door—Kolya didn't see the Mongolian until he reached the table.

"Well," Ushka snarled, standing up, "there's the whoreson himself!" The Mongolian towered over the wiry Kolya, who stepped back in surprise.

His heart racing, Arkady stood up as well. Faces turned toward the trio from up and down the long table. Several *zeks* rose to their feet.

In seconds Ushka found himself circled by ten or twelve prisoners. His eyes darted around him, his ruddy face, weathered by too many winters in the far north, paled. "Listen, comrades," he stammered, feeling all the accusing eyes on him, "this is none of your affair."

"Maybe it is. Maybe it isn't."

Ushka turned to find himself facing Romanenko, a Ukrainian with arms like tree trunks, a barrel chest, and a look of hatred on his face. Romanenko, a full head taller, looked down at Ushka and jammed a finger into his chest. "Where's your Kalashnikov now, worm?"

Ushka backed away, but found his way blocked by a solid wall of *zeks*. Murmurs began to rumble across the mess hall as word spread that the murderer of five brother *zeks* was among them. More *zeks* gathered around, and the murmurs grew to ugly taunts.

Romanenko stepped forward. "What's the matter, Ushka,

don't you care for our company? Why the sudden hurry to leave? You haven't even had your gruel yet." He picked up Ushka's bowl. "Here, let me help you." He hurled the contents into Ushka's face, splattering the watery yellow liquid all over the Mongolian, then slammed the bowl down onto his head. "And here's a new hat for you."

A warder stuck his head out from the kitchen, alarmed at the disturbance. Seconds later, two others shoved their way past the edge of the crowd and disappeared through the doorway.

"Guards are on their way, Romanenko!" someone shouted. The Ukrainian looked ready to kill. He grabbed Ushka by the throat and started to shake him like a rag doll, before Arkady, Kolya, and the rest pulled him off.

"They'll throw you in the cooler," Arkady pleaded, stepping between Romanenko and Ushka. "He's not worth it. He's just not worth it!"

Romanenko glared sullenly at Ushka, but made no move toward him. A term in the cold, dark dampness of the cooler meant almost certain tuberculosis.

"Here they come!" voices shouted from the doorway.

Kolya pulled Romanenko away. Ushka saw his chance and shoved his way past them, then ran for the door. By the time a squad of armed guards burst through the doorway, he'd slipped away in the darkness and everyone was seated again.

The squad leader's questions led them nowhere. The *zeks* reported the fracas as a simple quarrel over a spilled bowl of gruel. The warders, stool pigeons to a man, hadn't seen enough to finger anyone.

The squad leader, a lanky Uzbek, had been around long enough to know when to press and when not to. He satisfied himself with a brief tongue-lashing and led the squad out again. The less fuss made the better—charges meant questions from his superiors, questions meant written reports, written reports meant an inquiry. Who knew where it all would end? The job was shitty enough without looking for trouble.

Seated together, Kolya, Arkady, and Romanenko watched the

guards shuffle out. When the mess hall door slammed shut behind them, the mess hall erupted immediately in excited chatter as the *zeks* hooted over the guards' ignominious exit and Romanenko's rough handling of the hated Ushka. Several came by to pound the Ukrainian on the back in congratulations, but he sat in stolid silence, oblivious to everyone around him.

Puzzled at his lack of reaction, one by one they drifted off to their tables. Calm quickly returned to the crowded hall. Soon the only sound was the low murmur of hushed voices.

Kolya, sitting next to Arkady, looked across the table at Romanenko. "I thank you, comrade. The bastard would have broken me clean in half."

Romanenko nodded woodenly.

Arkady stared disconsolately at his half-empty bowl of gruel. "We haven't seen the last of him, I'm afraid," he muttered. He looked over at Romanenko. "I thank you as well. He would have done for me too."

Romanenko seemed to shake off his black mood. "He hasn't seen the last of me either, comrades."

"You don't have to get involved, he—"

"I *am* involved." Romanenko's thin lips compressed in white-hot anger. "The rat killed a friend of mine, a fellow who saved my life in Stalingrad. One of your work gang, he was. Ivan Petrovich and I fought side by side from the Volga to the Vistula. . . ."

Arkady glanced at Kolya, then back at Romanenko. "You knew Kalinin?"

"He was like a brother to me."

Kolya shook his head. "Poor Kalinin. Never bothered anyone. You remember him, don't you Arkasha?"

Arkady nodded. "We shared the same saw a few times."

"And now he's rotting out on the taiga, food for wolves," Romanenko said. "Thanks to Ushka and his itchy trigger finger."

"What are you going to do, comrade . . . ?"

Romanenko met Arkady's direct gaze. "Nothing stupid," he

said at last. "But Ushka isn't long for this world, I'll tell you that. He's murdered one brother too many, comrades. One brother too many. . . ."

Arkady pushed away his bowl of gruel. Despite the rumbling in his stomach, his appetite was gone. He felt ill—sickened by the hatred and brutality that ruled Penal Camp Ust-Izhma, the bitterness that made beasts of men and fed the jaws of hell with a daily ration of emaciated souls. He was worn down by a demonic system that set brother against brother, that ruled by those dark angels Fear and Coercion, that polluted the basic goodness in men by drowning them in the filth of a false gospel and made them the hapless agents of their own destruction.

Chapter XXVII

US 20TH Air Force
Tinian, the Marianas
August 6, 1945

I

Wilson Lindberg looked up from the latest issue of *Stars and Stripes* as his bombardier, Captain Hank Callahan darted into their Quonset.

"Hot damn, have you heard, Lindy?"

"Heard what?" He saw the excitement on Callahan's face and knew something big was up. Hank Callahan was the kind of man who wouldn't bat an eye if a grenade went off under his bunk. Lindberg sat up in his chair and took his feet of the desk.

"The 509th dropped some new kind of bomb on Hiroshima. Scuttlebutt has it that the whole damned city's gone!"

"What . . . ?" Wilson stared at him. Visions of the horrible hour over Osaka returned to haunt him. He could almost smell the burning flesh. . . .

Callahan grabbed Wilson's service cap from the table by the door and tossed it to him. "Come on, let's go over there and get the scoop."

Wilson caught the cap, then set it down on the bunk beside him. "Go ahead, Hank. I think I'll just stay here."

"Aw, what the hell, Lindy, you *still* in the dumps about Osaka?"

Wilson stuck his nose back in his newspaper. "What if I am?"

Callahan came up to the bunk. "Jeez Louise, Lindy, how long you gonna stew about *that?* Hell, you're starting to act like *we* started this damn war."

"Look, go over there if you want, Hank. I'm not interested, okay?"

Callahan stared down at him. "You know, you're not the only guy on this base who's had a bellyful of the war, Lindy!"

Wilson looked up from the paper. "Never said I was."

"Well, you're sure as hell acting like it."

"Look, what do you want me to do, Hank? You want me to go down to the 509th with you and smoke and joke about another fried Jap city?"

Callahan went white with anger. "Goddammit, what's your problem, Lindberg? Ever since Osaka, you've been moping around like some monk without his monastery!"

Wilson returned the glare. "Leave me alone!"

"Not until you tell me what the hell is going on!"

They glared at each other for several seconds. Wilson was the first to look away. Callahan stood over him, confused, hesitant. "Look," he said at last, breaking the painful silence, "I just thought I'd ask, all right? Just forget it."

He headed toward the door.

"Hank . . . ?"

Callahan stopped in the doorway, his back to Wilson.

"Yeah . . . ?"

Wilson grabbed his cap, feeling like a self-righteous jerk for reacting as he had. Hank hadn't liked Osaka any more than he had, none of the crew had.

"Wait up."

They walked out to the waiting jeep and climbed into the bucket seats. Callahan started to turn the key, then paused. He glanced at Wilson. "This sounds big, Lindy, real big. It could end the war."

"Let's hope so, Hank, let's hope so." Wilson slapped him on the shoulder. "Buy you a beer later?"

"You're on."

Callahan fired up the jeep and gunned it across the sprawling bomber base toward the 509th. "There's brass up the yazoo over there," he yelled over the rumble of the engine. "Lots of reporters too."

Wilson saw most of the 509th's B-29s parked at their revetments as they neared. He remembered hearing two or three planes taking off around 0400, thought nothing of it, and went back to sleep. As they pulled to a stop, he saw only three empty revetments. Yet Hank said the whole city was gone. How in hell could the 509th have destroyed Hiroshima with only three planes? He shuddered at the thought. What fiendish new gimmick had Lemay come up with now?

The jeep skidded to a halt next to a group of officers. Beyond them, a larger group was gathered at the end of Runway 2 Left. "Hey, Captain!" yelled Callahan over the idling motor. "When are they due back?"

"They're about thirty minutes out, Captain."

"How many planes went out?"

"Three. The one with the bomb, a weather plane, and an observer plane."

Wilson's mind balked at the reply. He stared past Callahan at the captain.

"One bomb?" asked Callahan.

The captain nodded.

"You're shittin' us! What the hell kind of bomb can blow up a whole city?"

A major named Waller spoke up. "It was an atomic bomb."

Wilson stared blankly at him. "What in hell is an atomic bomb?"

"It's a device that releases energy when an atom is split by fission. The bomb the *Enola Gay* dropped on Hiroshima this morning released energy equivalent to twenty thousand *tons* of TNT."

Wilson stared at him. "Twenty thousand *tons?* "he heard himself ask.

Waller nodded.

"Holy Christ . . ."

"How many of these things do we have?" Callahan asked, awed at the power of such a weapon.

"Couldn't tell you even if I knew."

"How the hell do you *split* an atom?"

Waller shrugged. "Damned if I know, I'm just a lowly navigator. All I know is you don't want to be within *miles* of that baby when it fixes to split."

Wilson paled suddenly. If the 509th was a special atomic bomb squadron they must have some of the damned things stored somewhere on Tinian. What if one went off? What if the *Enola Gay* had crashed on takeoff? The whole damn island would have gone up. . . .

Callahan looked past Major Waller at the storage Quonsets ringing the 509th's B-29 revetments. The same thought seemed to be on his mind as well. He spoke before Wilson could.

"How are these contraptions triggered?" he asked, eyeing the Quonsets uneasily. "I mean, hell, how do you guys control it when an atom decides to split? We could be sitting here and . . ." His voice trailed off.

"All I know is they aren't armed until the plane is airborne." Waller shrugged. "I don't know diddly about the scientific mumbo jumbo involved."

The airmen gathered around them relaxed somewhat, but glances drifted frequently toward the Quonsets. Waller grinned. "I know you fellows were steamed at us never getting sent along when you headed for the Empire. Or maybe a little disgusted at some of the special treatment we got, or the fact that we avoided the other squadrons. But hell, we didn't have a choice. When we got assigned to this, we found out quick that a guy would land in Leavenworth with a lifetime pass if he blew the secret. We had people watching us all the time: OSS spooks, Army G-2, MPs. . . . Hell, we couldn't take a leak without filling out a report in triplicate. The 509th isn't a bunch of stuffed shirts, guys, we're not prima donnas who thought we were too good to associate with you. We simply didn't have any choice."

Wilson flushed in embarrassment. He remembered giving the 509th guys a hard time more than once. "Hey, I want to apologize, Major. We've all been pretty unfair to you."

"Forget it. We'd have felt the same in your shoes. No one likes to see another outfit get special treatment, especially when it looks like they're sitting on their asses doing nothing." He grinned again. "All you ever saw us do was take off in twos or threes and come back after what must have looked like a joy ride over the ocean, while the rest of you were pulling three raids a week over the Empire. Well, after today, you might not have to go anymore. If the Japs don't give up now, we'll drop another bomb or two on them. They'll see the light soon enough."

Wilson made an effort to ignore Waller's callousness, telling himself it was just habit. War hardened people, especially strategic bomber crews.

He nodded gravely. "Okay if we hang around a while, Major?"

"Sure."

Hank pulled the jeep off to the side of the tarmac. They looked out to sea. Sunlight sparkled off the waves. Seagulls soared placidly over the water, their cries carrying faintly to shore on the breeze.

"Hey, I'm sorry I lost my temper, Lindy." Callahan cut the engine. "Guess the shit's been getting to all of us, huh?"

"Yeah." Wilson drank in the tranquillity of the day, unwilling to think of the latest horror unleashed on Hiroshima. If it meant peace, maybe it wasn't so bad. . . .

"You gonna get out when all this is over, Lindy?"

Wilson watched the gulls winging gracefully over the bay. He sighed, thinking of all the plans he'd made. He'd had it all figured out—he'd make lieutenant colonel, get his own squadron, go to the War College in a few years, maybe even make general someday.

"I don't know, Hank." His eyes began to fill. He pulled his sunglasses out of his shirt pocket and put them on. "I just don't know anymore. . . ."

II

Bill Lindberg, Reggie Blackwell, and Al Foster stood in the shadows of the new USO Club on Okinawa, leaning against the side of the Quonset, passing a flask of Jim Beam bourbon around. The sky was studded with stars. Out in the harbor, the fleet of warships and transports gathered for the invasion of Japan was ablaze with lights. Searchlight beams crisscrossed the darkness over the ships, swinging wildly to and fro in celebration of VJ Day.

The aluminum walls of the Quonset vibrated steadily with the blare of big band music as an impromptu band of sailors and marines played Glenn Miller and Tommy Dorsey tunes for the people jammed inside and the mingling throng out in the compound.

Bill Lindberg took a long pull of bourbon and handed the flask to Blackwell. His head buzzed pleasantly from the liquor. The soft breeze off the harbor reminded him of summer evenings camped out on the shore of Lake Michigan back home. He closed his eyes, drinking in the sensations of the night, his foot tapping to the driving beat of "In the Mood," his back pressed against the trembling walls.

The war's over . . . it's finally over. . . .

Oblivious to Bill's sudden silence, Blackwell tipped the flask back, only to find it drained of all but a drop of bourbon. "Oh, way to go, Billy boy," he said, staring at the flask in frustration. "You drank us clean out of booze."

"Huh . . . ?" Bill's eyes blinked open. Confronted with the

evidence, waved upside down in front of his face, he shrugged happily. "Sorry, Reg."

"Gentlemen . . . ?"

They turned toward Al Foster. With a flourish, he pulled another half pint of Beam from his back pocket and held it aloft in triumph. "A good marine such as myself never runs out of ammunition!"

Blackwell threw an arm around Foster's shoulder. "All right, Alvin!" He winked. "You know, it might not be a bad idea to start rationing Private Lindberg here, before he drinks us dry again."

Grinning, Bill took a step toward Blackwell, who gave him a friendly shove. He tripped over his own feet and stumbled backward, then landed on his rear right in the path of two nurses coming around the corner. The one on the left, not seeing him lying there in the shadows, walked right into him and stumbled headfirst onto the ground beside him.

Her friend, standing over them, started giggling. "You sure fell for *him,* Sally!"

Aghast, Bill picked himself up and helped the nurse to her feet. "I'm sorry, Lieutenant, sir," he blurted, visions of lengthy KP duty dancing in his head.

The nurse brushed off her skirt, then regarded Bill with flashing eyes, trying to ignore the helpless laughter of her friend. She glanced at Foster and Blackwell, standing stiffly at attention, eyes wide, then back at Bill.

"Well don't just stand there, Sally, have him shot," sputtered her companion.

"It was my fault, Lieutenant, sir," offered Blackwell, stepping forward.

Sally ignored him. "What's your name, marine?" she asked Bill.

Bill saluted. "Private William Lindberg, sir."

"Well, Private, may I ask what you were doing there on the ground?"

"I . . . uh . . ."

Sally waited, staring him down.

"I must have tripped, Lieutenant, sir. I'm sorry."

"Seems to be contagious." Sally's friend giggled.

"Begging the lieutenant's pardon, sir," Blackwell volunteered. "Like I said, it's my fault. I gave him a little shove."

"A *conspiracy,* Sally! Have them *all* shot."

Sally glanced at her friend, convulsed in tipsy laughter, but found her eyes drawn again to Bill. He looked so contrite. . . . "Private Lindberg," she said, a twinkle in her eyes, "what do you have to say for yourself?"

Sensing her fading resolve, Bill decided to throw caution to the winds. After all, what could they do to him, send him to Okinawa? "Well, sir," he explained, straight faced, "tripping women was the best way to meet them back home. Force of habit, I guess. . . ."

Sally's friend roared. Even Sally had to laugh.

"Well, Private Lindberg," she replied, smiling broadly, "considering that it's VJ-Day, I'll overlook your tactics and compliment you on the results." She turned toward her friend. "Your defender here is Lieutenant Barbara Thompson."

Lieutenant Thompson nodded at Bill. "In recognition of your courage on the field of battle, Private, considering your courage in refusing to retreat in the face of superior forces, I hereby bestow upon you and your comrades in arms the temporary rank of lieutenant."

"Temporary, sir?" Bill asked, playing along.

"Promotions will expire when that flask the lieutenant is trying to hide over there is empty," she explained, grinning at Al Foster.

They found a spot to themselves down on the beach, away from anyone who might be such a stickler for regulations as to report the fraternization of officers with enlisted men.

They talked and laughed and drank as the stars twinkled overhead and the spotlight beams from the fleet offshore danced off the scattered clouds. Al Foster passed out within an hour, unnoticed by the others. Not long after, Reggie Blackwell and

Barbara Thompson wandered off down the beach, leaving Bill and Sally alone.

They greeted the first faint light of dawn together, admiring the amber glow in the eastern sky. As the sun finally peeked above the gray sea, Bill worked up the courage to kiss her.

Pulling gently away after the lingering kiss, Sally smiled up at him. "It *took* you long enough, Captain Lindberg."

"You're beautiful, Sally. . . ." Bill mumbled awkwardly, lost in the warmth of her embrace, the sweet sensation of her lips on his.

"I bet you say that to all the lieutenants you trip on VJ-Days."

"Only the ones who promote me, Sally." They kissed again, long and passionately, then sat side by side, hand in hand, savoring the beauty of the first sunrise of peace.

III

Sinclair Robertson sat in the lounge of the Palace Hotel in San Francisco, feeling out of place in a barful of civilians. For three years, first in London and then in countless rear area officers' clubs in France, he'd drunk elbow to elbow with servicemen. But as he scanned the crowd, he saw only a handful of uniforms among the suits. Even more unusual was the fact that everyone spoke good old-fashioned American English.

"Excuse me, is this place taken?"

Well almost everyone, Sinclair mused. *That* accent was pure Boston Irish. "It is now. Have a seat."

"Thanks." The man smiled gratefully. He waved down the bartender and ordered a martini. "And get my friend here another," he added, tossing a fifty-dollar bill on the bar. He turned toward Sinclair. "What'll you have?"

"Gin tonic I guess, thanks."

"My pleasure."

Sinclair noticed him wince as he sat down. The fellow had the look of a former serviceman, but in a way he didn't. His suit was expensive, but didn't seem to fit him right and the tie was a horrible mismatch. Probably some rich kid who'd spent the war as a staff officer to some general in the Pentagon.

The bartender brought their drinks and blinked as he was handed a five-dollar tip. "Thank you, sir!"

"You're welcome. Just keep them coming 'till I say stop, all right?"

"Yes, sir."

He turned again to Sinclair. "You from the Bay Area?"

"No, I'm here covering the United Nations conference."

"Well! So am I, as a matter of fact." He raised his glass to Sinclair. "I thought I'd run into a reporter or two here. Here's mud in your eye." They clinked glasses.

"Working for a Boston paper?" asked Sinclair.

The smile, rivaling Ike's now world-famous grin, flashed across his tanned face. "Do I sound like I am?"

"Sure do."

He laughed. "Actually, I'm on assigment for the *Chicago Herald-American.*"

"Got much experience?"

"None. Just got out of the service." He did a double take at a table of women who'd been glancing his way with obvious interest. "Remind me to send those ladies a drink, will you?"

"Sure thing." The guy had style. Maybe he'd be able to line up some companionship for the both of them.

"How long have you been in the business?"

"Since '41. Covered the war for *Harper's.*"

"Oh yeah? Europe or the Pacific?"

"Europe."

"Pacific myself. PT boats."

"See much action?"

The cub reporter took a long drink, his ever-present smile fading. "Enough to get my boat sunk in the Solomons." He waved the bartender over, seemingly reluctant to go into detail about the incident. A round of drinks were duly ordered for his admirers at the corner table.

"So, you think you'll like being a journalist?" Sinclair asked. The fellow's smile returned, but it seemed wistful.

"I'd enjoy it I think, but my father has other plans for me."

"I see."

They watched the bartender deliver the round to the ladies; the ball was in their court now.

"Wants me to get into politics back home," he explained.

Sinclair ordered them a round. "You don't sound too interested."

"I'm not. I don't think I'm cut out for politics. My brother Joe, now he was a natural. . . ."

Was? Sinclair saw the cloud cross his new friend's face. He paid for the round and they sat in awkward silence for a moment.

"Oh, thanks for the drink." He held out his hand. "By the way, my name's Kennedy, Jack Kennedy."

"Sinclair Robertson." They shook. "Kennedy . . . Kennedy . . ." The name was vaguely familiar, a Joseph P. Kennedy had run the S.E.C. for FDR, been ambassador to Great Britain a few years back. . . . "You any relation to Ambassador Kennedy, Jack?"

A wry smile crossed Kennedy's face. "He's my father. Or more to the point, I'm *his* son." He took a long drink of his martini, set it down thoughtfully, then held up two fingers to the bartender. "We lost my brother Joe a year ago, Sinclair. My father was devastated. . . . Joe was his favorite, his eldest, a natural at anything he did. Dad had Joe's career all planned out—congressman, senator, a run for the presidency somewhere down the line. . . . When Joe got killed, those plans got transferred to yours truly."

Sinclair sipped his gin, at a loss as to what to say. Joe Kennedy had a lot of money, a *lot* of money. He was well connected politically, both in Massachusetts and on the national level in the Democratic Party; getting a son nominated for national office was certainly within his reach. But winning an election was quite another matter. He could throw his influence around to wrangle a nomination, but he couldn't buy a general election.

He glanced at the kid as he paid the bartender for the new round. Jack Kennedy was certainly personable, the type who made a good first impression on people. But could he give a good speech? Could his rail-thin body hold up to the rigors of a long political campaign? He seemed to be in frequent pain, perhaps something to do with his PT boat getting sunk. *That* certainly wouldn't hurt him politically. Not only was he a veteran, but a veteran who'd been wounded in action.

"Drink up, Sinclair." Kennedy was smiling at him, his glass held aloft between them. "Here's to . . ."

"Your political career," Sinclair offered. He tapped his glass against Kennedy's.

Kennedy laughed. "Just the thought of it scares the hell out of me." He set his drink down. "You know how an Irishman campaigns back in Boston, Sinclair? He sings 'Danny Boy' at every union hall and ladies' aid picnic from Cambridge to Dorchester Heights. Gawd, you wouldn't believe it."

"Can you sing, Jack?"

"Not a note. I'll lose by a landslide."

They looked at one another for a moment, then burst out laughing, drawing stares from the other patrons. They managed to stop after several seconds, but the vision of Jack warbling "Danny Boy" in a smoky union hall filled with tattooed longshoremen set them both off again. Sinclair laughed so hard, his sides ached. Then he doubled over as Jack crooned the first words, way off-key:

" 'Oh Danny boy, the pipes, the pipes—' "

"Please stop," Sinclair pleaded, tears of laughter streaming down his face. They howled.

Finally, with their chests heaving, lack of oxygen forced them to stop to catch their breaths. Kennedy wiped his eyes. "Well, now that we've made complete fools of ourselves, perhaps we should apologize to the fair damsels behind us."

Sinclair glanced at the table. "I'm right behind you, Mr. President."

After another fit of laughter, they approached the table. Kennedy flashed his best smile. "Ladies, I'd like to apologize. I imagine the ungodly racket we've been making has made conversation somewhat difficult for you."

"Not at all." The woman who had been facing the bar smiled. "Would you care to join us?"

Part V
Crisis

Chapter XXVIII

Westminster College
Fulton, Missouri
March 5, 1946

I

Winston Spencer Churchill stepped to the podium, clad in a scarlet robe and fortified against the unseasonable heat by a drop or two of gin. The audience, Westminster College students and faculty, as well as a good turnout from Fulton and the surrounding area, greeted the famous man with polite applause.

The former prime minister of Great Britain thanked the assembled notables, including and especially the president of the United States, seated on the platform behind him and fully supportive of the speech he intended to deliver. Then Churchill cleared his throat and launched into the speech itself.

Sinclair Robertson, standing in the press gallery to the left of the platform, scanned the attentive audience as Churchill began to speak. It wasn't every day these people could see a president and a prime minister in the flesh, and their faces were glowing with excitement.

He was only half listening to the famous voice, expecting a wholesome but rather boring speech on the values of higher education and the rewards in store for good students who studied hard. But soon his eyes were drawn from the Missourians to the podium, for Mr. Churchill seemed headed in another direction entirely.

He was speaking of Europe, more pointedly, of Soviet actions in Europe.

Sinclair sat up and took out his notepad. He fumbled for a pen, finally finding one in the inside pocket of his suit coat. He began to take a shorthand account, writing furiously as Churchill reached the peak of his speech.

"From Stettin on the Baltic," the master of oratory intoned, "to Trieste on the Adriatic, an Iron Curtain has descended upon the Continent. Behind that line lie all the capitals of the ancient states of Central and Eastern Europe. Warsaw, Berlin, Prague, Vienna, Budapest, Belgrade, Bucharest, and Sofia, all these famous cities and their populations around them lie in what I might call the Soviet sphere, and are all subject, in one form or another, not only to Soviet influence, but to a very high, and in some cases, increasing measure of control from Moscow."

Churchill's words rang out over the hushed crowd, calling for a fraternal association of the English-speaking peoples to guard against Soviet expansion. Sinclair glanced at Harry Truman. The president's jaw was set, his gaze riveted upon his fellow Missourians to gauge their reaction to their renowned guest's indictment of Soviet behavior.

As Churchill concluded, Sinclair silently thanked his editor for his uncanny prescience. He had resisted the assignment when first offered, not interested in doing yet another journalistic retrospective on the recently ended political career of the former British prime minister. Even the dangled bait of a promised interview had failed to excite him.

But when Chief Editor Jameson Robbins sensed something on the wind he was usually right, so Sinclair had boarded a plane for Missouri, and now, as the old fox had suspected, a major story had broken. Winston Churchill had taken the Soviet Union to task for its postwar boorishness and at the same time thrown down a challenge to President Harry Truman to do something about it. Better yet, an interview with Churchill had already been arranged for Sinclair. He would have a precious ten minutes with the former prime minister that very evening, thanks to the foresight of Jameson Robbins.

At precisely ten o'clock, he was ushered into Churchill's stateroom. The ex-prime minister rose from his chair, his ever-present cigar clenched in his jaws, and thrust a hand out at him.

"Mr. Robertson, come in, come in." Sinclair shook the proffered hand, surprised by the iron grip of the aging statesman.

"Thank you, Mr. Prime Minister."

Churchill nodded toward the chair opposite his. "Care for a drink, Mr. Robertson?" It was more of a statement than a question. Before Sinclair could frame an appropriate reply, Churchill handed him a snifter of brandy. "Beastly hot here, reminds me of South Africa."

"Unseasonably warm, Mr. Prime Minister, "Sinclair agreed, recalling that a much younger Winston Churchill had experienced his first fighting in the Boer War back at the turn of the century. A young imperialist then, a staunch defender of the British Empire, had he not changed over five decades? Was he perhaps seizing the issue of Soviet intransigence in Europe as an excuse to maneuver the United States into propping up the Empire and its far-flung domains? That had been the initial reaction of Sinclair's colleagues in the press contingent. Most of them suspected that Churchill was more concerned with the communist threat to British India, Hong Kong, Singapore, and Palestine than he was with Eastern Europe. After all, what real British interests were there in Sofia or Prague?

Churchill settled into his chair. "Well then, shall we get to the business at hand?"

Sinclair took a sip of brandy, more to indulge Churchill's hospitality than because he thought it particularly appropriate at the moment. "Excellent brandy, Mr. Prime Minister."

Churchill smiled appreciatively. "Medicinal," he replied, winking. "My physician *insists* upon a daily dose of this fine elixir."

Sinclair grinned. He set his glass down on the table between them. "Shall we begin?"

"By all means."

"Mr. Prime Minister . . . immediate reaction toward your remarks today has been mixed. Some people feel that your speech is counterproductive, that it will offend the Soviets and further strain relations between East and West. They claim that the responsible course at this critical time would be to stress the issues upon which we agree with the Soviet Union, not those which foster disagreement and distrust."

Churchill's pink complexion darkened. Anger seemed to flash across his eyes, before some inner control mechanism asserted itself. He leaned forward, his hands on his knees. "I consider myself a student of history, and history teaches us that those who ignore the past are condemned to repeat it."

He frowned, and reached for his cigar smoldering in the ashtray on the table between them. "Have these people already forgotten the lessons of Munich? Have they forgotten what a bitter harvest we reaped when we accommodated tyranny, when we allowed Adolf Hitler territorial concession after territorial concession in the false hope that peace and security could be purchased through the diplomatic equivalent of turning the other cheek? By the time we ran out of cheeks to turn, our political credibility was bankrupt, our desire for good relations and a spirit of cooperation was misread as cowardice."

Churchill stoked his cigar to life, the end glowing cherry red as he drew in. Then he exhaled a swirling cloud of white smoke. " Today we find ourselves in a similar situation. A totalitarian system is establishing control over sovereign lands and peoples beyond its own borders. As the Nazis expanded by occupying the Rhineland, Austria, the Sudetenland, and Czechoslovakia, *without opposition by ourselves,* so is Moscow expanding its power by maintaining occupation troops throughout all of Eastern Europe. My fear, Mr. Robertson, is that through *passive acceptance of these* unilateral measures, taken by the Soviets in violation of wartime agreements between us, we are sending the *same* signal to the Soviets that we sent to the Nazis ten years ago—that appeasement of aggression is *once again* the policy of the Western democracies."

Churchill crushed the remainder of his cigar out in the ashtray. "We must not repeat the tragedy of 1936. Had we stood up to Hitler when he first moved into the Rhineland, we might well have prevented the catastrophe of the world war and the horrendous loss of human life those terrible years inflicted upon mankind. As we now know, Hitler bluffed us into backing down over the Rhineland. His army was a hollow shell, a small, poorly trained, poorly armed conglomeration of conscripts, militia, and paramilitary units."

Churchill sighed, his right fist clenching and unclenching in frustration as he relived the lost opportunity. "Had the French responded with military force," he continued, his voice bitter, his eyes ablaze, "the Germans would have been humiliated, utterly defeated, and Hitler's reputation irretrievably damaged. He would have been crushed before he got started, sparing the world sixty million dead, entire continents in ruins, national treasuries drained, and the human spirit crushed by the specter of six million innocents slain for their religious faith."

Sinclair nodded, jotting down the last of the remark in his special shorthand. He glanced at his watch—time for only one more question. "You have drawn certain parallels, Mr. Prime Minister, between the Soviet Union and Nazi Germany, a tactic certain to draw vehement reaction from Moscow. Furthermore, you have called for an Anglo-American alliance against Soviet expansionism. In your view, is the present geopolitical situation growing so serious that direct conflict between East and West is likely in the next, say, five to ten years?"

Churchill took a sip of brandy. "It would be the greatest tragedy should our differences become so solidified that military conflict ensue." He set the glass down, clamped a fresh cigar in his jaws, and lit up. "Returning once again if I may to the example of history, I would point out that most wars break out due to simple miscalculation, by one side or both, as to the intentions of the other. By my remarks today, I have sought to introduce a policy which will leave no doubt in the Kremlin leadership as to what our position is regarding their illegal hegemony over Eastern Europe. History teaches that stating a clear position leads to war less often than having no clear position. Having no clearly defined policy all too frequently invites an adversary to form his own conclusions, which often prove to be sadly mistaken.

"So, I of course hope, and expect, that we can resolve our difficulties without resort to arms. But our first obligation is to those ideals upon which our civilization has been founded—personal freedoms, religious freedoms, government by the consent of the governed, and all the other inherent human rights set down in our constitutions. Should these sacred rights be threatened, they will have to be defended. For to allow tyrants to trample them at will is to betray our heritage, to make a mockery of the ideals our ancestors fought and died for and for which our own generation has sacrificed so much. . . ."

The famous voice dropped in timbre as Churchill concluded, leaning forward earnestly, his cigar clamped in the corner of his mouth, his hands forthrightly on his knees. "I am confident that our forebears will not find us wanting. We shall meet the challenges ahead and we shall prevail, no matter what the cost, for our cause is just, Mr. Robertson. Our cause is just."

II

Bill Lindberg climbed into the cab, gave the cabbie Sally's address, lit up a cigarette, and looked out the window as the cabbie pulled away from the train depot and swung into traffic. Minneapolis looked a lot like Grand Rapids, except on a larger scale. The people seemed friendly—most Midwesterners were. He hoped Sally's parents weren't the exception.

As the train had chugged across Indiana, Illinois, and Wisconsin, he'd rehearsed appropriate responses to every possible parental reaction to his arrival. But by the time the train had crossed into Minnesota, he'd resigned himself to total and complete disaster, convinced that he would undoubtedly make the worst impression possible and have to endure an entire weekend in embarrassed disgrace.

As the cab crossed Hennepin Avenue, he struggled to get control of himself. After all, Sally had sounded excited when he'd phoned from the depot and assured him for the hundredth time that her parents weren't going to devour him raw.

He snuffed out his cigarette and popped some Wrigley's gum into his mouth. She was right. How bad could it be?

Five minutes later the cab pulled up to a white, two-story house. Bill glanced at the meter and handed the cabbie a five-dollar bill with a shaking hand.

"You're white as a sheet, pal. What's wrong?" the cabbie asked as he made change.

"Meeting my girlfriend's parents."

"Ah . . ."

"Keep a buck for yourself, sir."

"Thanks." The cabbie handed him the rest. "Look, I'll bet they're as nervous as you are, buddy. Relax!"

Bill managed a smile. "Maybe you're right. I hadn't looked at it that way." He climbed out of the backseat, feeling much better. "Thanks."

"You bet." "Gotta go. Good luck." The cab pulled away, leaving Bill alone on the sidewalk. He remembered the terror of Iwo and smiled at the thought of the ridiculous panic he'd endured all morning. No matter what happened, he wasn't going to get his ass shot off today.

Sally met him at the door with a smile and a hug for moral support. "Nervous?"

"Yeah."

"Dad and Mother are on the back porch. I saw the cab pull up and haven't told them you're here yet." She took his hand and he followed her through the living room and kitchen and out onto the screened-in porch.

Her mother glanced up, then rose from her wicker chair in surprise. "You must be Bill," she said, a welcome smile on her face. She was plump, her naturally blond hair done in a permanent wave, her dress simple but pretty.

"Yes, ma'am." They shook hands as Mr. Lindquist rose from his rocker.

"Arthur Lindquist," he said, extending his hand. There was no smile.

"Bill Lindberg, sir. Nice to meet you."

Mrs. Lindquist cast a bemused glance at her husband, then smiled at Bill again. "My husband smiled once in '27, I don't recall the occasion."

Bill wasn't sure whether to laugh or not. Mrs. Lindquist saved him the decision by apologizing for not greeting him at the door. She turned to her daughter. "Sally, why didn't you call us when Bill's cab drove up? Heaven knows what he must think."

"Oh, Mother."

"Don't give it another thought, Mrs. Lindquist."

Arthur Lindquist gestured toward a chair. "Sit down, Mr. Lindberg."

"Thank you." Bill sat down as Sally giggled.

"Mr. Lindberg? Daddy, his name is Bill. Would you call him Bill, please?"

Arthur Lindquist frowned at his daughter. "I always call a man I've just met by his last name. Who doesn't?" He looked Bill in the eye. "So you're the fellow Sally met in the Fae East, eh?"

"Yes, sir."

"What do you do, son?"

"For goodness sakes, Art," Mrs. Lindquist said, "you're giving the poor boy the third degree and we haven't even offered him anything to eat or drink, or asked him how his trip was." She turned to Bill. "We have Coca-Cola, coffee, iced tea, or something stronger if you'd prefer. Supper will be ready at six. In the meantime, I'll bring out a plate of sandwiches if you'd like."

"Oh please, ma'am, just a Coke would be fine."

"You must be hungry—"

Bill held up his hand. "No, I had lunch at the depot, Mrs. Lindquist. Just a Coke, thank you."

"Okay." She turned to her husband. "Arthur?"

"I'll have a beer and a sandwich."

"Sally?"

"A Coke, please, Mother. Oh, do you need any help?"

"No, I'll bring a tray out."

Mrs. Lindquist vanished into the kitchen. Sally pulled a chair next to Bill's and sat down beside him. "So what do you think of Minneapolis, Bill?"

"Seems very nice." Her perfume stirred memories of VJ Day. He looked into her eyes for a moment, remembering it all. She seemed to be thinking the same thing, and flushed ever so slightly.

"Here we are." Mrs. Lindquist returned with a tray of Cokes, sandwiches, and beer. Sally handed Bill a Coke, Mrs. Lindquist handed her husband his beer and an egg salad sandwich.

"Thank you, Mrs. Lindquist." Bill held up his bottle of Coca-Cola. "I remember dreaming about one of these all the time when I was overseas. A Coke . . . it seemed so, well, so out of reach, like something on another planet."

Mrs. Lindquist beamed. "He's very easy to please, isn't he, Sally? I like him."

Arthur Lindquist cleared his throat. They looked his way. "Can I ask the young man what he does for a living now, Lucille? Or can't a man indulge his curiosity in his own house?"

"Arthur, don't be silly." Lucy Lindquist waved off the jibe good-naturedly.

"I'm working in a filling station right now, Mr. Lindquist. I hope to start classes at Michigan State in Lansing next term."

"Are you satisfied that Bill's not a hobo now, Arthur?"

The senior Lindquist grunted. He began to reply, but Sally cut him off. "Bill," she said, glancing at her father, "did you know Daddy was in the Marine Corps?"

"No, I didn't." Bill took a sip of Coke, feeling more relaxed. They had something in common at any rate.

"World War I. France. Right, Daddy?"

"Yeah."

Sally's eyes narrowed. "Well, isn't it interesting that you and Bill were both marines?" She stared expectantly at her father.

Arthur Lindquist's eyebrows rose. He set down his bottle of Hamm's and looked at his daughter. "I thought you said he was in the navy. . . ."

"No, I didn't, Daddy. I told you he was in the marines." Sally shrugged, oblivious to the rivalry between the two services. "Anyway, what difference does it make if Bill was in the navy or the marines?" She stared at her father, confused at the sudden animation in his eyes.

Art Lindquist noticed Bill's widening grin and started laughing. "What difference does it make . . . ? What difference does it make!" He leaned forward in his chair, a twinkle in his eye. "Tell my daughter here the difference between a United States Marine and a swabbie, Bill!"

Bill, pleasantly surprised at the sudden transformation in Arthur Lindquist, set down his Coke. "Well, Sally, it's like this. Sailors aren't too popular with marines."

"Damn right. Ain't met one I liked yet!" Art Lindquist turned toward his wife. "Well, don't just sit there, Lucy, get the boy a beer!"

Lucy Lindquist excused herself and headed toward the kitchen. On her way past Sally, she winked. Sally stared after her a moment, then jumped from her chair and vanished through the doorway after her mother.

Bill listened as Arthur Lindquist began to tell sailor jokes. By the time the women returned, they were laughing together like long-lost comrades. Sally sat down beside Bill. He took her hand.

Everything was going to be all right, she thought, smiling happily. All because Bill wasn't a sailor!

III

Wilson Lindberg stared through the glassed-in nose of the B-29 at the sparkling sea twenty-five thousand feet below. Twisted like a broken necklace of emeralds, the islands of Bikini Atoll glittered in the tropical sun, almost lost to sight amid the vastness of the Pacific.

His headphones crackled with last-minute instructions and Wilson applied left rudder. The B-29 banked gracefully to the west until it was on a heading which would bring it into a position where it would be upwind of the test area at zero hour.

He pressed the intercom button at his throat. "Pilot to crew, let's get the goggles on." He pulled down his dark-tinted protective goggles and checked the clock on the instrument panel before him.

Thirty seconds . . .

Major W. P. Swancutt, commander of *Dave's Dream* droning high over Bikini Atoll some five miles to the east, felt his B-29 leap upward as its cargo, America's third atomic bomb, plunged from the forward bomb bay and whistled earthward. He pulled the bomber into a steep, banking dive to put as much distance as possible between Ground Zero and *Dave's Dream* before the bomb, now descending beneath a parachute to slow its fall, went off.

In *The Big Stick,* Wilson Lindberg felt his heart begin to pound in anticipation. The handful of pilots who'd witnessed an atomic explosion had been at a loss to describe the experience. The crews who'd gone to Hiroshima and Nagasaki, of course, had been under such intense pressure to perform flawlessly that their strained psyches couldn't be expected to respond to descriptive analysis of the results. Today was different. Observation of the explosion and its effect on the ships moored around the atoll was the primary goal of the witnesses.

Wilson watched the cockpit clock tick down to zero and stared through the tinted goggles at the tranquil atoll below. An eternity seemed to pass. He turned to glance at the cockpit clock, wondering if it was on the blink.

An unearthly light flooded the cockpit.

"Gawd Awmighty!" crackled over the intercom. Wilson turned toward Bikini just as the flash faded. A massive, writhing column of blue-gray vaporized seawater was billowing skyward, even as its churning base obliterated from sight the anchored warships at the atoll.

Wilson stared at the rapidly expanding mushroom cloud, hypnotized by the sight of tons of gaseous seawater hurtling toward the stratosphere. The behemoth broiled upward, building upon itself, twisting inward even as it curled outward, seeming to reach up for the sun itself, to grasp the offending light in its writhing embrace and plunge the world into darkness.

Seconds later, the shock wave slammed into *The Big Stick,* tossing it sideways like a toy. The world spun crazily through the cockpit Plexiglas. Shocked by the impact, Wilson tore his gaze from the hell over ground zero. He squeezed the control column between his knees and yanked it sideways, jammed his feet against the rudder pedals, and wrestled the big plane back to level flight.

Sweating, stunned, his heart pounding like a runaway jackhammer, he looked to the east to find the summit of the mushroom cloud already at eye level and still rising. Far below, Bikini Atoll was hidden by the widening base of the monster, now several miles wide.

Wilson shuddered. Could he really drop one of these things on a city?

As the intercom came alive with the awed reaction of the crew of scientists and observers aboard, Wilson Lindberg knew he couldn't. Until that moment he hadn't been sure. He'd buried his doubts deep inside, telling himself that he had a job to do, that he was a pilot, that if worse came to worst the moral issues were on the shoulders of other men, not his.

But Osaka still haunted him, the smell of burnt flesh had never really left him; the ghosts of faceless civilians would go with him to his grave. *He* had been the man dropping fire and death, not General Lemay, not President Truman. *He did it, he was the instrument of destruction.*

Wilson stared fixedly ahead, unhearing, unseeing.

"You okay, Lindy . . . ?"

He turned toward his copilot, Lloyd Pruitt.

"Huh? Oh, yeah."

"You sure? You're white as a sheet."

"You don't look so hot yourself, Lloyd."

Pruitt stared past him at the cloud churning relentlessly skyward some ten miles away. "God in heaven, that . . . *thing* . . . must be ten miles high."

Wilson forced himself to look one more time at the beast. It did have a certain terrible majesty to it.

He frowned, fighting the seductive appeal of the demonic spectacle. Who were men to presume the right to unleash such a deadly force upon the world? This thing was godlike, its elemental might dwarfed its creators. Once set free, who would be able to control it . . . ?

The sound waves finally reached them. A low, growling rumble swept through the cockpit, then faded away, smothered by the steady drone of the four Wright-Cyclones.

To Wilson, it sounded like a moan of warning, as though the soul of the world itself had spoken.

Chapter XXIX

Leningradsky Prospekt
Moscow
March 6, 1946

I

The gleaming black Packard limousine sped down the center lane of the Leningradsky Prospekt, trailing a long motorcade in its wake. Every third car was a Packard identical to the one privileged this night to carry Joseph Vissarionovich Djugashvili to his isolated *dacha* at Zavidovo. To foil assassination attempts, Stalin chose one of the armored Packards at random before leaving the Kremlin for his *dacha* or vice versa. No one, not even his closest comrades, would know in advance which armored limousine would be carrying the Supreme Leader.

Stalin had considered it obvious that he was most vulnerable to the plots of his enemies when traveling, thus the elaborate precautions. He was not about to fall victim to a "tragic automobile accident" or be blown to smithereens by some cleverly concealed bomb. Not now. Not especially now, with Hitler defeated and Western Europe in ruins, ripe for socialist revolution. Everything was falling into place as the forces of history demanded. All of Europe would be his in a year or two. In the Far East, Mao would be a puppet whose strings he could pull to bring all of China and Indochina into the Soviet sphere. The backward African continent, ripe with minerals, was virulently anticolonialist and there for the taking. By his seventieth birthday, if all went well, only the Americas and perhaps England would remain to be dealt with.

Stalin frowned as the Packard slowed. He glanced out the tinted rear window. A heavy snow was falling despite the bitter cold weather of the past few days. Blue-haloed street lamps flashed by.

If some bumbler had failed to keep the route cleared of snow, he would soon find himself shoveling the streets of Irkutsk with a spoon. Stalin's smile of anticipated vengeance faded. Could something more sinister be afoot? Khrushchev had been acting strangely lately. So had Beria . . .

His throat tightened as he pictured the motorcade blocked ahead, while traitors in league with his rivals raked the trapped motorcade with machine-gun fire from the flanks.

The Packard accelerated and Stalin was soon at ease. His thoughts returned to the strategic moves he must make to fulfill the iron laws of history. There was one fly in the ointment, one fat *English* fly! That devil Churchill had the American simpleton Truman in his clutches, hissing in his ear, provoking him into a harebrained scheme to plunge the world once more into war.

Well, if they wanted a war, he would give them one, the devil take them! But it would not be the kind of war they expected. Until he possessed the bomb, direct conflict with the West must be avoided. The wise course would be to lure the West into unwinnable guerrilla wars through proxies such as Mao in China.

Stalin smiled as he lit his pipe, savoring the rich tobacco flavor as he stoked it to life. The ideal scenario would be for the West to get dragged into the civil war in China. A war on the Asian continent would bleed the imperialists white while the Soviet Union recovered from her struggle against the Hitlerites. Then, perhaps in three or four years, he would have atomic bombs of his own and would be in a position to give as well as he took in a final showdown with the imperialists.

If the Americans knew that a strike on Moscow would cost them New York, if a devastated Leningrad meant a devastated Chicago, would the harsh reality of atomic stalemate lead to a renewed isolationism and the withdrawal of the United States from world power politics as was the case after 1918? It was quite possible, if the USSR had the atomic bomb and could produce them as quickly as the Americans.

That was the rub. Stalin's smile faded at the thought of American atomic bombs rolling off the assembly lines like so many sausages. How many bombs did Truman have? What kind of lead would he have by the time Beria's spy networks delivered the great secret of atomic fission to Moscow? If Truman had one hundred bombs by the time he had five or ten, what hope was there in winning an atomic war? Yes, the USSR was a huge country, capable of enduring terrible punishment, but a basic infrastructure of industry and agriculture had to survive for the crippling of the imperialist beast to be worthwhile. . . .

Stalin pondered the results of a full atomic exchange. Even at a ratio of five or ten to one against, the Soviet Union, with as few as ten bombs could destroy the major industrial and population centers of the American northeast, while the Americans would have a harder time destroying Soviet industry, even with a hundred bombs, since the Nazi invasion had forced the relocation and wide dispersal of Soviet industry into the Urals.

Perhaps the final confrontation could be forced far sooner than he'd thought. The centralization of American industry was their Achilles' heel. Truman could be held hostage to the vision of a crippled economy and millions of American dead. American society could not survive such losses. The Soviet Union could. Twenty million had died to defeat the Hitlerites. If another twenty million must die to defeat the imperialists, that would still leave two hundred million survivors.

Stalin's smile returned. One becomes a great leader when one finally understands that the ends justify the means. Since world

communism was the ultimate goal of mankind and the culmi-
nation of the laws of history, it mattered little that a single generation suffered, if the results of their sacrifice benefited the
countless generations yet to be born. It would be criminal to
spare the present generation if it meant condemning *every* generation to follow to capitalist oppression and slavery.

Still, one must be cautious. The Motherland had been devastated by the Hitlerites—heavy industry was still in tatters. Soldiers could be replaced quickly, but it took years to rebuild
factories.

Stalin took a contemplative puff of his pipe, to find the bowl
cold, the tobacco consumed. Frowning, he stuffed the pipe in
his pocket, and took out a package of American Lucky Strikes.
The pipe had long ago become part of his image, so he continued to smoke pipe tobacco, but he preferred cigarettes, *American* cigarettes.

The Packard slowed as it reached the outskirts of Moscow.
Out in the more open areas of the outlying districts the wind
was fierce. No longer restrained by the urban sprawl of the
inner city, the wind howled with reckless abandon, buffeting
the heavy Packard and piling drifts over the road. Visibility fell
drastically as the motorcade experienced the full fury of the
blizzard.

Stalin peered out the window, fuming at the delay. He could
see nothing but white. The air seemed a solid wall of windblown
snow. Several minutes passed as the motorcade crawled forward,
following the heavy plows clearing the way to the *dacha*.

The hour drive took nearly four hours, but Stalin never considered turning back. One accomplished nothing by retreat. Success depended, he'd learned long ago, on relentless
perseverance, on brute force.

He smiled in grim satisfaction as he entered the *dacha,* then
turned in the doorway and looked out for a moment at the
grounds of Zavidovo, buried under ten-foot drifts. As the wind

howled in his ears, and the driven snow whipped past his boots into the *dacha,* he raised a hand and extended a finger in obscene contempt for the blizzard.

"Fuck you," he muttered, glaring out at the fury of nature. "I am Stalin! I am *Stalin!"* he roared, shaking his fist at the elements. He slammed the door closed behind him.

Nature must not have heard him. In the morning, it took the KGB guards two hours to dig him out.

II

Yuri walked along the south bank of the Towper Canal, remembering the bitter fighting of May, 1945. Thoughts and faces of those days flashed through his mind—the German woman he'd saved from rape . . . the treachery of Igor Konstantinov . . . the euphoria he'd felt when the guns had fallen silent at last and he'd known that he'd survived.

The weather was cold; a heavy overcast hung low over the linden trees. The mood in occupied Berlin was as somber as the weather as the first winter of Soviet occupation waned. He'd passed several Berliners, not a one had so much as acknowledged his presence. He'd noticed quickly that Soviet soldiers were ignored by the populace, treated as if they weren't there. Only when actually addressed would a Berliner deign to speak to a Russian, and then only in the briefest of replies.

Yuri sighed. The attitude of the people was understandable, but just the same, it annoyed him to be treated like a leper because he was a Russian and they were German. The war was over—a war begun by the Germans. If anyone had a right to be bitter, it was a Russian such as himself. But he was willing to put the war behind him and turn a new page, to treat the Berliners as fellow human beings, and get along in a spirit of friendship.

Instead, he was a nonperson, an object of contempt and hatred simply because he had fought to defend his country against the Hitlerite invaders.

He found himself standing on a familiar corner. Most of the rubble had been cleared away. The demolished homes were now vacant lots, but the street was still recognizable. It was here, in a dark cellar halfway down the block, that he'd confronted Konstantinov and Rogev.

What had become of the woman? Had she lost her husband in the war? Had she herself even survived the last days? Yuri walked down the street and stopped where the ruins of the house had stood. All that remained was the foundation of the cellar, the cement ringing an empty hole in the ground.

He stood there, trying to remember her face, but all he could see was a dark form struggling under that lout Konstantinov, his fist smashing into her face, the look in his eyes when Yuri had pulled him off and shoved the barrel of his Kalashnikov under his nose.

He felt an odd compulsion to seek her out, to find her. But what was her name? Without a name it would be all but impossible to find her. Even then, if she weren't in East Berlin, he would not be free to search. He was a garrison soldier, not permitted to travel beyond the Soviet sector of the capital.

Yuri walked back toward the house on the corner, one of the few still intact in the area. Perhaps one of the people still living here knew of her, remembered her. He paused outside the house. Even if they did, why would they tell a Soviet soldier? Would they not be suspicious of his intentions and deny they knew her, even if by some chance they did?

He walked to the door. Couldn't hurt to ask.

An elderly woman appeared in the doorway, eyes wide in fear. Yuri smiled. "Good day, *frau.* . . . I am looking for a friend," he stammered in passable German, having picked up a fair portion of the language during the war, and then on his own back in Leningrad. "I was wondering if you could help me?"

Someone spoke from inside. The woman turned and spoke

rapid German which Yuri had trouble following, but he picked out enough to understand that she wanted the man to get rid of him somehow. The man appeared behind her in the entry hall. He was a man in his middle years. He told the woman to go back to the kitchen, then smiled obsequiously at Yuri.

"May I be of some assistance?"

"Yes, please." Yuri looked him in the eye, anxious to make a good impression. "You see, I was here, in '45. . . . I . . ." He paused as the man's eyes clouded over, obviously remembering the brutal assault, the frenzied rapes, the sacking and pillaging of his city. "I was here, on this street on May third," he explained quickly. "I discovered two of my men mistreating a woman who was hiding in a cellar down the street and stopped them. I . . . that is, I was wondering if you might know her. I've wondered all this time what became of her, her family . . . her first name was Kathe. . . ."

The man stared at him for the longest time. Yuri's hopes rose. If he knew nothing, he'd have said so right away. He seemed to be fighting some inner battle, debating the wisdom of telling a Russian anything. His eyes took in the absence of officer's epaulettes on Yuri's tunic. It seemed to make up his mind.

"She spoke of you once, long afterward. But I'm afraid I am not certain where she is now. Her husband came and they left soon after."

"Then she's all right." Yuri smiled in satisfaction. It was a relief to learn he hadn't risked his neck only to have some other soldiers finish the job Konstantinov couldn't. She had survived after all.

"Do you know where they are? I would like to write her. Them." He shrugged, searching for a way to explain. "It is time to put the war behind us, our peoples must become friends, we must have peace now. Enough have died."

The German hesitated a moment, appraising him. "Come in for a moment," he said at last, pulling the door all the way open. "I'll see if my mother has their address." Yuri followed him into the kitchen, and sat down when his host nodded toward the chairs around the kitchen table. He tried not to hear the conversation coming from the other room, but couldn't help but discern that the older woman wasn't about to give the address to a Russian, while her son maintained that it wasn't right for her to decide.

Yuri's hopes fell as her voice grew increasingly strident, then fell silent altogether. He rose as the son appeared in the doorway, embarrassed.

"I am sorry, I don't have the address for you." He shrugged, his eyes rolling toward the room behind him. "Come."

Yuri followed him outside. "Look," he said, "the best I can do for you is be a message bearer. I will pass along whatever you wish to Frau and Herr Dietrich. If they wish to reply, that is their business, and yours. Fair enough?"

Yuri smiled. "Yes. Thank you."

"Well?"

"Oh. Well, just tell Frau Dietrich that Sergeant Yuri Arkadovich Rostov is back in Berlin and hopes that she and her family are well. Tell her that I . . ." Yuri paused. This was getting too complicated. He frowned at the complexity involved in just saying hello to an acquaintance. "Just tell them that I am here and say hello."

"I'll do that." The German smiled. "Good day, Yuri Rostov."

"Good day."

Yuri lingered on the step a moment, then walked down the sidewalk, turned north, and headed back for his barracks. The old woman's voice echoed in his ears. She distrusted all Russians, that much was plain. But perhaps she had good reason for her feelings. Who knew what horrors she had seen when Berlin had fallen? Who knew if the poor old thing hadn't been raped herself?

Yuri forced her from his mind. He had come here on a long shot to find out about Kathe Dietrich and on his first try had stumbled on someone who knew where she was. She had survived! He could reach her if he wished. Not perhaps directly, but it was a start.

His spirits soared. He had a friend in Berlin, a woman who owed her life to him. Certainly she and her husband would offer him some refuge from the boorishness of barracks life, even if only a few times a year.

Chapter XXX

The White House
Washington, D.C.
January 4, 1947

I

Harry Truman's hand shot up, cutting off Chairman of the Atomic Energy Commission David Lilienthal in midsentence. "We have *four* atomic bombs? You're standing there and telling me that two years after Los Alamos we still have only *four* atomic bombs? I'll be a son of a bitch. . . ."

A painful silence ensued—the only noise in the Oval Office was a muted crackling from the fireplace opposite the president's desk. A brisk wind buffeted the French doors that opened onto the Rose Garden. Standing beside Lilienthal, Secretary of Defense James Forrestal stared abjectly at the Oval Office carpet.

Lilienthal cleared his throat. "Four operational bombs, Mr. President. . . . Several others are in various stages of completion."

Truman took off his spectacles and tossed them on his desk. "What in hell have those fellows been doing out there in that desert since '45?" He rose to his feet, his anger rising. "If Joe Stalin decides to throw us out of Berlin tomorrow and chase us all the way to Paris, what in damnation am I going to do about it? Send in the 82nd Airborne? Call up the National Guard? Jesus Christ and General Jackson! We don't have an ice cube's chance in hell of keeping Stalin out of Western Europe unless he knows we can hit Moscow with B-29s. The only leash on the Red Army is our atomic bombs, and you're standing there telling me we have a whopping total of four of them!"

"We were as shocked as you are, Mr. President," said Forrestal. "The problem is, Los Alamos has lost a lot of people since the war ended. Many of the project's top scientists have returned to civilian life, leaving too many critical positions vacant. Production has suffered accordingly."

"Well, this just can't get out. The national security of the United States and the freedom of Western Europe may well depend upon our possession of atomic bombs—*enough* atomic bombs to prevent the Russians from taking advantage of their superiority in ground forces."

He turned from his guests and looked out across the Rose Garden. When he spoke, his voice was low but intense. "We have to light a fire under Los Alamos. Get those people off their asses. Find out why so many of the original team have left and do what it takes to get some of them back. In the meantime, until a sufficient rate of production is restored, we must see to it that this appalling information stays out of the press."

"What about Capitol Hill, Mr. President?" asked Forrestal.

Truman turned to face them. "I am a former congressman, gentlemen. I have the highest regard for the legislative branch and the abilities of those who serve there . . . but by God, we're sitting on a powderkeg here. If this leaks out, we'll all be up the creek without a paddle." He shook his head sadly. "We'll fudge the figures if we have to. I don't like it, but there it is."

"If *that* gets in the press the Republicans will have a field day, Mr. President."

Truman glared at Forrestal. "I don't give a damn about the press or the Republicans. I *do* give a damn if Joe Stalin finds out we have four bombs and sets the Red Army loose."

Agitated, the president gripped the back of his chair. Atomic bombs were inhuman weapons, but by God, if he had to use them, he would damn well use them. He wasn't about to go into the history books as the man who stood by while Stalin spread godless communism worldwide.

"All right, gentlemen, are we clear on this? I want more atomic bombs and I want them now. The more we have, the more Stalin *knows* we have, the more likely he is to behave himself."

"Yes, Mr. President."

"Well, get cracking."

Lilienthal turned to leave.

"Give me a call tonight," Truman added, before dismissing the chairman. He turned to Forrestal. "How's General Marshall's plan coming along?"

Forrestal filled the president in on the progress of Secretary of State George Marshall's plans to provide massive economic aid to rebuild Europe. The war-torn continent lay in ruins, its economy shattered, its people scraping out a meager existence in the ruins.

"It's a breeding ground for trouble," muttered Truman as Forrestal concluded. "We've got to do whatever it takes to get Europe back on its feet."

"We're about set to present it to Congress, Mr. President." Forrestal paused. "The only loose end to tie up yet is whether we offer to include the Russians."

"It'll look like hell if we don't. . . ."

"Congress won't like it."

"No country suffered more devastation than Russia," Truman replied, sitting back down in his chair. "The way I see it, if we help them now, they might not be tempted to plunder what's left of Europe."

"I see your point—feed the hungry Bear before it looks elsewhere for honey."

"Exactly." Truman frowned. "I doubt Stalin will take us up on it though. He needs a foreign threat to unite his people behind him. He always has, and we're the only possibility left him. Still, it's worth a shot."

"If our friends on the Hill know he's likely to refuse help we just might be able to include Russia in the package," Forrestal hinted. "Otherwise, I don't know if it would pass."

"We'll work that angle on them then. It's important that the offer be made." Truman pulled a handkerchief from his coat pocket and began to clean his glasses. "Okay, the Marshall Plan's on course. What about this spy business?"

"We're still working on the details with the agencies involved and people on the Hill, Mr. President, but a consensus seems to be forming."

"Good." Truman sighed. "I don't like it, I don't like it at all, but we've just got to have a larger, centralized intelligence-gathering apparatus. We've got to keep an eye on the whole world now. We can't afford to have all this competition and infighting between Naval Intelligence, Army G-2, the FBI, and the OSS anymore. This new Central Intelligence Agency will fit the bill. We can combine all of our intelligence assets into one agency." Truman put on his glasses. "But I damn well want sufficient Congressional oversight on those people—an espionage system is dangerous. By its very nature it's a threat to civil liberties."

"The CIA's authority won't extend to domestic spying, Mr. President," Forrestal reminded him. "All counterintelligence and internal security authority is vested in the FBI."

"Hell, I know that." Restless, Truman rose from his chair again and began to pace. "It's just that I fear we're opening a Pandora's box of troubles here. I know the Russians are masters at this spying game and that we've got to fight fire with fire, but we've got to make damned sure we don't wake up one day to find an American KGB in our midst. Congress will have to watch those spooks like a hawk."

The president turned again toward Forrestal. "What about this new Defense Department business, how's that coming along?"

"The services are against it, but Congress is ready to pass it."

Truman nodded. "Some of those folks at the Pentagon need

reminding now and then who's running this country. By God, if the generals and admirals ever quit fighting each other for a few minutes, we might be able to get something done." He resumed his pacing. "We can no longer afford to allow inter-service rivalries to fester like they have. We need one boss, a secretary of defense, to keep them all in line."

"Congress agrees, Mr. President. Reorganization of the military should become law by summer."

"No problems with an independent air force, equal under the secretary of defense with the army and navy?"

"It'll pass too."

"High time, if you ask me. The air force is our first line of defense now. We can't have a bunch of army generals running the show anymore."

Truman turned toward the French doors behind his desk and looked out onto the white blanket of snow covering the Rose Garden. More snow had begun to fall, heavy flakes swirling down from the leaden skies, driven on a rising north wind.

"Getting worse, Jim," he muttered, his back to Forrestal.

"There's a storm coming down from Pennsylvania, Mr. President. I'm afraid things are going to get worse before they get better."

Harry Truman smiled bitterly at the irony. The same could be said about the postwar world. "I guess we'll just have to ride it out, Jim."

"Yes, Mr. President."

Truman watched the wind whipping across the sleeping garden, stark and colorless in the icy grip of winter. "I miss the roses, Jim."

"Spring's coming, Mr. President."

The president shivered. "Not today, Jim. Not today . . ."

II

Arkady Rostov staggered through the knee-deep snow of the taiga forest, puffing heavily through aching lungs as he dragged a section of sawed-off tree trunk toward the nearest pile. Any deep breath of the frigid air set him to coughing, so he took short, shallow breaths as he struggled along. His partner, Kolya, looking up from the hewn sections of the tree they'd felled that morning, set his saw down, and came over to lend a hand.

Along the frozen Pechora River, winter was in its deepest days. The thermometer back at the main camp had registered thirty-three below zero at sunrise, yet the ragged black columns had been counted, frisked, and sent out into the taiga. Only during a full-scale blizzard, when the snow drifts isolated the logging camps from the main camp and the winds cut the visibility to nothing, did the *zeks* remain inside.

This was not one of those days. Despite unearthly cold that froze any exposed skin in three minutes, that rendered metal saws so brittle that they snapped at the slightest strain, the *zeks,* bundled up in every rag they could lay their hands on, plodded through the morning.

"You should have reported in sick last night, Arkasha," Kolya scolded, his vaporized breath drifting away on the wind as they set the log next to the pile. "You'll catch pneumonia for sure if you keep working like this."

Arkady sank down onto the log for a moment, wheezing from the strain. The constant trips across the thirty meters of deep snow between their tree and the pile of lumber, combined with his heavy cold, was quickly draining what little reserves of strength three years in Penal Camp Ust-Izhma had left him.

He looked at Kolya through watery eyes and started to explain, but a sudden coughing spell doubled him over. Clouds of vaporized breath burst in rapid sequence into the frosty air. "I would have," he gasped, recovering enough to speak, "if that weasel Ushka hadn't wangled an orderly job there."

"I forgot Ushka was there."

"I haven't."

Kolya spat in disgust. The stream of saliva glazed in midair, steamed for a moment in the snow, and froze solid in seconds.

"Romanenko should have done for that bastard when he had the chance."

"Well, he's long gone to the Kolyma now."

"You two! Get to work!"

They looked up to find the escort commander glaring at them from across the lumber pile. *"Do you louts think this is a rest home?"* he bellowed, stalking toward them, waving his arms.

They got up quickly. It was too cold to sit still for long anyway. He followed them to their tree, gloved hands stuffed again in the pockets of his greatcoat, shapka flaps pulled down over his ears and forehead, lumbering along through the snow like a great white polar bear.

"What are your numbers, *zeks?!*" he demanded as they reached the tangle of cut logs and branches lying in the snow. "I'm going to write you up!" He brushed off the powdered snow clinging to the backs of their peacoats. "Oh . . . it's you fellows," he said, his anger fading. Arkady and Kolya were two of the better workers in the gang, not known for goldbricking.

"My comrade is sick," Kolya explained as they turned to him. "He shouldn't even be here."

"Who isn't sick?" The escort commander's mustache had caught the steady breathing from his nostrils and was coated in frozen frost, the brush of white icicles completely hid his upper lip. He glanced at Arkady, saw the rheumy eyes, the sagging posture, the ragged breathing, and shook his head. If anyone was a candidate for a week in the camp infirmary, it was K-578.

"I don't want to see you here tomorrow, 578," he said. "You are the property of the State, your body is not your own. I'm ordering you to the infirmary. Report in as soon as we get back." He trudged off toward the fire his guards kept stoked outside the perimeter, muttering at the idiocy of some *zeks*. Most of them howled for a day or two off if they had a hangnail and here was 578, obviously sicker than a dog, out in thirty-below cold.

Arkady picked up his saw and began trimming the branches

from the next section of trunk. "Thanks, Kolya, now I'm in for it."

"I'm sorry, Arkasha, maybe I shouldn't have said anything to him."

"Well, it's too late now."

Kolya picked up his saw. "Look, if you catch pneumonia out here, you're a goner. This is Ust-Izhma, not Leningrad."

"I'm a goner at the infirmary too—Ushka will stick a knife in me the minute my eyes are closed." Arkady sawed through a branch and watched it drop to the snow.

"Maybe you could talk to the doctor about him. If old Krasnov finds out Ushka has it in for you, the bastard won't dare do anything."

"I wouldn't count on it."

They worked through the bitter afternoon, exchanging few words, each lost in his own thoughts.

Finally, as the pale yellow sun waned above the western wastes, the escort commander had enough and called it a day an hour early. The inevitable head count was conducted as thoroughly as ever, but the frisking ritual was waved. The *zeks* were formed up in marching columns and sent slogging back toward the main camp.

It was pitch dark by the time Arkady left the mess hall to report to the infirmary. Kolya walked beside him under the stars, determined to have a word with Krasnov if Arkady wouldn't.

"He won't see you," Arkady argued as they neared the cabin.

"I'll report in sick too."

"He'll see through it. You're not sick."

"It'll give me a chance to talk to him."

They stepped into the entry. Clouds of steam billowed around them as the freezing outside air met the warmer air inside.

"Close the damned door!" A trustee glared at them from behind a desk of knotty-pine planks. Kolya shut the door behind them.

"We're here to see Dr. Krasnov," he declared, taking off his cloth cap. "By order of Comrade Belyanin."

"You'll have to wait," the man grunted, waving them toward a crowded bench in the corner. Several *zeks* eyed them sullenly. The infirmary contained only two dozen bunks. When they were filled, there were no further admissions until a vacancy occurred.

An hour passed before their turn came. One after another, the *zeks* ahead of them were sent back to their barracks. Kolya went in first, emerging short minutes later. "I told him," he said, pausing on his way to the door. "I'm off for the barracks." Their eyes met.

"Thank you, Kolya."

Kolya nodded. "It'll be all right, Arkasha—our friend landed himself in the cooler for filching infirmary supplies. Turns out he had quite a black market going."

"In the cooler, eh?" Arkady asked in relief. "How long?"

"Ten days I guess." Kolya grinned. "Krasnov won't take him back, even if he survives."

"The fool had it made here. . . ." Arkady shook his head.

"I guess he just couldn't resist the temptation—thought he could bribe his way back into the NKVD. Got caught trying to sell a few syringes and some morphine to one of the escort commanders."

"An escort commander!"

Kolya nodded, his grin widening. "The fellow had it in for him and set him up; told him he'd gotten addicted to morphine after getting wounded in the war—promised if Ushka kept him supplied, he would pull some strings and get him his old job back."

"Krasnov told you all this?"

Kolya shrugged. "Our doc gossips like an old woman, probably what landed him here in the first place—"

"You, 578!"

They turned to the trustee glaring at them again from his

desk. Arkady stepped toward the examination room door. "Sorry, comrade, we were just talking."

"This isn't a debate club, *zek!*"

Sarcasm ruled Ust-Izhma.

Kolya patted Arkady on the back. "Make sure you get at least a week, Arkasha."

"This isn't a rest home, Kolya!"

They laughed, drawing another glare from the trustee. Arkady's laughter quickly turned to coughing. He doubled over suddenly, hacking uncontrollably. Kolya helped him into the examining room before being shooed away by Krasnov.

The old doctor, a *zek* himself, examined Arkady and admitted him at once. "Well, you've got pneumonia, 578," he grunted, taking off his spectacles and slipping them into a pocket of his peacoat. "I'll do what I can for you, but we just don't have enough supplies for proper treatment."

Arkady felt almost relieved, despite the sudden knot of fear in his gut. For the first time in one thousand and twenty-four days he was going to get some rest. . . .

He took a shallow breath, just enough to speak. "How long will I be here, comrade?"

Krasnov stared at him. "Perhaps I didn't make myself understood," he said at last. "You have pneumonia. I can't treat it properly. It will probably kill you."

Arkady stared back. The harsh reality of his situation finally sank in in full force, but the instinct to deny it was still strong. "But I don't fell *that* badly, Doc. . . ."

Krasnov shrugged. "You're malnourished, at least twenty or thirty kilos underweight. You don't have the necessary reserves of strength to fight off the disease and I don't have the medicines to help you. If you'd come in sooner . . ."

"I . . . couldn't. . . ."

"Ah, the Ushka business."

Arkady nodded.

Krasnov sighed. "Well, if it's any consolation, that snake

won't last five days in the cooler in this weather, much less ten."

Arkady stared at the floor. "I want to go back to my work gang, comrade."

"Nonsense. We'll put you in a bunk. You'll be as comfortable as possible here."

"Would I make it?"

Krasnov shook his head. "If it were summer . . . if you were a little stronger . . . if my supplies weren't so short. . . ."

Arkady rose unsteadily. He had to grip the examining table for support. "I'm going back to my friends."

"You won't last a week."

"Thank you for telling me the truth, Krasnov." Arkady patted the old man on the shoulder and left for the barracks.

When he got back, Kolya and the others gathered around him, amazed at the apparent vitality he displayed.

"Arkasha, what happened?" Kolya asked, eyeing him closely. "I thought for sure he'd admit you."

Arkady shrugged. "He stuck a needle in me, shot me full of some new antibiotic, and told me to come back every evening for a week or so. Said I'd be a new man in no time."

"Lights out, comrades!" shouted Smirnov, the work-gang leader, walking down the center aisle between the rows of triple-bunks. "Dawn comes early!" He paused at Arkady's bunk. "Rostov, what are you doing here? I thought you were out sick."

"Not too sick to fell trees for Comrade Stalin," Arkady replied with mock enthusiasm, drawing bitter smiles from the *zeks* around him. "We must cut them down without mercy—I haven't met one yet that wasn't an anti-Soviet wrecker!" He thrust a forefinger into the air. "Just think of all the socialist saws they have snapped clean in two, the villains. It's obviously a sinister plot to ruin the Five-Year-Plan."

Smirnov frowned. "You'd better not let a warder or a guard hear you talk like that."

Arkady smiled. The pent-up fears of a lifetime drifted away, the dread of retribution from an all-seeing state and its legions of informers faded to nothingness. He was beyond punishment now. He could cleanse his soul of the lies he'd lived with his forty-eight years. His last days would be days of truth, he would be free at last. . . .

The *zeks* shuffled off to their racks. The bare lightbulbs hanging from the raftered ceiling winked out, leaving them in the gloomy darkness of yet another hopeless night behind the barbed wire of Penal Camp Ust-Izhma. Outside, beyond the windows coated with two inches of ice, the winds howled as they swept across the taiga from the arctic wastes of the Barents Sea.

But Arkady didn't hear the wind. As he drifted off to sleep, he was back once more in Leningrad, back home at the kitchen table by the steaming samovar, with Nina, with Yuri, with Natasha.

He never awoke.

They found him in the morning. Grieving, his friends in Work Gang 571 carried his body with them to the logging camp and when the sun had set and another day of labor had been put behind them, they set him on a bier of logs and kindling and cremated him.

The black column of *zeks,* the growling of their guard dogs heavy on their ears, marched back to camp as the crackling flames consumed their comrade. Across the brittle snow the smoke and ashes of Arkady Pavlovich Rostov rose gracefully into the bitter Siberian air toward the stars above.

Chapter XXXI

Grand Rapids,
Michigan
June 1, 1947

I

The cab pulled up in front of the house and to Bill Lindberg's immense relief disgorged a familiar passenger. Dressed in his new Air Force blues, Wilson Lindberg ran up the walk, carrying a garment bag over his shoulder.

Bill met him at the door. "You made it!"

Grinning, Wilson held up his wrist and pointed to his watch. "Four hours to spare."

"Guess again."

"Huh?"

Bill pulled the sleeve of his tuxedo up past *his* watch and tapped its face with his forefinger. "We're three hours ahead of you, remember?"

Betty Lindberg stepped past him and hugged her chagrined eldest son. "Never mind, Bill, he's here, isn't he?"

Wilson gave his mother a peck on the cheek, then smiled sheepishly. "I guess I almost blew it. . . ." He looked toward the kitchen. "Where's Dad?"

"At the church." Betty Lindberg grabbed her purse and pulled the front door shut behind her. "Where we should be by now."

Bill was sweating freely in his tuxedo as he stood before the altar of the packed church, waiting for the "Wedding March" to begin and Sally to come down the aisle on the arm of her father. The humidity, as ever in Michigan in June, was high. The sweltering heat was bad enough outside, but was worsened by the scores of friends and relatives jammed inside the church. He glanced at Wilson standing beside him as best man, and rolled his eyes. Wilson winked, then leaned toward him. "We'd have jackets on if this were Tinian," he whispered. "Relax."

Bill nodded. Maybe it was more nerves than weather. Then, finally, mercifully, the first notes of the "Wedding March" rang out over the crowd from the organ loft.

When Sally, glowing behind her veil, joined him at the altar and the service began, he forgot the heat and focused his attention on Reverend Halliday. The elderly reverend helped them through with barely perceptible nods at the appropriate moments and the service rolled along smoothly toward the exchange of vows.

When the moment came, the church grew hushed. He listened carefully as Reverend Halliday led Sally flawlessly through her vows. Then came his turn. Halliday turned to him and intoned the first words: "I, William Robert Lindberg, take thee, Sally Lindquist. . . ."

He took a deep breath, then echoed the line in a steady voice. "I, William Robert Lindberg, take thee, Sally Lindquist."

Halliday smiled encouragingly. "To be my wedded wife. . . ."

"To be my wedded wife."

"To have and to hold. . . ."

"To have and to hold."

"Till death do us part. . . ."

"Till death do us part."

"By the powers vested in me, I now pronounce you man and wife." He nodded. "You may kiss the bride."

Bill lifted Sally's veil. Their first kiss as man and wife was long and lingering. Finally, Reverend Halliday cleared his throat. Their lips parted at the subtle hint and Sally looked up at Bill. "Now don't trip me again when we go down the aisle," she whispered.

Bill grinned. "Worked once, didn't it?"

Behind them, Halliday looked over them at the congregation. "My friends, I give you Mr. and Mrs. William Lindberg, Jr."

They turned and walked out arm in arm past their beaming parents, family, and friends.

The reception was brief. Everyone knew they were anxious to get a good day's driving behind them by nightfall.

But after running the gauntlet of rice throwers outside the church, they lingered beside the wedding gift from their parents, a shiny black 1938 Ford sedan, accepting congratulations and exchanging good-byes with everyone.

Bill, uncertain of what kind of future he wanted, had waived his peacetime discharge option and elected to remain in the Marine Corps at least until June of '48, when his four-year enlistment officially expired. With a new wife to support, he wanted the security of a steady paycheck while they got settled into married life. He had to report to Camp Pendleton, California, on the fourteenth. The long drive west would be their honeymoon trip.

One by one the well-wishers departed, until only their parents and Wilson remained. Long separations were nothing new to either family in the wake of the war, but the farewells were tearful just the same.

Lucy Lindquist hugged her new son-in-law. "Take good care of her, Bill," she said.

"I will." He shook hands with Arthur Lindquist.

"Welcome to the family, Bill."

"Thank you, Art. Come out and see us now."

"We'll try."

Sally hugged her parents as Bill turned toward his.

"Oh, Bill . . ." Betty Lindberg kissed her son and wrapped him in her arms.

"Take care of yourself, Mom."

"Now you listen to Sally, you hear?" She pulled away and smiled bravely. "You go back to school when you get out, like she says."

"Okay, okay."

His father put his arm around his shoulder. "Hope you and Sally like the car, son."

"It's beautiful, Dad."

"Wish we could have gotten you a new one."

"Are you nuts? It's a great car."

William Lindberg smiled proudly. "I guess it's all right, huh?"

"Sure is!"

"Well, good-bye, Bill." To his surprise, his father hugged him—William Lindberg had never been the demonstrative sort, especially in public. "You call us collect when you get there, you hear?"

"We will, Dad."

Wilson shook Bill's hand as their father stepped over to say good-bye to Sally. "You've got a great girl there, Bill." He grinned, nodding toward Sally. "How'd a marine ever get a gal like her?"

"He tripped me, remember?" Sally replied, joining her husband. Everyone laughed. The incident was already a family legend. "You ought to try it on some WAAF sometime, Wil. I'll give you a year—if I don't have a new sister-in-law by then, I'll make the arrangements *for* you."

"Uh-oh." Wilson opened the car door for her. "You'd better get your wife out of town before I get in more trouble, Bill."

"I guess so."

Showered with the last of the rice, Bill and Sally climbed into the Ford and, with final farewells ringing in their ears, waved good-bye and drove off.

Sally turned for a last look at her parents and in-laws as Bill turned the corner at the end of the block. "We'll miss you!"

she shouted through the window. They waved back, then faded from sight beyond the trees lining 28th Street.

She slid over to sit beside Bill and he put his arm around her. "Well, Mrs. Lindberg, I don't know about you, but I can hardly wait to get to Des Moines."

She kissed him on the cheek. "Our first stop doesn't have to be Des Moines, honey."

His eyebrows rose in pleasant surprise. "Okay . . . how about Kalamazoo?"

Her hand was warm on his thigh. "How long to Kalamazoo?"

"About an hour."

She giggled. "I think we can wait a *little* longer than that, don't you?"

"I don't know, honey." Bill sighed theatrically. "An hour can be a real long time. . . ."

She snuggled closer. "I'll leave it up to you."

"Great!" He braked and pulled over to the side of the street.

Sally laughed happily. "Don't make me slap you, Bill Lindberg."

"All right, all right." Grinning, he pulled away from the curb. "I'll try to make the state line, how's that?"

"You've got yourself a deal."

II

Yuri Rostov sat on a park bench on the Pottsdammer Platz, watching the couples strolling by, searching the unfamiliar faces with growing disappointment. Every few minutes, he glanced at his watch, wondering if Kathe had gotten his letter, wondering if she and her husband would come, wondering if they even *could* come, or would want to. . . .

He had written that he would like to meet and said that he would be at the park every Saturday afternoon. He had given no address and asked them not to contact him, that it could get him in trouble. Then he dropped the letter in a corner mailbox.

For two years he'd studied German so he could write them, and, if they ever met they could talk freely, as friends.

It was a beautiful day. Yet despite the warm sun, the birdsong and the peaceful serenity of the park, his spirits fell as the afternoon wore on. He began to berate himself for getting his hopes up.

After all, what was he to them?

He frowned. Nothing but a bad memory, a reminder of the horrible days known to Berliners as "The Russian Time," when some fifty thousand German women were raped in and around Berlin by victorious but vengeful Red Army troops. *"Frau, komm!"* had been the dreaded command barked from countless Russian lips. To ignore it was to die.

He sighed. Maybe he *did* save Kathe from his own comrades, but what about the tens of thousands of second-line troops who followed the elite assault regiments into Berlin? With a few exceptions, such as Konstantinov and Rogev, the lead units had been too disciplined, too professional, too proud to stain their honor by rape and pillage. But who knew what brutality she might have experienced when the dregs of the Red Army poured into the city? Who knew what horrors might have befallen her at the hands of those thugs?

And what of her husband? Even if she felt inclined to meet, why should he approve? Why should he want to meet some anonymous Russian, especially if she'd been raped anyway after he'd gone?

Kathe might never even have told him of the incident. Why should she?

Yuri rose from the bench. He'd been a fool . . . his loneliness had led him to assumptions of friendship that couldn't exist— not after the bitter war of extermination between their two countries.

He started walking, too upset to sit still. It was a pity, but probably for the best, for it was forbidden for Russian soldiers to fraternize too closely with the populace. Beyond the ordinary, everyday contacts the troops of an occupation army had to deal with there was a line that could not be crossed. A soldier seen too often with the same Berliners would fall under suspicion, would invite NKVD surveillance, and likely land himself in the Gulag as a spy.

Yuri thought of his father sentenced to ten years in a penal camp on trumped-up charges of "anti-Soviet activity."

His crime?

Nothing more than telling a handful of his students how many of their fellow Leningraders had likely starved to death during the Nazi siege. Such talk, Yuri had learned from one of the students involved, had been interpreted by the NKVD as implied criticism of Stalin's leadership. To criticize Stalin was to criticize the Soviet Union. To criticize the Soviet Union was anti-Soviet activity. Anti-Soviet activity was treason.

Yuri frowned. If such an innocent act as recording the martyrdom of one's fellow citizens was a capital crime, it only followed that having unauthorized contact with former enemies was as well.

Yuri shivered suddenly, despite the warmth of the day. What could he have been thinking? For all he knew some NKVD stooge could be watching him right this minute. . . .

He turned around and headed back in the direction he'd come, anxious to put the whole silly idea behind him. Better to be bored silly back in the barracks than risk the attention of the NKVD. One Rostov in the Gulag was enough.

"Excuse me . . . ?"

He stopped and turned toward the voice to see a young woman rise tentatively from the bench he'd been sitting on not more than a minute before.

"Yes . . . ?"

He didn't recognize her. Despite his decision to forget the whole matter, he was disappointed it wasn't Kathe. A part of him still wanted to see her again—NKVD or no NKVD.

The woman took a step toward him, then hesitated. She seemed to study him for a moment, then a timid smile appeared. "Private Rostov?"

He stared at her. This couldn't be Kathe—she bore no resemblance to the sobbing waif he remembered from the cellar. Her figure was much fuller, her hair longer and lighter in color, her eyes—

He blinked. As long as he lived, he'd never forget the look in her eyes when he'd paused on the cellar stairs and told her his name.

They were the same eyes.

"Kathe . . . ?"

"Yes, it's me."

"You look so . . . so different."

Her smile wavered. "I must have been quite a sight that day."

"I didn't—that is, I meant . . . that . . ." His words trailed away in confusion.

"I know, I know." She gestured toward the bench. "Please, sit down for a minute, Yuri Rostov."

"I'm touched that you remember my name, Kathe." They sat down, half facing each other on the narrow seat. Yuri glanced around quickly. To his relief, no one seemed to be taking any interest at all in them.

"I'll never forget you."

Yuri looked away to hide the tears welling up in his eyes. He affected a sudden interest in the children romping in the grass beyond the pathway until he regained his poise.

"Is something wrong?"

"No." He turned to her again. "Thank you for coming, Kathe. It means a lot to me."

"It was the least I could do. God knows what would have happened that day if you hadn't been there."

"Those were bad days . . . bad days. . . ."

Kathe nodded.

"I would have liked to have met your husband," Yuri added quickly, anxious to change the subject. "He is well, I hope?"

"He . . . never knew. . . ."

"I thought it might be better that way. . . ."

"I should have told him, but—"

"You don't have to explain, I understand." Yuri smiled. "It would have been hard. . . ."

"Gunther was a POW for several months," Kathe explained. "Thank God it was the Americans and not—" She stiffened. "Oh, I'm sorry, I just meant—"

"My own father is in the camps," Yuri cut in. "I'm glad that the same fate didn't befall your husband."

"Your father . . . ?"

Yuri nodded. He looked away again, ashamed to admit that such things occurred in Russia.

"How terrible."

"But he is back now, your Gunther?" Yuri asked.

Kathe took the hint and dropped the subject of Yuri's father. "Oh yes. They held him for a few months and then released him." She found herself looking at the children again. "When he came home, he was terribly depressed." Her voice fell. "He saw the death camps. They put him to work for several weeks, burying the poor people Himmler's beasts had murdered. For the longest time I was afraid he was going to kill himself. He felt responsible."

"He was a soldier, I take it?"

"Yes, a pilot. On the Western Front," she added quickly, anxious to avoid further awkward moments. "Anyway, he was in such a state when he got home that I just couldn't bear to trouble him with my problems."

"I hope you didn't . . . have more trouble. . . ."

Kathe sighed. "He was an officer at least, not a beast. He felt badly afterward, put me to work as a cook for himself and his staff. He protected me—never touched me again. It could have been worse. Much worse."

"I'm sorry."

"So am I, for all the cruelty—on both sides." She shook her head. "Thank God it's over."

"Yes."

Kathe rose. "I must go now. I told Gunther I wouldn't be gone long."

Yuri got up. She rose up on her tiptoes and kissed him on the cheek. "Thank you, Yuri Rostov."

"Thank you again for taking the trouble to come down here."

"My goodness, it was the least I could do." She smiled, reached out, and grasped his hand in hers for a moment. "Your German is quite good, Yuri Rostov."

He blushed with pride. *"Danke . . .* Well, *auf weidersein,* Kathe Dietrich."

"Auf weidersein."

He watched her until she was lost in the crowd of Berliners, saddened at the thought that they would probably never meet again, but grateful for the friendly reunion, brief as it was.

Chapter XXXII

National Airport
Washington, D.C.
June 15, 1948

I

Sinclair Robertson leaned back into the cushion of the window seat and watched the sparkling Potomac drop away below. As the DC-4 banked into a turning climb, he could make out the gleaming white dome of the Capitol at the east end of the National Mall and followed the gray ribbon of Pennsylvania Avenue as it ran northwest from Capitol Hill through the city toward the White House and the river beyond.

He stared down at the tiny Executive Mansion, nestled between the greenery of Lafayette Park and the urban sprawl of downtown Washington. Somewhere down there in that old house, Harry Truman was probably wondering why he had ever left Missouri.

Sinclair frowned. Why was *he* leaving the States? He had enough seniority to beg off the Berlin assignment. He'd paid his dues, covering World War II for three years, from North Africa in '42 all the way to the finish line on the Elbe three years later.

The DC-4 climbed steadily. Sunlight streamed through the cabin windows as the airliner broke through the overcast. Washington was lost to view below the clouds and Sinclair finally eased his grip on the arms of his seat. He'd never liked takeoffs or landings and never really relaxed until they were at altitude or safe on the runway.

He exhaled, drawing an understanding smile from the stewardess passing in the aisle. Next stop, Gander, Newfoundland, then across the North Atlantic to Shannon, Ireland, then to London, then to Berlin. It would be good to be on solid ground again after such a marathon, even if it was the disputed soil of Berlin.

Berlin.

He'd never gotten there in '45 like he'd expected. They'd flown him to San Francisco right after VE Day, then sent him to Japan for six months. Ever since, he'd been in the D.C. bureau. But now, three years later, he'd finally given in to the restlessness that had plagued him since the end of the war, feeling somehow that only by returning to Europe could he close a personal and professional chapter of his life and move on.

He couldn't forget Maggie O'Reilly any more than he could forget the frustration of never having seen Berlin. Both awaited him, twenty-four hours, four landings, and three takeoffs from now.

He smiled wryly. What kind of reception could he expect from either. *If* he survived so many ascents and descents. He'd had no contact with Maggie since '46. . . . Berlin was a bleeding wound draining the life blood of the Grand Alliance and threatening to kill it outright. Would Maggie respond to the telegram he'd sent and meet him at Heathrow? Would Berlin be the Sarajevo of the Third World War?

"Care for anything to drink, sir?"

He looked up to find a stewardess smiling down at him.

"Uh, yes . . . I'll have a gin and tonic, please."

She jotted down the order. "And you, sir?"

The Air Force major in the aisle seat next to him ordered a beer. Sinclair glanced back out the window.

Why had he ordered a gin and tonic? He hadn't had one

since . . . ah, that was it. It had been *their* drink, his and Maggie's. She'd been on his mind and the order had come from his lips automatically.

"Nervous flier?" The major nodded toward Sinclair's hands, white knuckled on the arms of his seat.

" Yeah." He grinned sheepishly.

"Relax, I've been flying for years—only crashed three or four times."

Sinclair stared, not sure if the guy was kidding or not. "Doesn't seem to have cost you any promotions, Major," he said at last, glancing at the silver oak leaves on his collar, then at the multicolored campaign ribbons on his chest. The fellow had seen a lot of action.

"Air Force went through a lot of pilots during the war." The major shrugged. "If a guy lived long enough, promotion was automatic."

"I suppose." Sinclair offered his hand. "By the way, my name's Robertson." They shook.

"Lindberg. Pleased to meet you."

The stewardess arrived with their drinks. Major Lindberg handed her a five. "Keep the change, honey." He turned to Sinclair. "So . . . headed for England, huh?"

"Germany, actually. Berlin."

"Oh yeah? That's where I'm headed."

"Berlin?"

"Frankfurt." Wilson frowned. "Although I've got a hunch I'll be seeing Berlin before too long."

"You still flying or have they got you sitting at a desk now?"

"Still flying—C-54s, the military version of this baby."

"Ahhh." Sinclair grinned. "Maybe I'll sleep better knowing we've got an extra pilot aboard."

Wilson chuckled dutifully. "So . . . what on earth brings you to Berlin, Robertson? If you don't mind my asking."

"Not at all. I'm a reporter."

Wilson smiled wryly. "When you mentioned Berlin I figured you had to be press or government." He took a sip of his beer.

"Berlin's not exactly the place to be right now unless you have to be."

"Think there'll be real trouble?"

"Maybe. Maybe not. What have you heard?"

"You must know more than I do. . . ."

Wilson laughed. "Don't bet on it. Hell, I'm just a pilot. All I know is that the Pentagon is beefing up our transport units over there." He looked expectantly at Sinclair.

Sinclair took a sip of his drink. "It's this currency thing, Major, if you ask me. The Russians don't want economic stability in Germany—or Europe, for that matter. It's in their interests for the whole continent to wallow in economic chaos. That's why they're tightening the screws on Berlin. If Germany's currency is stabilized and hyperinflation reversed, it would be a political defeat for communism, which can only flourish in conditions of mass economic hardship. That's why they're against the Marshall Plan as well. They *don't want* Western Europe rebuilt with American aid, they *don't want* the German economy saved."

Sinclair shook his head. "I'm afraid Berlin is going to be the test of each side's determination to have its way. All of Europe is going to be watching what happens there. If the Russians blockade the city and force the Western Allies out, it will make all of Truman's promises to rebuild Europe ring hollow.

"If the Russians blockade the city, I just don't see how we can stay there." Wilson stared at his beer. "If they block the road and rail routes to Berlin from the west, three million people are going to starve."

"Can't an airlift keep supplies moving?"

Wilson emptied the rest of his bottle into his glass. "Do you know how much food a city of three million people consumes a day?"

Sinclair shook his head.

"Fifteen thousand tons. A C-54 can carry roughly ten tons."

Sinclair did some quick arithmetic. "That's what, fifteen hundred C-54s a day . . . ?"

Wilson frowned. "It would be, if we had that many. Problem is, we only have about two hundred of them, and they're scattered all over the world."

"Looks impossible."

"Can't say I like the odds, Robertson. Look, even if we flew in every C-54, even if we used every old C-47 we had, even if Tempelhof could by some miracle handle *three thousand* take-offs and landings a day, even if the Russians let us fly over their zone of occupation, there's still the matter of electrical power—the Russians control all the city's power plants. They could just turn off the switch and three million Berliners would have no lights, no heat, no nothing." He drained the rest of his beer. "Much as I hate to say it, staying in Berlin is going to depend on whether Truman is willing to fight for it. Nothing short of war is going to keep us there. An airlift is a pipe dream."

Sinclair shook his head. "I bet there's a few people kicking themselves now for letting the Red Army beat us to Berlin."

"No shit."

"I was on the Elbe, you know, with the Ninth Army when Ike pulled the reins in."

"Oh yeah? You covered the war in Europe?"

"From Normandy to VE-Day."

"I was in England myself, flew B-17s with the Eighth."

"Really? I guess I assumed you were in Transport Command the whole time."

"Nope. Did a tour in Europe, then flew B-29s in the Far East 'til VJ-Day."

"I'm impressed."

Wilson shrugged. "Nothing special about it—lots of guys pulled two tours."

"So why'd you transfer from bombers, Major? I'd think, what with all that combat experience, you'd have made colonel by now, maybe even general."

Sinclair saw Wilson's expression darken and instantly regretted his remark. "Not that it's any of my business, really," he added quickly. "Force of habit—reporters ask questions, you know? Sorry if I was out of line. . . ."

Wilson waved away the apology. "Forget it." He paused, recalling Osaka. "I guess I had my fill of it, Robertson. Figured I'd get into transports, maybe fly C-54s for a few years, then land an airline job somewhere."

"Uh-huh." Sinclair flagged down the stewardess and ordered two more drinks. "You know, Major, it's been bugging me the last few minutes. . . ."

"What's that . . . ?"

"Well, your name seems familiar somehow." He laughed. "I'm pretty good at remembering names—got to, part of the job. And yours rings a bell."

"I'm sure we've never met."

"No, that's not it." Sinclair struggled to dredge up the connection. Lindberg . . . Lindberg . . ." You flew B-17s during the war, you said."

"Yeah. Winter of '43-'44." Wilson looked quizzically at Sinclair.

"You would have been, what, a lieutenant, a captain?"

"Captain."

Foggy memories began to stir. Sinclair closed his eyes, shutting out the distraction of the cabin. Captain Lindberg . . . flew B-17s. . . . "I remember hearing something about a Captain Lindberg, I'm sure of it," he explained, opening his eyes again in frustration. "But I just can't remember what."

Wilson grinned at the perplexed look on Sinclair's face. "Must have been some other Lindberg."

"Maybe."

"Had to be. I sure didn't do anything that warranted any press attention."

"No special missions? No spectacular brushes with death?"

"Nope." Wilson shrugged. "I *was* shot down once, but so were about a million other guys."

"Shot down . . . maybe that's it. But hell, I only did one story on—"

Sinclair sat up suddenly. Images of a wrecked bomber in a French field rose in his mind. He saw the face of a young girl, an old farmer.

Could it be?

"Did you happen to crash-land in France? Get rescued by a fellow name of . . . uh . . . Lafleur?"

Wilson stared at him in astonishment. "Why yes." "How did you know . . . ?"

Sinclair grinned in triumph. "I *knew* I'd heard about you!" He gripped Wilson's arm in excitement. "I was with the Third Army in, what . . . must have been August or September, '44. Stumbled across this farmer who had a wrecked B-17 in his field—heard the whole story."

"You met Lafleur?"

"Yeah! Lafleur, his daughter. . . . They told me all about it."

"I'll be damned."

"I even tried to track you down for a week or two. I'd promised the girl I'd try—she wanted to write you."

"Ah, Gabrielle." Wilson smiled.

"Anyway, I guess things just started to happen too fast— never did find you, then forgot about it, I guess. Figured you'd look her up on your own if you wanted to."

Wilson sighed. "Never did . . . got sent to the Marianas right away, then stateside after the war." A plan began to form. Maybe he could get away from Frankfurt long enough to look them up. They *had* saved his life.

Sinclair was thinking the same thing. "Pity," he said. "I sort of feel responsible. Look, it's just a thought, but if you have any interest in seeing them again, I might like to do a story on it. What do you think?"

"I'd like to see them again, but hell, we might be in the middle of a shooting war any day now."

Sinclair's smile of anticipation faded quickly. "I'll be damned if I hadn't almost forgotten about Berlin."

"*I* haven't."

"I guess you've got enough on your mind, huh?"

Wilson noted the chagrin on Sinclair's face. "Look, if Berlin doesn't blow sky high and I can work it out, I'll let you know, all right?"

"That'd be great!"

"When I get to Frankfurt, I'll write you."

Sinclair jotted down his paper's office address in Berlin and handed it to Wilson. "Maybe we'll even run into each other."

Wilson frowned. "If the Russians don't run into us first. . . ."

II

Bill Lindberg sat alone in the waiting room, staring at the delivery room doors, wondering if something had gone wrong. Sally had been in there a long time now. He glanced at his watch. Almost midnight, she was in her tenth hour of labor. . . .

He shifted in the chair, picked up a copy of *Life* magazine, and paged through it again. Hospitals had always made him uneasy. The antiseptic smell, the unnatural silence of the corridors, the paleness of the patients—

"Mr. Lindberg?"

Mrs. Ida Barrow, the head nurse on duty in maternity, was looking at him from the gray double doors of Delivery Room 1.

He jumped to his feet. "Yes?"

She smiled. "Congratulations, your wife has just delivered twins."

Bill stared at the her.

"Twins . . . ?"

"That's right, Mr. Lindberg, twin boys."

He stared at her, mute. Finally, the meaning of the words sank in. *Twins. Two* babies instead of one. "Sally's okay?" he heard himself ask.

"She's fine, just fine."

"When can I see her?"

"Soon. Just sit down, I'll let you know."

"Okay." He sank into the chair. He was a father! Twice!

Twenty minutes later, Ida Barrow led him into the recovery room. Sally, obviously exhausted, lay in bed, a tiny bundle in each arm. "Daddy's here," she cooed, first to one, then the other. He went to her side and looked down at his sons.

"Sally . . ." he fumbled for words.

She beamed. "Aren't they beautiful, Bill?"

"Oh, they are." He reached out to touch the soft little face, flushed red, eyes squeezed tightly shut, tiny fingers clenching and unclenching against the blue blanket. "They're so tiny," he said, wonder in his voice at the miracle she'd given him.

"They didn't *feel* small, Bill."

"Sally had quite a time, Mr. Lindberg," said Ida Barrow. "But she's a trooper, she is. You should be very proud."

"I am. " He leaned over and kissed her. She held up the other for him to see.

"He's the youngest, came into the world three minutes after his brother."

"Your wife needs her rest, Mr. Lindberg," hinted Mrs. Barrow. "She's had a long day. We all have."

"Okay." Bill looked at his family, his heart bursting with pride and love. "Well, we had Matthew picked out for a boy's name, Sally, but it looks like we're one name short."

"How about John?"

"Well, that'd cover two of the apostles," Bill joked. Sally had been big on Biblical names when they'd discussed it. "How about Luke and Mark for the next two then?"

"The next *one* will be a girl," Sally replied.

Bill grinned. "You're the boss. Matthew and John, then?"

"If you agree."

"I do." He laughed happily. "Seems like those were the words that got me into this name-picking business in the first place." He kissed her good night.

"You'll call everyone?"

"You can bet on it. I don't care if it is after midnight."

Ida Barrow cleared her throat.

"I'm off, Mrs. Barrow. Thank you for everything." He paused at the door. "I'll see you in the morning, Sally. Uh, and Matthew and John too."

He left the hospital in a daze, and found himself out in the parking lot without remembering how he'd gotten there. He looked up into the star-spangled night, drawing deep breaths of the California air to calm himself. The moon had yet to rise; the heavens sparkled with countless stars. He drank in the silent majesty of the cosmos, his heart full.

He stood there under the timeless constellations, thinking of the two new souls who'd entered their unfathomable domain, of the two tiny bundles of life who'd become part of this awesome infinity of creation, to join the cycle of life and death on a small world lost in a vast solar system, a solar system itself in a remote corner of an average galaxy, a galaxy just one of billions of galaxies in a universe without limit, without end. . . .

What did it all mean? What *could* it all mean . . . ?

What would life bring to John and Matthew Lindberg? Would they stand under the same stars someday, asking the same silent questions? Would they get no answer either, or would their generation be the one to finally understand the bewildering immensity of the universe and mankind's true role in it?

They would be his age in 1968. . . . Bill rolled the odd-sounding syllables off his tongue. Nineteen-sixty-eight. . . . He would be forty years old, Sally thirty-nine, Matthew and John twenty.

Twenty . . . old enough to be soldiers. . . .

The haunting thought resolved into chilling clarity. A sense of terrible foreboding came over him—it was a rare generation that was spared the trauma of war. He thought of Iwo Jima— God forbid his sons would see anything like *that*. . . .

But Japan and Germany had been crushed—they would be no threat. Still, there was Russia now, a military juggernaut whose leaders seemed intent upon expansion, upon spreading their communist doctrine worldwide. A new phrase had been coined—*The Cold War*—to describe the growing tensions between the United States and the Soviet Union. Aw, but hell, all that would be sorted out long before John and Matthew came of age.

Wouldn't it . . . ?

A bus rumbled past, pulling Bill away from the future. He frowned. It was strange how a man's mind could wander when exhaustion broke down the everyday barrier between the conscious and the subconscious.

He climbed into the '38 Ford, stepped on the starter, and turned the key. He told himself he might have become a little too involved in that psychology course he'd enrolled in at San Diego State.

Miracle of miracles, the engine turned over on the first try. He released the parking brake, shoved her into gear, and headed for home and a night of long-distance telephone calls.

Chapter XXXIII

The Kremlin
Moscow
June 23, 1948

I

Marshal Georgi Zhukov turned from the huge wall map of Germany to conclude his report. "So as you can see, Comrade Stalin, the balance of forces in Germany leaves the West with no means of breaking a blockade of Berlin. We can close all overland routes to the city and respond to any subsequent military response with an overwhelming display of force."

Stalin leaned forward in his chair, puffing on his pipe. His gaze darted from the map to the commander of the Red Army, then back to the map. A heavy silence fell over the room as he weighed the possible American responses to a blockade. "You can guarantee," he said at last, "a stranglehold on Berlin? You can crush any hostile movement toward the city?"

Zhukov hesitated only a moment. "Yes, Comrade Stalin."

Stalin took his pipe from his mouth and examined the smoldering bowl, then reached for the tobacco pouch in his tunic pocket. "And if the Americans fill the skies with B-29s, what then, Zhukov? Would that not prevent us from massing our troops at critical rail and road junctions?"

He tapped the bowl of his pipe on the edge of the green-baize covered table. Spent ashes dropped to the floor. He glanced expectantly at Zhukov, then filled the bowl with fresh tobacco. "Well?"

Zhukov allowed himself the slightest smirk of condescension. "The tactical situation, Comrade Stalin, would allow us to use artillery and close air support to close the autobahn and rail routes to Berlin. There would be no need to mass troops. The Americans, to maintain their presence in Berlin, would need to supply the West Berliners with food and medical supplies. Such huge volumes of freight can only be moved on rail or highway by train or truck convoy. We would simply zero in our artillery on every mile of track and autobahn and that would be it. Then, our Stormoviks would pounce on anything that escapes the shelling."

Stalin relit his pipe, sizing up his marshal. The man was forgetting his place far too often, playing on his war reputation. Stalin frowned as he stoked the pipe to life. Zhukov *had* been indispensable in hurling the Hitlerites back from the gates of Moscow. He *had* indeed saved Stalingrad as well, and killed or captured three hundred thousand Nazis in the bargain. He *had* then proceeded to drive the fascist hordes all the way to Berlin and crushed the enemy for good. But he had allowed his successes to swell his peasant head insufferably. Even now, he could be plotting some Bonapartist scheme to overthrow the party and establish a military dictatorship.

He would have to be dealt with, that was clear. But should the West force a military showdown over Berlin and fighting break out, he would be needed. The soldiers worshipped him; the people adored him. For the time being, his arrogance would have to be endured.

"Do you think the Americans will go to war over Berlin, Comrade Marshal?"

"If they do, we will sweep them from Europe in a matter of weeks."

"Yes, yes, that is obvious. They do not have the numbers to stand up to the Red Army for long. But the atomic threat must be considered. The price of a socialist Europe may turn out to be Moscow, Leningrad, Kiev. . . ."

"One must not overestimate the capabilities of their B-29s, Comrade Stalin. They would have to fight their way thousands of kilometers through the Red Air Force to reach Moscow."

Stalin nodded. But the ultimate question was how many bombs the Americans possessed. Had they produced dozens of bombs or only a handful? His air force marshals insisted that they could shoot down at least fifty percent of any formation trying to penetrate all the way to Moscow. Minsk and Leningrad would be more vulnerable, being closer to potential bomber bases in England and Turkey. Only some thirty percent attrition of American bombers could be expected defending those cities from atomic attack.

Further complicating the issue was the expectation that the Americans would scatter their atomic-bomb-carrying planes throughout a formation of three to four hundred planes. How could the defenders tell which planes carried bombs and which were conventionally armed decoys?

Stalin rubbed his face in irritation. There were too many unknowns should full-scale conflict erupt, but the bottom line was the inevitability of socialist victory over bourgeoisie capitalism. It would be a pity to lose Moscow or Leningrad, but they could be rebuilt.

He rose from his chair. The Berlin issue must be settled. All of Germany must be brought into the socialist sphere so that she would never rise again to threaten the Motherland. If the West was allowed to remain in the western sectors of the capital and the country, they would soon enough allow *their* Germans to rearm. Then all the terrible sacrifice of the Great Patriotic War would have been in vain.

"Blockade Berlin, Zhukov," said Stalin at last, his mind made up. "Put the Red Army and Air Force on full alert. We must be ready to act decisively should it come to war. But I want no provocations, no bluster. Simply halt all Anglo-American traffic to Berlin. Do *not* be the first to shoot. If a train or a truck

convoy just barrels through a roadblock, simply block the route
again farther east. If war is to come, it will be of much use to
us politically if the West is seen as the aggressor."

"I understand, Comrade Stalin." Zhukov paused.

"Yes, yes, what is it?"

The marshal's eyebrows rose questioningly. "If the Americans open fire on my troops, how forceful should my response
be? Am I simply to drive them off with counterfire or am I
permitted to take tactical action against other potential threats
in the area, other convoys, other supply or support units?"

Stalin frowned. He suspected Zhukov was anxious for a
bloody confrontation, looking for any excuse to draw the Americans into battle, for if war broke out with the West, he would
find himself with the immense power he enjoyed during the
Great Patriotic War against the fascists. He must be kept on a
tight leash.

"You will take no offensive action without my express order,"
cautioned Stalin, his eyes narrowing. "As I said, returning fire
if fired upon is permitted, *locally*. But you will limit your reaction to driving off the enemy. Just *react*, Zhukov."

Stalin waved his hand in a gesture of dismissal. "At any rate,
the Americans will turn back when confronted with even the
slightest *display* of force. You won't need to demonstrate force,
Zhukov. Just the *appearance* of military units will be sufficient.

"The Americans can count divisions, Comrade Marshal.
They won't risk a military confrontation in Germany."

II

Yuri Rostov waited on the siding as the train slowed to a halt,
then followed the colonel and his aides toward the lead car,
coupled just behind the steaming engine. Before they could
board, an American officer emerged, followed by his aides and
a nervous pair of noncoms.

Yuri glanced at his unarmed counterparts. They eyed the

Kalashnikov slung over his shoulder warily and Yuri flushed in embarrassment. They were looking at him as an enemy would. . . . But why? He looked away, confused. America and Russia were allies . . . weren't they?

The delegations stood facing each other under the blazing sun. Overhead, a pair of Yak 9 fighter planes circled warily, the droning of their engines an ominous message to the Americans that ignoring the symbolic roadblock could lead to shooting.

Colonel Rossokovsky broke the tense standoff. "It is my duty to inform you, Colonel, that I am unable to allow you to pass through to Berlin."

Yuri stiffened. What was this? He glanced past the Americans at the freight train. It looked harmless enough. Then why was Colonel Rossokovsky so nervous? Yuri shifted uncomfortably, eyeing the train again. What could a freight train be carrying into Berlin that could possibly concern the Soviet authorities?

The American officer replied, his voice steady but determined. Yuri edged toward Rossokovsky as his aide, Ivanov, translated. "The American colonel requests your reasons for blocking an ally's access to Berlin."

The American spoke again. Ivanov stiffened, then repeated his words in Russian. "He also says that it is his duty to see this train through to Berlin. He says that you are violating the United Nation's charter by obstructing free access to Berlin."

Rossokovsky cleared his throat. "Tell him that I am sorry for the inconvenience, but that we must close this rail line for technical reasons."

Yuri relaxed. *That* was it. The rails ahead must be damaged, or a switch jammed.

The American listened to the aide's translation into English, then fixed a withering gaze on Rossokovsky as he responded.

"He wants to know when these *technical* difficulties will be overcome," repeated the aide, without the evident sarcasm.

"The Soviet side will inform the American side when the problem has been fixed," declared Rossokovsky. "In the meantime, I must ask you to pull this train off onto the siding."

The American colonel bristled at the translation. He looked away from Rossokovsky in obvious disgust, and directed his reply at the unfortunate Lieutenant Ivanov.

"My superiors find it quite astonishing that *technical* difficulties seem to have affected *every* rail line *and* autobahn route from the Western Sector to Berlin. I have been instructed to offer whatever assistance the Soviet side might require to rectify the situation," the American said. He waited expectantly for his counterpart's response.

Ivanov translated the statement, again leaving out the sarcasm.

Yuri stared at Ivanov, then at the American colonel. *All the rail lines were out? And* the roads? It made no sense.

"We are quite capable of remedying the difficulties without your help," replied Rossokovsky.

The American's tone was biting as he spoke at some length. Ivanov hesitated when he'd finished. He glanced nervously at Rossokovsky. The American glared at him, then gestured impatiently at his counterpart.

"He says," Ivanov said haltingly, "that a blockade is an act of war. The American side expects the Soviet side to recognize the seriousness with which the American side views this matter."

Yuri winced. Blockade . . . ? War . . . ? What the devil was going on?

Ivanov paused. The American colonel's aide spoke for the first time. "Tell him all of it, Lieutenant," he said in Russian. "We don't want any misunderstandings."

Ivanov's eyebrows rose in surprise. He turned again to Rossokovsky. "Obstruction of overland access to Berlin will be met with the appropriate response, Comrade Colonel. The American side will open access to Berlin through its *own technical* means, should that prove necessary."

"We shall see about that." Rossokovsky glared at the American. "In the meantime, I must insist that you pull off onto the siding."

As he listened to the translation the American colonel glanced at the circling fighters. His gaze fell on the platoon of T-34 tanks facing him from farther up the track. He barked a terse order to an aide, saluted stiffly, and disappeared into the train.

Yuri stared at Rossokovsky. The colonel was pale, his expression grim, his eyes fearful. Yuri felt a terrible sense of foreboding come over him. Numb, he watched as German brakemen threw the switch ahead that would divert the train off the main line. The locomotive belched steam and rumbled forward, pulling the cars onto the siding.

Rossokovsky turned on his heel, stalked to his waiting staff car, and climbed stiffly in. "Watch them!" he barked from the backseat. "I'll be back."

The Mercedes drove off. Yuri watched it for a moment, then turned as his immediate superior, Lieutenant Rogov, growled orders directing Yuri's squad to form up in a line alongside the tracks.

Bewildered, Yuri took his place in line, facing the train from a few meters away. He found himself just behind the engine, directly opposite the single passenger car. Behind it, a score or more of boxcars sat silently in the harsh sunlight, their mysterious cargo obviously the cause of the strange confrontation.

Yuri's gaze shifted from the boxcars to the passenger-car's windows in front of him, drawn by a sudden movement from inside. From the shadows of the interior, a face was looking out at him through the glass.

He looked back. It was one of the American colonel's escorts. The soldier reached up, slid the window down, and addressed him in English. Yuri froze. Was he permitted to talk to the Americans? He doubted it. He looked behind him. Luckily, Lieutenant Rogev was far down the line, walking past the freight cars some fifty meters away.

He met the American's gaze. *"Shto?"* he asked. He searched his memory for the few English words he'd picked up. *What . . . .* wasn't that the appropriate word? He leaned toward the window. "What?"

The American nodded toward the boxcars. "It's just food, Ivan," he explained. "It's just food."

Yuri stared blankly. *Eetsjusfoodivan?* What did that mean? He saw Rogov returning and stiffened, alarmed at the possible consequences of getting caught talking to the Americans. He shook his head at the American sergeant, desperately signaling him to close the window.

The American, interpreting Yuri's head shaking as blunt denial of his remark, slammed the window shut in disgust. Relieved, but dismayed at the sergeant's reaction, Yuri stared through the window, but the American was gone.

Chapter XXXIV

The White House
Washington, DC
June 26, 1948

I

Harry Truman stood on the balcony of the Executive Mansion and looked out across the South Lawn, green and lush in the warm summer sunshine. A faint drone in the distance drew his gaze across the Potomac River toward the hills of Virginia, where a DC-4, gliding into its final approach to Washington National Airport, stood out in sparkling silver against the blue southern skies.

Once again, as so often in the past weeks, his thoughts fell on Berlin and another airport, where other DC-4s—or C-54's, as his generals called them, were landing daily, on his express orders, at Tempelhof to show Joseph Stalin that the West intended to stay in Berlin, whatever it took.

The president frowned. How far was Stalin going to push him? Didn't he understand that a blockade was an act of war, a provocation which had led many powerful men in Washington to advise the use of military force to open the land routes to beleaguered Berlin? Didn't he understand that his bullying had led dozens of congressmen and senators, generals and admirals, diplomats and newspaper editors around the country to conclude that war had become inevitable and that the United States shouldn't hesitate to welcome it while it still held an atomic monopoly?

An airlift wouldn't work, they'd told him. A city of three million people simply couldn't be supplied by air, they'd told him. The only way to save Berlin was to push an armored column down the autobahn and defy Stalin to stop it, they'd told him. If war is to come, let it come now, they'd told him. . . .

The president slammed a fist down on the white railing of the balcony. It was easy for those fellows to talk tough. It was easy for them to rattle the sabres of war, to beat on the drums, to vent their frustrations by howling for a showdown. But if things went wrong, they would be the first to change their tune, the first to condemn him as a reckless warmonger. If he forced his way down the autobahn and Stalin unleashed the Red Army, smashed through the thin American lines in Germany and swept to the English Channel, who among them would stand with Truman?

Truman frowned. Maybe a few generals, a couple of admirals, a congressman or two. But the rest would scatter like sparrows on a wire. . . .

The thirty-third President of the United States looked through the trees to the southwest where the Lincoln Memorial lay at the far end of the National Mall. The sixteenth president would have understood his predicament. He too had presided over a capital thick with people calling for war, only to be abandoned when the disaster of First Bull Run had befallen the Union.

Truman looked beyond the Lincoln Memorial toward the Pentagon, lying on the far shore of the Potomac. Behind its gray walls, war plans were being polished, troop movements planned, air and naval armadas readied for deployment. If the storm broke, the Joint Chiefs would be ready.

But would the men? Would the sailors on lonely destroyers slashing through the cold waves of the North Sea be ready? Would the airmen sweating in their barracks in desolate Turkey be ready? Would the soldiers holding the thin line along the

Elbe be ready? The president listened to the soft rustle of the wind through the trees ringing the South Lawn. The world was at peace. But at what price? Was peace worth abandoning Berlin and its three million people to communist slavery? If the Russians gobbled up Berlin without a fight, what would keep them from wanting Paris next? Or London?

Or Washington?

Truman gripped the railing tightly. If Stalin wanted a war over Berlin, then he damn well would have to be obliged! But Harry Truman wasn't about to start it by ordering some poor bastards in a handful of Pershing tanks to clank down some damn German highway into the teeth of four Russian armored divisions!

Hell no.

The president turned from the railing, his decision made. An airlift was the step to take, the *only* step to take, at least for the moment. It would show American resolve. It would force the Russians to make the first hostile move—shooting down an unarmed transport plane would leave the world in no doubt as to who was the villian and who the victim. Whereas a sudden shootout on the autobahn would leave the United States open to charges that it had triggered World War III by forcing its way across the Russian sector of Germany to encircled Berlin.

"Mr. President . . . ?"

Truman turned to see the chief of the White House detail of the secret service, Fred Nicholson, standing in the open doorway to the family quarters. "Fred . . . what is it?"

"Mrs. Truman is looking for you, Mr. President."

Harry Truman shook his head. "So, Bess has turned you into a messenger boy again, eh?"

"Not at all, sir."

"I'll speak to her, Fred. We can't have the secret service running about like butlers." For the first time that day he smiled. Once a critical decision had been made, he'd always been able to put the agony of the process behind him. "Don't know if it'll do any good though," he added, his smile widening. "Bess doesn't listen to me much more than those fellows over on the Hill do."

Nicholson grinned at the presidential joke. "I'm certain Mrs. Truman meant no disrespect, sir. I just happened to be in the West Wing when she came down to see you about supper. I told her I was going this way anyway."

He stepped out onto the balcony and joined the president at the railing. "I don't really need much of an excuse to come up here, the view is so beautiful."

"Yes. Yes, it is." They looked out across the green swath of the National Mall toward the obelisk of the Washington Monument, gleaming in the sunlight. Beyond the towering monument to the first president, north of the dome of the Jefferson Memorial, the waters of the Tidal Basin sparkled peacefully, reflecting the images of the cotton-white clouds drifting by overhead.

They lingered on the balcony, admiring the sights for a few stolen moments longer. Finally, Truman sighed and turned toward the doorway. "I'd guess I'd better go find Bess."

"Yes, sir."

The commander-in-chief disappeared into the White House, leaving Nicholson alone by the railing. The secret serviceman's gaze fell on the fifty American flags rippling proudly atop the flagpoles encircling the base of the Washington Monument. His thoughts drifted to April 1945, when the same flags had drooped at half-mast after the death of FDR.

He shook his head. Since that day of national sorrow, Harry Truman had carried the weight of the world on his small shoulders. Burden after burden had fallen on him—facing Stalin at Potsdam, the atomic bomb decisions, finding and prosecuting Nazi war criminals at Nuremburg, demobilizing twelve million GIs, standing up to the Russians over Greece and Turkey, propping up war-torn Europe with the massive economic aid of the Marshall Plan, establishing the Department of Defense, establishing an independent United States Air Force, all despite the intransigence of a hostile Congress.

And now there was Berlin. *On top* of the strong political challenge of New York Governor Thomas Dewey. Nicholson frowned—as if the already bitter election campaign of '48 hadn't been brutal enough, the president now had something even worse to deal with—a potential world war.

Nicholson found his gaze drawn to the water fountains surging skyward from their basin out on the South Lawn. The frothy waters rose steadily, majestically, propelled into gleaming columns from the pressure of a seemingly endless reservoir of power hidden beneath the surface. Day and night, they flowed on, never flagging, never failing, never quitting.

Nicholson smiled. Just like old Harry. He never quit either. . . .

II

Sinclair Robertson looked out the window of the C-54 as it banked into its final approach to Berlin. The city looked much the same as it had three years ago when he'd seen photos of the shattered capital of the defeated Reich on a plane bound for the States after three years of covering the war in Europe. From five hundred feet, he could see that at least the streets had been cleared of rubble. But block after block of vacant shells of buildings were a stark reminder of the war.

Now, with the Soviets blocking the land corridor to Berlin, was the war that Patton had predicted that May morning in 1945 about to erupt? Was it indeed inevitable, or would calmer heads prevail and some understanding be finally reached on the status of divided Germany?

Sinclair swallowed to pop the growing pressure in his ears. Templehof Airport tilted into view out the cabin window, then drifted forward until it was hidden by the plane's nose as the pilot lined up with the runway. The whine of hydraulics sounded from below as the landing gear deployed.

Truman couldn't be expecting to be able to feed Berlin by

airlift alone. . . . A city of some three million people consumed far more food than a few dozen C-54s, even flying around the clock, could bring in. Berlin would slowly starve unless the president attempted to reopen the land corridor.

The C-54 touched down with a jolt and the screech of rubber tires on concrete. His seat vibrated from the landing roll and Sinclair gripped the arms, never calm until his feet were on solid ground again. He forced his thoughts again to the crisis.

Stalin was a wily bastard—through the tactic of blockade, with little risk to himself, he had forced Truman to react or lose Berlin. The Soviets could simply block the roads and tracks to the city from the west and the Americans couldn't get through, unless they were the first to use force, thereby putting Truman in the position of being the aggressor in the eyes of much of the world. Either way, Truman would lose face and American prestige would plummet in the developing countries which were the ideological battleground of the postwar world.

It took several phone calls from his hotel room to track down Wilson, but he finally reached him in Frankfurt. Four long weeks passed before they saw each other again, and then it was just a brief hello at Tempelhof as Wilson and his crew munched sandwiches and drank Cokes under the wing of their C-54—to save time, they weren't allowed out of earshot of the unloading crew chief. As soon as the transport was emptied of cargo, they took off again for another load.

Three more weeks went by before a mechanical failure grounded Wilson overnight in Berlin and he had time to set up a meeting. They'd agreed that it was far simpler for him to leave a message at Sinclair's hotel than for Sinclair to keep trying to track him down. When the telephone rang in Sinclair's room, he happened to be in and agreed to meet Wilson at a bar on the Wilhelmstrasse at eight o'clock that night.

Sinclair was ordering his second beer when Wilson walked through the door at eight-thirty. "Sorry, I'm late," he explained as they shook hands, "but my driver couldn't find the place."

"No problem, Major." Sinclair grinned. "I've been waiting

seven weeks to get the inside scoop on this airlift, a few more minutes doesn't matter." They sat down at a corner table. "Hungry?"

"Starving."

Sinclair waved a waitress over. "Well, they've got sausage, sausage, sauerkraut, or sausage." He shrugged. "Best menu in Berlin right now; everyone else, hotels included, is hurting, despite the show you fellows are putting on." He leaned closer. "The owner must have had his freezers full when the Russians cut the land routes. Anyway, the beer's good, what's left of it—American—Miller High Life or Pabst Blue Ribbon."

Wilson grinned. "I guess I'll have sausage. And a Miller."

Sinclair ordered in passable German. The waitress, a rail-thin blonde, brought the beer.

"Danke, fraulein." Sinclair raised his bottle. "Here's to Transport Command, eh?" They clinked bottles. "So, how's it been going?"

Wilson took a long drink. "Well, we're doing the best we can, but damn, it's like bailing the ocean out with a spoon, Robertson."

"I can imagine." Sinclair noted the dark circles under Wilson's eyes, the pasty complexion of a man driven to the limits of endurance.

"We got in this morning from Frankfurt. Ground crewmen found a crack in the main spar, so me and the guys grabbed some sack time. Phone call wakes me at 1800—turned out there aren't any available Skymasters here, so we probably won't go out until sometime tomorrow. I'll finally get some good sack time tonight, but I'm so far behind, I don't know how much it'll really help. I feel like I could sleep for days. . . ."

"Looks like you could really use it."

"We're all tired as hell." Wilson took another drink of his Miller's. "But two more squadrons just got here from the States, another two are on the way, and we might get a couple more from Japan and Hawaii, so we're going to have some more help."

"Glad to hear it."

"Yeah. We've been busting our tails, but like I said, it's just not going to be enough without more planes—a lot more planes. If this thing drags through the winter, we're going to have to haul coal in too. Up to now it's been mainly food."

"Do you think you guys can keep it up once winter hits, what with the coal requirements on top of the food?"

"I don't know, Robertson. We've been flying like crazy for what, seven or eight weeks now?"

"Something like that."

"Whatever it's been, we've been going at it as hard as we can, but yesterday was the first day we managed to haul in more than 4500 tons—that's what Berlin needs a day, *every day,* to survive. It took over seven hundred flights. . . ."

"Seven hundred flights?"

"Seven hundred and seven, to be precise."

"Every day?"

"Every day."

"Damn . . ."

The waitress brought their food, two plates of the sorriest-looking sausage Wilson had ever seen. The sauerkraut, white, dry, and withered, didn't look much better. "I can see we're going to have to wash this stuff down with more beer," he said, after the girl had gone.

"She'd probably have slept with you for it," Sinclair replied, a sad smile on his face.

"I shouldn't bitch, should I."

"I guess I'm used to it. I've been here almost two months."

Wilson stared at the plate. "I'm so damn worn out I just didn't realize how bad it really is here."

Sinclair shrugged. "If it weren't for you fellows, there wouldn't be anything at all."

Wilson waved the waitress over. She hurried up, the look in her eyes revealing her fear that a complaint was coming. Jobs were precious in postwar Berlin and her boss was a stern taskmaster. But Wilson, in struggling German, told her to take it home with her when she left. She stared at him, wide-eyed.

Sinclair shoved his plate aside as well. "Mine too, *fraulein.*"

She looked for a moment at what she considered a feast, then started crying. She explained that such things weren't permitted, that she'd be fired, her boss would suspect that she was trading her favors for food. Sinclair excused himself, spoke with the manager for a few minutes, and returned with a smile. "It'll be okay, *fraulein,*" he assured her. "I told him this was on the up and up and that if he didn't believe me, I'd have no choice but to take my lodgings elsewhere. It'll be wrapped up and waiting for you when you get off." He grinned. "My newspaper's poured a lot of reichsmarks into this place for my room and board, so I've got a little pull, I guess."

"Oh, danke, danke . . ." The rest of her gratitude poured out in such a torrent that neither Sinclair nor Wilson could make any of it out. Finally, embarrassed by all the fuss, Wilson cut in, patted her hand, and shooed her away.

"Poor thing," he said, "she can't weigh more than ninety pounds." Shaken by his first personal evidence of the bleakness of the average Berliner's existence, he drained the rest of his beer, his initial embarrassment replaced by a deep anger at the Russians for causing such suffering.

"Lucky you aren't wearing your uniform, Major. She'd have married you right here." Sinclair raised his bottle of Pabst to his lips, then lowered it. "Say, that reminds me—I wrote a letter to that French girl you told me about."

Wilson's eyebrows rose in surprise. "Gabrielle?"

"Yeah. Anyway, she wrote back."

"Really? How are her and the old man doing?"

"Okay, I guess. She said that they'd both like to see you if it could be worked out."

"I'd like to see them too." Wilson smiled, the Russians forgotten for the moment. "They saved my hide."

"I'll give you the address." Sinclair pulled out his wallet.

"Hmmm," he said after a fruitless search, "must be back in my room. I'll have to mail it to you."

"That'd be fine."

"Think you'll ever find any spare time to go see them?"

"Like everything else, that seems to be up to the damn Russians."

"I'd still like to do a story about you three."

"Maybe if we got them to Frankfurt."

"That's an idea. How about if I see if I can arrange it? I'm sure my paper would pay their fare."

"Great!"

"Oh, another thing. Did you say the main spar on your plane was cracked?"

"Yeah."

"Isn't that pretty bad?"

Wilson laughed. "You could say that. The main spar holds the damn wings on."

Sinclair went white. "You mean you guys flew all the way from Frankfurt in a plane that could have fallen apart at any second?"

"That's about the size of it. Look, we're under so much pressure to try to meet that 4500 tons a day that maintenance rules have gone out the window. We would have been grounded if anyone had seen the crack, but hell, the ground crews are as dead on their feet as we are." He shrugged. "They missed it, but I can't really blame them. They're so overworked they can't even keep up on the routine maintenance. Most of the transports flying into Tempelhof are way below standard operating condition and would have been grounded in a normal situation; but they're needed, so they fly. It's a miracle we haven't had more crashes than we have."

"What've there been, two?"

"Yeah. With five fatalities." Wilson leaned forward. "Say, I hope you don't write any of this up, about the maintenance stuff, I mean. We're all willing to take some risks to keep this thing going, but if the folks back home find out about the safety problems and General Tunner is forced to go by the book, Berlin is finished. We don't want that, any of us."

"I won't." Sinclair glanced at his watch. "I don't want to keep you, Major. Maybe you'd better go get some sleep."

"I think I will."

"Good. I'll write the Lafleurs, see what I can set up."

"Thanks." Wilson shook his head. "Might be Christmas before I get a free minute though."

"Now that's an angle."

"Huh?"

"I could fly them to Frankfurt for a Christmas reunion. It'd make a great story."

"God, I hope I'm not still here at Christmas."

"I wouldn't count against it."

Wilson sighed. "You're probably right."

Chapter XXXV

Frankfurt
American Zone of Germany
December 24, 1948

I

Wilson Lindberg acknowledged the clearance for takeoff from the control tower, signed off, and flipped a toggle switch to set the cockpit windshield wipers on high. As they rocked quickly back and forth, he glanced out at the weather. "Ceiling, zero feet . . ." he mumbled, half aloud. "Visibility, zero feet . . . heavy snow . . . winds from the north at twenty-five knots, gusts to thirty-five." He had to laugh, despite the churning in the pit of his stomach. "Other than that it's a great day to fly!"

He shook his head, took a deep breath, and exchanged troubled glances with Lt. Gary Warwick in the right seat of the Skymaster cockpit. Warwick, peered through the windshield at the swirling snow and sighed. The vague outline of the runway was visible only in the scattered moments when the gusting winds wavered.

"Even Santa Claus would stay on the ground today, Lindy."

"Yeah, well, ol' St. Nick doesn't work for General Clay, does he?"

"Clever old bastard."

Wilson blew out a long breath, collecting himself for the

blind takeoff. "Okay, let's roll. . . ." He shoved forward the throttles between the seats and the C-54 eased into its takeoff roll. Wilson held his breath as the plane built up speed, its four props spinning in silver disks, biting into the thick air, pulling the heavy transport into a hurtling, headlong bolt for the sky.

His gaze locked on the glowing instrument panel, Wilson never looked through the windshield at the murky wall of white swirling past the Plexiglas. As Warwick called off the airspeed, Wilson concentrated on keeping the course dial bearing-indicator needle locked on dead center by alternating pressure on the rudder pedals so the plane wouldn't careen off the runway and cartwheel into flaming debris across half the airfield.

When Warwick reported takeoff speed, Wilson eased the control column back and pulled the lumbering Skymaster off the gray blur of runway. He felt no sensation of climbing—it was rather a disorienting sense of hanging in midair, perched on the edge of a fatal stall.

Vertigo.

He fought it, glaring at the instruments as beads of cold sweat broke out on his forehead, forcing himself to believe what they told him instead of what his brain was insisting was happening. He checked and double-checked the dials—airspeed at one-eighty and rising . . . altitude, three hundred feet and climbing . . . wings level on the artificial horizon . . . angle of attack twenty degrees on a bearing of seventy-five degrees. . . .

They were right on course, dead center in the crowded air corridor between Frankfurt and besieged Berlin.

"You okay, Lindy? You look a trifle green. . . ."

Wilson nodded, despite the lingering dizziness. "Touch of vertigo, I guess. I'm fine now."

"You sure?"

"Yeah."

Warwick eyed him carefully. "When do we break out of this soup?"

"Five thousand feet."

"Want me to take it?"

Wilson grinned. "All right! I can take a hint."

"Got it." Warwick took hold of his control column and eased it back as Wilson let go of his. "Have some coffee, Lindy."

"Think I will." Wilson took his thermos from his flight bag beneath his seat, unscrewed the top, and poured steaming coffee into the cap. "Ahhhh . . ." he sighed, savoring the rich chocolate-brown brew. His head began to clear as he sipped the coffee. By the time the C-54 broke through the heavy overcast into brilliant sunshine, he'd almost forgotten the trauma of takeoff.

His thoughts turned to the reunion with Henri and Gabrielle Lafleur. If all went according to schedule, he'd be in and out of Tempelhof in under an hour and back in Frankfurt by evening. Robertson's telegram said that they'd arrive in Frankfurt by train around 1300, about the same time he landed at Tempelhof. Robertson would fly back with him, and they'd have all of glorious Christmas Day to spend together.

"I wonder how long we're going to have to keep this up, Lindy." Warwick finished setting the elevator trim, then settled back in his seat and stretched in the sun-drenched cockpit.

"Beats me. All I know is that Christmas Day off is going to feel real good."

"Yeah."

"I feel old as death. . . ." Wilson thought of hungry, freezing Berlin, somewhere below the clouds to the east. As exhausted as everyone was from the grueling schedule of assembly-line takeoffs and landings, from dodging harassing Yak fighters on the way, from groping their way through the winter weather out of Frankfurt into Tempelhof, out of Tempelhof back to Wiesbaden, then across to Frankfurt again to start the whole cycle over again, no one was going to quit until Stalin lifted the blockade.

Berlin needed food, Berlin needed coal, or Berlin was going to die. It was as simple as that.

"We've got company." Warwick pointed toward a dark dot dead ahead. In seconds, the tiny image resolved into the menacing silhouette of a Russian fighter plane, hurtled past them in a blur of white, and banked sharply to the north, red stars gleaming on its wings.

"Yak 9 . . . ?"

Wilson nodded grimly. "I thought we might get a Christmas present from Ivan today, but no such luck."

"At least they're not shooting at us."

"Yet." Wilson watched the Yak make its wide turn and zoom in for another pass. Like him, Warwick had been through these skies before, during the war, when Focke-Wulfs and Messerschmitts had come at them the same way, but with guns blazing.

The Yak made another head on pass, banked away, then appeared again off their left wing. The pilot edged closer until he was less than fifty feet off the silver wingtip.

"Now what?" Wilson looked across the wing at the Yak cockpit as the pilot shoved a hand-lettered sign against the Plexiglas. He leaned forward, squinting against the sun's glare to read it.

" 'Bang . . . bang . . . you're dead!' "

"What a smart ass," Warwick muttered. "Hundreds of Russian pilots in Germany and we've got to get a smart ass."

The Yak dogged them until they descended toward the top of the overcast for their final approach into Berlin. Then, with a final derisive gesture, the pilot banked away to the southeast.

"Yeah, Merry Christmas to you too, pal." Warwick shook his head. "Jeez Louise, what a grouch."

Wilson chuckled as he took the controls and brought the nose down to lose altitude more quickly. The distraction of keeping a safe distance from the weaving Yak had left them higher than they should have been for the final approach into Berlin.

The sun vanished as the heavy cloud layer swallowed them up. They descended through the murk, past four thousand, past three thousand, past two thousand feet. Wilson opened the frequency to the tower, still lost from view somewhere below and to the east. "Tempelhof Control, this is EC 84, inbound at angels two. . . ."

The response crackled into his ears immediately. "EC 84, Tempelhof. Come to bearing zero-niner-three, over."

Wilson glanced at Warwick. "Too far south."

"Must be high crosswinds, Lindy."

"Yeah."

Wilson banked the C-54 to the north with left rudder and slight pressure on the control column until their bearing was corrected. He watched the altimeter needle sweep past one thousand feet, then glanced quickly through the windshield to see nothing but heavy clouds and swirling snowflakes.

"EC 84, Tempelhof," his headset earphones crackled. "We have you at four-zero-zero at three point five from Runway Zero Two. Maintain heading, come to seven-zero-zero, over."

They were too low.

He pulled back on the control column. Tempelhof was right in the middle of the city, to make a low approach was to court disaster.

"Tempelhof, EC 84. Visibility is zero, over."

"EC 84, Tempelhof. Do you wish to declare an abort, over?"

Wilson glanced at Warwick. "Tempelhof, EC 84. What do you advise, over?"

"EC 84, Tempelhof. Ceiling is two-zero-zero over the runway. . . . We have you on course, over."

Wilson stared out the windowshield again, trying to get a glimpse of the ground. He blinked at the dizzying swirl of thick flakes whipping past the Plexiglas. "Doesn't sound like they want us to abort, Gary. . . ." He eased the nose down, the altimeter needle swung past three hundred feet.

"EC 84, Tempelhof," his headset hissed, a definite edge of alarm in the controller's voice, "you're drifting south, maintain bearing, over."

Wilson's pulse began to race. He pulled the column left, remembering the long row of ten-story apartment buildings along the south edge of the base. The C-54 roared ever lower as he fought the crosswinds.

Where was the runway?

He leveled the wings just as the Skymaster broke through the clouds a hundred feet off the ground. The looming bulk of the control tower flashed by just off the right wingtip.

His headset crackled ominously. "EC 84! Abort! Abort!"

Wilson tried to pull up. "Full power!"

Out of the corner of his eye, he saw Warwick slam the throttles full forward. The Skymaster, buffeted by the high surface winds, its four engines sluggish from months of wear and tear, was slow to respond. Flaps down, landing gear down, it staggered out of its descent and leveled off.

The end of the runway rushed toward them. Beyond it, the dark mass of trees lining the far end of the field formed a solid wall eighty feet high.

The port outboard engine sputtered and coughed, its mechanical guts unable to take the sudden transition to full power. The Skymaster's nose yawed slightly to the right as the starboard props poured out more power than the port props. Wilson stared at the onrushing trees, kicking left rudder in a desperate attempt to compensate.

Too late.

"We're not gonna make it. . . ."

He was amazed at the calm that came over him in those final seconds. The last thing he saw before the C-54 slammed into the trees was a Christmas candle glowing in the frosted window of the snowplow garage just off the right edge of the runway.

II

Gunther and Kathe Dietrich joined the tiny knot of people huddled in the darkness beside the mangled treeline where the C-54 had come to rest. The perimeter lights of Tempelhof cast their shadows across the scarred earth, the torn and twisted tree trunks, the ragged gap in the chain-link fence.

Kathe took a candle from her coat and walked slowly up to the base of a tree where someone had laid a wreath. She set the candle on the frozen ground beside the wreath, lit it, then rejoined her husband. Gunther put his arm around her shoulder and they watched the flame flicker for a moment, then begin to glow steadily in the silent stillness.

Kathe huddled against him for warmth. "I wonder who they were . . . ?"

Gunther took off his cap and held it at his side. "They were friends," he said simply.

"To die so far from home, to die for us." She began to sob and buried her face in Gunther's chest. From somewhere across darkened Berlin a distant church bell began to toll the arrival of Christmas. The handful of Berliners stood together in the faint candlelight, silent, as the lone church bell's distant tolling was answered by another bell somewhere in the night, then another, then another. The soft pealing of the bells echoed across the besieged city, ringing in the birth of the Messiah. But to the solemn Germans gathered in the flickering light, they were also ringing for three unknown American fliers.

As the bells faded, the Berliners drifted away, some alone, some in pairs, until only Gunther and Kathe and a lone figure bundled in a khaki trenchcoat, hands stuffed into his pockets, remained. He lingered, head bowed, seeming oblivious to them.

"A pity," Gunther said, breaking the long silence.

The man looked up, then slowly nodded. "It was nice of you to come here," he said in halting German. "All of you. . . ." His voice faded away as he looked beyond them to the west, where a C-54, wingtip lights glowing, broke through the overcast above the darkened city and glided, engines humming, against a backdrop of stars toward Tempelhof. They watched the transport descend to the distant runway, then touch down softly, winking lights marking the progress of its landing roll until it vanished behind the shadowed buildings flanking the airport.

"We had to come," Kathe said, wiping her eyes with the back

of her mitten. "We heard . . . and . . . well, it was the only thing to do. . . ."

Sinclair Robertson regarded the German couple through misty eyes. "I just heard myself."

"You are an American, yes . . . ?"

Sinclair nodded. "I'm a correspondent."

Kathe reached out and grasped his arm. "Please, if you will, sir, tell your readers how grateful we are for the help of your president, your people, these brave pilots. From our hearts, we thank them all."

"I will, *Frau* . . . ?"

"Kathe Dietrich, sir. This is my husband, Gunther."

"Sinclair Robertson." They shook hands. "I will convey your gratitude, Kathe, Gunther, but I will also tell them of the courage of Berlin and her people. An epic story is unfolding here."

He paused, taking in the scarred ground, the twisted trees, the plain wreath lit softly by the candle's flame. "But first, I must write of a friend of mine. . . ."

"A friend?"

"Yes." Sinclair thought of Wilson Lindberg, of Gabrielle Lafleur, of what might have been.

Kathe saw in his eyes the sorrow of a man directly touched by the day's tragedy. Herr Robertson wasn't here to cover a story—he was here to pay his respects to a fallen friend.

"You knew them . . . ?"

"The pilot was a friend of mine, Kathe. His name was Wilson Lindberg."

"Please, allow us to offer our sympathy," Gunther said. Kathe nodded.

"It doesn't seem real. He was so young. . . ."

Gunther was first to break the long silence. "I was a pilot during the war, *Herr* Robertson. I considered myself very capable." He shook his head. "But I have to tell you, I would not have had the guts to fly on half the days these fellows have. This is the worst winter we've seen in memory. The rain. The fog. The sleet. The snowstorms. Day after day. Night after night.

For weeks, and weeks, and weeks on end. Yet these men, your friend, and all the others, have climbed into their cockpits and, time after time, roared down icy runways into the murk, nursed ten tons of cargo into the air, groped their way somehow to Berlin, and brought us life through tiny Tempelhof."

Another C-54 appeared through the mist to the west, its engines throbbing steadily. They stared at the red and green lights sparkling from its shadowed form.

"Every ten minutes," Gunther said softly, awed by the magnificent display of logistics, by the relentless pace of the greatest supply effort in human history. Eyes brimming, he watched the Skymaster glide to a landing. "The determination," he mumbled, "the courage of these men is beyond words. I am ashamed to remember that I fought men like this, that I shot many of them from the sky. . . ."

Sinclair put a comforting hand on Gunther's shoulder. "They weren't bringing food then, Gunther, they were bringing bombs. . . . They were doing their duty, just as you were doing yours. They didn't like it any more than you did. In fact, my friend bombed Berlin himself, back in '44."

Gunther stared at Sinclair. "I fought over Berlin myself."

"You might have seen each other, who knows . . . ?"

Memories of that distant winter surfaced. Gunther smiled sadly. "I remember following a lone Fortress toward Berlin. It seems another lifetime now, but in a way it seems like yesterday. Anyway, this American had fallen from the formation, all shot up, and much to my amazement headed right toward the Reichstag instead of fleeing. Well, I got on his tail, but then I couldn't shoot, I just couldn't shoot—"

"Gunther!"

Gunther saw the wide eyes, the amazement on Sinclair's face. "Yes?"

That was Wilson.

Gunther stared at him, speechless.

"He told me one time about the Reichstag, about the German pilot who had him cold, but turned away."

"My God . . ."

"He never forgot it."

Numb, Gunther stared at the wreath, the candle, then at Sinclair. "I would have liked to have met him, this friend of yours, this Wilson Lindberg."

"He felt the same way. He told me you saved his life."

"And now he has given his for us." Gunther noticed the evening star twinkling far to the east beyond darkened Berlin and thought of the Magi who followed a brother beacon to Bethlehem, seeking the newborn Son of God so many centuries ago, seeking the Redeemer.

What is life, he thought, if not a journey toward redemption . . . ? Should it not be measured in deeds rather than days? If so, Wilson Lindberg's brief time on earth would not be found wanting.

III

Henri Lafleur picked up the phone on the third ring. Sitting on the bed of the hotel room, Gabrielle watched him with hushed anticipation. "Are they here, Father?" she asked, rising from the bed, unable to contain herself any longer.

Henri held up his hand to shush her. It began to tremble. "I see. . . ." he mumbled, his face suddenly pale. She stared at him.

"Papa . . . ?"

"We'll be here. . . . thank you." He set the receiver gently into its cradle. Gabrielle saw the look in his eyes and stepped back.

"He isn't coming, is he . . . ?"

Henri walked slowly to the bed. "There's been an accident, Gabrielle."

Gabrielle sank onto the bed. Henri sat down beside her, dazed, unbelieving. He took her hand as he fumbled for the right words. "It was *Monsieur* Robertson, Gabrielle," he managed at last. He took a ragged breath and forced himself to tell her the rest. "Major Lindberg's plane crashed at Tempelhof, I'm afraid there were no survivors."

"No." Gabrielle stared at him through welling eyes. "There . . . there must be some mistake, Papa," she pleaded, desperate for some glimmer of hope.

Henri could only shake his head.

"Oh Papa . . ." Gabrielle buried her face in his chest as the tears began to flow. "Why . . . ?" she sobbed, shoulders trembling, clinging to him in grief. "Why? Why? Why?"

Henri rocked her gently in his arms, at a loss for words. Who could ever say why?

Chapter XXXVI

Arlington National Cemetery
Washington, D.C.
January 15, 1949

I

Standing at attention at the head of the grave, the honor guard leader nodded at the eight airmen, resplendent in dress blues, facing each other in ranks of four across the flag-draped casket. They lifted the flag at each corner, then, white-gloved hands acting in choreographed unison, began to fold the banner with snappy precision into the traditional triangle. As the red and white stripes disappeared beneath the blue field of stars, four F-80 Shooting Star jets roared overhead in a missing-man formation, the vacant space in the formation symbolizing a fallen comrade.

As the jets faded from view beyond the bare treetops of Arlington, the last man handed the star-spangled triangle silently to the honor guard leader. He pivoted, then marched solemnly toward the family and presented the memento to Betty Lindberg. Beside her, gathered at the grave, stood her husband, her son, and daughter-in-law, their two-year-old sons Matthew and John, and a handful of Wilson Lindberg's hometown friends. The adults huddled together for warmth and comfort against the winter chill, staring at the casket in silent grief.

No one noticed the shiny black Lincoln roll slowly up the winding road from the entrance and brake to a stop. As another honor guard of air force officers raised rifles to the sky and fired the traditional salute to a fallen comrade, the president, hatless, clad in a black, knee-length coat, accompanied by General Omar Bradley in a green army greatcoat, walked across the grass toward the gravesite.

Bill Lindberg, dressed in his marine dress blues, noticed the visitors first. He blinked, did a double take, then nudged his father. William Senior glanced at him through welling eyes, then froze in astonishment as he saw Truman and Bradley. The president and the chairman of the Joint Chiefs of Staff paused several feet away and bowed their heads as the minister began to invoke the final benediction for Wilson Charles Lindberg.

As the words of the minister's last blessing faded on the wind, the first soulful notes of "Taps" echoed across the cemetery. The bugle rang out over the endless rows of headstones and carried through the bare trees, stirring a flock of sparrows to wing. When the last note died away, Harry Truman walked up to the family, followed by General Bradley. Bill snapped to attention and saluted crisply. The president nodded and Bradley returned the salute.

"I thought I'd come by to express my condolences," Truman said. "I wish I could have made it to the service but . . ." His voice trailed away. What did the press of government business mean to a family who'd just lost a son and brother?

"We're deeply honored, Mr. President." Bill nodded toward his parents. "My parents, William and Elizabeth Lindberg . . ."

The president shook hands. "My sympathy, sir . . . ma'am." He introduced Bradley. The highest-ranking officer in the armed forces shook hands with everyone as Bill and Sally's twin boys stared up at the five gleaming stars on his greatcoat shoulder tabs.

"I would be honored if you would come over to the Mansion for coffee. . . . I have a presentation I'd like to make," Truman said.

William Lindberg glanced at Betty, overwhelmed at the president's gesture. He swallowed the lump in his throat and tried to speak, but nothing emerged.

Betty squeezed his hand, and said, "We appreciate your kindness, sir . . . but you must be terribly busy. . . ." Her lower lip trembled. "Coming here was . . . was . . ."

Truman touched her gently on the shoulder. "Please."

They followed him toward the waiting Lincoln. Two other sedans had pulled up behind it and were idling with open doors. Bradley ushered Wilson's parents into the first car, and Bill and Sally and the boys into the second. The small caravan crossed the Memorial Bridge, rolled past the Lincoln Memorial, and five minutes later, pulled through the west gate of the White House.

They followed the president into the West Wing entrance, down the entry hall, and into the Oval Office, where they stood in an informal half-circle facing the president's desk. General Bradley handed the president a folio and came to respectful attention. Harry Truman opened the blue leather binding, glanced up at the Lindbergs, then began to read:

"On the 24th of December, nineteen hundred and forty-eight, Wilson Charles Lindberg, Major, United States Air Force, on his five hundred and second flight into besieged Berlin, fell in the service of his country. Major Lindberg displayed uncommon valor and devotion in flying that day. He knew, as his comrades in Transport Command knew, that the men, women, and children of Berlin were depending upon him. He did not falter. He did not turn back. Despite the near-zero visibility and threatening storm, he pressed on, determined to deliver his precious cargo of food and coal to the helpless city. In discharging his duties, Major Lindberg has fulfilled the highest ideals of the United States Air Force."

Harry Truman closed the cover and handed the folio to Betty Lindberg. "His sacrifice will not be forgotten, ma'am. Your son will be remembered by his proud countrymen, and perhaps most of all, by the grateful people of free Berlin."

General Bradley handed the president a flat white box. He opened the lid and handed it to William Lindberg. "Sir, on behalf of the people of the United States of America, it is my privilege to present you and your family, on behalf of your son, the Distinguished Flying Cross."

William Lindberg blinked back tears. "Thank you, Mr. President."

General Bradley put his hand on William's shoulder. "It's the highest award for valor we can award in peacetime, Mr. Lindberg."

"Thank you, General Bradley."

The president glanced at the medal, then looked into William's eyes. "I'm afraid it's not much compared to the loss of a son, Mr. Lindberg. . . . If there was anything I could do to bring him back, I would."

"I know, sir. . . ."

Harry Truman sighed. "I just want you to know that, well, it's only knowing that this country has men like your son Wilson that allows me any sleep at all these nights. When I think of the evils this world spawns, when I think of the tyrants who've come and gone across the stage of history, I thank God that this country has always been blessed with sons like yours. . . . I guess there'll always be Hitlers and Stalins and Tojos, but by God, let them do their damnedest—we'll come out all right in the end."

He tousled the blond heads of Matthew and John and smiled down at the two-year-olds. "Your uncle was a brave man, boys. A brave man. And you can tell anybody that asks that the President of the United States said so, all right?"

They stared up at Harry Truman, not fully understanding but sensing from the atmosphere in the room that they were part of something special this day, something very special.

Matt raised his arms toward the president, drawn by the friendly smile. Harry Truman picked him up. "I'll bet you're going to be a Marine just like your dad, huh?"

"Mawine," echoed Matt, delight in his eyes.

"And your brother can be a pilot, just like your uncle." Harry Truman glanced at Sally for approval. She smiled.

"We'll never forget this, Mr. President. God bless you."

Harry Truman, challenged day after day by the lingering crisis in Berlin, carrying the terrible weight of a possible world war on his shoulders, swallowed hard. For the first time in his life he found himself at a loss for words. He nodded, blinking back tears, touched by the simple expression of unqualified support from a young American mother.

Omar Bradley noticed his distress and nodded toward the door. "Shall we have that coffee now?"

They walked down the red-carpeted West Wing hall past framed portraits of Washington, Jefferson, Lincoln, Wilson, and Roosevelt, entered the mansion itself, and followed the president into the State Dining Room where White House stewards had set a table for them. Through the windows in the distance they could see across the Potomac the gentle hills of Arlington National Cemetery, serene and silent under the winter sun.

II

Washington, D.C., was sweltering in July heat by the time Sinclair returned to the States, fresh from the triumph of the Berlin Airlift. On the fourteenth, Stalin had reopened the road and rail routes to the besieged city, acknowledging defeat in the first postwar showdown between Washington and Moscow.

But it would not bring back Wilson Lindberg.

Sinclair kneeled at the grave, covered now with lush green grass. As he'd promised her, he set a lock of Gabrielle's honey-blond hair, bound in a blue ribbon, on the grave. Beside it, he laid a sprig of edelweiss from Gunther and Kathe Dietrich. He pulled the last memento from his pocket—a miniature bottle of water from the Volga River sent by a Russian friend of Kathe's. As she'd explained at Tempelhof before he'd left, it was a keepsake the soldier had carried with him from the Battle of Stalingrad to the Battle of Berlin. He'd heard of the fatal crash and had sought to atone in some small way for the actions of his government.

Following their wishes, Sinclair removed the cap and sprinkled the grave with the contents, touched by the gesture of goodwill from a common Red Army sergeant. He got slowly to his feet, hoping someday he might meet this Yuri Rostov.

Epilogue

Sverdlovsk
U.S.S.R.
August 19, 1949

I

Academician Andrei Sakharov peered out through the viewing slot of the concrete control bunker at the lone tower etched in silhouette against the setting sun. From ten kilometers away, the distant structure seemed lost amidst the endless taiga—a lone sentinel of steel girders erected on the orders of the man in the far distant Kremlin.

Sakharov sighed wearily. The past weeks had taken a heavy toll on the scientists gathered in the remote wastes of Soviet Asia. Tens of thousands of man-hours of labor had been poured into the project, the best scientific minds in the U.S.S.R. had gathered—many of them involuntarily, thought Sakharov with wry patience, in order that the West's increasingly irksome monopoly on atomic fission be ended.

He rubbed his eyes. August had been a blur to the scores of men toiling in this remote corner of the world to assemble the device which would, hopefully, explode at thirteen minutes past eight o'clock.

He glanced at his watch, then lowered his tinted goggles over his eyes. "Goggles on, comrades."

Silently, Sakharov's colleagues donned the protective glasses which would shield their eyes from the white-hot glare of raw nature unleashed, then stared at the summit of the tower where the Soviet Union's first atomic bomb rested.

A disembodied voice crackled suddenly over the bunker speakers and echoed through the dark interior as the countdown reached the final ten seconds: *"Desyat . . . devyat . . . vosim . . . sem . . . shyest . . . pyat . . . chetiree . . . tri . . . dva . . . adin . . . NOL!"*

A terrible glare burst over the taiga. Sakharov blinked and edged back from the wall. A beam of intense white light shot through the viewing slot, lighting the Russian's face in an unearthly glow and casting his shadow on the far wall behind him.

The bunker was silent as a tomb as the awed scientists stared at the expanding fireball. Seconds later, a wall of airborne dust, carried toward the bunker on the expanding shock wave, blasted through the viewing slots. In the blinding, swirling clouds of dust, the men choked and coughed. Before they could recover, the growling roar of the sound waves thundered over them, shaking the ground beneath their feet.

Sakharov leaned forward and gripped the edges of the viewing slot to steady himself. For several minutes, he watched the mushroom cloud surge skyward toward the stratosphere, until the winds dispersed the churning vertical column of smoke and ash into writhing fragments of iron-gray cloud.

Finally, he turned from the bunker opening. "Well, there's your bomb, Comrade Stalin. . . ."

Sakharov found himself facing Lavrenti Beria's NKVD stooge, General Anton Malinovsky, sent to observe the test as a representative of the secret police. Bursting with pride, he grasped Sakharov's hand and pumped it excitedly. "Congratulations, comrade! This is a great day for the Motherland! A great day!"

Sakharov nodded woodenly. Despite his pride that Soviet science had finally matched the West, the thought of the atomic

bomb in the hands of Joseph Vissarionovich Djugashvili chilled
him to the core. . . .

II

Joseph Stalin hung up the telephone, leaned back in his
swivel armchair, and closed his eyes in silent contemplation of
the news from Sverdlovsk. Since the humiliation of the Berlin
blockade debacle, he'd been desperate to restore lost Soviet
prestige. The American fliers had made a fool of him, their
cursed C-54s had created a veritable air bridge between the Elbe
and the capital, rendering his blockade an impotent joke.

He frowned—who in their wildest dreams would have predicted that the Americans could have supplied a city of three
million people by air for an entire year? It was galling. A handful of transport pilots had made a mockery of his threats, won
over a generation of Germans to the West, and swung a cowed
and wavering Europe away from the Kremlin and into the arms
of Washington. His plans for a socialist Germany were dust,
his goal of imminent communist revolution throughout Western
Europe a pipe dream, thanks to those devils in their C-54s.

Stalin sat up and rose to his feet, a smile spreading across
his face.

But all *that* was water under the bridge now. The Soviet Union
had exploded its first A-bomb. Academician Sakharov and his
comrades had provided him with the means to best the imperialists at their game of atomic blackmail. Yes indeed, *two* could
play that game. No longer would there be sleepless nights in
the Kremlin because that bastard Truman had dispatched B-29
atomic bombers to England or Turkey. The U.S.S.R. had its own
atomic bomber, the shiny new Tupolev 4, and at last, a Soviet
bomb to put in its bomb bays.

Stalin turned to the window and looked out upon Red Square,
delighted at the prospects for the future. With the might of the
Red Army *and* the atomic bomb, there would be no stopping

the glorious march to world communism. The era of capitalist imperialism would soon end, brought to a close by the genius of a simple cobbler's son from Tbilisi.

He smiled down on Lenin's Tomb, imagining the day he would stand on its marble ramparts to review the victory parade of a World Soviet Socialist Republic. *Next* time, nothing would save the imperialists. The Berlin fiasco was but a reprieve, a short breathing spell before the corrupt body of capitalism was liquidated and interred to rot away in a forgotten grave.

Yes, *next* time it would be different. An airlift could not save London, Paris, or Washington from Soviet atomic bombs. . . .

THE ONLY ALTERNATIVE IS ANNIHILATION ...
RICHARD P. HENRICK

SILENT WARRIORS   (8217-3026-6, $4.50/$5.50)
The Red Star, Russia's newest, most technologically advanced submarine, outclasses anything in the U.S. fleet. But when the captain opens his sealed orders 24 hours early, he's staggered to read that he's to spearhead a massive nuclear first strike against the Americans!

THE PHOENIX ODYSSEY   (0-8217-5016-X, $4.99/$5.99)
All communications to the *USS Phoenix* suddenly and mysteriously vanish. Even the urgent message from the president canceling the War Alert is not received, and in six short hours the *Phoenix* will unleash its nuclear arsenal against the Russian mainland. . . .

COUNTERFORCE   (0-8217-5116-6, $5.99/$6.99)
In the silent deep, the chase is on to save a world from destruction. A single Russian submarine moves on a silent and sinister course for the American shores. The men aboard the U.S.S. *Triton* must search for and destroy the Soviet killer submarine as an unsuspecting world race for the apocalypse.

CRY OF THE DEEP   (0-8217-5200-6, $5.99/$6.99)
With the Supreme leader of the Soviet Union dead the Kremlin is pointing a collective accusing finger towards the United States. The motherland wants revenge and unless the USS *Swordfish* can stop the Russian *Caspian,* the salvoes of World War Three are a mere heartbeat away!

BENEATH THE SILENT SEA   (0-8217-3167X, $4.50/$5.50)
The Red Dragon, Communist China's advanced ballistic missile-carrying submarine embarks on the most sinister mission in human history: to attack the U.S. and Soviet Union simultaneously. Soon, the Russian *Barkal,* with its planned attack on a single U.S. submarine, is about unwittingly to aid in the destruction of all mankind!

Available wherever paperbacks are sold, or order direct from the Publisher. Send cover price plus 50¢ per copy for mailing and handling to Kensington Publishing Corp., Consumer Orders, or call (toll free) 888-345-BOOK, to place your order using Mastercard or Visa. Residents of New York and Tennessee must include sales tax. DO NOT SEND CASH.

POLITICAL ESPIONAGE AND
HEART-STOPPING HORROR. . . .
NOVELS BY NOEL HYND

CEMETERY OF ANGELS   (0-7860-0261-1, $5.99/$6.99)

GHOSTS   (0-8217-4359-7, $4.99/$5.99)

THE KHRUSHCHEV OBJECTIVE   (0-8217-2297-2, $4.50/$5.95)

A ROOM FOR THE DEAD   (0-7860-0089-9, $5.99/$6.99)

TRUMAN'S SPY   (0-8217-3309-5, $4.95/$5.95)

ZIG ZAG   (0-8217-4557-3, $4.99/$5.99)

REVENGE   (0-8217-2529-7, $3.95/$4.95)

THE SANDLER INQUIRY   (0-8217-3070-3, $4.50/$5.50)

FLY THE DANGEROUS SKIES OF TOMORROW
THE WINGMAN SERIES BY MACK MALONEY

THE SEVENTH CARRIER SERIES
BY PETER ALBANO